# Wolf's Cage

## LAURA TAYLOR

ALSO BY LAURA TAYLOR

THE HOUSE OF SIRIUS

Book 1: Wolf's Blood

Coming soon
Book 3: Wolf's Choice

To Fabien.
For being both my greatest fan and my harshest critic. And for giving me
Nikolai, who has become one of my favourite characters.

# ACKNOWLEDGMENTS

Thank you Linda, for once again exceeding all my expectations and designing the dazzlingly beautiful cover art. I'm speechless.

Thank you Ellen, for your insights into psychology, and for fixing the technological timelines. And the technology in general. And for loving Nikolai. Vodka solves everything.

Thank you Narinder, for your exceptional knowledge of grammar, for noticing the little things, which can make such a difference, and for the fantastic coffee.

# CHAPTER ONE

**22 Years Ago**

Caroline Saunders opened the door to her rundown home and dumped her school bag by the door. She'd started secondary school this year and had homework to do, a science project that she was actually looking forward to. It was a study on the planets of the solar system, and there was a certain fascination to exploring a world far beyond the one she inhabited.

But there was no point trying to do any work now. Her oldest brother, Troy, was fighting with her father again. Her other brother, Greg, was fifteen and was playing video games on the couch. Shit. She'd hoped he was out. Every time she tried to do homework when Greg was around, he teased and mocked her, and went out of his way to spoil her work. Last week she'd all but finished an essay on a novel for English and he'd 'accidentally' spilled orange juice all over it, leaving her to either rewrite the entire thing, or explain to her teacher why she hadn't handed in her assignment. Again.

Fucking teachers. She tried to get her work done, tried to learn, tried to pay attention, but it was an uphill battle all the way, with her mother drunk, her brothers constantly in trouble for shoplifting or getting into fights, and her father… well, the less said about him, the better.

Her mother was an odd one, of course. She was only drunk half the time. The other half, she was wonderful, cheerful and affectionate, baking cookies for Caroline to take to school and generous with both hugs and praise.

It was an entrenched routine, and one that Caroline had come to loathe. Her mother would get on an 'up' and would attack the mountains of garbage around their house with vigour, clean, cook, go shopping… and then she would invariably end up buying something that Caroline's father deemed 'excessive'. Though Caroline couldn't figure out why buying steak for dinner or a small chocolate cake for pudding was such a crime, when her father blowing £100 on a horse race was perfectly okay.

But then her father would get in a rage and smack her mother around, triggering a plunge into drinking and depression, and Caroline would be left to fend for herself for weeks, scraping together dry bread crusts and mouldy cheese to make a sandwich for lunch, getting picked on by the other kids when they saw her meagre fare, and then struggling to concentrate all afternoon when she was too hungry to focus on school.

They were in the middle of a 'down' phase at the moment, her mother opening her first bottle at 7am and sitting like a glassy eyed shop mannequin for the rest of the day, not paying attention to anything other than when her bottle ran out and she had to go get a new one.

Caroline was about to head for her room, plotting ways to avoid her family for the rest of the evening, when her father burst into the living room, no doubt having heard the door close when she arrived.

"There you are, you little bitch," he snarled at her. "I'm sorry I ever had you, you useless piece of shit. It's your fault she's gone! You and your damned complaining. Always whinging you're hungry, you're cold, you're tired, you want a clean fucking shirt! Can't just keep your mouth shut, can you?"

What the fuck? "Who's gone?" Caroline asked, heart beating fast as she tried to feign indifference. Whatever this was, it sounded bad...

"Mum left," Troy told her, leaning against the kitchen doorway. "This morning. Just packed her bags and walked the fuck out."

Caroline didn't bother asking why. In truth, it could only ever have been a matter of time. Nor did she attempt to say that it wasn't her fault. According to her father, *everything* was her fault.

"What?" Her father snapped, stalking towards her. "Nothing to say? You don't even care, do you, you little shit. Just thinking of yourself the whole time, fuck the rest of us. I'll teach you some damned manners..."

The first blow hurt the worst, a loud crack against her cheek that made it feel like her face was going to explode. The second one wasn't as bad, Caroline already reeling from the first and less able to pay attention to it, and after that, she knew the blows were coming, which seemed to make them easier to bear. She shrank in against the wall, arms over her head to protect herself, and then, when he didn't stop, she slowly sank down onto the floor, curling up in a ball as his fists kept coming.

As Caroline lay on the floor, nose bleeding, head ringing, she didn't bother feeling sorry for herself, wasted no time or effort in wishing she had been born to another life, a different family.

No, the only thing in her mind was trying to remember which of the boys at school was the toughest, who won the most fights and elicited the most fear from the other students.

Because first thing tomorrow morning, the instant she got to school... she was going to persuade one of them to teach her how to hit someone back.

# CHAPTER TWO

## Present Day

*Noturatii Progress Report*
*Date: April 7*

*Author: Jacob Green*
*Title: Chief of Operations – British Division*

*Subject: Recent explosion in research laboratory*

*Casualties:*
*43 Security personnel*
*11 Administration staff*
*9 Scientists*
*5 Level Four Assassins*
*1 Satva Khuli*

Jacob paused as he typed the words, feeling a cold thrill go up his spine. The Satva Khuli was dead, the most highly trained, most lethal, most cold blooded killer the Noturatii had to offer. She'd been sent to defend their science lab from the shape shifter abominations.

And now she was dead, killed by those vicious bastards. Though how they had done it, he couldn't begin to guess.

*On 25th March, the Noturatii's main scientific research centre in northern London came under attack by a concerted force of shape shifters. An exact count of the assailants was not possible due to the security feeds in and around the complex being taken out of operation, however we estimate the total number to have been around 35.*

4

*Our security forces were unable to repel the attack in its early stages, largely due to logistical difficulties caused by narrow hallways and multiple security check points, which limited staff movement and prevented a wide scale assault on the shifters.*

*In anticipation of such an attack, I had previously requested, and been granted, attendance by a Satva Khuli.*

*It has long been known that the shape shifters employ a brand of assassin of their own. Even though this was a known possibility, it was anticipated that the Khuli should possess sufficient skills and weaponry to repel a shifter assassin. I am startled and disappointed to find that this was not the case, and would urge management to investigate the current standards of Khuli training to avoid this kind of defeat in the future.*

Jacob gritted his teeth, hoping he wasn't overstepping his bounds with that bold statement. The truth was, the training the Satva Khuli, literally the 'Blood Tigers', endured was already brutal to the point that only one in three children recruited for training lived to adulthood. Frankly, he had no idea why the woman sent to them hadn't been able to fend off the shifter invasion. After the sirens had sounded and the attack had reached the lower levels of the lab, Jacob had cut and run, a planned escape through a series of little known tunnels, leaving his not insignificant security detail to take care of the problem.

That the shifters had a member of their pack capable of killing a Khuli was a worrying prospect. God knew what sort of nefarious destruction they were planning next…

*In the course of the shifter attack, our Head of Science and Research, Phillip O'Brian, was killed. The shifters planted a large number of explosives throughout the laboratory complex, which were detonated after they exited the building, causing the total destruction of the complex including the warehouse facility above ground. Attempts were made to upload pertinent findings from our research to the central database, however it is believed that this process was interrupted before it could be completed. I am currently interviewing surviving science staff to determine the extent of information lost, and to implement plans for recovering recent advances made.*

Melissa Hunter, the sole surviving member of the science and research team, had been livid when she'd found out the extent of the damage. Normally a respectful, disciplined woman, she'd completely lost the plot when he'd told her exactly how much data they had lost. The team had been working on ground-breaking research, hoping to crack the secret of how the shape shifters converted humans into their particular brand of abomination – people capable of turning themselves into wolves. Months of planning had culminated in the capture of a shifter and the attempted conversion of three civilian women. At least one of the experiments was believed to have been successful, but the data from the last test subject had been lost, wiping out months of careful planning and research.

Melissa wasn't the only one who would be outraged by the loss. Jacob was trying to paint as rosy a picture as possible, implying that valuable data could be recovered. It was the second time his research team had been wiped out by the shifters and the second time priceless data had been lost. Headquarters was not going to be happy.

But neither would they be happy about Jacob hiding any of the facts, so he gritted his teeth and forced himself to continue typing.

*The captive shifter being held in our cage facility was freed during the attack and is believed to have re-joined the shifter pack in the north of England. Surviving security personnel are being interviewed with regards to his escape, however further experiments will not be possible until a new test subject is acquired.*

Jack Miller, in particular, would be a gold mine of information. One of Jacob's personal security guards, the man was observant, methodical, dedicated and had advanced combat skills, thanks to his time in the military. Now, if Jacob could just find the time to debrief him, given the thousand other tasks that needed seeing to in the wake of the lab explosion, he might actually learn something useful.

*On a more optimistic note, we have recently received hard confirmation that there are not one, but two shifter packs in England's north. Two days ago, a turncoat from the more primitive of the two groups sold information to the Noturatii in exchange for the extermination of one particular shifter, a woman by the name of Dee Carman, who was the subject of the first successful experiment we completed in our labs. Please refer to report 5694B for details of her conversion and escape, and subsequent efforts to recapture her.*

*I am putting a team together to begin investigating possible locations of the second pack, which is believed to be the more technologically advanced of the two, and the group responsible for the assault on the lab. I anticipate significant information to come to light within the next few weeks.*

*In the meantime, we have transferred our science operations to the British headquarters in east London, and are currently compiling a list of equipment required to resume our research into the shifters' physiology and possible ways to exterminate them.*

It was a bold attempt to paint a positive picture from 'anticipated gains', when all Jacob actually had to show for his efforts so far was a sketchy map of the shifters' possible locations and a group of soldiers cooling their heels while he scrambled to fill the gaps left by the colossal losses from the lab explosion.

Knowing there was little more he could do to improve the situation – the loss of the lab had been a disaster, and he and everyone else knew it –

he hit send, hoping his superiors were in a good mood today.

Deep in the heart of the Kielder Forest in the far north of England, Genna waited at the edge of the camp as the rustling sound of wolf feet came closer. The Grey Watch, the far more reclusive of the two shifter packs in England, lived hidden in the forest and shunned all contact with modern society, with a blanket ban on television, internet and mobile phones. But even they needed to venture out now and then for basic necessities, and the pack was gathered, waiting for Luna and Rience to return from their trip into town. They'd been to pick up flour, sugar, herbs and spices, milk powder… and far more interesting, the latest mail. Though letters were rare, they kept in contact with other Grey Watch packs from across Europe, messages still written by hand, in code, passing on vital information about the movements and activities of each pack and warnings about any unexpected developments from the Noturatii.

Moments later, two wolves dashed into the clearing, Luna coming first, the older and larger of the two, followed by Rience, a large satchel strapped to each of their backs. Sempre, the alpha female, was waiting in the centre of the clearing, and they went straight to her, standing patiently while she unstrapped the bags.

But then, instead of waiting for their leader to check the mail and announce any news-worthy snippets of information, Luna shifted immediately, diving into one of the bags without a word. She pulled out a small envelope, and then more surprisingly, a newspaper – such things were generally forbidden – and handed them both to Sempre with a bow, an apology for her impertinence. "It's from Il Trosa," she said simply, which made Sempre's eyes widen, and she snatched the envelope out of Luna's hand, ripping the thing open and reading quickly. Her expression went from concerned, to confused, to outraged, and she snatched up the newspaper next, a low growl rumbling from her throat as she read the front page.

"Pack up the camp," she announced, when she'd finished. "We're moving."

On a normal day, almost everyone in the camp would be in wolf form. The Grey Watch shunned not only human society, but all links to their human past, their natural human bodies included, and their members were expected to spend upwards of ninety percent of their time in wolf form. But today, more than half the gathered shifters were already in human form, some of their rules having been temporarily set aside while they all recovered from a vicious battle from a few weeks ago.

Dee Carman, a woman from Il Trosa, the other shifter pack in England, had sought refuge in their camp after being attacked by the Noturatii, and over the course of the evening, it had been revealed that she was no ordinary shifter. Rather, she was the reincarnation of Fenrae-Ul, the Destroyer Wolf, an ancient soul returned from the dead with the devastating ability to separate the two halves of a shifter, returning them permanently to either human, or wolf form: the embodiment of a prophecy that predicted the end of their species.

A battle had ensued, as Il Trosa sent their best warriors to retrieve her, and there was barely a member of the Grey Watch left uninjured after the fight. Two of them had been killed, with another having to be put down after Dee had used her destructive powers on the wolf, ripping the human half right out of her body.

As a concession to the serious injuries everyone had sustained, they had been temporarily allowed to remain in human form while their wolf side healed. It was a far more comfortable state of being, as the pain inflicted upon the wolf forms didn't affect the human side, and also a pragmatic solution, as it reduced the risk of infection, some of the wounds deep and easily contaminated.

Now, with so many of their number in human form, the automatic questions and objections flowed readily, a chorus of 'why?' and 'what's going on?' and 'what did the letter say?' filling the clearing.

Looking thoroughly irate, and more than a little nervous, Sempre held up the letter. "Baron sends his regards," she stated with no small amount of scorn. "And wishes to inform us that Il Trosa recently attacked a Noturatii base. He says they're likely to retaliate and will probably come north, hunting us in the forest." Then she held up the newspaper for them all to see. It showed the charred remains of a large building on the cover, along with the headline 'Warehouse Blaze Causes Mass Evacuation'. "They broke into a warehouse, shot a hundred or more people and then blew the thing sky high. Front page news! So once again, we have to turn tail and run, because Il Trosa can't keep their shit together for five fucking minutes. Pack your things. We're moving to the northern camp. Today."

The northern camp was the most remote camp in the forest, hidden deep in a gully where even the most determined hikers found access difficult, and as far from human settlement as it was possible to get in England.

It was also a dark, dank space where everything was constantly wet and leeches were plentiful, sunlight rarely making it to the ground even on a clear day, and there was a round of grumbling as everyone made their objections known.

"Damned Il Trosa!"

"They'd take every camp from us if they could!"

"Can't stop causing trouble."

"How about we show up on their doorstep and camp there, since they keep screwing things up for us here?"

"Or we could just turn Il Trosa over to the Noturatii and be done with it," Genna muttered… and was surprised when the pack suddenly fell silent around her.

"What did you say?" Sempre asked, looking at her like she'd just grown a second head, and Genna felt a wave of embarrassment as she realised that the entire pack had just heard her throw-away comment. But now that she had centre stage, why not make the most of it?

"Well, you know where their estate is," Genna pointed out, not understanding why it was such a strange idea. "It couldn't be too hard to let the Noturatii know where it is, and then Il Trosa is no longer our problem."

Sempre looked at her like she'd just suggested the woman remove her own liver and eat it for breakfast. "You stupid girl," she said, in a tone so cold Genna felt the blood drain from her face. "You know nothing of our culture, or our history." Sempre stalked towards her, face red with anger, and it took all of Genna's courage to stand her ground, when all she really wanted to do was run away and hide. "The Treaty of Erim Kai Bahn expressly forbids such a thing. What the hell do you think would happen if Il Trosa announced *our* location to the Noturatii? If one pack ever betrays another, the treaty is broken, and we may as well hand ourselves in to the Noturatii, line up and ask them to shoot us all!"

"What? Why? Why would the loss of one pack make a difference?" Genna had never heard of this treaty. She'd been with the pack for less than six months, converted in a rush before her official training period had been completed, and apparently there were important parts of shifter culture and history that the Grey Watch had yet to teach her about.

"If we betray the Lakes District Den," Sempre said, her tone condescending and impatient, "then the Council will get wind of it, and immediately betray us to the Noturatii. And then any Grey Watch pack from anywhere in Europe could take offence at that, and betray another Il Trosa pack, who will get revenge by betraying a Grey Watch pack, and the whole thing spirals into chaos until there are no shifters left. The Treaty was set up to prevent that exact kind of stupidity. When it was signed in 1437, it was expressly forbidden that any shifter pack should ever betray another to the Noturatii. We may fight amongst ourselves, kill each other, take revenge for a thousand perceived slights, but against the Noturatii, we are allies. For all Il Trosa's stupidity and recklessness, we stand as a united front against a common enemy. Never, ever forget that."

Genna nodded obediently, suddenly eager to be back in her wolf form as she felt her face heat. But it wasn't from embarrassment. Her gut churned as she realised that she had made a terrible, terrible mistake, and she felt rather faint at the enormity of what she had done.

After the attack on their pack, Genna had been horrified by the powers of Fenrae-Ul, the ease with which she could destroy a shifter, and had seen the woman as their greatest and most immediate threat. And so, in an effort to get rid of her, she'd sought help from the Noturatii themselves, had sold them information about the whereabouts of Il Trosa's Den, in exchange for assurances that they would kill the girl when they found her. It had seemed a simple, clever solution to a confounding problem.

Only now, it turned out it was nowhere near that simple. It seemed that, rather than helping her pack and assuring a more stable future for them, she had instead broken an ancient treaty – a treaty no one had ever told her about! – and in doing so, should she ever be discovered, she had risked an internal war amongst her own species that could get them all killed.

Oblivious to the cause of her apprehension, Sempre spun away from her and faced the rest of the pack. "Gather your things. Remove all traces of our presence from this camp. I want everyone ready to move in one hour. And Lita?" she snapped to an elderly woman hanging on the fringes of the clearing. "See to it that Genna is educated in the finer details of the Treaty. The girl's ignorance has been tolerated for quite long enough."

# CHAPTER THREE

In his temporary bedroom in the manor at Misty Hills, the estate that the Lakes District Den called home, Andre stood under the shower spray, letting the near-scalding water cascade over his back, relieved that his latest assignment was drawing to a close. It had been nearly two weeks since the Den had carried out their assault on the Noturatii lab, the operation an unmitigated success, as they had safely recovered Tank, one of the most senior wolves in the Den, blown the lab sky high, and escaped without a single casualty.

But the fallout from the battle was still being dealt with, as many of the Den's members were still carrying injuries, and Tank was struggling to recover from the torture he had endured while being held captive.

Andre himself had been working overtime, helping to return one of the Noturatii's other captives to her home, a young woman they had rescued from the lab who had been forcefully converted into a shifter, and then separated from the wolf again in a ground-breaking exercise that had been completed by Dee Carman, the Den's newest member, with a most unique talent. In addition to that, they'd had to deal with a traitor within their own ranks, Dee's boyfriend Mark, who had secretly infiltrated the lab late last year, and who had subsequently been demoted to the rank of omega and branded with a traitor's mark as punishment for his treason.

Finding a moment to unwind and take stock of the whole situation had been hard, and Andre let the hot water continue to run down his body, easing aching muscles and blocking out the rest of the world for a few precious minutes.

Finally he was ready to emerge, checking his healing wounds as he towelled himself off, rubbing his shoulder-length hair to stop it dripping down his shoulders. With a towel wrapped around his waist, he headed into the bedroom, then paused as he saw the flashing alert on his laptop. A few clicks of the mouse later, and he was reading a message that sent chills down his spine. *'Call us. Now.'* It was from the Council, the shifters' Italy based control centre, and it was as laconic as usual, the Council unwilling to send any important information through unsecure channels. But the message was imperative, nonetheless, so Andre grabbed a shirt and threw it on, not bothering with trousers as he took a seat in the chair in front of the computer. Then he spent a couple of minutes setting up a secure, encrypted connection to the Council.

His request for a video call was answered immediately. A long table came into view, the Council's twelve members staring at him from the screen with severe expressions.

No, not twelve. There were only eleven people seated at the long table in Il Trosa headquarters.

Eleanor, the oldest and longest running member of the Council, cleared her throat, her face pale, her aging form shaking ever so slightly.

"What's happened?" Andre asked without even saying hello. He had never seen the woman so upset.

"Amedea is dead," Eleanor said simply, and Andre felt himself pale. Amedea was an Italian woman in her forties, one of the younger members of the Council. For her to have died so young could mean one of only two things. Either she had been murdered, or…

"She committed suicide last night," Eleanor said grimly, "to safeguard the secrets of our species. May she find glory in the House of Sirius."

"May she find glory," Andre repeated. Then he closed his eyes and shook his head. "Why?"

"We had a situation in Italy a few weeks ago. We thought we had contained it adequately, but clearly we made some mistakes."

She went on to tell Andre the whole story. A prominent politician had somehow become involved with the Noturatii. A little too involved, it seemed. He'd started channelling funds into their cause, lending services to the group to assist them in their quest to exterminate the shifters, and so the Council had had to intervene. An assassin had been sent to kill the man – a dangerous and delicate mission, but the Council's assassins were some of the best trained operatives in the entire world. Andre could vouch for that personally, being one of them himself.

But the hit had gone wrong. Though the assassin had succeeded in killing his target, he had also been discovered – a known risk, given the high security presence around the man. So, as dictated by the oath he had sworn when enlisted to serve the Council, he had promptly swallowed the capsule of poison that every assassin – and every Council member – kept in a ring on their left hand. The lethal dose had rendered him lifeless in less than three seconds.

But the Noturatii's reach was longer and more insidious than the

Council could have predicted, and after weeks of investigations, under the guise of a 'police inquiry', they had somehow linked the dead assassin to Amedea.

The situation had been a dire emergency. With one of the Council exposed, there was the firm risk that she could be linked to the rest of them. And so Amedea had taken herself swiftly out of the equation. It was an act of reckless bravery, and also a sacred responsibility for each and every Councillor. Their ultimate duty was to ensure the safety of the shifter species, and upon joining the Council, each member swore an oath to forfeit their own life should they be at risk of exposing their secrets.

It was a stark tragedy... but Andre soon discovered that the reason for the Council's call was more complex than just breaking the bad news.

"The immediate complication from this is that you won't be able to return to Italy in the near future," Eleanor told him apologetically. "I know you would have liked to attend the funeral, but with the political environment the way it is, we've temporarily banned all movements into and out of the country. In a few weeks this should blow over, but for the moment you'll have to stay in England."

Andre nodded obediently. Remaining here for a while longer wasn't a problem. But then Eleanor went on.

"There are also two other reasons we would like you to stay. We have a couple of assignments for you..."


## 25 Years Ago

Andre walked into the library of the Lakes District manor, his heart in his throat. The Council emissary had arrived just six days ago to assess Andre's development and education, a process that normally took weeks, and this meeting had come far sooner than he had anticipated. At fifteen years old, and as the adopted son of a shifter couple, he was rapidly approaching the age where he would be considered for conversion – an event that couldn't come soon enough, as far as Andre was concerned – and he was terrified that the emissary had discovered something undesirable about him, something faulty that would jeopardise his future in Il Trosa. The wolf shifters were more than just a family to him – they were his pack, though he wasn't yet a wolf himself, his comrades, his friends, his entire world. To become one of them would be the highest honour that could possibly be bestowed upon him, and to be denied the opportunity to become a wolf was the most devastating disaster he could imagine.

His parents were already sitting at the long table, opposite the emissary, all of their faces stern and serious, and Andre fought to keep his expression calm and neutral. He took a seat, putting his hands in his lap to hide the fact that they were shaking.

"Adriana has some news for you," his mother said softly, offering the emissary a tight smile. His father said nothing, but Andre saw him take his mother's hand beneath the table, and his anxiety only got worse.

"Don't be nervous," Adriana said, no doubt having noticed his apprehension. "This is nothing to be worried about. Quite the opposite, actually."

Andre tried to relax, curiosity gnawing at him about what he could have done in so short a time that warranted such attention. But one did not question a Council emissary. And Andre was far too polite to risk antagonising one of the most elite members of their society.

"Before I came here, I was fully briefed on your progress," Adriana went on. "Lidia reports that you've been completing your lessons at an impressive pace. Heron says you've displayed a remarkable enthusiasm for your studies into shifter history and culture, and Raven thinks your combat skills have improved significantly over the past year."

Andre couldn't help but glow at the praise. Like all children of Il Trosa, Andre had been home-schooled, and along with the usual lessons in English, Maths and Science that any normal teenager would receive during their time at school, he had had additional hurdles to overcome during his adolescent years. With the Noturatii an ever-present threat, shifter children began learning hand to hand combat from the tender age of ten, they were taught to use their first firearm at the age of twelve, and by the time they were sixteen – the minimum age at which conversion into a shape shifter was permitted – they were expected to be able to survive a one-on-one battle with a Noturatii operative, whether that fight involved fists, knives or even guns.

And in addition to that, they were also expected to have mastered the various aspects of shifter culture, memorising each and every chant for the sacred rituals, learning the history of the four bloodlines, studying the Treaty of Erim Kai Bahn and the origins of the Endless War, which had begun in the 1400s and continued to rage to this day.

Andre had thrown himself into his lessons with vigour, genuinely captivated by the history and culture of his people, eager to take his place in the war and to do his part in securing a stable future for their species. It was heartening to know that his efforts had not gone unnoticed.

But if his studies were all going so well, then what was this meeting about?

"But since coming here and meeting you in person, I've had to re-evaluate your progress," Adriana continued, and Andre's heart rate kicked up a notch. Had he missed something? Had he failed at some task, or disappointed one of his tutors in a way that had escaped his attention?

"It seems," Adriana said, choosing her words carefully, "that you are not just a dedicated student and talented fighter." She fixed him with a steely look, and Andre fought not to squirm under her scrutiny. "It has become apparent that you are, in fact, an unusually gifted child. Most teenagers would not reach your level of study, nor your skills in combat, until they were at least eighteen. Some of them not even then. To say that your progress has been remarkable would be a significant understatement."

Andre held his breath. Such praise, coming from a Council emissary, was a rare thing, and the only reason he could think of for this meeting was that perhaps she was going to let him be converted early. The idea had his heart speeding up in excitement.

"The Council has taken notice of your abilities. So they would like to extend an invitation to you and your family. The decision is entirely yours, and it comes with a great deal of responsibility – certainly not a decision to be made lightly. But if you are willing, we would like you to come to Italy, and to be trained for a position in service to the Council."

## Present Day

Andre fought to banish the memories from his first dealings with the Council. The images were as clear in his mind as if they had happened yesterday, two long weeks passing before he had finally decided to accept the emissary's invitation and his family had bade farewell to their Den and moved to Italy. It had been a difficult, if exhilarating time of his life, but for the moment, he had far more important things to attend to.

He'd arranged a meeting with Caroline and Baron, to deliver his news to them, and they had assembled in the library. How many discussions had taken place around this table, Andre wondered as he took a seat. How many decisions made, lives altered by the words spoken from this very chair?

"I received a call from the Council this morning," he began, once Caroline and Baron were settled. "And they had some bad news." He outlined the details of the situation in Italy, the attack on the politician, the death of the assassin and then of Amedea, and the two alphas reacted with the predictable shock such news warranted. Baron gritted his teeth and folded his arms, looking like he wanted to punch something, while Caroline's eyes reflected a fiery rage, her fingers toying with the hilt of the dagger strapped to her side. But neither one said anything, waiting patiently for him to finish his report.

"The Council has placed a ban on all travel into and out of Italy," Andre concluded long minutes later, "so I'm going to have to impose on your hospitality a while longer. And as far as the rest of the Den is concerned, that is the full extent of the situation. Travel is too dangerous right now, so I'm to remain here." The explanation was no lie, and would be serious enough to quell any concerns within the shifter ranks – having a Council assassin hanging around the estate tended to make people nervous, and to keep the peace they tried to make such visits as short as possible.

"But there is an additional reason I've been asked to stay. Which you must not tell anyone else about."

That got Baron's attention, his head snapping up, his eyes promising retribution to anyone who threatened his Den, and it was that very protective instinct that made everyone on the estate respect him as much as they did. For Baron, the welfare of his Den came first. Every time.

"I don't like keeping secrets from my pack," he said coldly, "so you'd better have a damn good reason for whatever it is you're about to say."

Caroline sighed and rolled her eyes at his impatience. But she said nothing, and Andre reflected that if he hadn't been in the room, she might have had a sharp retort for his complaint.

"It has been requested that I assess one of your shifters for service to the Council," Andre explained, respecting Baron's concerns and not wanting to exacerbate them. "Caleb Anderson. The Council has taken note of his abilities, and they've been justifiably impressed."

At the sudden announcement, Caroline looked both surprised and delighted. For a member of their Den to be considered for service was a huge compliment to the alphas, and to the Den as a whole. But the look on Baron's face was one of open disbelief.

"Caleb's no assassin," he said flatly. "Aside from the fact that he hates violence, he's only got one eye, for Christ's sake. How's he supposed to go up against the Noturatii like that? Sorry, Andre, but you're barking up the wrong tree with that one."

"I don't disagree with you," Andre said, years of training in diplomacy and tact put to good use as he deliberately overlooked the rudeness of Baron's interruption. "But there are other roles he could fill. Historian, perhaps, or scientist. We're not all thugs and murderers," he added, with a hint of irony. It was a rare shifter who made it through life without having to kill someone at some point in time, skirmishes with the Noturatii all too common. But not everyone in service to the Council was employed as a full time killer-for-hire.

"Caleb is ranked fourth in this Den. He has the battle skills to stand up to the harsher situations the Council faces, and a temperament well suited to refined study. An eye for detail. A quiet presence that people tend to find calming and reassuring. Exactly the sort of shifter the Council needs."

"You're most welcome to stay," Caroline jumped in, no doubt wanting to head Baron off before he said anything else out of line. "And it would be an honour for Caleb to be assessed."

"As I said, no one else must know about this," Andre repeated. "Assessing a shifter for Council service requires careful observation, and I cannot have any interference along the way."

"Understood," Caroline agreed, and Baron nodded, perhaps not entirely happy with the situation, but willing to go along with it.

Andre nodded, satisfied with the outcome of the meeting. "Very well." Then he turned to Caroline. "If you would be so kind as to excuse us, I have a few other details to discuss with Baron. So as to minimise my impact on the Den while I'm here."

Caroline nodded, standing up smoothly, her body encased in black leather, half a dozen weapons visible as she headed for the door. "I'll leave you to it." She gracefully left the room, and Andre waited until the door had closed.

He turned to Baron, letting the weight of his gaze set the tone of the conversation to come, and when he was sure he had Baron's full attention, he continued, careful to keep his voice low.

"As you're no doubt aware," he began carefully, "the situation in Italy is more complex than I've implied. With one of the Councillors dead, it is now necessary to select someone else for the position." There was a strict set of rules regarding the Council. The office had to hold twelve members at all times, and when one of them was killed or died of natural causes, immediate plans were set in motion to fill the empty seat. Potential Councillors could only be chosen from those shifters who currently, or had previously held the rank of alpha, and emissaries had already been despatched to three other Dens to assess potential candidates, the Council being fortunate in that they already had enough operatives out in the field so as not to disturb the delicate political situation in Italy by sending any from there.

Il Trosa was not a democracy, the Council ruling with a firm hand and strict laws, but that wasn't to say that individual members of Il Trosa had no say in their ruling body. To reach the rank of alpha, a shifter had to garner the support of their entire Den, had to be a skilled warrior, a seasoned strategist, and have a personality amiable enough to maintain support on a social level for an extended period of time. And, if an alpha was deemed appropriate as a Councillor, their Den would be given the opportunity to vote on their appointment. A vote that came back negative in the majority removed the alpha from consideration, regardless of how suitable the rest of the Council might think he or she was.

"The Council has asked me to assess Caroline for the role." There was no hiding the surprise on Baron's face, though it wasn't possible to tell whether he thought the idea was a profound compliment, or a hideous mistake. "I realise that removing her from this Den would cause no small disturbance. You have no other females immediately capable of taking over the role of alpha, and bringing in a foreigner to lead always causes a certain degree of resentment. So as a courtesy, I'm making you aware of the potential for complications down the track. But more than that, I'd like to request your cooperation in her assessment. And an absolute guarantee of secrecy regarding this part of my duties."

"You think Caroline should be a Councillor?" Baron asked sceptically, ignoring the request for secrecy.

"What I think of the idea, one way or the other, is irrelevant. The Council has given me an order. I am duty bound to carry it out to the best of my ability." Was Baron jealous? Was he about to protest the Council's choice? He had been alpha for longer than Caroline, after all, he had brought his Den through some of the worst circumstances imaginable and emerged on the other side with a stronger, more skilled and more disciplined team than most alphas could ever dream of.

But then Baron snorted. "Well, I'd rather her than me," he said with a chuckle. Andre must have looked surprised, because he went on, "I don't have the patience for all that political crap. And the responsibilities they have to deal with on a daily basis would drive me insane. But Caroline? There is no shifter I would rather see be given that honour than her. My lips are sealed. And if you need anything at all, any time… don't hesitate to ask."

"I appreciate your cooperation."

"On a personal note though… tell me honestly. Do you think she's got what it takes to be a Councillor?"

It was a question Andre had been steadfastly avoiding since he'd been given the order by Eleanor, and he found himself surprisingly reluctant to face it now. Amedea's death had been a stark reminder of the risks that the Council faced every day, and he found it hard to think of Caroline being put in that kind of danger. "I think," he said carefully, "that she's managed to come through some extremely difficult circumstances, and has displayed remarkable strength of character throughout. The requirements for a Council member are strict and rigorous, and she's up against some stiff competition from other alphas across Europe. But knowing her as well as I do, I can say without a doubt that she's in with a fighting chance."

# CHAPTER FOUR

Three days later, out on the manor's back lawn, Andre faced off against Caleb, both of them sweating despite the cool, foggy day. Caleb came at him again, a smooth, lithe attack that feigned left, swung right, and then grazed past Andre's jaw as he whipped his head back just in time. He countered, moved right, lashed out with a leg that Caleb spun to avoid, then jumped to avoid a well aimed kick. It was invigorating. Caleb was an expert, that much was certain. Especially considering he was fighting with only one eye, the other a puckered mess from an injury sustained years ago.

But even so, Andre would have had to admit that he was taking it easy on the man, not hitting too hard, not making use of some of the more advanced moves that could, at times, make it seem like Andre was flying, the laws of gravity simply not applying to him.

But Caleb was a fast learner and a willing student, and after half an hour of training, a few pertinent tips thrown in along the way, he'd already made some notable progress.

They had a small audience for the session. Silas was standing to the side, already having completed an hour of training with Andre, now observing his techniques as he trained Caleb. Baron was sitting on a stone wall a short way off, watching with no small degree of interest. John was loitering near the formal garden, an expert in going undetected, but despite the attention he was giving the weeds, Andre was sure he was watching, learning, analysing each move.

And Tank was over by the memorial wall in wolf form, as he often was these days after his captivity with the Noturatii, a grim expression on his wolf face.

"How about it, Tank?" Andre called, stretching his muscles ready for the next round. It hadn't been a huge surprise when Silas had approached him this morning to ask for extra training, the man a dedicated soldier who was not likely to pass up the opportunity of having an assassin on the estate without trying to improve his own skills. And then a few others had joined in, watching, asking questions, and Andre was happy to take advantage of the opportunity to assess Caleb's fighting skills without being too obvious about his intentions.

The Den had, for the most part, reacted well to the announcement that Andre was to stay on a little longer, some people choosing to avoid him, others welcoming the extended visit, Heron among the latter. Andre had grown up on this estate and Heron had filled the role of aunt perfectly, playing with him as a youngster, then becoming one of his tutors in his teenage years, and after more than two decades apart and with Andre an adult now, they had the growing beginnings of a firm friendship.

Tank shifted, sighed, and marched over to where Andre waited.

"How are your injuries?" Andre asked, in case there were any lingering issues he needed to be aware of. Extra training was all well and good, but not if it reopened fresh wounds that would better be left to heal.

"Good enough," Tank said, stripping off his sweater and limbering up as he prepared himself for a fight.

The first round went well, Tank a solid fighter, but he had significant strength and weight behind him, and he was inclined to use that in preference to style and speed.

In the second round, Andre made a point of exposing a few weaknesses in Tank's technique, offering pointers throughout, and he was a little surprised when Tank responded with more aggression, anger bleeding through his usual focus. And it wasn't hard to figure out why. After being tortured in the Noturatii lab, he was likely to be carrying a grudge or two, with Andre becoming a convenient target for that anger. It was one of the reasons Andre was keen to fight him, to assess not just his physical recovery, but his mental one as well.

It wasn't until the third round that Andre began to get worried. Tank was eyeing him with all the predatory intent of a wolf stalking a deer. Poised. Focused. And lining up for the kill.

"Maybe we should take a break," Andre suggested, after fending off Tank's next attack. But Tank wasn't listening. He lunged for Andre again, and it was at that point that Andre realised he might have underestimated the man's skills. He wasn't paying enough attention to the blow, more focused on getting Tank to calm down, and it caught him on the side of the face, rattling his teeth and causing a spark of anger in return. Andre was a trained killer, after all, and his automatic response to being attacked was to respond in kind. He'd punched Tank before he'd even thought about it, the battle suddenly far more serious than a friendly training bout.

Tank registered the change in his opponent, heavy handed force giving way to lithe elegance, his body tightening, his stance drawing in to centre his balance, and Andre wasn't entirely sure where Tank was right now, whether he was still aware of being on the estate, fighting a friend and ally, or whether he was, in fact, back in the lab, fending off scientists with syringes and guards wielding instruments of torture. Then Andre was deflecting a volley of blows, part of his mind suddenly paying attention to whether or not Tank had any hidden weapons on his body, cautious of a knife suddenly coming his way as he gave ground… which only seemed to enrage Tank more.

"Enough!" Andre yelled, shoving Tank away and getting himself out of range quickly. "Get a hold of yourself."

Tank glared at him, not backing down an inch, and Andre was dimly aware of Baron standing up and stepping forward, looking uncertain as to whether he'd need to step in, and of Silas, still loitering nearby, ready to lend a hand if needed.

It wasn't that Andre thought he would need help to take Tank down – he'd killed a Satva Khuli very recently, and Tank was certainly less of a threat than she had been. No, the real problem was to stop Tank without doing him any serious damage in the process. Training fights were, to a certain extent, quite stressful for a career assassin. Andre was far more accustomed to battles in which the stakes were real, life or death, and in which winning was the same as killing, and losing was the same as dying. In a training fight, he constantly had to remind himself to hold back, to pull that punch or not follow through with that strike, else he end up breaking a bone or blinding an eye when he'd really just meant to leave a bruise.

"Walk it off, Tank," Baron barked from beside him, just as he was wondering what his next step should be, either aggression or capitulation equally likely to set Tank off, and thankfully, the huge man was more willing to listen to his alpha than to an outsider. With a growl and a show of teeth, he backed off, turned around and stalked off across the lawn, throwing a few angry looks over his shoulder as he went. Andre stood for a moment, taking a slow breath, a sideways glance at Baron conveying his gratitude for the intervention.

"Sorry," Baron said shortly. "I thought he was dealing with it all better than this. I'll have a word to him. After he calms down."

Andre nodded, well aware of the often unpleasant consequences from run ins with the Noturatii, and not inclined to hold any grudges over it. But still, Tank was currently something of a loose cannon, and one way or another, he was going to have to deal with the trauma of his captivity.

But the next surprise in store for him was perhaps even more unexpected than Tank's reaction to the fight.

Caroline stepped up in front of him, dressed for a work out, and she levelled a cool, if mildly hopeful look at him. "Do you have time for one more?" she asked flatly. "Or have they worn you out already?"

One of the things he remembered well about Caroline was that she didn't take disappointment well, even in so small a thing as asking for help with her training, and so he didn't take any offence at her almost disdainful request. She was likely just preparing herself for him to refuse.

He fought not to smile. There was no way in the world he was going to refuse her, even if he'd been exhausted to the point of barely being able to stand up. But he was actually still feeling quite fresh, invigorated by the work out, and though he wouldn't say it to her, for fear of embarrassing her, this was a paltry effort compared to his regular training regime. It wasn't uncommon for him to keep going for six or eight hours a day, running, martial arts, full contact sparring with one of his fellow assassins, then rock climbing, swimming, knife throwing, then more sparring in wolf form. The need to keep his skills sharp was relentless, and at times he did more training in a single day than the average shifter did in a whole week.

There was also no question that he would refuse her on the basis of her being female. Noturatii operatives weren't picky about who they killed, and female shifters were just as likely to meet their demise at the pointy end of a knife as males.

"I'm game if you are," he said, with just a hint of challenge, and Caroline almost smiled – as close to the expression as she ever seemed to get.

As Caroline prepared for the fight, she felt a cool thrill of anticipation that had nothing to do with combat.

When Andre had first arrived at the Den several weeks ago, it had been like seeing a ghost. They'd met fifteen years ago in Italy, not long after Caroline had been converted, and it had been a traumatic time for her, and a trying one for him. Though they'd only spent eight weeks together, it had left indelible memories in Caroline's mind that had come flooding back with Andre's arrival – lost longings and hopes, regrets, and even a few threads of happiness, faint reflections of a time when both their lives had seemed far simpler. He'd aged since then, worries now lining his face, though he wore the years well, more handsome than ever.

"Hit me," he said, adopting a fighting stance, and, as she had been taught since the day she'd been recruited, Caroline blanked her mind from all distractions, replacing the image of him standing before her with the image in her mind of a Noturatii soldier, with the knowledge that if she didn't win this fight, she was heading home to the Great Hall in the House of Sirius.

And then she attacked.

Most of Caroline's training had been done by Silas. Raven had helped back when she was a new recruit, a former alpha of the Den who had been killed ten years ago, and Tank had given her a run for her money a few times, but Silas had been the mainstay of her training.

When she'd started, he'd complained that she was too up front, too obvious about her intentions – 'You fight like a buffalo' was what he'd actually said – and she'd learned to duck and weave, to move fast, to dodge blows, to deflect them, and all in all, she had done remarkably well. After all, she'd risen to the rank of alpha, and held that position for the past six years. So while she expected to be taught some new tricks by Andre, shown some weaknesses in her defence and gaps in her attacks, she hadn't expected there to be *too* big a difference in their ability levels, assassin or not.

So when she came at him, tried to tease out his fighting style, to land a few experimental blows, it came as quite a shock to realise that each time she tried to hit him, he was simply... not there. One of Silas's first lessons for avoiding injury had been 'get out of the way', but Andre took that to a whole new level. He didn't sidestep, didn't duck or spin or dodge. He just... vanished, reappearing a split second later, behind her elbow, or landing a blow to her knee. She staggered, regained her feet and tried again, paying more attention to the way he moved, and trying to figure out whether this was pure physical skill, or if he was employing some kind of shifter magic to confuse her.

Nope, she concluded a moment later. It was pure physical skill. There was no blurring of his form, no crackle of electricity, though he was certainly capable of mixing things up with a few magic tricks, even if he was choosing not to now. So she tried to move faster, to grab hold of him to slow him down, to dodge and weave as lithely as he was.

And she failed spectacularly. If anything, she was even further from landing a blow now than she had been before. Fighting Silas had been like fighting a snake, lithe, slippery and fast. Fighting Andre was more like trying to grab quicksilver. It was there, but it wasn't...

Caroline paused, acutely aware of her audience watching the fight and weighing up her skills. It seemed to her that Andre was being far tougher on her than he had been on Tank or Caleb. Why would he go out of his way to make her look bad?

But then, before her anger could get the better of her, she reminded herself that this was *Andre*. He wasn't the type to deliberately humiliate her. So what was the point he was trying to make?

Fifteen years ago, if he'd tried to teach her anything with this technique, she would have thrown a tantrum and declared it to be entirely unfair – something she'd subjected Silas to often enough, much to his exasperation. Now, she stopped, replayed the fight in her mind, trying to analyse what she had done wrong, what she could learn from the failure... and came up with absolutely nothing.

"Okay," she said finally, wiping sweat from her brow. "What am I doing wrong?" It was an effort to swallow her pride enough to ask the question. She was a seasoned fighter, after all, and a niggling part of her mind insisted that she was smart enough to figure it out on her own.

Andre quirked a smile at her. "Anticipation," he said simply. "You fight as if you're going to hit a person where they stand. Which is fine most of the time, because most people in a fight stay in relatively the same place. But when you start fighting people at my level, it's not about where a person is. It's about where they're going to be. You need to learn to anticipate where I'm going to move to, and what I'm going to do next, and then arrange to be there before I arrive."

His answer was completely baffling to her. But rather than deride or dismiss it, she paused a moment to give it some thought. And then said, "How?"

Andre grinned. "An excellent question. I'm so glad you asked."

# CHAPTER FIVE

**18 Years Ago**

Caroline stood behind her bedroom door, checked her uniform, shouldered her backpack, and attached a firm scowl to her face. She glanced in the mirror to check that everything looked as it was supposed to. Daggy t-shirt with 'Dan's Pizza Parlour' printed on the front. Hair pulled back in a tight pony tail. Expression on her face that said she was bored and generally pissed off with life, and anyone who didn't like it could go jump.

All set.

She opened the door and stomped down the hall, deliberately ignoring her brother Greg as she reached the living room. He was sitting on the couch drinking beer and bitching at his girlfriend about the fact that she was refusing to give him a blow job.

The chit would give in in the end. She always did. But at least this time, Caroline would be out of the house by the time she did it. Because there was never any guarantee that they would bother to go into Greg's room when he decided to take his pants off.

"Look at the little princess," Greg said as she passed through the living room. "All ready to go out and do some hard work. Aw, aren't you just a special little worker."

"Fuck you," Caroline said, in the most disinterested tone possible. At seventeen years old, work was hard to come by, and her job at the pizza parlour was dull, a droning monotony at best, completely disgusting at worst. Last week, she'd spent an hour and a half cleaning mouldy pizza dough out of the bottom of the bins, and had come home stinking of garbage. She'd found lumps of dough in her hair for three days afterwards. But it earnt her a little money, and, more importantly, got her out of this God-forsaken house for a few hours.

Not that Greg had any appreciation for her efforts. He was unemployed, cruising along on government handouts, and of the opinion that anyone who did more work than absolutely necessary was an idiot.

But today, Caroline was more interested than usual in avoiding his attention. Because today, she wasn't going to work at the pizza parlour, wasn't going to get dough up her fingernails and come home with her clothes stinking of pepperoni.

No, today she had a job interview. Sales assistant for a clothing store. In reality, she knew, it was nothing more than standing behind the register and ringing up people's purchases – people who were all buying clothes that were far nicer and far more expensive than anything Caroline could afford. But it was a huge step up from kitchen hand at the dodgiest pizza place in town, and the next step forward in getting herself the hell out of this piss-hole. Permanently.

Her backpack contained a respectable outfit, the one blouse she owned, pale blue and quite plain but with a nice, feminine cut, and a pair of plain black trousers. To avoid her brother's attention, she would get a bus from her usual stop, then change buses the next suburb over, get changed in a public toilet and hopefully present herself as a decent, hard working young woman come time for the interview.

If she could just remember not to swear while she was in there.

In the back of her mind, she was a little surprised at her own tenacity at seeking a better life, given the chaos and violence all around her. Perhaps it was because of Old Joe, the war veteran who lived down the street, who told her each day without fail as she passed his house that she was turning into 'a fine young lady'. Perhaps it was due to that one teacher in eighth grade who'd taken a genuine interest in her, told her that life was a gift, and that dreams could come true, if only you were prepared to endure a season or three of hell to get there. Perhaps it was because of that movie she'd seen, the one where the skinny little kid got beaten up all his life, but then came out years later to become a gold medal winning Olympic sprinter.

However the seeds of her rebellion had been planted, Caroline was clinging to them now, though some days she seemed to be hanging off the edge of a very high cliff by nothing more than her fingernails.

But this job could make the difference she had been looking for. A legitimate career move. A reliable source of money. A chance to prove she was better than her drug addicted, jail-bound family.

"Where the fuck are you going?" her father snapped when she reached the front door, and Caroline very deliberately stopped to crack her knuckles, feigning indifference while keeping him firmly within her line of sight. *Never turn your back*, she'd learned years ago, and that rule, among a handful of others she'd learned to live by, had spared her some of the more severe beatings of her young life.

"To work," she said, her tone implying he was stupid. "Same as I do every week. Fuck, after six months, you'd think you'd have figured out that I have a job by now."

He wanted to hit her. The glow of violence was bright in his eyes. But she'd learned to hit back by now, vigorous work outs filling out her body with thick muscles, combat boots on her feet able to deal hefty blows, and fading bruises on his face testament to her success in previous scuffles between them. So he hesitated, and Caroline took the opportunity to open the door and escape through the gap, not wanting to take the risk that he'd follow through and she'd have to go to the interview with fresh bruises on her face. About half the time he thought better of his attacks, having learned that Caroline was younger than him, quicker and had an attitude that gave as good as it got. But the other half of the time, usually when he'd been drinking, he forgot that she could fight back, and he'd have a go at her anyway, and while she was quicker, he was still stronger, meaning there was no guarantee she'd win any particular bout in the boxing ring.

Out on the street, she set a fast pace down the road, glancing back now and then to check that no one had bothered to follow her.

"There you are, young lady," Joe called cheerfully as she passed. "As fine a young woman as I've ever seen. You've got great things ahead of you, I'm sure!"

Caroline waved half-heartedly and called "Good afternoon", unable to figure out how someone living in this neighbourhood managed to maintain such a positive outlook on life. Joe grinned back and raised his coffee cup in salute, then Caroline marched on, down to the bus stop, more determined than ever that this time, she was going to break free from her old life and make something of herself.

Caroline stared down at the letter in her hands and swore fluently. The owner of the café she was sitting in glanced up at her, the gruff old man no doubt ready to kick her out if she started causing a fuss. This was a rough neighbourhood, and he'd had too many cups broken, seen too many tables overturned to put up with riff-raff for long.

She hadn't got the job. She'd found the envelope in the letter box this morning and, not wanting to open it at home where Greg would give her a hard time about it, she'd brought it here, where there was some peace and quiet, hopeful and excited as she'd read the first line. It said she'd come across well in the interview – she'd bloody well better have, Caroline thought indignantly. She'd tried her hardest to play the part of well mannered, respectful teenager who would be polite and helpful to the customers, and had even managed to get through the entire twenty minutes without cursing.

But the letter had gone on to explain that her interview had been unsuccessful; the lady had found another candidate with some prior experience in sales, so she was going with them instead.

Caroline resisted the urge to throw her coffee mug across the room. With one last, heartfelt "Fuck!", she got up and left the café, sparing the owner the bother of throwing her out.

How the hell was she supposed to get anywhere in life when she couldn't get anything better than a minimum wage, crap-arse job? She'd be finishing school at the end of the year and had hoped to be able to afford to move out of her hell-hole of a home by then. Maybe get a flat with some friends. Save up for a shitty car and start clawing her way up the ladder, like a drowning rat trying to escape the floodwaters.

Outside, she turned left, then stopped, turned around and went back the other way, wandering aimlessly down the street. It was still early, and being a Saturday, no one would care what time she came home. Or if she came home at all. More often than not these days she stayed at her boyfriend's place. He was an arsehole, just like most men, but at least he didn't hit her, just called her names and left his filth lying around his flat. It was a small step up from living with Greg and her father, Troy temporarily not her problem as he was currently in jail.

As soon as she got her own place, she'd ditch the bastard, but for now, spreading her legs for him a few times a week meant she could keep using him for a place to stay.

Movement caught her eye, and Caroline swore as she recognised the man across the road. He was following her, and trying to act nonchalant about it. Fuck, not again. Caroline kept walking, deliberately maintaining her pace, but out of the corner of her eye, she watched the man as he tailed her down the street. He was middle aged, tough and toned, but not like the thugs in the gangs, not like the drug addicts who hurled abuse at random strangers, not like the petty criminals who nudged closer to serious jail time every day. No, for all his tough exterior, there was something unique about this man. Something quiet, studied. Peaceful, even, if Caroline would dare to call it that.

But he'd also been following her for the past week, and 'peaceful' was not a word she was willing to apply to a weirdo with a tendency for stalking women.

She considered her options. She could call the police. But she hated them with a passion, having been harassed repeatedly in the past few years, the cops convinced she was doing drugs and determined to catch her out for possession, or even dealing. She'd never done drugs in her life. But she had seen the downside of that lifestyle up close and personal, a friend passing out and having to be taken to hospital after taking a bad pill. Another friend, raped after she'd got so high she didn't know what was happening or where she was. Caroline had decided long ago that she was never going to go down that path. Not that the cops cared, no matter how many times she denied using.

She could continue to ignore the man, as she had done so far. He never approached her, never followed her home or showed up at school. Just watched her from a distance when she was out and about. And since she tended to haunt the same few blocks in her spare time, it wasn't like it was terribly hard to find her.

Or she could confront the man. See what the fuck he wanted. And since they were currently in a public place, on a crowded street in the middle of a Saturday afternoon, there wasn't likely to be a safer time or place to have it out with him.

Caroline was a tough bitch, hitting hard, taking no shit from anyone, telling it like it was, whether it was her drunk father, her thug of a brother or any one of the local boys getting in her face. She knew how to look after herself.

But she also knew how to avoid trouble. Don't get into cars with drunk boys. Don't linger in shadowy places. Don't be afraid to ask the bouncer of the club to call you a cab, pride be damned, because having a three hundred pound gorilla babysit you like a toddler was still preferable to being snatched into a dark alley and raped.

There was a public square up ahead, wide open spaces, plenty of places to go if she needed to run away, so she kept going until she reached it, stopped beside the ugly sculpture in the centre of it, and turned, arms folded, eyes fixed on the man. His long hair was in a ponytail, a motorbike helmet in his hands, and he was wearing a red t-shirt – it was worth making note of these things, Caroline told herself, in case she needed to make a report on him later.

He paused when he saw her stop, and Caroline wondered what she was going to do next if he simply walked away.

But he didn't. A moment later, he resumed his slow, easy pace, a calm confidence oozing from him as he crossed the square to reach her.

"What the fuck do you want?" Caroline snapped immediately.

"I mean you no harm," the man said quickly. "I just want to talk to you."

"Yeah, right. You get off on sneaking around with girls young enough to be your daughter? Cos I ain't into that shit."

"Not at all," the man said, his accent starched and proper. "I have a business proposition for you."

Caroline snorted. "A 'business' proposition? Well, you're out of luck, cos I ain't into that shit either."

The man smiled, a strange look that was almost bashful. "You misunderstand. The business I work in has nothing to do with prostitution."

Okay, she could humour him, Caroline decided. Since they were here, and he wasn't being rude. "What is it then?"

"I work for a covert operations unit. The exact nature of our business is… somewhat delicate. But we're always on the lookout for people with a particular skill set. A skill set that you seem to cover nicely."

Was he winding her up? "Look, Einstein, I ain't got no 'particular skill set.' I'm a kid from the wrong side of the tracks who's just trying to finish school and get the hell out of this shit hole, so-"

"On the contrary. How long have I been following you?"

What the fuck? "A week."

"When was the very first time you saw me?"

"Last Sunday. Outside the pizza place."

"And what was I wearing?"

"A black leather jacket and jeans. And you had that motorbike helmet with you."

The man looked briefly impressed. "Very observant. Last Tuesday you had a fight with a man outside the club on Nelson Street. He was twice your size, but you won the fight. Quite easily, I might add."

Caroline shrugged. "Kick a guy in the balls, and they all go down pretty much the same."

"And you've been getting solid grades at school. Impressive, given the difficulties you must have in completing your studies."

What the hell? "You've been going through my school files? Look, you fuck-head, you're messing with the wrong person. That shit is private, and you've got no right to-"

"Like I said," the man interrupted, his tone sharpening just a touch. "I work for a covert operations unit. We have access to files that the general public could never get their hands on. Getting into your school files was as simple as a few clicks of a mouse."

Interesting. Despite her reservations, Caroline was getting interested. "You work for the Government?"

"Not the Government, no. Our operations are a little more below the radar than that."

"Are you criminals?" There was no way she was getting involved in some sort of crime ring, no matter how sophisticated they might be.

"No."

"Then what are you?"

"All in good time. But first, I'd like to know a little more about your plans for the future. You've been looking for a job. Calling people about flats for rent. So tell me, Caroline, in an ideal world, what would your future look like?"

How the fuck did he know her name? "Who the fuck are you?" she demanded roughly.

"My name is Kendrick. I'm the leader of my unit. And we lost a few good agents recently, so we're on the look out for some new recruits."

"What exactly are you offering me? A job? Like, as a spy, or some shit?"

"That's not too far from the truth. But it's far more than a job. It's a whole new way of life. Money, though probably not as much as you might imagine. Training in skills you wouldn't find anywhere outside the highest ranks of the military. Membership into an organisation whose operatives are loyal beyond all reason. If you were to become one of us, there are nearly twenty men and women who would welcome you as a sister, and who would willingly put their lives on the line should yours ever be threatened. You would have the doors opened into a world of mystery and myth the likes of which the world hasn't seen since the Ancient Greeks erected temples for gods who walked the earth. This, Caroline, is the way out that you've been searching for. All you have to do is embrace it."

Fuck. It sounded far too good to be true, a wind up, a con-artist, a trap just waiting to snap shut with her in its jaws.

And yet...

"Okay, I'll bite," Caroline said, not quite able to believe her own words. "So what do you want from me in return?"

Half an hour later, Kendrick left the grimy town square, feeling cautiously optimistic about this first meeting. Caroline was a firecracker, that much was certain, her actions and attitude fuelled by anger, but not without good reason. Before coming here, Eric, the Den's IT expert, had run police checks on her entire family, had checked her school records, and they'd spent a month tailing her, in a far more clandestine manner than he'd been using himself. But then again, this time around he'd been *trying* to get her attention. And it had worked rather nicely.

She was perfect as a new recruit for the Den. No close ties to her family, no significant responsibilities, a marked aversion to any kind of illegal drugs, though she had started drinking alcohol at quite a young age. And she was desperate enough to get out of here that she was willing to overlook his often vague responses to her questions. But not stupid enough to let things slide entirely.

The shape shifters were an almost neurotically secretive society, and as alpha of the British Den, Kendrick knew he had to walk a fine line between giving her enough information to keep her interested, but not enough to put their Den at risk.

All things considered, their investigations into this young woman were going remarkably well. And now that she'd taken the bait... all he had to do was reel her in.

# CHAPTER SIX

**Present Day**

Jacob sat at his desk in the Noturatii's main base in east London and scowled at the reply he'd received from Headquarters. As predicted, his superiors were deeply unhappy about the lab explosion, not so much in regards to the loss of resources, but due to the lost results from the experiments on shifter conversions. The letter read:

*It seems that much of the loss of data was caused by your apparent strategy of withholding information from head office, presumably in order to delay progress made by other labs and thereby advance your own team's interests and prestige. This sort of behaviour is juvenile and entirely unacceptable for a man of your position. As such, we are removing your team from the Conversion Project and transferring all further research on the subject to our laboratories in Germany.*

Jacob bristled as he read the reply, resenting being told off like a small child. But fortunately for him, they weren't coming down *too* hard on him. The letter went on:

*While we do not approve of the way you have been running your lab, the fact remains that your team have made significant advances towards being able to create new shifters, and this gives us a solid foundation from which to continue our research.*

So despite the reprimand, there were to be no further repercussions for his actions. He wasn't being demoted, or worse, killed; other staff who had betrayed the Noturatii had had their 'employment' swiftly terminated. But despite HQ's harsh stance on detractors, Jacob would have been surprised if they'd resorted to such drastic measures in his case. He had an outstanding track record, after all – in his ten years as Chief of Operations, he'd doubled the size of the Noturatii's presence in England, secured new funding from two government departments and hired some of the best educated staff the country had to offer. The German head office knew he was worth his salt, and were prepared to give him another chance because of it. But that wasn't an excuse to rest on his laurels, Jacob reminded himself sternly. If he wanted to maintain his current good standing with HQ, then he'd have to do some serious repair work to make up for the disaster in the lab.

But there was other news in the letter that was more positive. As promised, they were sending a new science team to replace those who had been killed. Doctor Gianna Evans, a prominent scientist from the office in the United States, was due to arrive in two days' time, bringing with her a team of three, who would set up the new lab and continue experimenting on the shifters. They were, in fact, bringing a live shifter with them for that very purpose, one that the Noturatii had captured in Russia not two days ago. And Melissa Hunter, the only surviving member of his own science team, would be welcome to join them, as she'd proved her worth in the conversion experiments. He read on:

*Dr Evans and her team will focus on attempting to decode the methods by which the shifters transform their bodies. We are confident that electricity is involved at each step of the way and an understanding of this process may lead to the development of advanced weaponry which would greatly assist our efforts in combat.*

*We expect you to make Dr Evans and her team welcome, and to provide whatever equipment or office space is necessary for her to perform her work. She will be sending regular reports to Headquarters for review, and I trust there will be no attempts to interfere with her work or to hide new advances made.*

Jacob sighed. In addition to Headquarters' dissatisfaction with his recent strategies, he'd received more bad news just yesterday. It had been discovered that one of the subjects they had attempted to convert in the lab, a woman by the name of Gabrielle, had returned to her home. It was a startling development, but after a moment's consideration, Jacob had realised that, contrary to previous beliefs, the experiment to convert her into a shifter must have failed – yet another disappointment in an ever growing list. The shifters had taken the woman with them when they'd fled the lab, and if they'd allowed her to go home, it was a sure sign that she wasn't one of them. There was no way they would have allowed a wolf to wander about alone, or for the woman to leave their pack if she had posed any kind of security risk.

And now that Jacob's team had been removed from the Conversion Project, there wasn't even any point in recapturing her to reattempt the conversion. This one, he was reluctant to admit, was going to have to slip through the net.

But that was a secondary concern, he told himself firmly, closing the email and dismissing the issue for the moment. Of far greater importance than these experiments was discovering the whereabouts of this second shifter pack. Miller and his team were already putting a strategy together, dividing up the Lakes District to search for the bastards. And as far as Jacob was concerned, that couldn't happen soon enough. They had caused him no shortage of difficulties and had proved themselves to be capable of massive destruction and slaughter without mercy. He had to find them, the discovery certain to regain him a large measure of the favour he had lost due to the lab explosion.

And when he did find them, he promised himself grimly... they would be made to pay.


Caroline walked down the stairs into the foyer, a list of notes in her hand as she headed for a meeting with Baron. Il Trosa's annual summer gatherings, the Densmeets, were coming up and this year, as they did once every three years, the British Den was playing host to one of them. A contingent of shifters were due to arrive in a few weeks from all corners of Europe. Misty Hills wasn't large enough to host them all, their numbers more than doubling for the festivities, but there was an estate in Scotland that they had rented out for the summer on these occasions for the past fifty years or so, owned by an amiable family who were happy to guarantee them absolute privacy for the duration of their stay.

In the other two years out of the three, the Lakes District Den was split up, the shifters being sent in groups of four or five to other Densmeets across Europe. It was both a political and a social occasion, a member of the Council attending each meeting to discuss important matters of policy and the future direction of Il Trosa, and also a chance for everyone to meet shifters from other Dens, to make friends, strengthen alliances, and, for those that way inclined, the chance to meet potential romantic partners. It wasn't uncommon for the summer to end with new couples forming and various shifters requesting transfers to different Dens, to be closer to their newfound love interests.

It was also an opportunity to exchange useful skills, and this year, Skip had been asked to run a hacking workshop, with several other hackers among those hoping to learn some of her more refined techniques.

As the host Den this year, there was a mass of planning to be done, seminars prepared, food supplies brought in, security measures put in place, and, of course, the Games – athletic and strategic challenges that were partly a chance for the shifters to hone their skills in a friendly competition, and partly an excuse to blow off steam.

As she reached the ground floor, Caroline turned left, heading for the sitting room where she had last seen Andre. Though he wasn't an official member of the Den, his input into the planning process would be helpful. Tank was also joining them, and Caroline was hoping it would be a pleasant distraction for him, to get his mind off his recent battle with the Noturatii, and hopefully drag him out of this moody phase.

But just as she was crossing the foyer, the front door opened and John came in. He ignored her, as he often did, slouching across the room and up the stairs, but the sight of him made Caroline pause as she assessed the fresh bruises across his face, and she closed her eyes and fought back a sigh.

Fuck. She'd told herself time and time again that she wasn't going to interfere with his unconventional relationship with Baron, had had assurances from Baron himself that there was nothing for her to be overly concerned about, but every time she saw the bruises, her instinctive concern for the boy leapt to the fore.

Not your business, she told herself firmly, resuming her walk to the sitting room. It wasn't like there was anything she could do about it, anyway...

The door to the sitting room was ajar, so she didn't bother knocking, just pushed it open, glancing around for Andre.

But what she found inside made her pull up in surprise. Andre was there, sitting with one ankle crossed over his knee on the sofa. And sitting opposite him, sipping tea from a delicate china cup, was Heron. Laughing. Chatting. No doubt sharing stories about Andre's travels over the years. Caroline was aware that he'd grown up in this Den, and that Heron was much like an aunt to him, but upon seeing them so cheerful and friendly with each other, Caroline was shocked at the powerful wave of jealousy that hit her.

But no, it wasn't seeing them chatting together that was playing havoc with her emotions, she realised a moment later. It was that the instant she'd stepped into the room, the conversation had stopped. The laughter died out. The smile on Heron's face went from happy to polite. And Andre looked up at her with an unreadable expression, his eyes suddenly guarded, his smile vanishing into a carefully neutral look so that Caroline suddenly felt like an intruder, firmly shut out of the friendly moment.

She and Andre had their own shared past, she thought with no small amount of resentment for Heron, an intense eight week stint in Italy that had changed her life forever. But Andre had made no effort to rebuild *their* past relationship, no sitting around sipping tea and laughing about old stories with *her*.

"Sorry to interrupt," Caroline said, feeling awkward, "but Baron wants to talk about the Densmeet, and we were hoping you could join us."

"Duty calls," Andre said congenially, standing up and giving Heron a slight bow. "We must do this again, though. You've heard all my stories, but I haven't heard nearly enough of yours."

Caroline led Andre silently to the library, not wanting to appear surly or petulant, but unable to find a single thing to say that wouldn't sound horribly inane. Conversation had never been her strong point, after all.

# CHAPTER SEVEN

**18 Years Ago**

Caroline stepped back from the punching bag and pulled her gloves off. Sweat was dripping down her face and neck, the workout long and hard, but she'd never enjoyed herself so much.

She wiped sticky strands of hair out of her face and turned to face Kendrick, a shadow of a grin on her face. It was as close to really looking happy as she got these days, but he seemed to read her mood well enough, and grinned back.

"Very well done," he told her, and she was secretly thrilled at the praise. Since that first, awkward meeting in the town square, she'd been putting Kendrick through his paces, not willing to accept his claims of a secret spy organisation without the hard evidence to back it up. Did he even know martial arts, she'd demanded of him on their second meeting, before delivering the ultimatum that unless she could see this 'special training' for herself, she wasn't going to touch them with a forty foot pole.

She'd half expected the man to walk away, his bluff called. But instead, for the past six weeks, he'd taken her on a whirlwind tour of her potential new career, training in karate, taekwondo and boxing, attending a shooting range to have her first lesson in using a pistol, and then he'd slyly asked her if she liked dogs. She'd shrugged, not at all sure why it was a relevant question… until she'd been taken to an out-of-the-way park and a few of Kendrick's colleagues had demonstrated the most amazing display of dog obedience she'd ever seen. The dog, named Anna, had been hard to identify, a brown and grey medium sized creature that didn't seem to quite fit any of the breeds Caroline knew, but she'd demonstrated the ability to sniff out drugs from the most unlikely places, to obey her trainer with startling precision and to take down a 'criminal', in this case, a volunteer in a padded body suit, with ease. Should she sign up, Kendrick had explained, then Caroline would be working with a large number of canines, and it was important that she was comfortable with the idea.

Caroline had never given much thought to dogs before, but after seeing the skills this one had displayed, she found herself rather liking the idea of a team of guard dogs roaming the spy compound, attacking the bad guys, and she'd said as much, which had made Kendrick laugh for reasons that Caroline didn't entirely understand.

But the thing that had really drawn her to this secret group was the way they treated her. Each of her instructors had been patient, disciplined, polite, explaining each step of her training clearly and encouraging her when she failed, praising her when she succeeded. Most of her teachers at school had been harsh and belittling, scolding her for the slightest failure, so it was hardly surprising that she was finding the idea of spending more time with these people appealing.

Now, in the boxing gym, Kendrick handed her a towel and sent her off to the showers, waiting until she emerged fifteen minutes later, clean and dry in a fresh set of clothes. He'd bought them for her a few weeks ago, another gesture to demonstrate the organisation's ready access to funding, as well as a purely pragmatic necessity – Caroline neither owned, nor could afford specific clothes just for working out.

They headed out of the gym and back to Kendrick's motorbike. The first few times they'd gone anywhere together, Caroline had insisted on finding her own way there, not willing to trust a random stranger by getting onto his bike with him. Now, though, she'd started to trust the man, as each and every time he'd stated an intention to do something he'd followed through, on time, and accurate down to the last detail. And to be honest, there was something exhilarating about flying down the road on a bike, a borrowed helmet on her head and the wind cold against her skin. She'd enjoyed riding with him, and was looking forward to doing it again.

But instead of putting on his helmet and getting onto the bike, Kendrick instead turned to lean against the wall. He folded his arms and gave Caroline a steely look, and she braced herself for whatever was coming next.

Right up front, Kendrick had been clear about his expectations of her. She was to follow his instructions, show up on time, and never, ever tell anyone else what she was doing, or mention the slightest detail about her new acquaintances. To do so would not only disqualify her from ever joining their organisation, but would also place her in grave danger, he had emphasised more than once, as his team understandably had enemies who would happily use a stray civilian as bait or leverage to strike a blow at them.

And as far as she was aware, Caroline had lived up to her end of the bargain, lying to her family, her friends, her boyfriend, keeping her head down and managing to invent a dozen excuses as to where she was going at random times of the day and reasons why she couldn't hang out or make it to a party.

But the look on Kendrick's face now gave her a cool sense of foreboding, as if something had gone wrong, or was about to, and she tried to control her growing unease. This had all been going so well. A new start. An opportunity to have a real purpose.

"So," Kendrick said, looking her up and down, a wariness in his eyes that was at odds with his usually open and genial nature. "You've seen what we can do. You've seen some of the resources at our command. And you've met some of our operatives."

He fell silent for a moment, and Caroline realised that this was it. He'd delivered everything she'd asked, explained himself as well as possible, given the secrecy of his organisation, jumped through every hoop she could think of. And now she was going to be asked to choose. She looked away, let her gaze wander up and down the street, trying to imagine what it would be like to never come here again.

"So what do you think?" Kendrick spoke up finally. "Have we lived up to your expectations?"

"Yes. Absolutely."

"And what about joining us? Have you given that some thought?"

"It has a certain appeal," Caroline admitted. "I still don't know what the fuck you do, but whatever it is, you seem to know how to do it well."

Kendrick nodded. "Good to hear. Then let's move on to the tougher part. There are conditions to joining us. If you agree to sign up, then the full details of our operation, our scope of activities and your new living conditions will be made known to you once we arrive at the compound. Following that, there's a mandatory two year training period before you can become a fully qualified operative. But given the dangers of our operations, understand that resigning is not an option. There is only one way people ever leave our organisation, and that is in a wooden box. Do you understand?"

That sent a cold shiver down Caroline's spine. "Just for the sake of clarity, is it too late for me to back out now? I mean, right now, standing here on the street, if I decide this isn't for me, will you shoot me, or do I get to walk away?"

"At any time until you accept our offer and we arrive at the compound, you have the opportunity to leave," Kendrick answered in his usual straightforward manner. "After you enter the compound, that's it. So if you have any questions or concerns, I strongly suggest you voice them now."

Good to know. "So what if I join up and turn out to be a massive failure at your training? If I can't resign, then logically that implies you can't sack me either. So what happens then?"

"We have a large number of skilled trainers in bases right across Europe," Kendrick said seriously. "We're willing to devote a large amount of time and energy to training our recruits, and there are a variety of different positions you could fill, each requiring a different skill set. One way or another, we will find a role suitable for you."

Caroline thought that through, then nodded. Nice to know this mob was loyal to their trainees. "Okay, so what other conditions are there to me joining you?"

"Absolute anonymity," Kendrick replied. "As far as the general public is concerned, you will cease to exist. We'll ask you to drop out of high school. Quit your job. Break up with your boyfriend. Cut all ties to anyone you know, including all members of your family."

Caroline snorted. "Yeah, well, that's no great loss."

"I'm serious, Caroline," Kendrick said sharply. "By joining us, you agree to abandon all links to your past. You will never, ever see your family again. Never contact them, never phone them, never have anything to do with them."

Caroline didn't even have to think about that one. "Consider them forgotten," she said blackly. "The sooner I get out of that hell hole, the better."

"You are entering a world of danger, war and uncertainty, as well as of loyalty, camaraderie and devotion. Your life as you know it will never be the same. Last chance, Caroline. Do you want to join us, or do you want to walk away?"

"I want to join you."

"Good." Kendrick reached into his jacket and pulled out an envelope. "This is a list of requirements for you, things you'll need to do before we meet again," he said, handing it to her. "As I said, you'll have to quit your job. Drop out of school. Concoct some story for your family, maybe tell them you're moving to another city to look for work... there's a list of suggestions in here and you can choose the one you think is most plausible. I'll see you again in exactly one week, on the morning of the nineteenth, at the train station in the city centre. Bring any personal effects you desire, but don't worry about clothing, toiletries or the like. Everything you need will be provided."

"What if you don't show up?" Caroline asked, trying not to sound nervous. He was asking her to take a hell of a risk, cancelling out her entire life like this, and it was only good sense to plan for unexpected contingencies.

"If I don't show up, it means I'm dead," Kendrick told her flatly. "And in that case, one of my colleagues will contact you to make alternative arrangements. For security reasons, I can't give you a way to contact us, but rest assured, we will be keeping an eye on you between now and then. If anything goes wrong, we are here to help."

Caroline's heart was in her throat as she walked away. So much possibility, and yet so much risk. What if it all went wrong? What if Kendrick was not who he said he was? But what was her alternative, she wondered grimly. Keep working a minimum wage job and waiting for the day when her father tired of beating her up with his fists and picked up a shotgun instead?

She had one week to go. One week to make a series of nerve-wracking decisions, to burn her bridges once and for all. One more week to endure a living hell, and to hope that she managed to make it out alive before the whole damn thing came crashing to the ground.


When the day finally came, Caroline was both as nervous and as excited as a skydiver on their first jump. She'd done her duty, quit school, dumped her boyfriend, and told her family that she was going to America for six months. All going well, she'd find a job there and wouldn't come back. When Greg asked her where she'd got the money, she cheerfully replied that she'd stolen it, and then had to tolerate a round of degrading suggestions that she'd been hooking on the side and had earned the money that way. Fucking arsehole.

But that was all over now. She'd finished her last day at school, packed her belongings, meagre though they were, and after a last farewell with her old friends at a local pub, all she had to do was pick up her bag from her house and catch a bus to the 'airport', or so her family believed.

She knew something was wrong the instant she set foot inside the door. Rather than greeting her with insults and threats of violence, her father was standing in the kitchen doorway, beer in hand and a scowl on his face... and he said absolutely nothing. Just eyed her coldly and sucked on his beer.

Greg was on the couch, playing a video game, and he hit pause as she came into the room, a glint of glee in his eyes, though he, too, said nothing. Caroline paused, glanced around the room, and then continued on to her bedroom with no small degree of trepidation. It was going to be fine, she told herself firmly. All she had to do was walk down the hall, pick up her bag, and get the hell out of here. If they tried to stop her, she could fight them. If they insulted her, she could ignore them. If they...

She stopped in the doorway to her room, and her jaw dropped. What the hell had they done?! She spun around, marched back to the living room, picked up a stray plate sitting on the stained coffee table and smashed the thing over Greg's head. "You fucking arsehole! You hate me so much, but you can't even let me fucking leave, you mother fucking piece of shit! How could you?" She picked up a lamp and threw it at him, and it hit him squarely in the face, mostly because he was already dazed from the earlier blow to the head. But Caroline's father was suffering no such handicap, and he cheerfully smashed his now empty beer bottle against the wall and came at her with the jagged end of glass.

"You think you're so much better than us?" he asked, words slurred with alcohol. "You think you can just up and leave like your fucking mother? I've raised you, paid for your food and your clothes, gave you a fucking house to live in, and you think you can just walk out?" He swung the bottle at her, and Caroline had had enough. She wasn't going to stand by while he attacked her with broken glass. She picked up the coffee table, surprised at how easy it was, though rage was flooding her system with adrenaline, and she swung the thing at him, heard a satisfying crack as it collided with his ribs, fairly sure she'd just broken some of them. He grunted, hit the wall, but didn't go down, so she swung it again, thumping it down over his back, and he went down that time, hit the floor and lay still. Perhaps she had killed him, she thought with a wave of fear... but fuck it. All the better if she had.

Greg was writhing on the couch, moaning, so she wasted no more time with him. Just marched back to her room and surveyed the damage they had done in her absence.

Not a single thing was left untouched. Everything on the shelves had been tossed to the floor. Her clothes were scattered about, the ones in the wardrobe as well as the ones in her bag, and they'd had paint tipped over them. There were holes in the walls, no doubt the result of angry fists, her books ripped up, the clock broken into a thousand pieces, broken glass scattered through the debris. They'd destroyed everything she owned, every last thing she could lay claim to in the whole world, and Caroline felt a fiery hate settle in her belly. She'd put up with far too much shit over the years, felt the blow of too many fists, far more than any child should have to endure. And now they couldn't even let her leave without taking one final shot at her.

She picked up the bag she'd packed earlier to see if anything had survived.

Nothing. Nothing was left unbroken or undamaged. And she felt tears prick at eyes as she pulled out the small ceramic figurine of a dolphin that had sat on her bedside table for years. It was damaged beyond repair, the tail and flippers snapped off, the delicate blue curls of the ocean shattered beyond recognition. Her mother had given it to her for her twelfth birthday; the last gift she'd ever given her. And Caroline still felt an ache in her chest when she thought of the woman. She'd been a hopeless parent, an alcoholic, unable to care for herself half the time, but she'd also loved Caroline, and the few good memories she had of her childhood were all focused around the woman. Along with a black resentment that she hadn't taken Caroline with her when she'd finally left.

Perhaps it was better this way, Caroline thought bleakly. A clean break, with nothing left to bring up memories of the past. She swiftly wiped her eyes and banished the tears. There would be time enough for that later.

But right now, she had a bus to catch, a new life to discover, and she was running short on time as it was.

Caroline dropped the broken dolphin on the floor, determinedly refusing to care where it landed. Then she put her shoulders back, her head up, and marched herself straight out the front door, ignoring the insults and threats that echoed after her.

# CHAPTER EIGHT

Out on the street, Caroline tried not to think, tried not to dwell on anything other than getting to the train station and meeting Kendrick. If she stopped and thought about what her family had just done, she was likely to either break down into tears, or turn around, go back, and finish the job of killing them then and there.

She got to the bus stop and waited impatiently, tapping her foot, pacing up and down until the bus arrived, and then she got on, took a seat near the back and stared out the window, trying to slow her racing heart, praying that Kendrick would be there on time, that his promises would come true and that she hadn't just made one of the worst mistakes of her life.

She was so caught up in her thoughts that she barely noticed when two well-dressed men got onto the bus – unusual in this part of town – nor when they sat down, one in the seat in front of her, one beside her. "Excuse me, Ma'am," the one beside her said. "It seems we have something of a situation."

Caroline looked up, taking note of the two men for the first time. And she was instantly on guard. "What situation?" she asked, thoughts racing as to what the hell could be going wrong now. Was Kendrick dead? He'd said that if he couldn't meet her, he'd send his colleagues instead. But if that was the case, then why wouldn't they just meet her at the train station at the arranged time?

But on the other hand, who else could these men be? They were clearly out of place, blending in as well here as a prostitute in a nunnery.

"It's regarding a particular acquaintance of yours," the man said, and held out a small photograph of Kendrick. So Kendrick had sent them. It was both a relief and a cause for alarm. Kendrick was her best and closest link to her new life, and if something had happened to him, there were no guarantees that the rest of his organisation would honour the promises he had made.

Caroline was about to ask what had happened when her phone beeped, announcing an incoming text message. Unable to afford one of her own, Kendrick had given her the phone several weeks ago. "Just in case", he'd said, and Caroline had taken it without question.

Now, she quickly pulled it out to see what the message was. She didn't use it very often, didn't receive many messages as none of her friends were able to afford one, though now that the devices were growing in popularity, the prices were gradually coming down.

On second thought, she realised, feeling a growing sense of unease, if Kendrick was sending someone else to meet her, why wouldn't he have chosen one of the few people she'd met during her training sessions, rather than random strangers? She glanced at the message.

*Get off the bus. Now.*

"Excuse me, this is my stop," she announced, standing up and all but forcing the man beside her out of the way. He could make a fuss if he liked, but they were in a public place, surrounded by other passengers, and she was more than willing to press the issue if he forced a confrontation.

But he moved aside, letting her out, and she wasn't entirely surprised when he and his friend both followed her off the bus. They'd arrived at a long row of shops, the streets busy, and Caroline looked around, wondering where Kendrick was, wondering what she was supposed to do next.

"Ma'am, you need to understand you could be in serious trouble," the man tried again, following her as she weaved down the street. She found an out-of-the-way spot outside a solicitor's office, and stopped, scanning the road. No sign of Kendrick. "We've been investigating this individual – a man you've been seen with several times in the past few weeks – and we have reason to believe he's part of a terrorist organisation. You could be in grave danger."

"I don't know what you're talking about," Caroline said sharply. "I've never seen him before. You must have the wrong person."

"Ma'am," the man tried again, then stepped up close to her when she ignored him. And Caroline froze when she saw what else he had in his hand besides the photograph. It was a pistol, held close to his body, covered by the edge of his coat, and it was currently pointed directly at her stomach. "I'm afraid you'll have to come with us."

Damn Kendrick for getting her caught up in this shit! It was supposed to be a simple meeting, a smooth, clean exit from her old life, not a disaster zone at her house followed by creepy stiffs in suits trying to kidnap her!

A motorbike suddenly pulled up at the curb in front of her, and Caroline felt a rush of relief as she recognised Kendrick's bike. Two burly guards appeared behind the men harassing her, lumpy coats suggesting they were carrying concealed weapons.

"Let the young lady go," one of them said, and the two men looked around, then stood down, quickly realising they were outnumbered. Caroline eased around them and went straight to Kendrick, putting on the helmet he offered and climbing onto the bike. They were off a moment later, leaving the two guards to deal with the men.

Once they'd been driving for about ten minutes, Caroline tapped Kendrick's shoulder and indicated that she wanted him to pull over. He did, and pulled off his helmet so he could talk to her.

"I'm sorry I was late," he apologised. "I hadn't realised they'd got so close to you."

"Who were they?" Caroline asked, removing her own helmet and climbing off the bike. She wasn't going anywhere else until she got some answers.

"I've mentioned in the past that we have enemies," Kendrick said grimly. "You've just met two of them. And I guarantee, they won't be the last."

"They said you were terrorists," Caroline accused him coldly. "I've told you a hundred times, I'm not into that shit. I want to make something of my life, not become a criminal!"

"I promise you, we are not terrorists," Kendrick said, looking her square in the eye. "Your morals are admirable, and will be respected to the highest degree. And in just a couple of hours, we'll reach our base and explain to you what we really are. All your fears will be laid to rest."


Caroline was wound tight as a spring by the time Kendrick pulled up at a wide iron gate. They'd headed north along the motorway, then turned off onto a series of country lanes, each narrower than the last, stone walls lining the road and green fields dotted with sheep stretched out on either side, until they'd finally arrived at a large estate.

Kendrick tapped a code into the panel beside the entrance. The gate slid open without a sound, and the bike continued up the driveway. There was a high wall all around the property, a thick barrier of trees and hedges inside it, blocking the view for any overly curious neighbours. Whatever it was these people were doing here, it was clear they didn't want stray observers.

After the incident with the men on the bus, Caroline was having serious doubts about wanting to be a part of it.

The bike rolled to a stop in front of a huge manor, three storeys high, in grey stone. Apparently they were expected, as a number of heavily armed guards stood out the front, waiting for them. She recognised Silas, one of the men who'd taken her through the basics of firearms use, and Raven, who'd been her instructor for some of her martial arts sessions. The rest of them were unfamiliar, but they all carried the same air of menace and authority.

"This way," Kendrick told her, dumping his helmet beside the bike and leading her around the side of the house, the group of guards following them.

At the back, they reached a wide lawn with a patio leading up to a back door. On the patio, more people waited, a woman who greeted Kendrick with a relieved smile and a kiss, a young man who looked like an ex-gang member, dark scowl and resentful glare, a dark skinned woman in her mid twenties. In all, there were more than a dozen people loitering about, and Caroline couldn't decide how to feel about that. The almost military air fitted in with Kendrick's previous assertions that they were a covert operations unit, and yet the hostile atmosphere could also fit perfectly well with a bunch of terrorists, ready and willing to shoot their newest recruit if she wasn't what they expected.

"We had a run-in with the Noturatii on the way here," Kendrick announced without preamble, "and Caroline's feeling a little apprehensive about what she's got herself into, so we're going to get that side of things sorted before we go any further." He turned to Caroline. "Don't be offended by the cool greeting," he told her with a wry look. "Recruiting new members always makes people a little nervous, especially when the newbies don't know what the deal is yet."

It was too late to back out now, Caroline reminded herself, cold fear in her gut.

"Let's put all our cards on the table," Kendrick went on, "and then you'll see exactly why we have a very particular sort of enemy, and why we operate at the very highest levels of secrecy.

"We are the local division of a much larger organisation by the name of Il Trosa, which operates right across Europe. Our head office is in Italy, and we have close to three thousand members in total. The Noturatii are our main opposition. Their organisation is run from Germany, but they have local offices in every country across Europe, as well as North America, Russia and China. The two men who tried to apprehend you earlier were Noturatii operatives. They're treated with a strict 'shoot first, ask questions later' policy.

"As for who we are, and what we do… a physical demonstration is really the only way to explain it."

The group gathered around her in a large circle, making Caroline's heart rate kick up a notch. She unconsciously lowered her weight into a fighting stance, knowing she couldn't take on this many trained warriors in one go, but ready to do as much damage as possible on her way down if they chose to take issue with her. But then she saw that a few of the men had stood back, guns in hand, no doubt ready to shoot her if she caused any trouble. Fuck. What the hell had she got herself into?

"We are a secret society," Kendrick said seriously, "that has existed hidden from the public eye for nearly six hundred years. We have delved far beyond the reach of modern science, and operate in a realm which can only usefully be called magic. We are the best kept secret this world has ever seen." Kendrick nodded to the woman who had kissed him, and Caroline was shocked to see a bright crackle of electricity cover her skin, flowing back from her head, down her torso and over her legs. Her form blurred, shrank in on itself, *changed*… Caroline stared, open mouthed, at the lithe, brown and grey dog that now stood before her, the same one from the training exercise in the park, if she wasn't mistaken. What in the name of all that was holy…?

"We are shape shifters," Kendrick said, and Caroline glanced around, the pieces suddenly clicking into place. It wasn't a dog at all. It was a wolf. That was why she hadn't been able to pick the breed. She gaped in open awe as she stared at the rest of them, a wide circle of wolves now standing all around her.

"Now you can see why our secrets are so closely guarded. And why the exposing of those secrets warrants the death of those who betray us."

Silence, as Caroline stood and took in the scene around her. Her first thought was that she was dreaming, that this whole day was nothing more than a vivid hallucination brought on by the stress of leaving her home. But the minutes ticked by, everyone waiting patiently, no one willing to break the heavy silence, and Caroline reflected that if she was dreaming, this was the part where she would usually have woken up.

"Can I touch her?" she asked Kendrick, nodding to the female wolf closest to her, and he nodded. So she crouched down and reached for the wolf, surprised by her own lack of fear. The wolf stood patiently as she ran a hand through thick fur, felt down her legs, then eased around behind her to view her from all angles.

"You were the dog in the park, weren't you?" Caroline asked cautiously. The wolf nodded, and it was odd to see such a human gesture from an animal. "And you understand what I'm saying? You're like a human mind, in a wolf's body?" Another nod.

Caroline stood up and turned to face Kendrick. "That is the single most fucking awesome thing anyone has ever shown me," she said, feeling a rush of excitement. "You want a new recruit? Hell, yes… I'm in."

# CHAPTER NINE

**Present Day**

Inside the library, Caroline dumped her notes on the table and took a seat, ready for the meeting about the Densmeet. Baron was already there, a stack of papers in front of him, with Tank sitting beside him, pen in hand, ready to take down the details of the meeting.

"I've got the list of visitors," Baron began. "We're getting five shifters from France, five from Spain, four each from Norway and Poland, twelve from Russia – four different Dens there – and four from Ukraine."

"Ukraine?" Caroline asked in surprise. "We haven't had them here before. Do they speak any English?" Not every shifter who came would know the language, but at least one member from each Den coming would be fluent and be able to translate for the others.

"Nikolai, the alpha, speaks English," Baron explained, checking the guest list in front of him. And beside him, Andre quietly coughed.

Caroline glanced up at him. "What?"

"Nikolai is coming to Scotland?" Andre repeated, a strange note in his voice.

"You've met him?" Baron asked immediately. It was reasonable for them to expect to have met about half the visiting shifters before, while the rest would be strangers.

"Briefly. I had business in Ukraine a few years ago. What do you know of the Den?"

"Nothing, save what the Council tells us. I didn't know they were any different from any other eastern European Den."

Andre raised an eyebrow. "They live in the Chernobyl Exclusion Zone," he said, a touch of awe in his voice, and Caroline's eyes opened wide at the news.

"They what?"

"On the edge of it," Andre clarified. "Not right in the centre. But nonetheless, they're exposed to a significant amount of radiation on a regular basis. There are some benefits to the location, though. Since humans were evacuated, the local wildlife has proliferated. There's an abundance of deer and wolves in particular, and that gives them a great deal of freedom. Very few humans to spy on them, an established population of wild wolves to mask their activities, plenty of prey. And the shifter physiology seems to protect them from the worst of the effects of the radiation. But it has had a few unforeseen side effects, as well."

"Like what?" Baron asked.

"It's enhanced their magic. There have been a few new abilities to come out of that Den in the last few years, and not from any dabbling with the bloodlines. Nikolai himself..." Andre paused and swore softly in Italian, then continued. "There are Council reports that he's learned to teleport. He can initiate a shift in one location, and his other form appears anywhere up to ten metres from that point. The Council is eager to conduct a further assessment on him and his Den, but so far they've been busy dealing with other problems."

"Teleportation?" Caroline breathed in awe. "Wow."

"You had a shifter here in England a good while back," Andre went on. "I don't remember his name, but he had the ability to disappear for a few seconds each time he shifted. His human body would vanish, but he found a way to delay the arrival of his wolf body, effectively rendering him invisible for a short time. He was of the line of Fellor. Nikolai is of the same line, so there's a theory that he inherited the same ability, but the radiation allowed him to take it to new levels."

"And what about the man himself," Baron asked, no doubt eager to know more about any potential problems that might be arriving on his doorstep. "What's he like?"

Andre let out a chuckle. "Unusual," he said wryly. "Nothing dangerous. He's just... he's a character. Let's put it that way."

"It should be interesting to meet him," Caroline said, curious about this foreign man. "What about the wolves from France? Who's coming with them?"

France was the nearest Den to England, and as such, they were close allies, often traveling between the two countries to visit or assist each other, and they had several good friends there. It would be nice to have the chance to catch up with them.

"They're sending Henri, Marcel and Vincent," Baron said, reading from the list. "Vincent is new, recruited last year. And also Sabine and Annabelle."

Caroline made a satisfied noise as she heard that last name. Annabelle was a good friend, and a constant source of both sound advice, and mischief. She was also a fine warrior and had a gift for rituals and ceremonies similar to Heron's. Henri, too, was a familiar name, though Caroline hadn't met the others.

"The Council has requested that Annabelle perform the Nochtan-Eil," Baron said, literally the 'Midnight Chant'. It was a sacred ceremony honouring Sirius and the lives of those who had fallen in the past year, and was generally considered to be the highlight of the Densmeet.

"The Council has advised them that you'll be attending," Baron said to Andre. "And Marcel has sent a message saying he'd like to meet with you." And then he added, with a note of interest, "Apparently he knew your father."

Caroline turned to Andre in surprise. "Your father?"

Andre nodded slightly. "My father was French. Hence my name. He lived with the Den there for eight years before he met my mother and was transferred to England. That was two years before they adopted me. I haven't seen Marcel since I was fifteen. But before that, he was a regular visitor here. It's been a long time." That last part was said wistfully, and Caroline felt another unreasonable stab of jealousy. For all the time she'd spent with Andre in Italy, there was so much she didn't know about his past.

"On the subject of the Nochtan-Eil," she interrupted awkwardly, eager to change the subject, but not liking what she had to say. "Luke fell this year. And under normal circumstances, Mark would have taken part in the ceremony in his honour."

A heavy silence greeted her statement, the implicit question hanging over them all. Mark had got into significant trouble last year and had subsequently been branded as a traitor, as well as demoted to the rank of omega. But the death of his closest friend left them with a dilemma. It would be hugely insulting to Mark to forbid him from participating in the ceremony, a slap in the face that effectively nullified the close bond he'd had with Luke. But on the other hand, to let a branded traitor take part in such a sacred ritual would cause an uproar with the rest of the shifters. She looked at Baron for a solution, and then, when none was forthcoming, to Andre.

"As it happens," Andre said slowly, "the Council has already taken note of the issue. And they have requested that Alistair take part in the ceremony instead of Mark."

"Ah." That single word conveyed a great depth of emotion, and Baron's expression tightened at the news. Alistair was a freelance reporter, the Den's PR genius, tackling any media leaks that came a little too close to the truth about the shifters, and he had also been a close friend of Luke's… but Mark was not going to take this well.

"I think," Andre hedged cautiously, "that they made the decision to take any potential blame away from you and Caroline. I know it's a little heavy handed of them, but they also like to avoid any situations that can create a sense of divided loyalty."

It was very considerate of them, even if it was heavy handed, as Andre had said, an interference in the running of a Den that they would not usually take. But Mark had been a high ranking wolf, and they must have known that both Caroline and Baron continued to feel conflicted over his demotion.

"Let's move on then," Baron said a moment later. "George will be organising catering, but he'll need help with preparing meals for so many people. Eric and Heron have both volunteered to help, and I don't see any problem with that arrangement."

Caroline nodded, glad that at least one item on their agenda had such a simple solution. At the end of the table, Tank was dutifully taking notes, not having said anything so far, though he'd been listening attentively.

"Skip will be running a three day seminar on hacking," Caroline said next, consulting her own notes. "We're taking four laptops for the purpose, and the other hackers will each be bringing one of their own. One of the Russian wolves needs to attend the sessions, but he doesn't speak any English, so he'll have a translator working with him. Silas will also be running his usual combat training sessions, but the translator isn't a part of that, so if we run both groups at the same time, that'll cut down on time taken away from other things."

"I've asked Caleb to help arrange the Games this year," Baron said, throwing a covert glance at Andre.

The 'Games', as they were exclusively known, took a variety of forms. For new recruits, they were a chance to hone important skills as a wolf, tracking, digging, manipulating objects in wolf form without the benefit of human hands. For more seasoned shifters, they rapidly increased in difficulty, more difficult scents to track, obstacle courses, team challenges designed to measure the shifter's ability to work with wolves with an entirely different skill set from their own. Each year it was a challenge to come up with new and interesting Games for the visiting shifters, each one not just a test of skill, but an excuse to have some fun as well, but for the older wolves, it was almost as much fun to design the Games as it was to participate in them.

"Caleb's got a good imagination," Baron went on, "and he should be able to come up with a good variety of challenges." It was a sideways reference to Andre's ongoing assessment of the man for service to the Council, a more direct reference not possible with Tank sitting in the room, but Andre caught on quickly.

"As an assassin, I'm not qualified to enter any of the challenges," he said, giving Baron a nod, "but I'd like to help set things up. I'd be happy to work with Caleb to get things arranged." It would be a perfect opportunity for him to assess not just Caleb's organisational skills, but his personality as well, opening up the chance for subtle one-on-one conversations as they put in long hours together to design each challenge.

"Just one other thing," Caroline said, before they wrapped up the meeting. "I take it you're making the usual provisions for John?"

Baron nodded. "I've got it under control." Not good at socialising and prone to fits of temper, John found the Densmeets to be more than a little stressful, and Baron had learned to make arrangements to ease his tension. A quiet bedroom for himself and John, away from interruptions and noise. Regularly scheduled breaks when either himself or Heron could take the boy away from the crowd for some down time. And plenty of exercise to keep his energy levels under control.

"Tank?" Baron said, drawing the man into the conversation for the first time. "Are you still up for putting in a few sparring sessions with him?"

"No problem," Tank said, aiming for his usual easy going mood, and not quite making it. "Happy to help."

"Thanks," Baron said, and Caroline made a mental note to talk to him about Tank in the near future. His ongoing reluctance to deal with his captivity in the Noturatii's lab was worrying, and she wasn't keen on heading to Scotland, with all its potential dramas, with him in the condition he was in.

"We should also think about Dee," Caroline said. "There's going to be a reaction to her and her wolf. Rumours will have spread by now about Fenrae-Ul and the prophecy about her destroying our species, and I don't want anyone giving her a hard time about it." Dee herself had said several times that she had no intention of harming anyone in Il Trosa, and Caroline was more inclined to listen to the woman herself than a millennia-old prophecy in a barely-translatable language. "But at the same time, I don't want people upset because they're worried about what she might do."

"Mark is just as likely to be an issue," Andre added. "People aren't going to be happy about having a traitor in their midst."

"I think we'll need to play that one by ear," Baron said, after a moment's consideration. "Making an issue out of either of them is only likely to create more tension, and a little heckling is to be expected. We are wolves, after all," he added with a wry grin. "But if anyone steps too far over the line, we need a couple of people on hand who can step in for them. I'll have a word to Silas about it. And you, Andre?" Andre nodded, wordlessly offering his support. "Tank? You okay with putting out a few fires, if they come up?"

"For God's sake," Tank snapped, his pretence at a good mood vanishing. "I'm not a fucking invalid. I know my job, and I'm perfectly capable of doing it, so stop asking me if everything's okay like I'm about to break at any moment."

And that, Caroline thought blackly, was exactly why they were worried. Tank was known for his good humour, his extensive patience and his ability to see the funny side to just about any situation. And this latest display of temper was not doing anything to reassure her that he was still capable of fulfilling his duties.

## 18 Years Ago

Andre marched into the Council's headquarters, a large villa just outside Cison de Valmarino, feeling on top of the world. It was three years since he'd been converted – later than he would have liked, but an exhilarating moment, nonetheless – and now at the age of twenty-two, with the skills from new training and the weight of new responsibilities on his shoulders, he was, for the first time, feeling like more than an awkward child. He was becoming a man, a warrior, a valued part of his pack. And it was a heady feeling.

The villa was set in a remote part of the country, surrounded by forests and even a few wild wolves. Though small in number, the presence of wolves gave the shifters much greater freedom in their day to day lives; if one of them happened to be spotted by a stray hiker or farmer, they would be dismissed as merely one of the regular wolves.

In the past three years, Andre had completed two and a half of the possible four internships available to him. He'd spent a year with Il Trosa's science division, seeing in detail the experiments they ran to try and decode the complex shifter magic. He'd spent a year and a half with the historians, learning the ancient language, studying the myths and genealogies, and most recently, he'd spent six months in training with the assassins. It was tough work, mentally as well as physically, and while he now had a renewed admiration for the Council's last and most deadly line of defence, he also found the whole business to be rather distasteful. It was a noble duty, to be sure, safeguarding Il Trosa from any and all threats, but killing people, sometimes innocent people, and the sometimes gory methods involved – particularly where the Noturatii were concerned – left him feeling rather dirty, if he was honest about it.

Of course, the fourth possible role for him was that of Diplomat, the political geniuses who wooed politicians, lobbied for laws in favour of wolf conservation and the preservation of wilderness areas, cosied up to rich philanthropists… it was all unbearably boring, and Andre had never really given the role of Diplomat more than a passing thought.

But this third internship was not shaping up well, and so in the very near future, Andre was going to have to make a choice about his future. Assassin wasn't for him, he'd decided, but he was having a tough time deciding between scientist and historian, both roles equally fascinating, both containing the potential to make real progress for their species.

There was also the thought in his mind of a relationship with a female shifter. Andre had met two or three women over the past few years who had caught his attention, though he had yet to develop any serious attachments. Assassins, in general, did not form long term romantic relationships – a consequence of their nomadic lifestyle and the necessary dangers of their job – but it was a serious possibility if he became either a historian or a scientist, much more of his life spent in a safe, stable environment at the villa, and while he still felt himself a little young for a serious commitment, the idea of marriage somewhere down the track was appealing.

As he stepped inside the wide foyer, a white marble floor lending a bright, airy feel to the villa, he found Eleanor waiting for him. She was sitting on the bottom of the stairs, and when she looked up at him, Andre felt his body turn cold, such was the look of desolation on her face.

"Come into the lounge," she said simply, standing up and leading the way, and Andre's mind immediately started imagining all manner of horrors that might have occurred. Bad news was on the way, that much was certain, but what? Had a Councillor been killed? Had a Den been raided? Or had one of the other trainees been injured, perhaps? Their training was tough, physical, and at times dangerous, and it wouldn't be the first time a trainee had suffered a broken leg or a bad concussion. Perhaps the injury had been worse this time...

Inside the lounge, Andre took a seat on the edge of a sofa, waiting apprehensively as Eleanor composed herself, two other Councillors watching on from the side of the room.

"I have some bad news," Eleanor said, stating the obvious, and Andre simply nodded. "There was an attack involving the Agordo Den. They ran into a group of Noturatii operatives out in the forest. Five wolves died in the battle."

Andre's heart sank. While the Council and their emissaries lived in the villa, the main shifter presence in Italy was a large Den to the north. This was bad news indeed-

"I'm so sorry, Andre. Your mother and father have both been killed."

Andre felt his world tilt, and he actually grabbed onto the arm of the sofa to steady himself. "What?"

"I'm so sorry," she repeated, stark sorrow in her eyes. "Alessandro, the alpha, was also killed. He did everything he could, and without his efforts, more would likely have died. Your parents fought bravely. May they find glory in the House of Sirius."

It was an oft repeated sentiment, a mark of respect for those who had fallen and a reminder that this life was not the end of their existence. But as he heard the words now, Andre felt no comfort in them, no relief or bitter-sweet joy in the idea that his parents had returned home to the Great Hall in the divine house of the Wolf God.

He wasn't aware of the hot tears running down his cheeks until Eleanor reached for a box of tissues and held it out. He ignored it, so she set it on the coffee table.

"You'll be given leave to attend their funeral, of course," she said softly, "and remember that we're all here for you. If there's anything at all that you need."

Andre felt like a great, black wave had just swallowed him whole. His parents were dead. Both of them. He could barely process the avalanche of emotion swamping him. Grief, a black, aching sorrow… and an almost frightening surge of fiery rage overtook him, demanding revenge against those who had taken his closest family from him.

It was in that moment that Andre's future suddenly crystallised into a clear picture, a singular purpose.

The Noturatii had killed his parents. And Council assassins killed the Noturatii. Revenge, as a general rule, was frowned upon in Il Trosa, the Council all too aware that one act of retaliation tended to lead to another, and another, and that was how wars got started.

But to become an assassin was a neat sidestep around that irritating barrier. It was a free pass to hunt down those who had hurt him, those who continued to threaten his pack, and the feeling of power the idea gave him was intoxicating.

"Thank you," he said respectfully. "I'll head north this afternoon. But before I go, there is just one other thing…" He glanced around, seeing the grim expressions on the Councillors, the stark sorrow etched in hard lines on aging faces. "I've made my choice about which guild I would like to join," he told them, knowing this was a sudden change of topic, and registering the surprise it caused. "I have decided to become an assassin."

# CHAPTER TEN

**Present Day**

"Tank?" Baron had found the man out on the back patio, sitting on a wall and staring at the moon. It was faint, hazy behind a thin layer of cloud, and the air was cold this time of night, their breath misting in the air. "We need to talk."

There were a number of reactions Baron had expected. Tank might just storm off, refusing to speak to him. Or he might get upset and swear at him, annoyed at being treated with kid gloves. But thankfully, he did neither, taking the route that Baron had been hoping for. Tank was a smart guy, after all, well versed in the long term effects of intense trauma, and it was good to see that he was still capable of seeing past his own pain to recognise the symptoms he was displaying.

"I know."

Baron sat down on the wall beside him, staring off into the dark forest. A long moment passed, and neither of them spoke. "So talk to me," Baron said at last, and Tank let out a long sigh.

"It's not the torture," he said finally. "I know everyone thinks it is, but it's just physical pain. It's unpleasant enough, and I've had my share of nightmares over it, but the wounds heal and the memories fade, and that's that."

"So what is it?"

Tank made a noise of reluctance. "Two things. Neither of which are put to rest quite so easily. Number one: they drugged me." Tank paused, then forced himself to continue. "The whole thing was surreal. Like being in a dream, and not knowing who's good and who's bad, not quite knowing even who you are any more. You try to believe that staying silent is the best thing, and that you're fighting on the side of good, but they've got their propaganda and their ideals about protecting humanity and reality seems to have turned sideways; you come out of that with a whole pile of guilt about who you are and what you're doing. And it lingers. I have dreams about killing shifters. About killing Noturatii. And never knowing if what I'm doing at the time is right or wrong."

Baron considered that, then gently asked a question, immediately dreading the answer. "Are you having second thoughts about us? About the shifters?"

A quick denial would have been comforting, but not entirely believable. So it was something of a relief when Tank hesitated, chewing on the idea for a moment. "It's not that I think we're evil or that I agree with the Noturatii. But we've always known that in this war, there are innocent bystanders who get caught in the crossfire. I guess this just put that into a new perspective. Every innocent life that is taken in our quest to stay alive is a life too many. And at some point, you have to wonder how much blood there is on your hands, and how much more there's going to be, and how many lives are worth the price of our survival."

"The Endless Dilemma," Baron said, not nearly as flippantly as the simple statement might have implied. "Which goes hand in hand with the Endless War. If we could end this fight tomorrow, we would. You know that. But the Noturatii-"

"We can't just blame the Noturatii for everything we do," Tank interrupted. "They are the cause of a lot of it, certainly, but they don't force us to pull the trigger. We have a certain amount of responsibility for our own actions. I don't know of any other way it could be at the moment, but it makes you think, you know?"

Baron nodded, making no effort to dispel Tank's lingering sense of guilt. It was a dilemma he'd wrestled with himself often enough, and as Tank had said, there were no simple answers.

"And the second thing?" he asked, after a while, remembering that Tank had said there were two things bothering him.

"They took my blood. And used it to make new shifters. Those women had no say in the matter, they didn't volunteer, like we did, they didn't even know what was happening. Their bodies were taken without their consent and used for evil purposes far beyond their control. I feel like-" He broke off, the words sounding strangled in his throat.

"You feel like what?" Baron asked softly. He had no misconceptions about what was going on here. Tank was a warrior, one of the strongest wolves in the Den, and not just physically. The man had been in the military before joining them, and had witnessed things, done things, that had a strong tendency to produce post traumatic stress in former soldiers – something that Tank had fortunately never suffered from himself. Whatever was bothering him was no doubt a most serious issue.

"I feel like I raped them. Violated them. In the worst possible way. And I know that, logically," Tank rushed on before Baron could say anything, "it wasn't me, it was the Noturatii. But it's like if someone stole your semen and used it to make a bunch of random babies all over the world, and then you find out years later, and on the one hand, it's nothing to do with you, but on the other hand, there's a whole bunch of tiny people running around who are actually your children. And it would be so easy to spend the rest of your life wondering how they are, and whether you should try to do anything to help them, and worrying that they're in danger or that someone's hurting them." He sighed, staring at the ground. "These are not the sort of ghosts that are easily laid to rest."

Baron sighed. In a way, it was Tank's own kindness that was slowly killing him from the inside. His sense of honour had been betrayed, his compassion unable to let go of an act that was not his fault, but that, by his own logic, remained his responsibility.

Two of the women who had been converted were now dead, and Baron had nothing to add to that situation that would be of any use. But the third woman had survived, had successfully been returned to her home after Dee had removed the wolf from her.

"We've been keeping tabs on Gabrielle," Baron told Tank quietly. "I hadn't mentioned it because I didn't think you'd want to keep being reminded about that, but..."

"How is she?" The question came out with a heartfelt urgency, and Baron wasted no time in filling Tank in.

"She's doing well. After she got home, she went to stay with her brother for a while. He's got two children, and spending time with them seemed to help. Now she's back home, back at work – part time only, but it's a good step forward."

Tank seemed to relax with the news, a faint smile settling on his face. "Good to hear," he said softly. "She shouldn't have to put up with being caught in all this madness."

"And yet the Endless War rages on," Baron said, a sad acknowledgement that for every piece of good news, there was plenty of bad to go around.

"That it does."

The Grey Watch's northern camp was dismal. It had been drizzling for days, small trickles of water dripping from every leaf, flowing down every rock. The ground was permanently wet, the dampness creeping into the wolves' fur and making them constantly uncomfortable, most of the pack becoming irritable and grumpy as a result.

Now that she was getting more of a handle on her life as a shifter,

Genna had started to take note of small details in their daily lives, things she had missed earlier because she was too busy just trying to survive.

One of the often quoted rules was that the shifters had to spend the vast majority of their time in wolf form – an imposition that Genna found extremely difficult. Staying as a wolf for more than twenty-four hours was uncomfortable, like constantly having an itch you couldn't scratch. And after three days, the effort became impossible, wolves invariably shifting in their sleep, much to the derision of their pack mates, or sneaking off into the forest to shift in secret and spend a few hard earned minutes in human form.

The more senior wolves seemed to have less of a problem with it, and indeed it was they who most commonly scolded the younger ones for their failures, something Genna had taken at face value in the first few weeks of her life here.

But now she'd learned to watch more carefully. To look past the words and put more weight on the actions of those few elite.

And the reality was that every single one of the senior wolves managed to find a reason to shift every single day. Sempre, in particular, spent a great deal of time as a human, constantly needing to have 'meetings' with the other senior females, or using her status to make use of the privilege of pulling one of the few males into the tent to have sex – something that was always done in human form, never as a wolf. There were constant requirements to look up some passage in the few ancient texts they carried with them, or make an urgent phone call to another pack in Europe, or issue commands to the younger wolves – all things that needed either human hands, or a human voice, and once she'd finally seen the hypocrisy of the alpha's rules, Genna couldn't decide whether she was furious, or amused by it all. The endless charade, the belittling comments, the mocking and scolding… it all seemed far less weighty and much easier to deal with when she realised that she, herself, actually spent far more time in wolf form than Sempre did. According to Grey Watch rules, she was better at being a wolf than their alpha was!

But there was another aspect to the rule that was equally ridiculous, but far less funny. Not every wolf managed to climb the ranks, and the lower ranking wolves had less excuse to shift – no important meetings to attend, fewer opportunities to spend time with the males – so that some of the longer running members of the pack were still quite low ranking, and had spent *years* being forced to stay in wolf form.

And some of them, Genna had learned, by quiet observation and subtle eavesdropping, were beginning to lose themselves. When in wolf form, they were less able to reason as a human would, finding it more difficult to put aside their animal instincts to make logical decisions, rather than those based purely on hunger or fear. And when in human form, the results were even more scary. Those shifters seemed to be losing their human selves entirely, gaps in their memories of things they had done as a human, difficulty remembering people's names or the importance of particular dates. It was not a fate Genna envied at all, and so she had begun the long, slow process of climbing the ranks herself, to gain what privilege there was to be had, honing her fighting skills, challenging wolf after wolf to status fights, becoming more aggressive in battles for food or for dry places to sleep. But in the process, Genna acknowledged sadly, she was losing herself anyway, becoming more confident, yes, but also more aggressive, more angry, more prone to justifying her desires and greed to herself, when every step up the ladder she took was at the same time condemning another wolf to more years locked in their animal form, more risk that they, too, would end up losing themselves to the wild.

As a human, Genna had been naturally sociable, generous, if perhaps a little lazy, and willing to assist others in need. Her invitation to join the Grey Watch had been on the basis not of an antisocial nature, as a lot of their recruitments were, but rather on a lingering sense of displacement. She couldn't find a career that appealed to her, floundering in her role as checkout worker with little ambition to move forward. She couldn't see the appeal of many of modern society's pass-times; team sports held no interest, she had no musical talents, television and modern movies seemed banal and pointless, and the interests of many of her friends had been unbearably dull, as they spent hours at the hairdressers or getting a manicure. Getting her eyebrows waxed? What the hell was that about? She had been raised in a small town, where the general expectation seemed to be that she would find a man, get married and start having children, and she'd been struggling to break out of the entrenched social order.

So when the shifters had come along, the wilderness had appealed, a chance to step back and reconnect with humanity's more spiritual origins. It was a source of deep disappointment to her that this pack was more consumed with their own internal politics than with rediscovering the wonders of the natural world around them.

Now, though, she was forsaking her inherent curiosity and bent for spiritual pursuits, becoming a violent force of nature willing to stomp over others to get more for herself, and she hated it, even as she saw the unfortunate necessity of it.

But there was one other startling discovery that Genna had made in the past few weeks, one that had the potential to cause an even greater problem.

In addition to the ability to shift, roughly one in five shifters also inherited a particular ability, a quirk of the shifter magic as it interacted with their unique DNA and state of mind. The talent usually manifested sometime in the first two years after conversion, and at first, Genna had waited with a gnawing curiosity to see if she would develop one of the coveted abilities. Some of the talents were powerful and awe-inspiring, the ability to call down lightning, for example, or to hypnotise prey into surrendering.

But as she'd learned more, her enthusiasm had dimmed, as she'd discovered that many of the other talents were far less noteworthy; the ability to find water underground – hardly a necessity in England, with frequent rain and rivers flowing everywhere; or the power to manipulate electric currents – completely useless out here, as there was nothing that ran on electricity in the camp bar a few mobile phones, the batteries recharged via the small solar panels the pack had bought, with firm restrictions on any other form of technology.

Each bloodline had their own set of possibilities, but since the Grey Watch was restricted to the line of Grenable, theirs was a very limited subset of the full compliment of powers. Since her gaff over the Treaty of Erim Kai Bahn, Lita had been drilling her with lessons every day, not just on the details of the Treaty, but on a range of aspects of shifter culture, along with a long list of possible manifestations of these strange abilities, and Genna now had several dozen of the possibilities memorised.

But aside from the lack of excitement over many of the potential mystical talents, there was another reason Genna had become less than enthusiastic about developing one of her own. Some of the abilities could easily be exploited, enhanced with techniques that Il Trosa had forbidden, but which, due to the single bloodline of their pack and the limited abilities that came with it, the Grey Watch had chosen to embrace. Lita's ability, for example, was to trace a person's movements from their blood, able to deduce exactly where that person had been in the past twenty-four hours. Not satisfied with the results, however, Sempre had encouraged the woman to begin performing blood rituals, aided by the sacrifice of wild animals, delving ever further into the unknown, until Lita could detect not just shifters, but regular humans, animals, prey. She had effectively become a sentry for their pack, constantly checking to see who was around – a park ranger, perhaps, or a wildlife expert seeking out rare specimens, a group of hikers straying too close to their camp.

And the overstretching of the magic, the dabbling in blood rituals that defied the laws of nature, caused some unpleasant consequences for the practitioner.

To look at her, one would have assumed that Lita was in her seventies or eighties. She walked with a limp, her back was crooked, her skin frail and easily torn and her hair so grey it was almost white.

But just a few weeks ago, Genna had been shocked to learn that the woman's real age was a paltry thirty-eight years. What the hell was she supposed to do if she developed a similar talent, and Sempre insisted on slowly sucking the life out of her in a similar manner? Some shifters even said it was an offence to the divine Wolf God himself, the perpetrators forever banned from the Great Hall in the House of Sirius, and the thought was nothing short of terrifying.

Three weeks ago, while wandering alone in the forest, Genna had made a shocking discovery. She did, indeed, possess one of the mystical talents, but the greater shock had been in discovering which one.

She'd been searching out a buried bone, eager for something to chew and hungry enough to not care what it smelled like, and she'd tracked down the scent of one, hidden in a shallow depression out in a deserted part of the forest. Unfortunately for her, a storm had come through since the bone had been buried, a heavy branch falling right on top of her prize. As a wolf, she'd had no chance of moving the thing, and even after she'd glanced around and furtively shifted into a human, she'd found it impossible to move. It wasn't so much wide as long, and must have weighed three or four times as much as Genna herself did. As she'd sat there, smacking at the branch in frustration, she'd imagined how much simpler things would be if she could make a short section of the branch disappear, just enough to reveal the bone, much as her clothing disappeared when she became a wolf.

It wasn't a totally ridiculous idea, she considered after a moment, knowing that not just clothing, but weapons, small bags, even items of food could all be made to disappear if strapped closely to the body before a shift, so she'd huddled up beside the log, making sure her thigh was pressed tight against it, hands on the wood, her body curled around it, and initiated a shift...

Only she hadn't shifted. Instead, she'd all but fainted in surprise as the section of the log had vanished right out from beneath her hands. The bone had been forgotten in an instant, a far more interesting mystery now presented to her. She could make objects disappear! She could reach into the other realm, the one where their bodies went when they weren't using them, and she'd sent the wood there, instead of her own self.

Long, private practice sessions had followed, with Genna not quite able to believe the gift at first, and then eager to see how far it could be pushed, how large an object she could make disappear, how long she could keep the item hidden... but all the while, a slow, creeping fear had been gnawing at her mind.

If Sempre found out about this, then her life was effectively over. This was one of the rarest gifts, one that hadn't been seen in a shifter for over two hundred years. It was one of the most powerful abilities any shifter could receive, those bearing this talent said to be blessed by Sirius himself, and its uses were enormous. She could steal things, and if searched, no one would ever find them. She could open locked doors, simply by making the lock vanish. She could disable cars or weapons, a handy trick against the

Noturatii. There were a great many more experiments Genna wanted to try, but with the constant risk of being discovered, she found that more often than not, her fear outweighed her curiosity, leaving her development in her gift stunted and irregular.

Now, back in the camp, Genna heard the first rumblings of a disagreement, and furtively slunk out of her resting spot to listen to the older females talking.

"We have to go," one of them was saying. "There's no way around it."

"It's too great a risk," another said unhappily. "Fenrae-Ul is going to be there. You want to end up where Rintur did, her human half ripped right out of her? I don't care what Baron says, she's not to be trusted."

"We can make it as short as possible," Sempre put in, sounding tired and irritated, rather than her usual commanding self. "Two days, tops. And Fenrae can't attack any of us during the meeting. It would breach the rules of the Treaty."

"What are they talking about?" Genna asked Luna in a whisper, after shifting into human form. Luna was loitering near the older females, and while not exactly her friend, Luna was one of the more even tempered wolves, more prone to cooperation than confrontation, and Genna had developed a cautious admiration for her.

"Scotland," Luna whispered back. "Every year we have a meeting in summer with the Il Trosa pack, and this year it's set to take place in an estate up near the Cairngorm National Park. Sempre doesn't want to go. None of them do, not with Fenrae-Ul set to kill us all, and they're more pissed off than usual with Baron this year. Take my advice – when we eventually get there, keep your head down and don't make any waves. It's going to be unpleasant enough as it is."

"Maybe we could insist that Fenrae isn't present," one of the women went on. "Baron has to honour the Treaty just as much as we do, and it's not an unreasonable request."

"But it's one he'd never listen to," Sempre replied. "Come on, you've met him. He's as stubborn as a mule, with the personality of a rabid bear."

"If going to the meeting is such a risk," Genna asked Luna softly, "why do we have to go?"

"It's a condition of the Treaty," Luna answered with a shrug. "A mandatory meeting once a year between us and Il Trosa to discuss any potential problems, to take a census of our population, and to give a full report on our activities for the year."

Ah, that explained it, then. Genna had learned quickly that, for all their complaining about it, the Treaty was regarded as a sacred document, more important even than the shifter's doctrine regarding Sirius the Wolf God and his decrees on their lives and behaviour, and there wasn't a wolf among them who would dare break one of its commands.

"In the end, they'll decide we have to go," Luna added, nodding to the still-arguing females. "But they feel better if they complain about it for a while first. It makes them feel like they made the noble concession to attend, rather than that they were forced into it." She shrugged, then turned to leave. "Nothing ever happens at the meetings, anyway. They talk politics for a few days, agree to continue disagreeing, same as we have done for centuries, and then we all go home again." She smiled, a wry, almost sad look. "Back to the damp and the cold, and the grey, grey sky." And then she laughed. "Not like Scotland's much better, in terms of weather, but look on the bright side. At least it's a change of scenery."

# CHAPTER ELEVEN

Baron sat in the back seat of the van, staring out the window as they wound their way along the road to the estate in Scotland. John was curled up next to him, head on his shoulder, fast asleep. Outside the van, rolling hills dotted with sheep drifted past, dense pockets of forest and wide fields of heather giving the scenery a rugged, untamed look.

The estate they were heading to was on the outskirts of the Cairngorm National Park, far enough from the major tourist centres to afford them privacy. It was set in a wide valley, with high hills on all sides that protected it from snooping eyes, and a thick forest that was home to a decent population of wild deer and with a river running along the valley floor. The house was a grand affair, twice the size of the Lakes District manor, with peaked turrets and bay windows, grey stone rising to tall chimneys. There were several cottages off the side, perfect for extra accommodation for those preferring a little peace and quiet away from the main crowd, and inside the manor there was a huge dining room, industrial kitchen and several halls for meetings.

While most of the Den would be staying in the main house, Caroline, Baron, John and Andre had been allocated one of the cottages, a concession to John's need for privacy and to keep Andre away from the bulk of the shifters. For all their respect for the Council, having an assassin on site tended to make everyone a bit leery, and placing him out of the main house would go a long way towards keeping the peace.

But more than that, Baron had also made the arrangement for the express purpose of assisting Andre in his assessment of Caroline. The need for the utmost discretion made it difficult to manufacture situations of any importance where the two of them would be thrown together, but by getting them to live in adjacent bedrooms for a few weeks, he was confident that Andre would manage to make time for the occasional 'chat', discussions on protocol for the Densmeet, or the opportunity to witness Caroline defusing the odd argument between shifters on the estate. He wasn't sure exactly what the assessment procedure consisted of, or what specific criteria Caroline was being measured against, but it was a long and complicated process, that much was clear.

After a long drive through progressively narrower and more winding roads, the Den's four vans pulled up at the front of the manor and the shifters piled out, stretching muscles stiff from the long drive. Security was the first issue of the day, with Silas, Baron, Caroline and Tank going on a thorough inspection of the immediate area. As promised, the owner had cleared out, leaving the rooms already made up, the manor clean and tidy and the estate deserted. They paid a hefty price for the privilege of absolute privacy, but it was worth it, high stone walls surrounding the entire estate and prominent signs announcing that this was private property, leaving the shifters free to roam about in wolf form without fear of discovery.

"The food will be arriving around midday," George informed Baron, when he returned to the front entrance. "I'll let you know when it's all clear." With humans scheduled to be entering the estate, there was a strict ban on shifting until they were gone, and the Den would be anxious to get out and about and start exploring their new territory in wolf form.

"Security's fine," Baron announced, holstering his gun after the others had reported back. "Let's get these vans unloaded." Along with the bags of personal effects that each shifter had brought, there were also a few crates of weapons – primarily for training purposes, but also a necessary precaution against the unlikely risk that the Noturatii might stumble upon them out here, as well as several of the ancient texts from the Den's library. Some of the books were still half blank, and would be added to while they were here, an official census of both the Den and the English Grey Watch pack, an annual report from the Council on the progress of Il Trosa as a whole, and a report on the Densmeet itself, including a full list of every shifter in attendance and a record of those fallen, who would be honoured at the Nochtan-Eil.

Everyone set to work immediately, lugging suitcases up long flights of stairs, computers to one of the halls, weapons to another, and a collection of dog beds into the large foyer that also doubled as a living room. There were also four heavy duty vacuum cleaners, necessary for getting all the fur out of the carpet before they left. While the owners were aware that their guests would be bringing 'a few dogs' for their summer vacation, there would be little excuse for the sheer volume of wolf fur that would be left lying around, and it was both for politeness, maintaining a good relationship with the owner, and for secrecy, hiding any sign of their presence, that the Den would be conducting a thorough clean up before they left the estate.

The situation in Italy had finally settled down, much to everyone's relief, so the ban on travel had been lifted just a few days ago, allowing the Italian wolves to join the festivities, and more importantly, it meant that the Councillors themselves would be able to attend the Densmeets, a valuable opportunity to spend face-to-face time with the rest of Il Trosa.

The French shifters would be arriving that afternoon, coming by train from France, with the rest of the guests filtering in over the next few days. A lucky few would be coming by private jet; the Council owned a modest plane that could seat up to thirty people. But using the plane too often could arouse the suspicions of the Noturatii, so many others would be travelling via more conventional methods, small commercial flights or high speed trains, as shifters from dozens of different Dens were shuttled all over Europe to attend their respective meetings.

Inside their cottage, Caroline and Andre chose their bedrooms. Andre disappeared inside, while Caroline simply dumped her bag and headed back outside to oversee the unpacking. No doubt there would be a few squabbles over who got which room in the manor, and it would speed up the process to have someone on hand to keep the peace, and pull rank, if necessary.

Baron and John had a large room with a queen-sized bed, and Baron hefted their two suitcases inside, followed by John, lugging the case of precious books. John kicked the door shut, dumped the box by the wall, and then set about exploring. A small ensuite bathroom, fresh towels laid out. A bay window looking out into a private courtyard. The wardrobe, the bathroom cabinets, the dresser... he even checked under the bed and behind the picture frames, and if Baron hadn't understood the reason for his paranoia quite so well, he would have found the inspection to be quite amusing.

When he was done, John flopped down onto the bed, wriggling around, arms and legs splayed, then he lay still, a sigh escaping his lips.

"It's pretty comfortable," he concluded. "A little too bouncy, but I can live with that. We should try it out. See if it lives up to expectations." He spread his legs a little, possibly just a concession to comfort... but then he palmed his own groin, and Baron barely glanced at the growing bulge in the boy's trousers.

"Put your libido back in its box and help me unpack," he said mildly, knowing it was a waste of time. John didn't understand unpacking, had no concept of the need to keep clothes neat and tidy. It was a good day when dirty laundry even made it into the hamper, more often just tossed onto the floor, or worse, hidden under the bed. Baron had learned to go on a weekly hunt for it each time he did his own laundry, otherwise it was likely to sit there for weeks until it stank and was on the verge of going mouldy.

"How many people are coming?" John asked, not for the first time, and Baron braced himself for the first wave of the yearly anxiety that came with every Densmeet. It wouldn't be too bad this year, with the meeting in a familiar space and with John surrounded by his own Den members. Other years were far worse, with the Den split up and John having to cope not just with multiple strangers wandering around, but also with totally new scenery, foreign languages, alien cultures. It was exhausting, Baron having to constantly be aware of his boyfriend's moods and running interference between him and the other shifters when things got too tense.

"Thirty-four," Baron told him, shaking out a shirt and sliding it onto a hanger. "Plus our twenty means a total of fifty-four." He went on to list them all, each of the Dens invited, the number of shifters from each one, the languages they spoke and the ranks of each person. And all the while John lay on the bed, fiddling with the blankets, moving the pillows around, occasionally glancing out the window with a look that was designed to convey indifference, but which failed completely.

Finally, when Baron had finished explaining everything, John got up, stalking silently across the room and catching Baron in a hug, arms wrapped around his waist from behind. Baron stood still, unpacking abandoned for the moment, simply letting John feel his body against him, the regular inhale-exhale of his breaths, the slow thud of his heart.

"You sure you don't want to come to bed?" John breathed, pressing his groin against Baron's backside, and the alpha sighed.

"I have work to do," he apologised. "The French shifters will be arriving this afternoon and I need to check their rooms are set up. Then I have to check on George in the kitchen and discuss a few things with Caroline."

"Yeah, all work and no play," John said with a pout, letting him go. "Fine. I'm going outside. To have a look around."

"No shifting!" Baron called, as the boy vanished out of the room, and then he smiled as the predictable "Fuck you!" came drifting back at him just before the front door slammed. A lack of reply would have been worrying, but in John-speak, the rude exclamation meant 'I know, and it's fine'. Baron shook his head, then quietly turned back to the suitcase of clothes in front of him.

# CHAPTER TWELVE

**16 Years Ago**

Caroline slumped down on the sofa in the sitting room and closed her eyes. It was two years since she'd joined the Den of shifters, two years that had been one long, tough slog through intense training sessions and challenging lessons into shifter culture and history. There had been chants to learn, politics to understand, lists of rules and regulations to memorise, complex social structures and rituals to deal with.

There had also been more than a few battles, as the Noturatii continued to threaten their existence. She hadn't been involved in any of the battles herself, but had witnessed the fallout, had seen numerous shifters be injured, had heard the grim discussions on the Den's strategies for future survival.

Since her recruitment, she'd got to know the rest of the shifters in the Den. Kendrick and Anna were the alphas, a happily married couple who led the shifters with diligence and a keen eye for strategy. Heron was a middle aged woman with a refined elegance who had played a big part in Caroline's education. Eric von Brandt was the resident IT expert, a German man who had moved to the Den years ago after his recruitment, as he'd had too many close ties in Germany to remain there without the risk of being discovered, and who had also been chosen as Caroline's sire for her conversion. He was a cheerful, if introverted man, who seemed more at home with his computers than socialising with the Den. Raven was an Asian man in his sixties, the oldest member of the Den, and he'd been alpha before Kendrick. In some ways, he reminded Caroline of Mr Miyagi – calm, wise, patient... but he was also more of a badass than the 'Karate Kid's' instructor had been, a facial tattoo giving him a dangerous air, and he was more willing to kick someone's arse if they stepped out of line. He'd retired from the position of alpha fourteen years ago, when Kendrick had taken over, but Raven remained a cornerstone of the Den, his skills in battle formidable and his years of experience as alpha providing a constant source of good advice to Kendrick and the senior wolves.

Caroline's two years of training had culminated in her conversion into a shape shifter just two days ago, and she was still struggling to get used to the changes the ritual had caused. The conversion itself had been strange, like trying to fit two people into one pair of trousers. The instant her wolf had arrived, her mind had started working differently, seeing the world from a new angle, subtle changes in her priorities or unexpected alterations in her moods. She had been experiencing strange cravings, her mouth watering at the scent of raw meat, or she'd feel a sudden and irrepressible urge to chew things. She'd been warned about these odd occurrences during her training, Kendrick telling her that it meant her body was reminding her that she needed to spend some time in wolf form, and she was careful to obey her body's demands, shifting promptly and seeking out whatever it was that her canine half seemed to be craving. It was an important part of the merging process, she'd been told, and the last thing she wanted to do was end up going rogue.

But despite all her achievements, Caroline still felt like she was somehow out of place here. The training had been hard, but there were also large parts of her life that had seemed far too easy. She had been given a place to live and food to eat, with nothing being asked of her in return aside from her diligent attention to her training. She was given a monthly allowance for clothing and personal effects, which had been far more than she could have earned even with a full time job. And when she had been converted, it had seemed like a gift of immense value, handed over freely despite her having accomplished nothing of any significance for the Den, no battles won against the Noturatii, no bright ideas that had helped improve their strategies against their enemies. After so many years of fighting for every mouthful, every opportunity, every tiny bit of money, she was left feeling rather hollow, a disappointment to her colleagues, though none of them had ever expressed such feelings towards her.

There was nothing scheduled for this afternoon, no more classes, no combat sessions, though Caroline knew that her training in battle would continue for months to come, and she was feeling rather at a loose end. There was a newspaper sitting on the coffee table, so, with no particular interest in the daily report on the world's events, she opened it and started reading.

When she reached page six, a name caught her eye, in a brief article near the bottom of the page. 'Julie Saunders'. Her mother's name. Her immediate assumption was that the article had to refer to a different woman. There had to be more than one Julie Saunders in England, after all.

But out of curiosity, she read the article anyway... and felt her heart stop.

A woman's body had been found, bruises on her wrists and face, her throat slit. A man had been arrested on suspicion of murder, but later released due to lack of evidence. And though the article didn't give any names, it mentioned that the man had been the woman's estranged husband. But it wasn't until Caroline reached the part about the location of the body that the pieces finally clicked into place. The woman had been found in a small woodland, not five minutes' walk from her old house.

Her mother. It had to be.

A surge of rage filled her as she jumped to the most obvious conclusion: Her mother had returned to her old house for some unknown reason, and her father, still furious over her abandonment all those years ago, had killed her.

Her mind immediately began trying to fit all the pieces together. She'd heard nothing from her mother since the day she'd walked out on them, but it wasn't out of the question to think that she'd finally come back. Caroline had spent many years hoping, praying for such a thing, even as she'd hated the woman for abandoning her so suddenly. But the years had tempered her anger, as Caroline had come to understand her mother's actions better, had even agreed with them at times, as her own desire to escape her family had grown.

But why would she come back after all this time? A small, childish part of her wondered whether it was because she'd wanted to see Caroline again. Walking out on her abusive husband was one thing, after all, but abandoning her children must have left some sort of impression on the woman. Maybe she'd finally overcome her alcoholism? Got treatment for her depression? Come back, hoping to make amends? Maybe it was just wishful thinking, but Caroline couldn't think of any other reason she'd have returned. She could hardly suppose that her mother still loved her father and had come back for him. Even on the best of days, she'd never expressed any kind of affection for her husband. There would also be no point in coming back to ask for money – there had never been much of that in the first place.

And if he'd truly killed her mother, then Caroline's father had robbed her of the chance once and for all of ever seeing the woman again, of ever hearing an explanation for her departure. Of ever hearing that, despite all appearances, Caroline had actually mattered to her. She read the article again, cursing blackly as she read the part that said the suspect had been released.

But Caroline was sure her father was responsible. Who else would want to kill her mother? If Caroline had been angry at her abandonment, then her father had been livid, regularly venting his fury about the woman, calling her every filthy name under the sun.

In that instant, Caroline knew she had to find out the truth. Contacting her family, she knew, was forbidden, a betrayal of trust that carried weighty consequences. She'd assured Kendrick when she'd joined the Den that her family meant nothing to her, that she would be glad to never see them again.

But murder? That was too much to ignore, regardless of the consequences.

But she didn't need to see them in person to know the truth, Caroline reasoned, looking for an option that would pacify the raging anger boiling inside her, as well as pose the lease possible risk to the Den. She didn't need to speak to them, or even let them know she was still alive in order to know whether her father had been involved in the murder. She had her wolf senses now. All she needed to do was check out the house, see if she could pick up her mother's scent. Though days had passed since her death, a wolf's sense of smell was strong enough to still be able to detect whether she'd been there.

But only if she moved quickly.

A plan formed in her mind, one that was reckless beyond belief, fraught with complications and the risk of being caught, but now that the question had been raised, the need to know the truth was imperative. Despite the risks, Caroline was familiar enough with the routines of the estate to believe that her plan had a chance of working.

So later that afternoon, she asked Silas for a firearms lesson. Upon its conclusion, she obediently took her gun back to the vault where the weapons were stored when not in use, a secret compartment hidden behind one of the shelves in the library, waiting while Silas entered the code to open the door.

With her instructor waiting outside the vault, she quickly and quietly slipped a new clip into the gun, then screwed a silencer onto the end. Then she set it on the ground. Shifted into wolf form and picked up the gun in her mouth. And then shifted back. The gun vanished, along with her wolf, so that when she emerged from the vault, there was no sign of her being armed at all. She'd earned enough trust in the past two years that Silas simply assumed she'd returned the gun, without actually checking it was on the shelf, and she genuinely hoped that he wasn't going to get into trouble for any of this. Later, back in her room, she shifted again, bringing the gun back into reality, and the theft was complete.

Leaving the estate was tricky, but it was more straight forward than stealing the gun. While security was tight, it was more designed to keep people out than wolves in, and there were a few spots along the boundary where a wolf could squeeze through a gap, or jump over a fence without alerting anyone to their presence. Caroline left the house via the front door, prepared to tell anyone who asked that she was feeling restless and needed a run. Then, once she was safely off the estate, she headed for the nearest train station, relieved that her plan was working, but knowing that the hardest part was still to come.

Hours later, Caroline crouched in the bushes in the front yard of her old house, shaking in fury. Her suspicions about her father had been confirmed. Upon arriving at the house, she'd furtively shifted into wolf form, after checking that no one was around, and carefully scented the ground. As a newly converted wolf, identifying scents was still a difficult task – her sense of smell was excellent, but the sheer volume of information her nose could detect made it hard to pick out individual scents. But Julie had been her mother, had birthed her, nursed her, raised her for twelve years, tucked her into bed at night, and despite the intervening years, Caroline still remembered the smell of her like she'd seen her yesterday.

After a few minutes of careful investigation, Caroline was certain she was right. Her mother had been here. There was no doubt about it.

Which meant her father had killed her.

And Caroline was going to repay the favour.

The strength of her hatred for the man surprised her. After successfully escaping from his clutches and spending two years in a far better environment, she'd somehow assumed that she'd moved on from the traumas of her childhood. But now that she was back here, where so much misery had made her life a living hell, the memories came rushing back, the beatings, the insults, the lack of food, the filth in and around the house… it was making her feel ill. She pulled the gun out of her jacket, eyeing the house coldly.

It was late at night, the sky fully dark, the shadows deep in the poorly maintained yard, and with her black clothes and the beanie on her head, she was confident that no one could see her.

The curtains in the living room of the house hadn't been drawn fully, and Caroline had got a glimpse through the crack. Her father and Greg were both home, slouching in front of the TV. No sign of Troy, but according to his last conviction, he should still be in jail, and that meant he wasn't Caroline's problem. He was a bastard, that much was true, but he couldn't have been involved in her mother's death.

Her task was simple. She would knock on the front door. Either her father or Greg would answer it, it didn't matter who. She would shoot whoever it was in the chest, then force her way into the house to shoot the second man. The silencer on the gun wouldn't cancel out all the sound, but it would be quiet enough that most people would simply dismiss the noise as a car backfiring. That sort of thing tended to happen a lot around here. And then she would shift, ghost away into the night, a simple, stray dog, if anyone noticed, no evidence left behind, no trace of the gun, nothing to link any of this either to herself, or Il Trosa.

She glanced down at the gun in her hand. Checked the clip. The silencer. And took a deep breath as she steadied herself, ready to stand up and march over to the front door-

A cold, hard lump of metal pressed against her temple, and Caroline froze, suddenly aware of the large body beside hers, where she had been alone only moments ago.

"I will only say this once, Caroline," Kendrick said, his mouth scant inches from her ear. "Put the gun down, or I will put a bullet in your skull."

Fuck! Fuck, fuck, fuck! She'd known there was a chance someone would notice she was missing, but she'd been hoping they would be too slow, that she would be long gone from here before they figured out what she was up to.

And how the hell had Kendrick managed to sneak up on her like that, anyway? She had excellent hearing, she was all but invisible in the dark... Fuck!

Knowing that Kendrick was totally prepared to make good on his threat, Caroline slowly placed the gun on the ground, shaking both from the shock of being caught, and the unfulfilled need for revenge swirling inside her. Kendrick picked it up and made short work of removing the clip and unscrewing the silencer.

And then the verbal onslaught of displeasure started. "What the fuck do you think you're doing?" Kendrick asked, then went on without waiting for an answer. "You're about to murder two people in their own home. You think the police aren't going to notice that? The Noturatii, even? They tried to snatch you on your way to the estate, the first time. They know who you are. Anything happens to your family, and they'll be all over it! You think we don't have enough problems keeping them off our tails without you lighting up a neon sign for them? Do you have any idea how much work it is to cover up a murder? And in the middle of suburbia? Or did you honestly think people were just going to ignore the two bodies lying around in pools of their own blood? For Christ's sake, what the fuck were you thinking?"

"He killed my mother," she bit out, knowing Kendrick was furious, but wanting to justify her actions nonetheless.

"You forget, Caroline," Kendrick snarled at her. "The instant you joined our Den, you ceased to have a mother! You ceased to have any family at all. Now, stand up." She did, then followed him churlishly as he led the way back towards the van, parked a few streets away.

As they arrived, Silas and Raven came out of the darkness, silent on booted feet, and it wasn't a surprise that Kendrick had brought backup. Silas was the best tracker in the Den, and he would have had no trouble tracing her scent from the train station.

The look on Raven's face was one of utter disappointment, and Caroline was surprised at how keenly she felt the brunt of that failure. Raven had been a patient and diligent teacher during the past two years, expecting a lot of her, but understanding her struggles as she trudged through some of the tougher lessons, and he'd never stopped believing in her, encouraging her, reminding her that there were great things to be achieved in the future, and it made her feel cold to know how badly she'd let him down.

Silas was harder to read, his expression blank, and she couldn't decide whether he was angry at her for trying such a reckless stunt, or simply pissed off that he'd had to drag himself out here at night when he could be at home with a glass of bourbon in his hand and an action movie on the television.

She didn't want to go back to the Den, Caroline realised suddenly. Her fury at her father was still vivid, a living beast that had not yet been sated, and most likely never would be, now that the Den knew what she had been up to. And she still had no idea what had driven her mother to return after all these years. The lack of closure left her feeling lost.

No, she couldn't go back with them. Not to the welcoming lights and sympathetic glances and warm bed. Not to be locked in a cage and lectured until the truth of her betrayal hit home, and then to spend the rest of her life dealing with the emotional conflict of being grateful beyond measure for her new life and the honourable people in it, and yet wishing this one act of betrayal had been more successful.

But Il Trosa wasn't the only wolf pack in England, Caroline remembered, her thoughts in turmoil. The Grey Watch lived to the north, in the isolated forests near the Scottish border. They lived in the open, no houses, no creature comforts. They lived wilder lives, raw and untamed, and far more brutal than their civilised counterparts in Il Trosa.

Caroline glanced around, seeing dark alleyways and overgrown yards. Kendrick was occupied with stowing the gun back in the van, Raven climbing into the passenger seat, Silas distracted for a moment checking the street for passers-by… so Caroline shifted in a split second, canine paws silent on the cold concrete, and took off, dashing down an alley, jumping a low fence into a construction site, then off down an overgrown path. She was wild inside, unable to tame her fiercer emotions, base instincts clawing at her mind for freedom. And so the wilderness was where she would go.


At Silas's startled shout, Kendrick lurched out of the van, just in time to see Caroline racing off into the darkness. And in wolf form no less! Thank God the streets were deserted. That small blessing would hopefully minimise the risk of public exposure. He rolled his eyes, not even considering going after her, resigned to the knowledge that the situation was now well and truly out of his control. The only way to follow her now was by scent, and he'd already taken a big enough risk by allowing Silas to track her in wolf form on the way here. Having three wolves roaming the streets in plain sight was a greater danger even than allowing Caroline to escape.

But this latest complication wouldn't last long. He reached into his pocket and pulled out his phone, dialling the number for the Council's headquarters in Italy.

"Susie?" he said, when someone answered the phone, using the code name that indicated an emergency situation to the Council. "It's Henry," – the code name for the British Den. It was far too easy to tap phone lines and listen in on calls, so nothing of any importance was ever discussed without either being in code, or on a secure link. "I'm going to need you to send Helga to us for a short visit." He hung up without waiting for an answer. None was required. When he got home, he could call the Council on a secure line and explain the situation in detail, but for the time being, he could rest easy, secure in the knowledge that the Council was at this very moment choosing one of their most highly trained assassins, and sending them with all haste to England.

# CHAPTER THIRTEEN

**Present Day**

Melissa sat at her computer, analysing the latest results from the experiments Dr Evans had been running. The new lab was set up – a smaller facility than the last one, within the administration block of the Noturatii's east London base. The new science staff had proved themselves to be devoted and hard working, and Melissa had been accepted as one of the team, praise for her work on the Conversion Project flowing freely from her new boss's lips. By all reasonable standards, the work was going extremely well.

And Melissa was hating every minute of it.

Conceptually, of course, this was still a dream come true. Since the day she'd found out what had happened to her brother Mark, that he'd become one of the shape shifter abominations, she'd been determined to wipe the hideous creatures off the face of the planet. And meeting him again earlier this year, face-to-face for the first time in over a decade, had only strengthen her resolve.

But this current situation was infuriating. She'd had her valuable research on the Conversion Project ripped out from under her, the experiments now being conducted in the lab in Germany. She and her team had made such progress, on the verge of a breakthrough with their last experiment, and now she'd been forever denied the chance to crack the mystery not only of how to make new shifters, but far more importantly, of how to un-make them.

On top of that, the new experiments were, as far as Melissa was concerned, a dismal failure. Their current objective was to determine the specific voltage and current for the electrical charges that allowed a shifter to change forms. The new shifter captive had been most cooperative, regular threats of pain and torture sufficient to motivate him to shift whenever they requested it. They had begun by attaching electrodes to his body, but had quickly realised that such a plan would never work – the shift caused the electrodes to vanish, along with his human body, and they'd quickly solved the problem by embedding the electrodes in the table instead, the greater mass preventing them from being caught up in the matter transformation. And once they'd got some useful readings, they'd fed them back into the shifter, each time hoping that he could be forced to shift by their technology, rather than by their threats.

But each time, the result had been a complete failure. No shift. No change in his physiology. Not the slightest waver in his form that might indicate they were on the verge of solving the mystery. The whole thing was becoming a total waste of time, and Melissa found herself resenting her boss's cheerful demeanour and her blind persistence in repeating the same experiment over and over again when it was clearly leading nowhere.

"How's it going?" Dr Evans asked, arriving in the lab where Melissa was working, and she immediately adopted a perplexed frown, indicating that the experiments weren't going well, but withholding any hint of her personal dissatisfaction. Politics, after all, were just as important as science in these labs.

"No luck," she said succinctly. "Even after we increased the sensitivity of the electrodes, the new voltages haven't caused any detectable change in the shifter. I've been thinking, though…" she said, deciding to go out on a limb. It was a risk, discussing her theories with Evans, with the firm chance that the woman would take the ideas and claim them as her own – no one got far in the Noturatii by playing fair, after all – but if she said nothing, then there was little chance they would ever reach the breakthrough they were seeking. "We've been working on the theory that each shift is caused by a single burst of electricity, one voltage, one discharge of current. But what if we're wrong? What if, instead of one charge, the shift is stimulated by a series of unique voltages."

Evans looked perplexed by the suggestion, so Melissa explained herself further. "The electrodes have been detecting the maximum voltage in each shift, which has consistently been around the 7000 volt mark. But if you look at the readings, there's actually a waver in the signal. It takes up to 0.6 seconds to achieve that voltage, and then there's a lag phase where the voltage lingers around 3000 volts for anything up to 1.2 seconds. So what if it's not a smooth rise to 7000 volts, but rather a series of steps? 0.2 seconds at 2000 volts, for example, then 0.2 seconds at 5000 volts, then the peak of 7000, then a drop back to 3000 volts to complete the shift. With some modifications to the equipment, it should be possible to detect changes in voltage as rapidly as every 0.05 seconds. And if we can isolate the voltage at each point in the process, we should get a much clearer picture of what's going on throughout the shift."

"It's an interesting theory," Dr Evans said, no doubt attempting to sound supportive, but Melissa could detect a patronising undercurrent in her voice. "But there's one other detail you're overlooking. When the shift occurs, the human body disappears and the wolf body emerges. That causes a certain amount of 'wobble' in the readings. Physical movement of the electrode against the skin can cause minute inaccuracies. Unfortunately, it's unavoidable, given the nature of our test subject. I think we need to focus our attention in a different direction. Perhaps, instead of having the electrodes in contact with the shifter's body, we need to find a way to detect the charges from a distance. A few centimetres should be enough, and if we insulate the lab to keep extraneous electrical signals out – there's a huge amount of electrical equipment in the offices, after all, which could be interfering with the signal – then we should be able to narrow things down to a much more defined voltage for each shift. But," she went on, with a much more genuine smile, "I like the way you think. Stepping outside the box, looking for new possibilities. Keep it up, Hunter. It's a pleasure having you on the team."

Melissa smiled and nodded, managing to look pleased with the feedback, before turning back to the analysis in front of her. Evans was overlooking serious avenues to further their research, and for all her condescending praise, by dismissing Melissa's ideas and running with her own, she was as much of a glory hog as if she had stolen the ideas for herself. The fact was, she couldn't handle having someone on her team capable of doing a better job than she could.

Melissa deliberately calmed herself, willing to bide her time. There was more than one way to skin a cat, after all. More than one way to win a war.

And more than one way to deal with an imposter in the lab, taking over what should have been her domain.


The Densmeet was slowly gaining momentum. The shifters from across Europe had been trickling in, with the Russians as the most recent arrivals. Now there were just the Ukrainians left to arrive before the main events of the summer could begin.

Skip was in two minds about the whole thing. Each year it was the same, an unsettling mix of excitement and apprehension as she looked forward to meeting new people and seeing old friends, but also dreaded the social anxiety that invariably came with large gatherings.

The Russians had just taken over the upper floor of the manor, a large group from four different Dens who had arrived in a cacophony of shouts and greetings, gifts presented to Baron and Caroline as the hosts for this year, and then a thunder of booted feet heading up the stairs, followed by more shouting as they all fought over which rooms were the best. Most of the Russians knew each other, it seemed, close ties existing between the eight Dens across the large country, and Skip hoped that Baron would remind them at some point that they were here to see other people as well, not just sit around and speak Russian with their comrades all summer.

Overcome by the noise and exuberance of the group, Skip retreated outside, taking Albert, her third-favourite teddy bear with her. Having a bear by her side was always a comfort, but she hadn't wanted to bring Rupert, her best bear, for fear of him getting lost or damaged in all the goings on.

She was sitting quietly on a low stone wall, admiring the rose garden, when she heard a rude snort behind her. She looked up to see two of the Russians standing there, staring at her and laughing. She shot them a quizzical look.

"You brought your teddy bear?" one of the Russians said in a thick accent, mockery strong in his voice. "Are you having a tea party with him? Or does he want to smell the roses?"

"Does he have a name?" the other one piped up. "He does, doesn't he? What's his name?"

Both the men were young, possibly even younger than Skip herself, and she immediately assumed they were new recruits. No seasoned wolf would be so rude. Putting on a front far braver than she was feeling, she rolled her eyes at the pair and tried to ignore them. It wasn't the first time people had been surprised about her bears, and it wouldn't be the last.

"Are you ignoring us?" one of the men asked, stepping closer. "That's not polite."

"Neither are you," Skip said defensively. "Why don't you go back inside and leave me alone?"

"Aw, the little wolf's afraid," the man said, putting on an expression of false sympathy.

"Wolf?" the other mocked her. "That's no wolf. She's just a puppy. Aren't you, little girl? Are you new here? Haven't quite found your teeth yet?"

"Let's see if she has any teeth," the first man said, and then he darted forward, ripping the bear right out of her hands. "Do you want it back?" He dangled the bear in front of her. "Will you come and get it?"

Coming out of the stables where the combat training would be conducted, Tank's mind was focused on the list of tasks Baron had given him; set up the shooting range, hang up the punching bags, check the flight schedule for the Ukrainian arrivals. But as he headed for the main house, he spotted Skip sitting on the wall by the garden. She seemed to be talking to two other shifters... but his head snapped up and a low growl rumbled from his throat as he saw one of the men snatch her bear. No doubt the poor kid was feeling a little overwhelmed with all the people, and fuck, if these two jokers had decided to give her a hard time, they had another thing coming. Changing course, he set a quick pace in her direction, all too ready to whip these young pups into shape.

"Give it back," Skip said firmly, not falling for the ploy of trying to chase the bear. The two men were bigger than her, and no doubt thought themselves quicker – which may or may not be true, but with two against one, she knew her odds of getting the bear back on her own were slim.

"Don't you want it back?" the man asked, dangling the bear just out of reach. "He's such a nice bear. It would be a shame if anything happened to him."

Skip stood up, weighing her options. She could shift, of course, and teach these rude boys a lesson, her wolf lithe and quick... but there were two problems with that. If they shifted as well, there was a strong risk Albert would get damaged in the fight. And if they didn't, then there were strict rules against wolves attacking people in human form. While Baron would no doubt see that she had good reason, she would still be in a load of trouble, and she frantically tried to think of another option. There was no way she could beat the two men in human form, after all...

But as she watched, searching for any obvious weakness in either man, they both suddenly turned pale. The one holding the bear held it out. "Here. Take it," he said quickly, looking genuinely frightened. But Skip didn't take the bait. Another trick, no doubt-

"I'm serious!" the man snapped. "Take it. It's yours." He glanced behind her, just a split second flicker of his eyes, and Skip suddenly became aware of a presence standing behind her.

With a wry smirk, she looked over her shoulder, and then let out a chuckle as she saw the line up behind her. There was Silas, front and centre, standing with his arms folded and a look on his face that threatened unspeakable pain. And beside him were Kwan and Aaron, both wearing matching scowls and trying to look tough.

She turned back, about to take the bear... but then, when she saw who had arrived during her moment of distraction, she snorted out a laugh. Tank and John were standing behind the two men, in a mirror image of Silas's pose, and, seeing the direction of her gaze, the two men spun around quickly, turning even paler as they saw the rear guard.

Skip reached forward and took the bear, cradling him carefully in her arms.

"Sorry," the men said hastily, glancing at her bodyguards nervously.

"We're really sorry." Skip merely rolled her eyes at them. She didn't find it the least bit embarrassing to be rescued by five strong men. It was a bold statement of solidarity, proof that her Den stuck together and looked out for each other, and she felt a warm burst of joy at the reminder of just how willing her friends were to stand up for her. With a smile and a wink at Silas, she slipped away, Kwan and Aaron falling in behind her.

Tank watched Skip leave, waiting until she was out of earshot, and then he glanced at Silas, giving the man a slight nod. The two boys were still standing there awkwardly, no doubt wondering if they were allowed to leave.

"We're really sorry," one of the men said again. "It was a bad joke."

"Not funny," Silas said, unsheathing a knife, tossing it once or twice, and then stepping forward until his face was a few scant inches from the men's. "Let that be a lesson to you, *pup*. You mess with our sister, you mess with us. Now," he went on, fingering the handle of his knife. "Have I made my point? Or should I make it clearer?" Beside Tank, John let out a growl. Tank cracked his knuckles, eyeing the boys like they were a tasty meal.

"You have made your point," the men assured him, attempting to back away, until they realised that John was blocking their path. "Very clear."

Silas waited a moment longer, then smiled and sheathed his knife. "Good. I look forward to seeing you around."

John stepped aside, and the two boys scurried off, both white as a sheet. John made a satisfied noise and wandered off, leaving Tank and Silas alone.

Tank eyed his comrade with wry amusement, surprised at his own good mood. Then he rolled his eyes when he saw the sceptical look Silas was giving him. "Shut up," he said, not quite able to keep the smile off his face. "That was fun."

"First time I've heard that word out of your mouth in a while," Silas said drily, falling in beside him as he headed for the house.

"Yeah," Tank admitted, seeing nothing to be gained in arguing the point. "I've been a moody bastard. I get it."

"For a while there, I thought you were starting to have a permanent case of PMS."

Tank glared at him, a look full of amusement, as he knew he'd made the same statement about Silas often enough. "You watch it," he griped good naturedly, punching Silas in the arm.

Silas grinned and slapped him on the back in reply. "Life puts us all through the wringer every once in a while. And climbing your way back out of the hole can take some time."

"I know," Tank said, aware that one good day wasn't going to make all his problems disappear. "But it's still good to see a light at the end of the tunnel every now and then."

"That it is."

The following morning, Baron stood in front of the mansion, watching as Tank drove the van up the drive. He'd been to Inverness to pick up the Ukrainians – the last of the shifters to arrive – and Baron was both curious and cautious about these foreign men. Andre had filled him in a little more about Nikolai's 'quirks', and though the man was no doubt a fierce warrior and a loyal follower of the Council, some of the stories had made Baron more than a little nervous. Living in the Chernobyl Exclusion Zone, the man seemed slightly unhinged, and having received no specific information from the Council about the Ukrainian Den, Baron felt he was stumbling about in the dark where these newest arrivals were concerned.

The van pulled up, and the doors slid open, a volley of words in Ukrainian pouring out even before the shifters emerged. There were four of them, all male, and Baron felt himself tense as he took in the size of them. They were all tall, broad shouldered, thick muscles evident beneath a healthy layer of fat – winters in Ukraine were cold, after all, and if they'd been living at the edge of civilisation, in an area with no electricity or running water, they would have had to perform a lot of daily tasks by hand and make do with wood fires for warmth, with no modern heating.

The oldest of the men looked around at his new home, grinning with satisfaction as he took in the grand, grey manor, the wide lawn, the thick forest... until his gaze settled on Baron.

This was the alpha, Baron realised immediately. Nikolai. And for a moment, the two of them merely sized each other up. It was always awkward, having two or more alphas on the same property for the summer, and sometimes they managed to get through it all with politeness and diplomacy, but other times serious arguments and occasionally even fights broke out as some dispute or other had to be resolved. This year, they had four alphas, Baron, Caroline, Nikolai and a female alpha from Norway, and when you threw Andre into the mix, a Council emissary with no official status in any Den, thing were bound to get tense.

Nikolai stalked towards him, his eyes never leaving Baron's, and he stopped just two feet away, head held high. Baron saw an immediate reflection in their human selves of the stand-off that would have taken place if they were in wolf form, hackles up, tails high, each assessing the strengths and weaknesses of their opponent.

Suddenly, Nikolai grinned, lunged forward and caught Baron in a bone-crushing hug that actually managed to lift him off the ground for a moment. "Baron! My friend! It is good to finally meet you," he declared, his English fluent, though his accent was strong. "I have heard many stories of your victories. Here." He reached into his coat, withdrawing a tall bottle. "I have brought you vodka! A gift for you, my friend." He looked around, taking in the scenery again. "Welcome to Scotland!" he declared, when Baron should really have been the one to offer the greeting. "Your weather is dreadful. And this is your other alpha?" he asked, making Baron realise that Caroline had arrived beside him. "Caroline. I have heard good things about you. Your wife, no?"

"No," Baron and Caroline answered simultaneously, which made Nikolai laugh.

"No? That is fine. I am not married to our alpha, either. She is a total bitch. A fine warrior. We argue all the time."

Baron grinned, suddenly deciding he liked this man, status issues aside. He offered his hand, pleased when he felt the man's firm grip. "Welcome to Scotland," he said belatedly. "Grab your bags, and I'll show you to your rooms."

# CHAPTER FOURTEEN

**16 Years Ago**

Caroline stalked slowly through the undergrowth, testing each step with a careful paw. The ground was damp, rotting leaves cushioning her feet and rendering her steps all but silent, but that was no excuse for getting careless. To her right, Rintur, one of the Grey Watch's wolves, crept forward with just as much care, their bodies held low, tails tucked down to avoid rustling any bushes. And up ahead was their prize: a handful of rabbits, grazing on fresh clumps of grass, ears twitching as they remained alert to the slightest hint of danger.

The two of them crept closer, their grey bodies camouflaged perfectly in the dim light of the undergrowth, ferns blocking the rabbits' view of them. A dozen yards from their prey, Rintur paused, and Caroline followed suit. Hunting was still very new to her, but Rintur had been an excellent teacher, and Caroline glanced her way, reading her intentions from her body language. They could get no closer without being detected, and she watched as Rintur braced herself, her canine body like a coiled spring ready to pounce. Caroline copied her, gathering her legs beneath her, her balance perfect, ready for that final sprint that would, with any luck, land them both a meal.

She peered through the leaves, picking out her target, a small rabbit on the fringes of the group that seemed not quite as alert as the rest. Breathed out. Breathed in... and attacked, a short, sharp dash out of the undergrowth, twisting as the rabbit bolted, going left, then right, then left again, Caroline responding on razor sharp reflexes, lunging forward... and she screeched to a halt, almost surprised at herself as she came up with a rabbit in her teeth, a high pitched squeal coming from the animal as it kicked its back legs in terror.

Caroline bit down hard, breaking the animal's neck swiftly and ending its pain. She glanced around, pleased to see that Rintur had been successful as well, a larger rabbit in her mouth, and she wagged her tail to show her joy at her accomplishment.

Rintur glanced around, checking that no one else was hovering in the background, waiting to steal her meal, and then she slunk away, lying down beneath a bush to enjoy her prize. Caroline chose a similar spot, a cosy nook inside a hollow log, and set her sharp teeth to work.

It was not quite two weeks since she'd joined the Watch, and the first few days here had been fraught with tension and drama. Sempre, the alpha, had been outraged when she'd learned that Caroline was a wolf from Il Trosa. She'd spent hours snarling at her, first in wolf form, then as a human, accusing her of spying, of trespassing, of being a weak, domesticated wolf with no business in the wild.

But Caroline had stood her ground, determined in her intention to join them. She'd made no complaint about their rugged existence, content to sleep outside in wolf form that first night. She'd embraced their competitive lifestyle, throwing herself into battles over food and other resources, and she was comfortable with the lack of amenities – a bare minimum of cooking facilities, no electricity or hot water, and only the most basic items of clothing available.

When they'd finally seen that she was serious about this life in the wilderness, the Watch had accepted her as one of their own. Tough, rugged females were hard to find in this modern society that provided every conceivable convenience, they'd said, and any shifter who could embrace their canine side with such zeal was an asset to their pack. For her part, Caroline had thrown herself into every aspect of this life, hunting, tracking, learning to use her enhanced wolf senses to their full potential. Life here was a constant battle for survival, with none of the ready comforts of life in Il Trosa, and she was feeling more alive, more useful as she performed necessary tasks for her new pack, carting water, chopping firewood, hunting for food.

Once the meal of raw rabbit was finished, Caroline followed Rintur back to the camp. Her mentor seemed to enjoy her company as much as Caroline enjoyed hers, and while she would have had to admit that she missed some of her friends back at the Den, she was also far from lonely. While the senior wolves remained aloof, the younger ones had welcomed her, and three or four of them were becoming close friends.

Back at the camp, Caroline passed the small huddle of males that the Watch kept on her way through the clearing. There were three of them, toned men with the faces and bodies of male models, but they were small as wolves, skinny and unremarkable to look at. Behaviour-wise, they were meek and passive, and as she watched, one of the senior females wandered over, her human form covered in a long grey cloak, and she issued a sharp command to one of the males. He responded by shifting into human form, his hairless chest naked, a pair of thin trousers covering his legs, and followed her towards the tent without a word.

If she'd been inclined, Caroline could have fought for mating rights with the males, sex being a privilege of rank, like all resources in their camp, but in all honesty, she found little about the idea appealing. Her past experience with sex had been dull at best, painful at worst, with her previous boyfriend far more concerned about his own pleasure than hers, always eager to push her to comply, even when she wasn't in the mood, and he'd loved to call her filthy names in the process, something Caroline had borne with resignation and a slowly growing resentment.

But despite her disinterest in sex in general and her dislike for overbearing men, the males of the Watch were unappealing for an entirely different reason. They were weak men, Caroline had learned quickly, beaten down and submissive, responding eagerly to gifts of food or flattery over their looks, but showing no hint of defiance or will of their own. More pet than person, they seemed to seek nothing but physical pleasure from life, and the quiet acceptance of their empty existence left Caroline cold.

Further on through the clearing, she saw two of the younger wolves fighting over a bar of soap. It was almost comical to watch, neither wolf wanting to take the thing in her mouth – it must taste disgusting, after all – but equally unwilling to shift and claim possession of the thing in human form. Caroline herself had no use for such luxuries. If she wanted to get clean, she would simply strip off and bathe in the stream naked, using sand to scrub the dirt from her body. But baths were not a regular necessity, with most of her time spent in wolf form, and she snorted derisively at the pair as she passed, heading further on to the very edge of the camp, where a clear stream would provide a refreshing drink of water.

Out here in the forest, the ghosts of her past seemed more easily laid to rest. While she still thought of her mother now and then, still wondered at her reasons for returning and still felt occasional bursts of anger towards her father, she was finding that the dark memories were coming less and less often the longer she spent here. Far away from civilisation, it was easy to think that she'd escaped her past, not just her traumatic childhood, but her days with Il Trosa, the Den seeming a far away memory now. The cool forest seemed more real than thick carpet and soft couches ever had, and Caroline felt she'd finally found somewhere she belonged, amongst the rustle of the trees, the call of birds overhead and with the damp mist and light drizzle seeping into her fur.

Adriana perched in a tree high above the Grey Watch camp. She was perfectly camouflaged, wearing mottled clothing that blended in with the tree's greens and browns, her scent disguised with the smell of pine needles, her body still and silent.

After arriving at the Den, Kendrick had wasted no time in taking her to Caroline's room to let her learn her scent. He'd shown her photos of the woman, in both human and wolf form, and then Adriana had headed out to Caroline's old house, beginning the slow process of tracking her from there.

Now, she waited patiently, watching as Caroline made her way across the camp. Adriana had been here since last night, sneaking in under cover of darkness, having chosen a vantage point above the stream that flowed past the camp. Sooner or later, it was almost certain that Caroline would come this way, either to get a drink, or to collect water for the camp, and now, Adriana's patience was about to pay off. She watched as the wolf strolled across the clearing, heading for the stream. She stopped to sniff at a bush, scratched her neck with a flexible back leg, then trotted over to the water for a drink.

Adriana lined up the tranquiliser gun in her hand. Waited a moment more, until she could get a good shot at Caroline's back leg... and pulled the trigger.

Caroline leapt in the air and snarled as she felt the dart, her startled yelp calling other wolves from nearby... and then she went down, the sedative taking effect quickly.

Howling and yipping from the others, and Sempre and the senior wolves were at the scene in seconds, examining the dart in Caroline's leg, and then they were on full alert, guns out, scanning the surrounding area for enemies.

This was the tricky part. Adriana now had to get out of the tree and convince the Watch that she wasn't breaking any laws, without getting shot in the process.

Carefully, slowly, so as not to alert them to her presence, she extracted a small, spiked disc from her pocket. On both sides of the disc, displayed in clear black and white, was the symbol of the Council's emissaries, an inverted V with a slanted dash above it. A flick of her wrist sent the disc spinning to the ground, where it embedded itself in the soil via one of the spikes, and she held her breath as the shifters spun around in alarm.

Then they noticed the symbol on the disc. Sempre swore, her words clearly audible from Adriana's vantage point. "Fucking Council..." she heard her mutter, but then Sempre sighed and reluctantly put her gun away, folding her arms and tapping her foot impatiently as she waited for their intruder to appear.

Taking her cue, Adriana moved, sliding down the tree in a graceful descent that had her landing squarely on her feet a few metres from the fuming leader of the Watch.

"You trespass," Sempre accused her coldly, when she reached the ground.

"On the contrary," Adriana said. "You harbour an Il Trosa fugitive amongst your ranks. I have come to collect her."

Sempre glanced at Caroline, and Adriana stepped quickly over to her, checking that the wolf was breathing and unharmed. She was out cold, her breaths slow and even, and she carefully retrieved the dart from her leg and put it safely away.

"Fugitive? What has she done?"

"Attempted to murder her natural family, and then defied her alpha when he sought to apprehend her. My orders are to return her to the Council for trial."

More swearing, growls from the wolves waiting nearby. "Are you going to kill her?" Sempre asked, looking like she was more than willing to make an issue of it, if the answer was yes.

"My orders are to deliver her to Italy alive," Adriana said calmly. "What the Council chooses to do with her after that is beyond my control." As it was, her instructions were already a surprise to Adriana. Usually, when a wolf committed such an act of betrayal, putting the perpetrator down was the standard course of action. But apparently Kendrick had pleaded for leniency when he'd spoken to the Council, and they'd agreed to take a more diplomatic approach on this occasion. "The Treaty of Erim Kai Bahn demands that you release her into my custody," Adriana reminded Sempre. "She has committed crimes against Il Trosa, and as such, we have the right to determine her punishment." The reverse would also be true – a shifter who betrayed the Grey Watch would be handed back to them should they attempt to seek shelter with Il Trosa, and both packs had respected the agreement for hundreds of years.

"I'm well aware of what the Treaty says," Sempre snapped, looking none too happy about it. She bent down and stroked Caroline's head, an act of tenderness that was at odds with the woman's usual cold manner. "This wolf has great potential," she said, stepping back reluctantly. "She could be a great asset to your pack. Or to ours. Mention that to your Council when you arrive."

Interesting. It seemed that Kendrick wasn't the only one to have recognised the value of this woman, and Adriana nodded. "I'll inform the Council of your plea on her behalf."

Sempre waited another moment, glaring at Adriana over Caroline's still body, the wolves around her growling steadily, a clear display of their anger at this intrusion.

But eventually, Sempre stepped back, clearing a path for her to leave.

Adriana took a thick metal collar from inside her coat. She attached it around Caroline's neck, much to the displeasure of the watching wolves.

Then she snapped a handcuff around her own wrist and attached the two with a short length of chain. There were no guarantees Caroline would cooperate, once she regained consciousness, and after two weeks of tracking her, Adriana was not inclined to take the risk of losing her again. Then she hefted the wolf's slender body onto her shoulder, and turned to leave.

"May Sirius guide your days and guard your nights," she said politely to Sempre. For all their disagreements, the Watch were still shifters, allies to Il Trosa in the fight against the Noturatii.

"Get off my territory," Sempre replied coldly. "We've had enough interference from Il Trosa to last a lifetime."


Caroline came awake slowly. Her head felt foggy. There was a strange sensation around her neck, and she tried to move... but found that she couldn't sit up. Tried to move her hands, and found them firmly secured behind her back.

Panic drove the last of the drugs out of her system, and she snapped her eyes open, struggling desperately for a moment as she realised she had no idea where she was.

"You're on a plane bound for Italy," a female voice said, and Caroline peered up at a tall woman who stepped into her line of sight. The woman held up her left hand, and Caroline's heart sank as she recognised the Council brand on the woman's palm. An assassin. Fuck.

"I'm Adriana," the woman said. "I am returning you to the Council for trial."

It wasn't just her hands that were bound, Caroline realised. Her feet were also tied, and a collar around her neck was chained to the wall, preventing her from moving more than a few feet. She was helpless, laid out like a hunting trophy, and the situation was as insulting as it was terrifying.

"Why didn't you just shoot me?" Caroline asked, feigning bravery. Given the potential punishments waiting for her in Italy, it was entirely possible that death was a better option than capture.

"It's your lucky day," Adriana said, complete disinterest in her tone. "It seems the Council may have a use for you yet."

# CHAPTER FIFTEEN

Caroline followed Adriana up the steps into the Italian villa, her heart pounding in her chest. It was just over three hours since she'd woken up, an hour more of the flight, and then a slow journey north from Venice, and she'd spent the time imagining all manner of horrors that could occur once they arrived. She'd heard plenty about the Council in the past two years, everyone in the Den regarding them with a strange mix of respect and annoyance, and in her experience, that meant that they were hard task masters, setting arbitrary rules for the sheer pleasure of it, but more than willing to kick anyone's arse if they broke them.

The foyer was beautiful, white marble and ornate light fittings, and in her long grey robe, smeared with dirt and grass stains, Caroline felt completely out of place. They were going to take one look at her and kick her out. Or tell her to go and have a bath.

Footsteps, and Caroline held her breath. If not for the leash around her neck, she might have been tempted to run away…

An elegant looking lady stepped into the foyer from behind a carved wooden door, and Caroline tried not to cringe. This woman was aristocracy, there was no doubt about it. Tall, dressed in a flowing blue dress, a light application of make up giving her a sophisticated look that made Caroline feel like pond scum. She wore no make up herself, and her hair looked like she'd been dragged through a hedge backwards, as the Grey Watch had placed very little importance on physical appearance, far more interested in one's capabilities at hunting and tracking.

"Eleanor," Adriana said from beside her, offering the woman a respectful bow. "This is Caroline."

Eleanor took one look at the collar around her neck and let out a heartfelt sigh. "Is that really necessary?" she asked of Adriana, without even saying hello, and Adriana held her gaze unapologetically.

"Yes, it is."

Eleanor's mouth tightened in an expression of displeasure. "Well you can take it off her now." Adriana didn't look convinced. "There are guards at the door," Eleanor said patiently. "And Caroline... no doubt you understand by now that there are some very serious charges against you. This is not intended to be a prison, but if you attempt to leave-"

"I know, I know," Caroline said, unable to overcome her own impertinence, nervousness showing itself as irritation. "The next assassin you send will just shoot me." Adriana had informed her of that possibility on the way here, along with a long lecture on how lucky she was to still be alive, and for all her earlier bravado and her resentment of her capture, the idea of dying, now that she'd had the chance to think about it, was rather more frightening than it had been a few hours ago.

Eleanor looked faintly amused. "Good to see you have a grasp of the situation. Please, Adriana, release her." Adriana did so without a word, unlocking the padlock and sliding the collar off from around her neck. "Now, if you'd like to come upstairs, I'll show you to your room, and I'm sure you'd like a shower, after your trip."

Well, she'd been right on the bath side of things, at least, Caroline thought, not quite able to understand the woman's congenial attitude. She'd rather expected to be locked up straight away, and if anything, the luxurious room she was shown to only made her feel more out of place. Her heavy boots were still caked with mud from the forest, and she paused at the bedroom door to take them off, not wanting to track dirt across the thick carpet.

"There's a spare change of clothes in the wardrobe," Eleanor told her, her expression never changing from the look of calm politeness she wore. "Once you're ready, come downstairs. The rest of the Council is eager to meet you."

Yeah, right, Caroline thought, as Eleanor left her alone. More like eager to punish her. But there was nothing to be gained from waiting. She headed for the bathroom, scowling at the thick, fluffy towels hanging on the rail, and stripped off her clothes. Time to make herself presentable, before she faced her doom.


Half an hour later, Caroline sat at a long table in a room that looked a lot like the Den's library, only larger, its high shelves containing thick volumes that seemed ancient. The titles on the spines were in many different languages, Caroline recognising some of them as Spanish, Italian and French, and then there were others, in a script and language she had never seen before.

The room was bright and airy, wide windows giving a view of a sundrenched garden outside, a perfectly blue swimming pool set amongst colourful potted flowers, stone statues and creeping vines. Exactly the sort of setting she'd imagined for a bunch of hoity-toity aristocrats.

But then there were the Council themselves, twelve men and women of various ages, and Caroline was a little startled to see that not all of them were dressed like Eleanor. One of the men wore simple jeans and a t-shirt. One of the women looked like she'd come in straight from the gym. And there were several who seemed to be dressed for combat, encased in black leather, weapons secured about their bodies. Huh. Not quite the rich, poncy line up she'd been anticipating, and the realisation left her feeling a little off balance. She found herself feeling a grudging respect for some of them, the warrior types in particular, and her initial resentment slipped a little. There was no sign of Adriana or any other guards, and Caroline wasn't sure whether it was because they were confident she wouldn't try to run away, or because the Council was more than capable of stopping her themselves, if she tried anything.

The hearing was brief. Kendrick had already filled the Council in on Caroline's actions, and she was given the chance to either confirm or deny the story – she didn't see any point in denying it, so she simply admitted to everything he had told them – and then she was asked to explain her actions.

The explanation was simple, as far as Caroline was concerned. Her father had killed her mother, possibly with Greg's involvement, and since the police investigation was not achieving anything useful, she had taken it upon herself to deliver justice. Her anger was understandable, the Council conceded, but in the end, it still broke Il Trosa law, and so they delivered their decision. She was to be 'retrained', and Caroline shuddered as she tried to imagine what that could mean.

What were they going to do to her? Would they cage her, as the Den did with new recruits who struggled to merge with their wolves? Beat her? Fuck, she'd put up with enough of that to last a lifetime. Torture her? Starve her? Each new idea conjured up an onslaught of even more terrifying options, Caroline's imagination running wild as she tried to envisage what her life was going to look like in the near future.

"Excuse me a moment," Eleanor said, rising gracefully from the table, and she let herself out of the room. Moments later she was back, a young man in tow, and Caroline braced herself for the first wave of this unknown new horror.

"This is Andre," Eleanor told her. "He'll be overseeing your training."

Caroline stared at the man in front of her. He was tall, slightly older than herself, but not by much. He had a warrior's body, toned muscles, shoulder length hair and two days worth of stubble on his chin. But at the same time, he had a gentleman's air about him, a look of refined intelligence that made

Caroline feel common and stupid.

"Ma'am," he greeted her respectfully. "It's a pleasure to meet you."

Caroline said nothing, confused by such a congenial greeting from the man who had just been assigned to making her life hell for the foreseeable future.

But it was the man's quiet peacefulness that held her attention. Odd, for someone no doubt trained in violence and prepared to enforce strict rules. There was something unnervingly calm about him, and though Caroline was reluctant to admit it, something inherently trustworthy as well.

"What are you going to do to me?" she asked, her anxiety finally getting the better of her, and the man smiled in a way that was supposed to be reassuring.

"Don't be concerned," he said calmly. "We have only your best interests at heart. If you'll come this way, we'll get started."


Andre led Caroline out of the villa and into the wide gardens. Though he was making an effort to appear calm and in control, he was actually nervous as hell. When the Council had been informed that Adriana was bringing Caroline in, they'd called him in for a meeting and told him he was being assigned to retraining duty for the young woman. After Kendrick's appeal, they'd decided that option was worth a try, rather than putting the young wolf down, and their decision would only change if Caroline herself proved to be unreasonably uncooperative during the meeting.

While he'd been expecting such an assignment sooner or later – studies into psychology were a mandatory part of an assassin's training, after all – he had become concerned when he'd read the woman's profile.

"I was wondering if you would consider reassigning Caroline to another trainer," he'd said to Eleanor, after grabbing a moment to speak to her in private.

"Oh?"

"She's had a highly traumatic past and is in a very fragile mental state. Her recent actions have been fuelled by a great deal of anger and fear. Perhaps she would be more suited to someone who could better empathise with her situation."

"On the contrary," Eleanor replied enigmatically. "I believe you are far better suited to this job than you realise."

Andre shook his head. "I was raised in a stable, loving home, with a supportive community and a clear purpose for my life. She was raised in a nest of violence and turmoil and has had to fend for herself since she was a young girl. I loved both my parents from the bottom of my heart. She wants to kill one of hers. With all due respect, I'm failing to see any common ground here."

Eleanor eyed him with an air of indulgence. "Let me first say that I admire your concern for her wellbeing. Even if that concern is a little misplaced. You are more talented than you realise, and I wouldn't be assigning her to you if I didn't think you were capable of fulfilling your duties. But aside from that, keep in mind that this is as much about your training as it is hers. Find your common ground. And then everything else will fall into place."

Eleanor's confidence in him had done little to reassure him – despite the fact that he was to be overseen by a more experienced staff member. So as he led Caroline outside, his mind was working overtime, reviewing the information he'd been given about her, and trying to come up with a plan of action that had at least a moderate chance of success. Digging up her past was going to be unpleasant for her, and the last thing he wanted to do was make things worse.

They came to a pergola where there were cushioned seats and a view of the forest stretching out below them. "I realise this must all be quite unsettling for you," he began, seeing the scowl on Caroline's face, which, if he was right, was a cover for her fear as much as it was an expression of her dissatisfaction with her current situation. "So I thought we would begin with teaching you some meditation techniques."

Caroline snorted. "Meditation? You want me to sit in the lotus position and say 'om' for hours?"

Andre allowed himself a small smile. "There's far more to meditation than that. It's a process that quiets the mind, turns it inwards and allows you to discover your own motivations and re-evaluate your beliefs. It allows you to travel to the source of your own thoughts and feelings, and to view them with a level of objectivity."

Caroline raised a sardonic eyebrow at him. "Believe me, the last place I want to be spending time is inside my own head."

And that, right there, was one of their first problems. Caroline's impulsiveness and rebellious attitude were likely due in part to her own reluctance for introspection.

"We'll be taking small steps. And you're free to discuss any concerns with me as we go along. So please, take a seat. Make yourself comfortable. We can start with some simple breathing exercises."

"Look… what's the deal here?" Caroline interrupted, completely ignoring his instructions. "I thought I was brought here for 'retraining'. Aren't you supposed to lecture me on loyalty and how breaking the rules is a betrayal of your values and a risk to security, and then assign me to toilet-cleaning duty if I don't agree with you?"

Andre shook his head, grateful that he had a naturally patient disposition. Because he was beginning to get the impression that Caroline was going to be pushing his patience to the very limit. And they hadn't even begun yet. He'd never met anyone quite so defensive about the simplest things.

"Coercion and force have never made anyone change their mindset in the slightest," he explained, "unless it was to make them even more stubborn and rebellious. My job here is to help you see new perspectives on life, to consider points of view that you haven't considered before. The idea is to let you reach your own conclusions about all this, not force my views upon you."

Caroline looked utterly confused, and if it was possible, even more defensive.

"Please, sit down," Andre said again, taking a seat himself. "There's nothing to be worried about. Let's just take this one day at a time."

# CHAPTER SIXTEEN

**Present Day**

Driving slowly along a winding road, Miller glanced at the map on the passenger seat of his SUV, a frown appearing on his face as he considered his progress. The turncoat shape shifter had said there was a second pack of wolves living in England, somewhere in the Lakes District.

On the surface, that had seemed like a fairly large area to search. But Miller had an excellent team of men working with him. After the explosion at the lab, they'd lost a lot of good men, men Miller had known personally, some of them with families, and he still found himself jerking awake at night, sweat covering him as he remembered the way the shifters had shot Phil in the head, the cold, ruthless way they had attacked the base, nightmares of his colleagues' bodies lying in pools of their own blood disturbing his sleep again and again.

So it had been gratifying when, in the aftermath of the disaster, Jacob had given him the freedom to assemble his own team, hand picked from the surviving security personnel, or from those who had been working in the Noturatii's other English bases at the time of the explosion. He'd chosen the very best – not necessarily the most seasoned soldiers, but those with a clear head and a keen sense of strategy. After a few days of floundering about at the sheer size of the region, they'd put their heads together and managed to wipe out at least half the area in quick strokes of the brush. A pack of wolves wouldn't live in close proximity to humans, so they could cross out every town, every tourist centre or manor open to the public, every public walking track and any properties clearly visible from a major road.

After that it had got harder, but nothing they couldn't tackle with a little refined intelligence. No one knew how big the pack was, so they'd taken an extremely conservative estimate of ten wolves, and assumed that they all lived together in more or less the same place. That ruled out more locations, where the property sizes wouldn't support that kind of population all in one spot, or where there was too much open countryside. Wolves would want trees, Miller reasoned. Forest where they could run without being spotted.

They had to be careful, though. At one point, it had seemed like they could discount every single property on the map the shifter had given them. Each one had a legitimate purpose, a productive farm, a tourist centre, cabins for hire, a wildlife sanctuary. They'd had to loosen their criteria, realising that given the technological skills of the pack, they'd have set up the property to look legitimate. They couldn't just set up a huge barbed wire fence around a slab of forest and hope no one would notice, after all.

At first, his men had come out in force, teams of four or five, weapons, surveillance equipment, until they'd realised that the sheer number of properties to cover meant that they'd be spending years on the project if they didn't find a way to cover more ground.

So today, Miller had come out alone, half a dozen other operatives out and about in their cars, each doing some preliminary reconnaissance work to target the most likely properties. But after days of this, Miller was starting to lose enthusiasm for the task. Hours of endless driving, checking properties, talking to locals who started out curious, and then became suspicious, knocking on doors to meet dozens of blank stares as he made up cover story after cover story. A complaint about excessive barking. Had they heard anything? Reports of suspicious activities. Had they seen anything? Foreigners? Well, this was a tourist area, after all. There were foreigners everywhere. And for his trouble, Miller had got a flood of useless information, the locals wanting to discuss everything from teenagers painting graffiti on things to wheat fields overrun with deer.

He came to his next stop, a conference centre owned by a company based in Italy. He'd checked the business records, and it all came back legit – the company had bought the estate about thirty years ago after the previous owners had decided to sell. Before that, it had been owned by the same family for generations, passed down from father to son, but the last owner had been getting old and had had no children of his own, so he'd decided to sell. A check with the locals had confirmed the story – they saw regular visitors in town from overseas, attending the estate for some conference or other, along with the estate's permanent staff, all very friendly people, and if Miller was honest, the whole arrangement sounded perfectly mundane, so he wasn't expecting anything much here. But for the sake of completeness, he should at least check it out. He pulled up at the heavy iron gates and wearily got out of the car. A sign on the gate read 'Misty Hills' in beautiful iron letters, and he peered through the gaps, trying to get a look at the estate.

He could barely see the manor from here, just a few windows on one corner of the house, but an aerial shot had shown a large building with a wide lawn, surrounded by acres of forest – a pretty standard set up for a lot of the old estates, so that didn't mean anything in particular. The drive was only visible for a short distance before it disappeared into thick rows of hedges, but the place seemed deserted.

The gates were locked, so Miller pressed the call button beside the gate, not really expecting anyone to answer.

But only a moment later, a tinny voice came through the line. "Good morning, can I help you?"

"My name is James Gardner," Miller said. "I understand this estate is a conference centre? I was hoping to speak to someone about renting it."

There was a muffled rustling sound, and then the voice came back. "One moment, sir. I'll come down and see you at the gate."

The intercom shut off, and Miller waited patiently. After a few minutes, an ageing man came down the drive, grey haired but still spritely enough, with a quick stride and a cheerful look on his face.

"Sorry to keep you waiting. You're looking for a conference centre, you say?"

"That's right. Do you have a brochure of your facilities? Or a website I could look at?"

The man immediately took out a notebook. "Which company do you represent?" he asked, leaving Miller momentarily floundering for a reply. "Pacific Software Solutions," he said, blurting out the first name that came to mind. "They're based in America, but we've been looking at expanding into England."

"And how many people were you thinking of catering for?"

Another painful pause as Miller's mind raced. All he'd really been looking for was a brochure, something to legitimise this estate as a real business. He hadn't even been able to see the manor so far, so any figure he put on the size of things would be a stab in the dark. The guy was just as likely to tell him they couldn't cater for his needs, when what he really wanted was a guided tour of the place. "Thirty," he guessed, waiting as the man jotted down more notes.

"We're generally fairly fully booked," he said congenially, "but I can pass your details on to the manager and have someone call you. Do you know how long your booking would be?"

"Something small," Miller said, not wanting to get himself in too deep. "A weekend, maybe. Three days tops. Is there any chance I could talk to the manager now?" This man was clearly not the one in charge, and if he was connected to the shifters, he hadn't shown up on any of their intel reports. His face was totally unfamiliar.

"I'm sorry sir," the man said, "but the conference centre is closed for the summer-"

"Or do you have a website I could look at?"

The man shook his head. "Most of our bookings are done through an agency, so we don't tend to advertise directly. But if you'd like to leave a card, I can get the manager to call you when she returns."

"Any chance I could have a look around while I'm here? I won't take long, I just want to check the meeting rooms are big enough, maybe look at one or two bedrooms?"

"I'm sorry sir, but I'm just the caretaker for the summer," the man said, sounding genuinely apologetic. "I'm not authorised to take visitors through. But if you leave your details, I'll be sure to pass them along."

"James Gardner," Miller repeated, then rattled off a random phone number, not really caring if anyone called back or not. The place was deserted, and this guy seemed more than willing to actually try and make a booking for him. That crossed it off his list on two counts – firstly, a shifter den wouldn't be open to the public on any terms, regardless of the season, and secondly, he didn't think the entire pack was likely to just up and leave for extended periods of time. Where the hell would they go? The emptiness of the place confirmed his suspicions that he was once again wasting his time here.

"Thank you for your help," he said to the caretaker, then climbed back into his car, crossing yet another name off his seemingly endless list. Next stop, a farming property down the road.


Sean Dalton watched the Noturatii agent drive away and glanced down at the description of the man he'd written on his notepad, along with the man's ramblings about a supposed 'booking' for the estate. A retired cop, Sean was one of less than a dozen humans in the world who knew the truth about the shifters. The dozen who weren't members of the Noturatii, that was. He'd done the shifters a few favours, back before he'd retired, helping them out before he'd known what they really were, and then he'd stumbled across the truth in a set of bizarre circumstances several years ago, just before he'd retired, shocked as he'd attended a reported shooting, only to find himself in the middle of a firefight, scrambling for his radio to call for back up, before he'd dropped the thing as one of the men had turned into the largest wolf he'd ever seen right in front of his eyes. Minutes later, with dead bodies all around him, he'd got on his knees and begged for his life as Baron, that huge brute of a man, had pointed a gun at his head and apologised for having to shoot him.

Somehow they'd found an amicable solution, though in truth, Sean didn't remember much of the conversation, too busy trying to wrap his head around the impossible things he'd seen, half convinced he was dreaming, while his mind raced to find a reason for them to let him live. His first grandchild had just been born, he'd rambled, he was due for retirement in a few months, he'd steadfastly supported the shifters in their various questionable activities throughout his career. He'd unknowingly met several of them throughout the years and, considering himself to be an excellent judge of character, had decided along the way that they were fighting on the side of good. They'd been operating outside the law, certainly, but Sean was experienced enough to know that not everything outside the law was outside the limits of morality. Perhaps they were fighting international sex slavery, he'd reasoned to himself, a worthy cause that would draw the attention of some violent opposition. Or perhaps they were helping illegal immigrants. Sean had been to Sudan in his younger days, had seen the horrors the people there had experienced first hand, and as a result, he had a soft spot for those seeking out a better life away from the threat of death or imprisonment. So he'd looked the other way, made a few unusual investigations disappear, and received heartfelt thanks in return.

That pledge of loyalty had, in the end, earned him the right to continue breathing, and he'd stumbled away, resolved to keep his mouth shut and his eyes open. Months later, he'd received a most unusual phone call, offering him a short summer job, caretaker for the estate while the shifters temporarily went... somewhere else. He'd asked no questions, filed no reports, told his wife he was going 'fishing', and hightailed it up here for a couple of weeks, eager to continue helping those who had spared his life, and brimming with curiosity to know more about this bizarre quirk of nature.

It was now his fifth year looking after the estate for the group, but never before had he met one of their enemies quite so up close and personal.

For a moment there, he'd considered simply shooting the Noturatii man, Baron having explained the bare bones of their conflict in a way that made Sean want to hunt down every single Noturatii operative and shoot them himself. Damned blind, bigoted fools. In this case, there had been just the one man. There was no one else he could see in the car, and shooting him was a quick, simple solution to the problem literally knocking at the shifters' door.

But then he'd rethought the impulsive plan. Perhaps this agent had brought backup that was waiting further down the road. Perhaps his car was fitted with a GPS tracker that would lead the Noturatii right to their doorstep. Tempting as it was to simply kill him, there were a dozen things that could go wrong that would make this situation even worse for the shifters. So Sean had played the part, taken notes, and let him walk away.

For now.

He pulled out his phone as he reached the manor. First things first. He ducked into the sitting room where a temporary security office was set up, and checked that the perimeter electric fence was live. Hidden just inside the stone wall, it would provide a nasty surprise for any overzealous operatives who tried to do a little snooping. That, combined with the motion sensors, set to sound the alarm if anything bigger than a squirrel moved out there, was the first line of defence while the shifters were off the premises.

That task seen to, he dialled Baron's number, waiting impatiently for the man to pick up the phone. When he did, he sounded out of breath, like he'd been running. "What?"

Sean didn't bother introducing himself. Baron would know who was calling from the number alone. He glanced out the window again, checking no one was trying to sneak up the drive. "Bad news, sir. We've just had a visit from the Noturatii."

Baron hung up from his call with Sean, turning to the anxious faces all around him. The topic of the conversation had been easy to pick up from his startled questions and alarmed tone, and Caroline, Tank and Andre had quickly taken note, leaving their preparations in the foyer of the manor to gather around, waiting eagerly for an explanation for the tense call.

But rather than explaining the situation, Baron instead thrust a small piece of paper at Caroline, a phone number written on it. "Call this number," he told her, knowing that Sean had told the man at the gate that the manager of the estate was a woman. "Ask for James Gardner. Apparently he wants to book Misty Hills for a conference, so find out what he wants, then tell him we're booked out."

"Noturatii?" Caroline asked, tapping the number into her phone, and Baron nodded.

"Most likely. I just want to know if this number's legit or not."

Less than a minute later, they had their answer. The woman who had answered the phone had never heard of James Gardner, and Caroline apologised and hung up.

"Wrong number," she said with a frown. "What the hell is going on?"

Baron explained it briefly, grateful that the estate was being watched by an ex-cop. Sean had an eye for detail and knew how to deal with unexpected situations. "From Sean's description, it sounds like our visitor was the guy we met in the lab. The black one, who was with Melissa." Most of the people they'd met before they'd blown up the lab were now dead, but those two in particular they knew were probably still alive. Tank let out a growl, holding a very personal grudge against the man, and then Silas arrived at his side, having overheard the last part of the conversation. He took a seat without a word, expression grim, ready to lend whatever help was needed.

"Sean's fairly sure the guy just went away," Baron went on, "but he's going to keep an eye out, just to be sure. If this was just a scouting mission, we might be in the clear, but if we start getting repeat visits, we could be in deep shit."

"What I want to know," Tank said, "is why the hell are they sniffing around our neck of the woods anyway? We've always done our business in the east, in Grey Watch territory. How did they find out we're in the Lakes District?"

"Could be a number of things," Silas pointed out. "They have some of us on file. Dee. Tank. Caroline. Could be facial recognition software. Could be someone canvassing the neighbourhood with photos to see if any of the locals recognise us. Could be that the Noturatii have just finally got their act together and started doing their jobs." The news was unwelcome, but hiding from it wouldn't do them any good.

"Can Skip still get into their system?" Caroline asked. Skip had successfully hacked the Noturatii's database earlier in the year, but there was no guarantee they hadn't upgraded their systems since then.

"She can still get in," Baron said, "but I don't like to ask her to do it unless it's an emergency. Every time we mess with their system, there's a good chance we'll get caught."

"I think this qualifies as an emergency," Andre said, and Baron nodded reluctantly.

"Yeah. I'll ask her to take a look around, see what she can find."

Silas let out a snort. "So Skip's going to hack their system to see if they're hacking ours? God, I just love technology."

Baron turned to Andre. "Can you call the Council? Tell them Misty Hills may have been compromised? If things go south, we're going to need help , and we're going to need it fast."

"On it," Andre replied quickly. "And here's an idea. Since we're more or less stuck here for the time being, I could ask for a couple of assassins to head over to the estate. Take a look around. See if anything's going on that shouldn't be."

Baron nodded, grateful for Andre's insight. He should have thought of that himself. "I'll call Sean and tell him he's going to be having a few visitors. I don't like the idea of him being left there on his own anyway, not with the Noturatii hanging around. But make sure the assassins know he's there. I don't want anyone getting shot by mistake."

"He knows what a Council brand looks like?" Andre asked.

"He will in a few minutes. And tell Simon I'm going to want a review of our security cameras the instant we get home," Baron told Silas. "No one threatens my home and gets away with it."

# CHAPTER SEVENTEEN

Andre sat in the main meeting hall, listening to Caroline address the gathered shifters, completing the formal welcome to the visitors for this year.

There had been a few arguments in the corridors as all the shifters settled in, disagreements over status or who was entitled to which rooms, but nothing serious had resulted aside from a few heated words, no one resorting to physical violence or challenges in wolf form. He'd also heard of Skip's encounter with the Russian recruits, Tank having exchanged a few strong words with the more senior Russians about acceptable behaviour, and the ranking wolf from one of their Dens had pulled the pair aside, firstly scolding them for their behaviour, and then assigning them to cleaning duties for the duration of the Densmeet, the pair now expected to wash the kitchen floor and clean the toilets daily. All things considered, it was a relatively peaceful beginning to the summer season.

"I'd like to commence the formal discussions," Caroline was saying, "by asking each Den to report on their experiences with the Noturatii this year. We have lost a number of good wolves, but also landed some solid victories against our enemies." She waited while those fluent in English translated the words for their Den mates, then turned towards the group of French shifters. "Henri? Would you like to begin?"

"Before we get started on the reports," a voice interrupted her, and everyone looked around to see Marianne, the female alpha from the Norwegian Den, on her feet, "I would like to raise an issue that is of concern to many of us here today. Rumours have reached us of a new addition to your Den this year. Dee Carman. Also known as Fenrae-Ul, the Destroyer."

A wave of muttering filled the room, a predictable response to what many shifters considered to be a serious threat, and Andre waited with interest to see how Caroline would react.

"What exactly is it that you wish to know?" Caroline asked, with absolute calm.

"Is it true?" Marianne asked, glancing around the room for the mysterious Dee. "Is she able to separate us from our wolf side?"

Caroline looked over to Dee, seated beside Mark, and Dee gave her a tiny nod. She got up and came forward, standing nervously in front of the group.

"Good morning, everyone. I'm Dee Carman. I joined Il Trosa last year, after I was kidnapped by the Noturatii and converted in one of their labs. What you've heard is true – I was not able to merge with my wolf. She considers herself to be an independent being, quite separate from me, and over the winter, we discovered that we do indeed have the ability to separate human from wolf. I have done so twice – once to a member of the Grey Watch who was attempting to kill me…" That brought another round of muttering, and Dee waited patiently for it to subside. "…and once at the request of Andre, the Council's emissary. Another woman was converted in the Noturatii lab, against her will, and was at risk of turning rogue, so I was asked to remove the wolf side of her to prevent her from going mad. I have never attempted to use my abilities on any other shifter, and frankly, I have no desire to."

There was a burst of words in French, and then Annabelle spoke up. "Sabine has asked about your wolf," she said diffidently, translating the words though she seemed uncomfortable with the question itself. "If she is separate from you, what is to stop her lashing out and killing us all?"

To her credit, Dee took the question with respectful calm. "Faeydir thinks that-"

"Faeydir?" someone interrupted.

"The name my wolf is known by," Dee said, which caused an eruption of protests.

"Faeydir was our creator, our origin," people shouted angrily. "You dishonour her name by using it for this creature of destruction!"

Caroline shouted for silence, waiting until the room was in order before speaking. "Faeydir's name was chosen for her when we first discovered that Dee and her wolf were two separate beings. That was long before we learned the truth of her abilities. It is a name. Nothing more."

"Faeydir sees Il Trosa as her home and her family," Dee went on, when the room was quiet. "She understands that there is sometimes the need for violence in our lives, but she has never had any quarrel with Il Trosa or the Council, and she has no intention of harming you in any way."

"So you say," one of the Russians said angrily. "But we have only your word that that is the case."

"The Council has assessed Dee, and does not regard her to be a serious threat." Caroline snapped. "Andre has their report available if you'd like to read it for yourselves. They have invited Dee to Italy to conduct a more thorough assessment, but they have expressed no serious concerns about either her behaviour or her abilities for the time being. For my own part, I have spent half a year with her, and know her to be one of the most gentle, kind and compassionate shifters I have ever met. Her wolf is unusual, to be sure, but she has made no sign of aggression towards either our Den or other shifters. She has followed our rules, respected our laws and gone out of her way to assist us when and where it was required. And as far as I'm concerned, that says far more about her intentions towards us than any prophecy written thousands of years ago in what is now a dead language."

"I think it would be wise," Nikolai spoke up from the back of the room, his English stilted in his heavy accent, "to take some time to get to know Dee. This is not the sort of thing we are going to solve overnight. Take a few days. Speak with Dee yourselves. Then we can talk about this more."

Reluctant agreement rumbled across the room, and Caroline nodded to Dee, who returned to her seat so that the rest of the meeting could continue.

Andre sat back, pleased, though not entirely surprised by Caroline's handling of the issue. It would have been easy to duck responsibility, simply announcing that the Council had assessed Dee and accepted her into Il Trosa, and left it at that. It was a valid argument, and one that the other shifters would have had to accept, but it also sidestepped the larger issue, and would have made life more difficult for Dee. At least this way, while the other shifters weren't exactly welcoming her, they had been challenged to investigate the issue more thoroughly before jumping to conclusions. Which gave Dee the firm chance to win some of them over.

And more than that, he was impressed with Caroline's willingness to stand by a member of her Den. It put Caroline's reputation on the line, as well as that of her entire Den, but then again, Caroline had never been one to shy away from a challenge, or back down from her beliefs. Andre discreetly took out a notebook and made a few pertinent notes. He was beginning to think he'd have a most interesting report to send to the Council, once his assessment of Caroline was complete.

Dinnertime at the Densmeet was both a warm social celebration, and a period of tension and spontaneous quarrels, and everyone was at pains to be both patient and forgiving when tempers flared.

The problem was that, far from being a human mind with access to a wolf's body, a properly merged shifter was equally influenced by both sides of their personality – the human one, and the wolf one. And wolves were very particular about meal times, the dominant members of the pack privileged with first go at the food, down through the ranks until the omega wolf was left to clean up whatever scraps might remain.

Within any given Den, the problem was dealt with through routine and ritual. The shifters sat at a long table, the alpha at one end, the omega at the other, and everyone knew their own rank, who they must wait for, and who must wait for them.

But at the Densmeet, there was the sudden problem of having to deal with fifty shifters crammed into a small space, with no clear lines as to who was the ranking wolf in any given situation.

For convenience, dinner was served as a buffet, with each person left to help themselves, but who got to stand where in the line was a matter of some heated discussions. Some of the ranks were obvious – the alphas went first, with Baron and Caroline given priority as a mark of respect for their efforts in hosting the Densmeet. Other people, knowing they were of low rank, gathered beside the wall and waited anxiously for their turn, letting the bulk of the group go first. But in between, there were twenty or thirty wolves who weren't quite so clear on their order, and while there was a certain amount of human politeness at play, awkward offers to let a visitor or a host go first, there were a number of inevitable squabbles as well. The Russians, in particular, seemed very focused on rank, making an effort to use physical size and prolonged eye contact to intimidate others into giving way.

But the problem was that a person's size or stature in human form wasn't always indicative of their rank as a wolf. Some large men, being of a rather more placid nature, were lower ranking than expected, while some rather small people – John being one of them – were actually ferocious fighters, skilled at both hand to hand combat and fighting in canine form. So Baron wasn't entirely surprised when he sat down at his table, plate of food in hand, only to hear his boyfriend engaging in a loud and prolonged argument with one of the Russian shifters. But John spoke no Russian, and the woman who'd picked a fight with him seemed to speak little to no English, so all that resulted was a lot of shouting, which came ever closer to the moment when one of them would attempt to shove the other out of the way and risk a sizable brawl right there in the dining room.

Baron glanced around, seeing Nikolai joining him at his table. Despite being an alpha, and without a doubt one of the toughest warriors Baron had ever met, the man seemed to be remarkably level headed.

"You speak Russian?" he asked quickly, knowing that many Ukrainians were fluent in the language.

"I do," Nikolai replied, already standing up, seeing where the problem was. While he could have asked one of the Russian translators to assist, given their apparent tendency for conflict, he was far more inclined to enlist the aid of someone who would help solve the problem, rather than just pour more fuel on the fire.

The two of them arrived beside the arguing pair, and John immediately shut up, folding his arms and waiting for Baron to do something useful. The woman, on the other hand, let rip with an onslaught of accusations in Russian. Nikolai listened patiently, then turned to Baron with an air of boredom.

"She feels that the English shifters are taking advantage of their superior numbers to secure higher positions," he translated drily, "and she would like to see some evidence of the young man's rank."

John raised an eyebrow at that. "Permission to shift?" he asked, turning to Baron with a scowl. "With no challenge intended."

Baron nodded, and John waited while Nikolai translated the information, then shifted into his wolf form.

As the members of the English Den already knew, his wolf was fearsome to look at. Battered and scarred, with cold, grey eyes that could look straight through your soul, he turned his gaze on the Russian woman. Who took one look at him and turned pale. She said something in Russian, and Nikolai laughed.

"John may go first," he said with a chuckle, then, without waiting for any more discussion, returned to his seat where his meal was getting cold.

John returned to human form, and sent a sardonic smile the woman's way. She backed up a step, and gave him a tight nod. Baron waited just long enough to send a warning glare John's way, a silent instruction not to cause any more trouble than was absolutely necessary, and then he returned to his seat.


At the far end of the line, Mark was faring rather worse in his efforts to secure his own dinner. His day had gone badly right from the start, with Caroline pulling him aside early this morning to explain that he had been forbidden from participating in the Nochtan-Eil, the official summer recognition of those who had fallen during the year. The news had been heartbreaking, a sharp reminder of all he had lost when Luke had been killed, and a blow that completely disregarded any friendship the pair had shared. He'd vented his anger at Caroline – apparently the order came from the Council itself, rather than from her or Baron – and he'd been surprised when she'd refrained from retaliating. Usually she was quick to tell people off when they stepped out of line, but she'd simply listened to his rant with calm patience, apologised for the situation and told him that Luke had been an honourable wolf and he would be sorely missed. Mark had spent the rest of the day brooding, even Dee unable to pull him out of his dark mood.

There had also been the reaction of the other shifters to the obvious traitor's brand on his left cheek. The hostile reception had been predictable, the shifters generally embracing strict standards of loyalty and solidarity, and his betrayal would be felt keenly, but it had been disheartening, nonetheless. And now that it was dinnertime, that hostility was coming out in new ways.

Branded as a traitor, he was automatically the lowest ranking wolf in the room, the omega of his own Den, and easily pushed aside even by the low ranking wolves from overseas. At first, he'd accepted the position with resigned dignity, joining the very end of the queue, waiting patiently while everyone else served themselves.

But when it came time to get his own food, he found out rather quickly that things were not going to be quite as simple as that.

"Second helpings," a large Polish man announced, pushing Mark out of the way as he reached for a plate, and he served himself a second portion of the roast meat and vegetables. The man took his time, and Mark waited for him to move out of the way... but he was just reaching for a plate again when another man stepped in front of him, a Russian of medium rank, who muttered a few words in his native language, and rudely pushed Mark aside.

Mark gritted his teeth, seeing several more shifters take notice of his predicament, and not liking the calculating gleam in their eyes. He was getting seriously hungry by now, but it looked like it was going to be a long night.

Seated at her own table, finishing her plate of food, Dee watched the ongoing argument at the buffet with growing distress. Though she would have loved to go over and get some food for Mark herself, or better yet, lay into the bullies and throw her rank around a little, she had been expressly forbidden from doing so when she'd been informed of Mark's demotion several months ago. It was part of his punishment for betraying his pack, she knew, and while they both understood that his low rank came with significant disadvantages, it was becoming more and more obvious that the other shifters were intent on stopping him from eating anything at all. And it wasn't just the foreigners. Even among their own Den, feelings still ran hot about his betrayal, and garnering any significant support for him was going to be difficult.

Faeydir was none too happy about it either, offering to bite the legs of those who were giving Mark a hard time, and Dee had to concentrate to rein her wolf in. Biting humans was forbidden, she reminded the wolf, who merely snarled at her, and then offered to pee on the shoes of the troublemakers instead.

Dee glanced at Mark, who gave her a helpless look, but she could only shrug, both of them knowing she wasn't allowed to interfere.

But there were others in their Den not subject to that particular restriction, Dee realised, and she immediately turned to Skip, sitting beside her, her teddy bear tucked safely in her lap. "Is there anything we can do about that?" she asked, nodding to where Mark was once again being shoved out of the way.

"Alistair would probably help," Skip suggested immediately, Alistair being one of Mark's closest friends, and Dee scanned the room to find him. Fluent in French, he was seated at a table with two of the French shifters, all of them laughing as one of them attempted to say a few words in English – clearly he hadn't learned any of the language before coming here – and Alistair had yet to notice the stand-off at the buffet table.

But just as she was about to get up and go ask him for help, another woman stepped up to the buffet, Annabelle, from the French Den.

"Excuse me, Mark," Dee heard her say, her table not too far from the buffet. "But can I just get a little more meat. Thank you so much." She stepped in ahead of Mark, and Dee was momentarily taken aback, having thought the woman to be more reasonable and compassionate than most of the crowd here. But Annabelle wasn't done yet. "I hear you are a carpenter," she said, starting up a conversation with Mark, who was looking like he was reaching the end of his patience. "You make tables, yes? And they are profitable? I would like to know more of how you do this."

Just then, another woman from the Norwegian Den approached the table and tried to step in between Annabelle and Mark.

But Annabelle was having none of it. "I am having a conversation!" she snapped loudly as the Norwegian woman rudely butted in, and the woman drew back in surprise. "Don't look at me like that," Annabelle went on, her accent thick in her anger. "I know you speak English. And you know that I outrank you. So remember your manners, and get back in line."

Too startled to respond, the woman did just that, and Dee watched, a grin on her face as Annabelle took her time selecting her meat, keeping up a running conversation all the while with Mark, who loaded up his plate as quickly as he could, knowing he wasn't likely to get another opportunity. Then Annabelle led him over to her own table, shooing Sabine out of the way so that Mark could sit beside her. Annabelle was a warrior and a physician, ranking fourth in her own Den and taking responsibility for the vast majority of their medical care – a high responsibility, when battles with the Noturatii were so common – and Dee could think of no reason why she would suddenly take an interest in carpentry. She was going to have to thank the woman later, she thought to herself, impressed at the way she played politics, and finally able to quiet Faeydir from her unhappy internal rant.

# CHAPTER EIGHTEEN

After dinner was over, Dee found herself alone. Skip had headed off to bed, exhausted from a long day of dealing with so many strangers. Heron was talking intently to Sabine from the French Den, Mark had headed out, sick of the constant harassment for his status, and Tank was caught up in politics, planning out some future event in the Densmeet that needed urgent attention.

Dee would have loved to take the opportunity to meet some new people – that was the point of this event, after all – but every time she caught someone's eye, hoping for the opportunity to start a friendly chat, they immediately turned away, pretending to be busy or already caught in conversation. But though she was feeling lonely and altogether rejected by the cold treatment, Dee couldn't really blame the shifters for their feelings towards her.

After she'd learned the truth about her wolf's unusual history, she'd finally managed to track down the much-debated prophecy in the Den's library. It had been hard work, sifting through a dozen thick volumes which talked about ancient shifters, their magic, their allies and enemies, myth mixed with factual history, until she'd finally found the record of Fenrae-Ul and the prophecy of destruction that haunted her. After reading it through a dozen or more times, captivated and horrified by the words recorded in beautiful, cursive handwriting, she'd easily memorised the verse.

'*Thus be the truth of the wolfe Fenrae-Ul,*' the words had read, no doubt translated into English a century or two ago. '*The daughter twice removed from Faeydir-Ul. The cause of the death of her mother's unhappy tale. By magicks deep and ancient, she shalle return henceforth to life anew. Ye shalle know her by the separation of wolfe from man. And under her reign, the shyfters shall be restor'd to the natural order. No more divided, but united as one being. And peace shalle reign as the old discord is laid to rest.*'

Dee sighed, feeling a heavy weight settle in her chest as she recalled the words. The message seemed clear enough. Fenrae-Ul had indeed returned, Dee's wolf able to separate the wolf half of a shifter from their human half. From the sounds of it, Fenrae had been the granddaughter of Faeydir, an ancient wolf indeed, and according to the prophecy, at some point during her life, she would restore the natural order to the shifters. No longer divided, they would become one being again; wolf, or human. And so she would become the 'death of her mother's unhappy tale', the end of the shifter curse that the original Faeydir had unleashed on the world.

No wonder no one wanted to talk to her.

Dee suddenly felt a cold pressure against her neck, and she jumped in surprise, spinning around to see that huge Ukrainian shifter standing behind her. He was grinning wryly, holding out a glass of liquid with ice in it, and she took it hesitantly.

"Go on, it won't bite you," the man said. "You looked like you were away in another world. I thought I should bring you back."

"Thank you," Dee said, but then she took a careful sniff before she drank. And lowered the glass again without tasting.

"You don't like vodka?" The man seemed taken aback, and Dee's heart sank. The one person who actually wanted to talk to her, and she'd inadvertently offended him.

"I like it," she assured him hastily. "But I'm not used to drinking it straight. Usually I have it with tonic."

To her great surprise, the man burst out laughing. "English wolves," he said, with equal parts disdain and amusement. "I've been told you're fierce warriors, killing *hundreds* of Noturatii this year, say the rumours. But you're frightened by a little vodka? Ha! Warriors, my great fat arse!" He took a sip of his own drink, then grinned at her. "I'm Nikolai," he introduced himself. "Alpha of the Ukrainian Den."

"Dee Carman," Dee replied. "But I'm sure you knew that already."

"Taste the vodka," Nikolai said, and then waited, the conversation apparently going no further until she did, so Dee lifted the glass and took a tiny sip. It was strong, but good – Nikolai wouldn't settle for second rate vodka – and he grinned with satisfaction as she coughed.

"Good, yes? You will learn to like it. Now, do you want to know a secret?" he asked, with a look that suggested that whatever he was about to say was a statement of the highest importance. Dee nodded, not knowing what else to do.

He bent down, putting his mouth right beside her ear, and then whispered, "I am not afraid of you."

He stepped back, looking smug, and downed the remainder of his drink.

This man was not like the others, Dee realised quickly. Strong, confident, but with an undefinable quality that was both peaceful and violent, a creature totally at ease with who and what he was. And as far as humans went, that was a rare quality indeed. So she asked, genuinely curious, "Why not?"

Nikolai looked pleased with the question. "We live in the Chernobyl Exclusion Zone," he said, enunciating the words carefully. "A dead world. The forest died with the explosion. The people fled. The insects and the birds suffered great losses. And the tourists come to see the gravestones, the remnants of lives ended by the folly of mankind. But the wolves?" He smiled again, a strangely peaceful expression. "The wolves and the deer grew in number. The trees slowly take back the towns. The roads give themselves up to weeds and grass. The humans left, and so the wild creatures roam free. That is where we live. So if the prophecy is not true, we will continue to live as we have, on the fringes of civilisation, wild and free. And if it is true?" He shrugged. "We will re-join our wolf brethren, and rule the land that humanity forgot." He levelled a serious, contemplative look at her. "What have I to fear, when the worst that will happen is that we will return to the wild where we belong?"

"That's an excellent philosophy," Dee said, relieved to have finally met someone who could see past the rumours and take the time to have a real conversation. "I admire your outlook on life." Faced with the prospect of her own death, by whatever means, Dee didn't think she could remain quite so composed.

"I have an idea," Nikolai said, lowering his voice to a conspiratorial whisper. "These wolves… half of them don't know what they are, jumping at shadows, blaming you for their fears. But the Ukrainians? We know where we stand. We face our enemies without fear." He eyed her glass, seeing that it remained largely untouched, and a scheming look appeared on his face. "I grow tired of this endless politics," he said, nodding at the shifters around the room, stiff faces and forced politeness at every turn. "Come over to our cottage," he invited her, and she recalled that the Ukrainians had been given exclusive use of one of the buildings set away from the main house. "You will help us practise our English," he said, more command than request, "and we will teach you to drink vodka like a Ukrainian."

As a general rule, Dee steered clear of hard spirits, preferring wine, or beer on the odd occasion. But she was short on options at the moment, the rest of the group continuing to snub her, and while a bunch of rowdy Ukrainians wouldn't have been her first choice for company, she wasn't yet tired enough to go to bed, and not inclined to spend the rest of the evening being the proverbial wall flower.

"That sounds like an excellent plan," she said, forcing herself to take another sip of the liquor in her hand, though she winced at the taste. Much to Nikolai's amusement.

"Let me find the others, then," he said with a wink, "and we'll go and start a party of our own."


Half an hour later, Dee sat in the lounge room of the Ukrainians' cottage, laughing as Nikolai finished a story about the shifters' escapades scaring poachers who wandered into the Exclusion Zone. Just last month, the pack had surrounded a pair of hunters, terrifying them to the point that one of them had wet his pants, and the other had run away screaming, coming very close to shooting himself in the foot with his own gun. The Ukrainian Den, she was quickly learning, had a twisted sense of humour, as well as a calmly philosophical view of life, accepting both hardship and good fortune with equal stoicism.

As a concession to her 'weak constitution', they had allowed her to drink her vodka with a good splash of lemonade in it. The others were drinking it straight, but Dee had been pleasantly surprised to discover that the four tough, no-nonsense men, though loud and boisterous, were also charming and friendly. There was Alexei, the newest member of the group, a twenty-five year old who had been converted only two years ago. Bohdan and Olek were both in their mid thirties, with Bohdan speaking a small amount of English, while Olek and Alexei both knew nothing of the language.

Dee had also learned that, due to Ukraine's conscription laws, it was standard procedure in the Ukrainian Den to fake their converts' deaths to avoid the chance of being called up for military service.

Taking a break to refill his glass, and then Dee's when he noticed it was empty, Alexei glanced sideways at Nikolai and said something hesitantly in Ukrainian.

Nikolai let out a laugh, while the others made various jeers and catcalls. "Alexei thinks you are very beautiful," he translated with a grin.

Dee laughed. Alexei was quite handsome himself, cheeky with an infectious grin, but she shook her head. "Tell him not to get any ideas," she said with a smile. "I have a boyfriend."

Nikolai translated, and Alexei sighed dramatically, then said something else.

"Then this man of yours is very lucky," Nikolai told her. "But if you ever change your mind, Alexei says he is available. What is your boyfriend's name?"

Dee hesitated. "It's Mark," she said warily, knowing that however open minded these men might be, this might be an issue for them. Silence fell over the group, everyone by now aware of the name of the traitor in their midst, and even Nikolai seemed to pause at that one.

"I have not heard the full story of this man," he said speculatively. "What is he accused of doing?"

Well, at least someone was bothering to stop and ask for the real story, Dee thought, trying to find a bright side to this mess. "He broke into a Noturatii lab and saved my life."

Nikolai's eyes opened wide, and he let out a hearty laugh. "Ah, I see. There is more to it than just that, I think, but sometimes we can focus on the wrong details, no? Well, you should keep him, then. Any man who will risk his life for yours is worth something."

Dee stared at him in surprise, then let out a laugh herself. "You are a most unusual man," she told Nikolai, who shrugged dismissively.

"If you could convince the Ukrainian women of this, I would be most grateful."

After that the discussion turned to the topic of her unusual wolf, Dee trying her best to explain her odd relationship with Faeydir – having another sapient being in her head was a huge advantage at times, a significant challenge at others, and she worried a little that her explanation would be lost in translation as Nikolai struggled to explain it to the other men.

But as a series of questions came back at her about her conversion and the exact nature of her wolf, Faeydir herself perked up. She'd been behaving well since the Densmeet had begun, being given plenty of exercise outside and treating the other wolves with polite caution, not inclined to get too close – apparently, meeting strangers from outside her pack was quite stressful for the wolf – so Dee was a little surprised when she made her next request known.

"Faeydir says she would like to meet you," she said awkwardly, knowing how strange it would sound to them to want to introduce her wolf separately from herself.

But Nikolai merely shrugged and explained the request to his comrades. Nods and words of agreement followed, so Dee gave the all clear to Faeydir. She shifted, then Faeydir stood in the middle of the room, slightly perplexed as she regarded the four large men in front of her.

Perhaps picking up on the reason for her confusion, Nikolai stood up, then shifted himself, his wolf large and grey, and the others followed suit.

Faeydir approached each of them cautiously, sniffing them thoroughly, and standing to be sniffed in return. Once she was satisfied, she sent a wave of wholehearted approval to Dee. Wild wolves, these were. They smelled of wilderness and snow. Strong, high ranking wolves. She laid her ears flat back and dipped her head, letting out a soft whine, and in his wolf form, Nikolai looked entirely pleased with the reaction. He took a step forward, head high, tail up, and Faeydir backed up a step, lowering her tail respectfully. Then Nikolai bounced towards her, a move that could have been part play, part threat, and Faeydir dropped to the ground, lying on her side, while her tail thumped on the floor.

A moment later, Nikolai was back in human form, a hearty chuckle filling the room. Dee shifted too, returning as a human sitting on the floor, peering up at the tall man, and he offered her his hand to help her up.

"Your wolf is very polite," he said with a grin. "She knows her place."

"She respects you," Dee told him sincerely. "And she's looking forward to seeing you at the deer hunt. She thinks you might have a few things to teach her."

Nikolai translated for his comrades, now back in human form, and they all laughed at the news. "That's a smart wolf you've got there. Now," he said suddenly, reaching for the bottle of vodka. "It's time we taught you how to drink like a Ukrainian."


It was nearing midnight when Mark knocked on the door of the cottage. After roaming the estate for a while, he'd returned to the dining room and shared a drink with Alistair, before searching for Dee. He'd finally learned from Heron that she'd been seen leaving with the Ukrainians several hours ago, and, not knowing what to think of that, Mark headed for the cottage where the four men were staying.

He was rather apprehensive about the reception he was going to get. The Russians had been none too pleasant to him so far, and while he hadn't had any particular run-ins with the Ukrainians, there was always the risk they would object to his presence. So he was a little surprised when the door opened and Nikolai cheerfully invited him inside.

He followed him into the living room, to be greeted by the sight of Dee sitting on the sofa, glass in hand, with three men lounging about the room around her.

"It is your noble boyfriend," Nikolai announced, taking his seat again. "I think he has come to rescue you again. Perhaps he feels you are in mortal danger, sitting here with us."

Mark didn't know how to react to the introduction. The traitor's brand was plain as day on his face, but then again, they knew he was Dee's boyfriend, and they seemed to have accepted her easily enough, so he wasn't sure whether Nikolai's comment was meant seriously, or sarcastically. But his confusion turned to consternation when Dee called hello and waved at him, slurring her words and looking more than a little unsteady.

"Are you drunk?"

"No!" Dee replied emphatically. Then she conceded, "Maybe just a little bit. I've been teaching them to speak English!" she said with glee.

"How much wood," one of the Ukrainians piped up helpfully, "would wood chuck-a-chuck if he could wood?"

That made Dee break into a fit of giggles.

Another man snorted in laughter, said something in Ukrainian, and then made his own attempt. "How much wood would chuck chuck if he was chucking wood?"

"We have been sharing some best Ukrainian vodka with Dee," Nikolai said, sounding more than a little inebriated himself. "You want to try?"

"No, thank you," Mark said, more interested in getting Dee safely to bed at the moment. "I think you've had enough," he told her seriously, and to his relief, Dee nodded.

"Tired now," she said, climbing unsteadily to her feet. "Goodnight everyone. Nadobranich."

A chorus of goodnights came back at her, and then one of the men stood up, approaching Mark. He held out his hand for him to shake, which Mark did, though he remained cautious as to the man's intentions.

"I am Bohdan," he said respectfully. "We is... happy... meeting Dee." He was not quite so drunk as the rest, but struggling with his English nonetheless. "Dee is..." he thought for a moment, then enthusiastically proclaimed, "top girl!"

"Thank you for looking after her," he replied, with just a touch of warning in his voice, as if he would have something to say about it if they hadn't taken good care of her – excess of alcohol notwithstanding – and guided her out the door.


Dee followed Mark across the courtyard, leaning on him so as to be able to walk straight. "They're really nice people," she told him, aware that her words were slurring slightly, but wanting to make the point nonetheless. Mark had seemed less than impressed with the men, and after their unperturbed acceptance of her explanation about him, she hoped that as the Densmeet continued, Mark would get the chance to spend some time with them as well, to get to know them better, and they him, so they could see that despite the rumours and gossip, he was every bit as honourable as she knew him to be.

But Mark wasn't so easily convinced. "That doesn't make it a good idea to get drunk with a group of strangers," he said, avoiding looking at her.

"They're shifters," Dee protested. "They live by Il Trosa's honour code. You know, if you fall I will carry you, I will measure your steps each day that you run, and all that," she said, quoting part of the Chant of Forests. "Besides, if they'd done anything wrong, Baron would have kicked their arses all the way back to Ukraine."

Mark didn't reply, but then Dee looked at him again... and snorted in laughter. "Oh, I get it. You're jealous!" she proclaimed gleefully. And perhaps he had reason to be, she thought, with just a hint of what she was reluctant to call satisfaction. The Ukrainians were very handsome, after all.

She'd never been the type to attract any significant male attention in the past. But her hosts for the evening didn't stand a chance. Her attention was already taken up with a far more interesting prize.

"You've got nothing to worry about," she told Mark, leaning up to press a kiss to his cheek. "I've already had my heart stolen by the most daring shifter in the whole of Europe."

Mark looked mollified by that, and slid an arm around her waist. "Let's get you back to bed," he said warmly. "And then we can talk more about this daring shifter you like so much…"

# CHAPTER NINETEEN

Closeted away in her tiny flat in east London, Melissa sat at her desk, her laptop in front of her, typing furiously.

The experiments into creating a device that could force a shifter to change forms had yet to yield any real results, though Evans continued to come up with more and more complex ways of running the tests, ordering close to ten thousand pounds worth of new equipment for the lab, having the walls insulated, the metal surgery table exchanged for a plastic one, even going so far as to implant electrodes within the shifter's body. But at no point had she reconsidered Melissa's suggestions as to the electrical dynamics of the shift, while Melissa became more and more convinced that she was right, as each new set of test results came in.

The wolf was clearly suffering from the ongoing tests, losing weight, his fur becoming bedraggled, his eyes puffy from lack of sleep and his skin had taken on a grey tinge. As pleased as Melissa was to see him suffering, there was a more pragmatic issue at hand – if they didn't take care of him well enough, they ran the risk that their only test subject would die before they completed their experiments, and she knew from first hand experience how difficult it could be to catch another one. But her suggestions to Evans that they pay more attention to the shifter's health had been met with incredulity, followed by outright laughter. She was going soft, Evans had told her with a sardonic grin. The shifters were tough, some of them having survived not weeks, but years in captivity, undergoing far more unpleasant things than this team was doing to their current prisoner.

But with their present limitations, it could take years for them to crack the mystery of the mechanics of the shift, and despite Evans' reassurances, Melissa was far from convinced that their captive was going to last that long.

Unless she did something to speed up their progress.

So here she was, at midnight, after putting in a full day in the lab, now sitting at home still working on her life's purpose, but in an entirely different way.

After long minutes typing, she paused, and took the time to re-read the letter she had composed. It was addressed directly to Headquarters, to Professor Ivor Banks, the most senior scientist in the whole of the Noturatii, and it detailed all of her ideas concerning the shifter experiments, each and every avenue that Evans had either blocked or ignored. And then it went a step further.

*During the raid on our former laboratory facility*, it read, *I encountered a small group of shifters attempting to flee the lab. Knowing that to allow them to escape was a great threat not just to our organisation but to humanity as a whole, I attempted to shoot one of them. Unfortunately, my firearms skills are not what they could be, and I missed, receiving a serious injury from the shifters in the process.*

*Traditionally the Noturatii has focused its combat training on its security staff – as well it should – but in the process, we have perhaps overlooked what has become a significant hole in our strategic planning. I propose that each and every staff member, whether administrator, scientist, diplomat or even a cleaner, should be given comprehensive weapons training. Had I been more competent with a gun, I would have been able to kill the shifters attempting to flee, and it could be supposed that several more of them might be dead, and many of our staff still alive, had they been appropriately trained and armed.*

*While I realise that it would take significant time and money to achieve this level of training across all of our offices, I would like to propose that this strategy should be considered, as I believe it would go a long way towards strengthening our team as a whole, and preventing future setbacks of this nature.*

Melissa finished re-reading her work, and nodded to herself. Satisfied that it came across as both polite and urgent, detailed but not boring, she took a few moments to set up a secure link to Headquarters, and hit send.

Jacob would be furious if he found out. Evans would be livid. The other scientists would be ropable about her having gone behind their backs.

But the opinions of those at Headquarters were the only ones that mattered. And if Melissa's ideas led to the strengthening of their cause, the opportunity to put more of her ideas into practice and win this war all the quicker, then it would all be worth it.

## 16 Years Ago

Andre watched Caroline in consternation. They were in the middle of another of their counselling sessions, and Andre was currently being forced to admit to himself that he'd reached a dead end.

It was five weeks since Caroline had arrived in Italy, and long discussions had occurred during that time, conversations about Caroline's home life, her relationship with her mother, her feelings when the woman had left, and her feelings about her Den.

None of it was simple, every event or relationship wrapped up in both bitterness and joy. She'd loved her mother, and yet also hated her for leaving. She was immensely grateful for her new life in the Den, and yet felt that she wasn't worthy of it, having done nothing to earn her place there, and having made no particular contribution to the community since her recruitment. Her childhood had been hellish, and yet she still managed to find bright moments, a birthday party when she was a young girl, or the day she'd got her ears pierced. Her joy when she'd got her first job, for all that it had been a miserable place to be.

The only thing she really felt clear about was her father. She hated him with every ounce of her being, with no hint of happiness or pleasure to temper her anger.

And now she'd just told him what her father had done just before she'd left her home for the last time, the total destruction he had wrought in her bedroom, and the fury she had felt, more tempted than at any other time in her life to give in to the rage and simply kill him.

And then, years later, when she'd thought there was nothing left that he could do to her, nothing left that he could take from her, he'd killed her mother. Or at least, she believed he had. Andre was keeping in mind the pertinent fact that the police had found no clear evidence of his involvement in the murder, and so the true events of that night remained uncertain.

But Andre's job in all this was to convince Caroline that killing her father was neither a necessary or nor a viable option, that clinging to family bonds was inappropriate, and he was to somehow come out the end of it all with firm assurances that Caroline would never again feel tempted to betray her pack and put her species at risk, whether for familial ties or for personal revenge.

How the hell was he supposed to do that, when he could empathise far too strongly with her, the rage, the helplessness, the overwhelming sense of injustice about it all.

Eleanor had done well, he had to admit, with no shortage of irony. He and Caroline had far more in common than he had realised, both of them losing parents to a force of evil, and both of them bent on revenge, and he could see no clear path out of their current conundrum. Evil had been done. Justice was required. How did one just walk away from that?

He was tempted to call an end to the session for today, needing time and space to get his own thoughts in order before he continued trying to muddle through hers. But just as he was about to speak, Caroline beat him to it.

"It's not like I would have gone with her anyway," she murmured, almost to herself.

"What do you mean?" Andre asked, feeling exhausted and wrung out from the dark memories the conversation was bringing up.

Caroline looked up at him, a bleak despair in her eyes. "I was waiting... I was hoping she'd come back one day. I always thought... When she left, I thought she must have decided I was as worthless as my father. I couldn't think of any other reason why she wouldn't have taken me with her. There are plenty of reasons, I suppose, but I couldn't see them at the time. So for all these years, I've been hoping she'd come back, and tell me she was sorry, that she wanted me to leave that hell hole and go and live with her. And when I went to my father's house... I thought that was why she'd been there. She'd come back for me. And he'd taken that away from me, the last, final chance to know that she'd thought I was worth something.

"But what would I have said, even if I'd had the chance to speak to her face-to-face? I have – had – the Den," she went on, correcting herself as she recalled that she might have lost even that part of her life, now that she'd betrayed them in such a reckless manner. "I've spent two years being trained for a covert war. I have new friends. I've cut all ties to any life I had before. So what the fuck did I think I was going to say? 'Hey, mum, great to see you again after all this time, but you're a couple of years too late, so how about you just fuck off again?' Jesus..."

It seemed she was feeling as wrung out as Andre was, and he searched for something intelligent to say. "Just because you couldn't go with her doesn't mean you didn't love her. Or that you didn't want that final validation of yourself. Regardless of the circumstances, your emotions about the whole thing are still important."

"True," Caroline agreed. "And I'm still furious. I feel hurt, and betrayed, and unbelievably angry. Not just at my father, but at my mother as well. But I also... It's like what you said yesterday. Even before Kendrick found me, I'd already moved on. I'd left that house, mentally, if not physically. I'd got a job and was looking for a place to live and I had plans..." She peered up at him, looking tired, and world-weary, and yet there was an odd spark of something else. Joy, maybe? Peace? Or a kind of freedom that Andre couldn't quite understand. "I can grieve for everything I've lost, and everything I never had in the first place. But it's also time I let it go. I don't want to let him keep controlling me for the rest of my life. I've moved on. I just... It would have been nice to know, in the end."

"To know what?"

"Whether she really loved me."

That was something Andre understood. For all her bravado and fiery attitude, he'd known some time that there was still a small, childlike part of Caroline that just wanted someone to tell her she was deserving of praise. "Do you think your Den loves you?" he asked simply.

"I don't know. I haven't exactly made life easy for them."

"Then let me tell you this: The usual protocol for someone who had done what you did would have been to put them down. But after you ran away from him, Kendrick spent no less than three hours on the phone, trying to convince the Council to give you a second chance. Why would he do that if he didn't care about you?"

Caroline tried to smile. The expression came out wobbly as sudden, hot tears slid down her cheeks. "He really did that?"

"He really did."

"Wow." She wiped her eyes, sitting quietly as she gazed off into the garden, lost in thought.

Andre tried not to stare at her, while her attention was elsewhere, and completely and utterly failed. In the last few days, along with his own growing disquiet about his parents' deaths, he'd also been having to deal with the slow realisation that he was finding it harder and harder to maintain a professional distance in his feelings towards her. When they had first met, Andre had thought she was the total opposite of himself in every way, impulsive where he was thoughtful, brash were he was painstakingly polite, derisive where he aimed for empathy. But he had slowly come to realise that Eleanor's prediction was true – they were far more alike than he could ever have expected.

And as he watched her, he finally managed to admit to himself the thing that was causing him the most discomfort.

She was... beautiful. Wild black hair that emphasised her eyes. High cheek bones that gave her a look of unexpected elegance. Lips that were thin, but expressive, always ready to tighten in displeasure, or quirk upwards in a smile that she was trying to hide.

She was, in a word, captivating.

And she was completely and absolutely off limits.

"Can we call it a day?" she asked suddenly, jerking Andre out of his illicit thoughts. "I'm exhausted."

Andre felt just as tired as Caroline seemed to be, and he was more than happy to end the session. "Get some rest," he said, closing his notebook and standing up. "I'll see you again tomorrow."


"How is the young lady doing?" Eleanor asked Andre later, after dinner was finished and the villa was quiet.

"Very well," he replied, feeling more together now, after an hour of meditation and a stern review of his own emotions. "She's still got a way to go to understand everything she's been through, but we're slowly working towards the point where she can let go of the past and move forward." Andre didn't fool himself into believing that today's session was the end of it. Caroline would come back with doubts, with questions, with a justifiable anger. But today she'd seen life from a different perspective, which was a huge step forward in his efforts to help her deal with her past.

"Good news indeed." Eleanor looked at him speculatively. "And what have you learned about yourself in the process?"

Andre closed his eyes and sighed, immediately seeing where she was going with this. "You knew exactly what you were doing when you put me with Caroline."

"That I did," Eleanor admitted easily. "You didn't think it had escaped our attention that you chose to become an assassin immediately after your parents were killed? So let me ask you this: How many Noturatii members do you need to kill in order to avenge your parents?"

"A few weeks ago, I would have said all of them," he admitted quietly, feeling the swell of emotion he'd felt that afternoon come rushing back.

"An impossible quest," Eleanor observed, knowing that Andre had already realised that. "And one that would slowly eat away at you, as each kill served as a reminder of how far away from your goal you were. So what would your answer be now?"

Andre stared at the floor, not quite able to meet her eyes. "None."

Eleanor reached out, laying a gentle hand on his shoulder. "So now you understand," she said softly, "why Caroline was assigned to you."

# CHAPTER TWENTY

**Present Day**

With the shifters once more gathered in the manor's main hall, Baron nodded to Nikolai, having just invited him to address the meeting. He'd pulled Baron aside earlier, saying he had a matter of great importance to discuss with everyone, though he'd refused to specify exactly what it was all about.

"I bring news," Nikolai said, regarding the room with a serious expression, "of an issue that is of great interest to our species. I have discussed this with the Council, and they have asked that I share the news with you. Earlier this year, I needed to travel to China with three others from my Den. The reason for our visit is not important now, but the result of it was quite startling.

"As many of you know, we are not the only shifter species on the planet. In particular, the Asian continent is home to the leopard shifters. They are becoming more reclusive, retreating into the mountains as the human population grows and their habitat is reduced. For centuries, we have known of their existence, but they have kept to their territory, and we have kept to ours. So our knowledge of the leopards has declined, I would argue to our detriment. But on my trip to China, I had an unexpected encounter with one of these cats."

The room, up until now, had been silent, but at this last statement, a collective gasp filled the room. The leopards hadn't been seen or heard from in decades, and their sudden reappearance was more than a little startling.

"They have their own enemies," Nikolai went on. "Not as extensive as the Noturatii, but a threat to them nonetheless. I assisted this cat with an incident involving her enemy, and in return, I was given a small amount of information on their situation.

"Years ago, decades, maybe even centuries ago, all of the cat shifters were leopards. And it was believed that this was still the case. However, during my visit, I witnessed this woman shift. And I was greatly shocked to see that she had become not a leopard, but a lynx."

A wave of muttering filled the room. But Nikolai wasn't done yet.

"We discussed our respective species briefly, and it seems that the cat shifters have achieved the impossible. This woman also reported that the cats now include not just lynxes, but clouded leopards, snow leopards, fishing cats. They have discovered a way to cross the species barrier – not once, but multiple times."

Baron was absolutely staggered by the news, his mind racing as cries of alarm and a volley of questions filled the room. For the shifters to cross species was thought to be impossible – indeed, the wolves themselves had tried it in the past. Their tests with coyotes had been a failure, with the new shifters unable to convert other humans. Attempts to convert other subspecies of wolf had been mildly more successful, with the converts able to turn new humans, but still ultimately a failure, as their progeny had reverted to the usual grey wolf form after a single generation.

"How did they do it?" Baron asked, equal parts concerned and fascinated, raising his voice to be heard above the din.

"I didn't get the chance to ask," Nikolai said apologetically, "and I doubt she would have told me if I had. The Council is discussing plans to form alliances with the cats. But they are exceptionally cautious of us, due to the dangers of the Noturatii – it amazes me that our enemies know nothing of the cats, or any other shifter species, but understandably, the Asian shifters would like to keep it that way. And they guard their territory closely. We would need to offer something of significant value to them, if they were ever to take an interest in an alliance."

More questions followed, Nikolai doing his best to answer each of them, with his limited information on the subject, but Baron's mind was in turmoil as the conversation continued around him.

Shifters jumping species. It was unheard of, the magic simply not able to make the transition successfully. There had been other species of shifter in the world, of course, the magic by no means limited to wolves alone. The bears were now confirmed to be extinct – they had fallen victim to the witch hunts of the middle ages, unable to rally together as the wolves had done. And in North America, rumours still persisted of another species, no one quite willing to believe the stories, as tales continued to be told of a type of shifter magic that defied all natural laws, a magic so powerful it made the wolves' own abilities look like they were nothing more than children stumbling about in the dark.

Skip felt a wave of trepidation as she walked down the hall towards the room where she was to run the hacking workshop. Up until a few days ago, she'd been looking forward to it, eager to spend a few days discussing the intricacies of computers in a way that she never had the chance to at home.

But then there had been that horrible incident with the Russians, and after that, she'd checked the list of attendees for her seminar, and her heart had sunk as she'd realised that one of the rude Russians was going to be among them – not as a student, but as a translator. She'd been dreading it ever since.

But as Skip reached the door to the meeting room, she was startled to find someone else waiting for her. John pushed off the wall, where he had been leaning with his arms folded, and looked her up and down. "How'd you like me to sit in with you?" he asked, a scowl on his face, and most people might have taken his offer the wrong way, a concession to her weakness, perhaps, or a grudging fulfilment of an order from higher up the chain of command.

But Skip and John had a close bond that frequently surprised those not familiar with their respective pasts. They'd both endured exceptionally brutal childhoods, had both been rescued by the Den, not just physically, but also from their own mental hell, and thanks to Heron's innate mothering skills, the pair of them had become as close as brother and sister – a most unlikely pairing, to be sure, but as a result, John was one of the few people Skip trusted completely, and she was one of the few people who could truly say they understood him.

Skip broke into a bashful smile, clutching her notebooks and clipboard tightly. "I'd appreciate it," she said, knowing that John would see no weakness in the admission of the need for help.

Inside the room, the others were already waiting for her. There were four of them, including a woman from Russia who was to be Skip's trainee, and the infamous young man who had given her such a hard time. And apparently he still needed a few lessons in manners. He looked her up and down, clearly unimpressed... and then did a double take when Skip took her seat at the main desk where three laptops were set up.

"*You're* our teacher?" he asked in surprise.

Skip didn't get the chance to reply. John stepped forward with a clear growl. "You watch yourself," he warned the man sharply.

Taking John at face value – none too impressive in human form – the Russian sneered. "And who are you?"

"I'm John," John said simply. The man looked momentarily confused, until something about the name suddenly registered, and his face paled.

"You mean... *the* John? Baron's John?"

"That's the one," John said, not sounding at all surprised that his reputation had preceded him.

"Ah." The man couldn't seem to decide whether to be impressed or terrified. He looked from John, to Skip and back… then sat down and shut his mouth.


In one of the rare moments of free time throughout the Densmeet, Andre found himself at a loose end, and so, hearing that the Russians had brought with them a rare and ancient text on shifter history, he headed for the room that was serving as a makeshift library.

But when he opened the door, he realised he was not the first one to have the idea. Caleb was already sitting at one of the desks, a thick book open in front of him, a notepad to one side in which he was jotting down the odd phrase.

He looked up as Andre came in, and immediately asked, "Do you speak any of the old language?"

"Some," Andre replied. He would have liked to learn more, but when he'd chosen to become an assassin, his studies into the intricacies of the language had stopped, leaving him with only basic lessons in the more common texts. "What are you looking at?"

"The prophecy of *Negur Ulis*. The Black Wolf."

Andre's eyebrows rose in surprise. It was an obscure myth, even the best historians unable to quite agree on what it meant, and he was surprised that Caleb would take an interest in it.

"The story always fascinated me," Caleb explained, "but I've never been able to get a good translation of it. And since Marianne brought the volume in its original language, I thought I would take a look."

"You read the old language?" Andre asked, surprised yet again. He'd known that Caleb knew a certain amount of it, but hadn't realised he was fluent enough to translate a text from scratch. He pulled up a chair and sat down beside him, peering at the book over his shoulder.

"Bits of it," Caleb admitted with a frustrated sigh. "But there are a few passages I can't figure out. Nor can anyone else, I guess," he said wryly, "which is why there hasn't been a decent translation yet."

"What are you stuck on?"

"This word," Caleb said, pointing, "and this one. *Vortos* usually means enemy, or threat, but if that's true, then this sentence seems to say that the Black Wolf is both our enemy and our ally. Or am I mistranslating *symuznyk?*"

"This doesn't say *symuznyk*," Andre replied. "The characters are similar, but there's a missing accent here, and an extra vowel here," he explained. The text of the old language was unique, containing elements of the Latin script, but also characters with a similarity to Greek and the Cyrillic script from eastern Europe. "The word is *symuchnek*, which-"

The pair of them were interrupted suddenly as Nikolai flung the door open, pulling up short when he saw them both.

"I am sorry," he said, closing the door much more softly. "I did not realise anyone was in here. I need a place to escape the politics for a while," he admitted, running a hand over his face. "Become alpha, and everybody thinks they can ask you a thousand useless questions." He headed for the side of the room and collapsed into a chair.

Andre nodded politely to him, then turned back to the book. "The meaning of *symuchnek* is not entirely clear, but from its use in other texts, it seems to have connotations of 'traitor'."

Caleb frowned. "So the Black Wolf is our enemy, and a traitor. That's sounds fairly grim."

"You study the story of the Black Wolf?" Nikolai was on his feet in an instant, rushing to look over Caleb's shoulder. "No, no, no, you have this wrong. You see, the preposition comes before the noun, not after it. The Black Wolf is an enemy, it says, and then he *becomes* a traitor. He betrays our enemies, which makes him an ally. I believe there is a pun in the original language. Subtle, but very clever."

Caleb looked up at Nikolai, both impressed and fascinated. "You know this text?"

"Like the back of my hand."

"There was something else I was trying to work out," Caleb rushed on, turning the page and searching for the appropriate passage. "Most of the prophecies refer to wolves who lived in the past and will be reincarnated. They refer to a distinction between wolf and human, similar to what Dee is experiencing. But every single one that does so also refers to the wolf by their original name. Faeydir-Ul, Fenrae-Ul, Kinos-Muz, the Mountain Ghost. But this just lists him as 'The Black Wolf'. There's no name, no mention of his past life. So what I want to know is, is he a reincarnation, or a new being? Just because it's a prophecy doesn't mean it's necessarily about a wolf with a past life."

As Nikolai bent down to examine the words more closely, Andre was secretly impressed. It was an angle on the story that he himself had never considered, having jumped to the same conclusion as many a historian that the wolf had to have existed before.

"This is a smart one, no?" Nikolai muttered, quirking a bushy eyebrow at Andre. "What is your expression? To read between the lines?"

Andre was inclined to agree. And he made a mental note to add the observation to his assessment of Caleb later. When studying a dead language, it was all too easy to simply accept everything your tutors told you, without stopping to question whether they were correct or not. It was a significant point in Caleb's favour that he was able to think outside the square where the old prophecies were concerned. The Council was going to be most impressed.

"It is hard to say one way or the other," Nikolai concluded a few minutes later. "But this is odd. It says here he is 'forged of lightning'. Converted, in other words, in a lightning storm. That is extremely rare these days, now that we have electricity to do it instead."

"Are you certain he hasn't already come and gone?" Caleb asked, studying the page again.

"Quite certain. This passage here refers to the witch hunts of the middle ages," he said, pointing, "and this one, to the Eil-Mei-Kyntrosi. The Black Wolf is to arise between the two events, and we have not performed the Kyntrosi since the year 1436." The most sacred of shifter ceremonies, the Eil-Mei-Kyntrosi, or literally, the Chant of Gathering Shifters, was only performed in the most dire of emergencies, as had been the case in the middle ages when the wolves had found themselves on the brink of extinction. The mere mention of the phrase was enough to make most shifters shudder, as it generally indicated a major turning point in history – and not always for the better.

"So there is a Black Wolf, who is yet to arise," Caleb said, summing up what he had learned, "who will be forged by lightning, who will betray our enemies, and who will... what is this? Cast down the Man of Jars? What does that mean?"

Nikolai frowned at Caleb's fumbling translation of the words. "This one is ambiguous as well. It could mean to kill someone, presumably a literal man of some description, or it could be to destroy, or deconstruct something. Some scholars have speculated that it means he will destroy an organisation or a business of some sort."

"So who, or what, is the Man of Jars?"

Nikolai shrugged, an enigmatic look on his face. "Remember, this was written thousands of years ago. We have many new inventions that the prophet would not have understood. How is he to explain anything related to cars, or trains, or computers? He would never have seen these things, and yet, with the world so far progressed, some of them could well be involved in these prophecies. So as far as the Man of Jars is concerned... your guess is as good as mine, my curious friend."

# CHAPTER TWENTY-ONE

Dee stood ramrod straight out the front of the manor, along with each and every member of her own Den, and several of the other shifters. At her hip was a pistol, a knife attached to her belt, and another in a sheath strapped to her ankle.

As a recently converted wolf who had not yet completed her combat training, it was a rare day when Dee was required to carry weapons. Around the estate, there was plenty of security – cameras, alarms, electric fences – and whenever she left the estate it was under escort, Tank usually acting as her bodyguard.

But today was a very different situation, and despite the fact that they were on their own turf, the Den was alert and watchful, the lower ranking members carrying knives and semi-automatic pistols, the higher ranking ones holding submachine guns. To say that security was tight was a gross understatement.

The sound of approaching vehicles broke the silence, and everyone was instantly on guard, Tank and Silas front and centre, while Baron and Caroline stood in the middle of the drive, awaiting the arrival of the Grey Watch.

Baron had received a phone call two days ago, a curt conversation that had merely sought to confirm the timing and location of the Densmeet, and informed Baron that the Watch would be arriving today.

Given the way their last encounter with the group had gone, with the Watch trying to kill Dee, and several of their own being killed in the process, it was a fair assumption that tensions would be running higher than usual this year.

After a short wait, three white vans came into view, slowly climbing the driveway. But rather than approaching the manor, they instead stopped a hundred metres away. Sempre got out of one of them and waited, and

Baron glanced at Caroline, then at Tank and Silas in consternation.

"Looks like we're going down to meet them," he said, clearly annoyed by the situation. Then he turned to Nikolai. "These wolves are crazy," he said shortly. "Even more crazy than the Watch usually is. And I don't trust them any further than I could spit. So if they do anything stupid, you're in charge, and you're free to make whatever call you think best."

It was an extravagant move, delegating control to a foreign shifter. Even though Nikolai was also an alpha, relations with the Grey Watch were generally handled on a country-by-country basis, meaning Sempre, Baron and Caroline were the leading authorities here. The precaution made it clear just how nervous Baron was; if Nikolai was to take control, it would be because Baron was no longer able to do so himself.

In slow, measured steps, weapons at the ready, Baron and Caroline proceeded down the road to the waiting vans, Tank, Silas and Andre close behind, and Dee watched them go with a strong sense of trepidation, knowing that she was the cause of a great deal of the tension, but not having a clue what to do about it. Beside her, Mark was watching the procession just as grimly, and she turned to him and asked, "Why do we bother doing this if it's all so likely to go pear shaped?"

"We have to," Mark replied. "It's a condition of the Treaty."

That meant nothing to Dee. "What treaty?"

Mark looked down at her in surprise. "Caroline hasn't covered that with you yet?" As a new recruit, Dee was less than a year into her mandatory two year training period, and it constantly amazed her how much there was to learn. No one had mentioned any kind of treaty to her, so she shook her head.

"It's the Treaty of Erim Kai Bahn, of Destruction or Victory. It was written in the 1400s. The shifters were being wiped out in the witch hunts – pretty good evidence of black magic, right there, if a person suddenly turns into a wolf. So the last remaining wolves in Italy organised the Eil-Mei-Kyntrosi, the Chant of Gathering Shifters. It's a ceremony which taps into the natural electromagnetic radiation of the planet. A large number of shifters are required, and it sends out a huge burst of radiation that acts as a beacon to all other shifters, summoning them to a single place.

"Weeks later, every single wolf shifter left in Europe had descended on Cison de Valmarino, in Italy. Ninety-eight wolves. That was it. All the rest had been killed. At the peak of our culture, we've had more than ten thousand shifters alive at once.

"A meeting was held to try and figure out how to preserve the species. The rough beginnings of the Noturatii had already started to form, dedicating themselves to wiping us out, with the blessing of various Christian sects. The shifters who later formed Il Trosa believed we needed to band together, to form a cohesive pack and take a stand to defend ourselves. Those who eventually became the Grey Watch disagreed. They thought they could disappear into the wilderness – of course, there was a lot more wilderness at that time – and evade their enemies, living basic lives, abandoning their human ties. There are pros and cons to both approaches, of course. One large pack is a lot more conspicuous, if someone is searching for you, but also much better able to defend itself.

"The end result was that the wolves split into two factions – Il Trosa, which eventually grew large enough to implement the Council to oversee them all, and the Grey Watch, who retreated into the forests and abandoned their human lives.

"The talks went on for weeks, every possible detail of our lives analysed and weighed up. The shifters of that time were extremely insightful, I'm glad to say. They knew the treaty would have far reaching effects long into the future, so nothing was left to chance. There are provisions in it for almost every imaginable circumstance – the proliferation of the species, the destruction of the species, the creation of new bloodlines, the loss of old ones, the expansion of humanity, the rise of better weapons. The very first guns were just beginning to be used around that time, and they imagined that further developments along that line were inevitable.

"But one thing everyone managed to agree on was that, whatever their internal disagreements might be, the shifters must always stand as a united front against the Noturatii, or any other organisation like them. But that was only possible if ties were maintained between the packs. So one of the provisions in the treaty was that Il Trosa and the Grey Watch must meet once each year to reaffirm our common bonds, to share information on our enemies and to discuss plans for the year ahead."

"So what happens if they break the Treaty and don't show up?" Dee asked.

"In extreme circumstances, that might be allowed. And by extreme, I mean a tsunami has flooded half of England, for example. In 1941, during World War 2, they missed a year. Travel was too dangerous, supplies too limited. But aside from that, deliberately failing to attend the meeting breaks the treaty, and then… God knows. Best case scenario, the Grey Watch pack that didn't show up gets culled. In its entirety. Worst case, war breaks out between Il Trosa and the Watch right across Europe."

It was a grim prospect, which made Dee understand why the Grey Watch would agree to this meeting, though they seemed reluctant to the extreme about the whole thing.

"One more detail of the treaty," Mark said, as Baron and Caroline reached the vans, and a heated discussion started up between them and the Grey Watch. "No one from either side is allowed to harm anyone from the other pack during the meeting. To do so is a declaration of war. So no matter what anyone does, or says, you and Faeydir both need to take it on the chin."

"Got it," Dee said, conveying the weighty importance of that command to Faeydir. At the same time, she shuddered. The prophecy stated that she would cause the destruction of the shifters, but reading between the lines, it didn't actually specify that she would do it by separating them all from their wolf selves. So perhaps this was what it was referring to. If Faeydir caused a fuss, she could inadvertently start a war right here, completely unintentionally, and with devastating consequences for all involved.

Baron strode down the road, gun at the ready. He wasn't prepared to take any shit from the Watch, having already agreed to their sharp demands and willing to fulfil the bare minimum of the terms of the treaty to get this thing over with. Sempre had stated on the phone that they intended to stay for one day only, not a moment more. The discussions would be held outside – it was a disgrace to expect wild wolves to have to enter a human house, she had decided, though in previous years, there had been no problem with holding the talks inside the manor, and when Baron had informed her that his Den would be armed – treaty or no treaty, he wasn't putting his Den mates' lives at risk – she had swiftly replied that they would be coming fully armed themselves. Rather than a friendly gathering of allies, this was turning into something more like a war negotiation between rival arms dealers.

So when he arrived at the van where Sempre waited, it was with a scowl on his face and a tight rein on his flaring temper. "What?" he demanded sharply.

"Fenrae-Ul," Sempre said, her tone just as sharp as his. "She is a threat to our pack. To our entire species. And we will not concede to these talks until she is removed from the property."

"Dee is no threat to you," Baron replied, letting a hint of his anger show. He'd fought Sempre before, and won, and the woman didn't scare him in the slightest. "The only reason she attacked you before was because you were trying to kill her."

"With good reason!" Sempre snarled. "The prophecy states that she will destroy our species."

"So you're going out of your way to give her a reason to do that very thing? Great plan!" Baron's voice was dripping with sarcasm. "Let me know how that works out for you."

"So you concede she is a danger?" Sempre pressed, which made Baron snarl.

"I concede nothing of the sort."

As the argument went on, Baron listening with gradually shortening patience while Sempre expounded the risks and insults that Baron routinely exposed them to, he noticed that the women inside the vans were getting restless. There were close to thirty of them, packed into just three vans, and it had to be getting uncomfortably cramped inside. One of the side panels was slid open, two or three of the more senior shifters stepping out to stretch their legs, and then, when Sempre seemed to ignore the breach in protocol, the second van opened its door, and then the third. Shifters piled out, women all covered from head to toe in grey robes, glancing anxiously at their leader, and Baron let himself suppose for a moment that it wasn't because they were nervous about the talks to come, but because they were fed up with their alpha's theatrics. Sempre seemed to have some extreme views, even by Grey Watch standards, and he wondered for a moment whether all the women here shared her views, or simply put up with them for lack of a better option.

As he watched, he caught sight of two males, lurking in the doorway of the vans, and felt a wave of pity for them. Both wore collars around their necks and avoided the gaze of any of the women. The Grey Watch had different standards on male-female relationships than Il Trosa, and while he didn't like to criticise other cultures too much, he felt that this particular pack had taken things too far. That the women subjugated their men to this degree was distasteful, but the thing that Baron couldn't wrap his head around was why the men put up with it. As shifters themselves, they weren't exactly at liberty to leave, but they could always appeal to the Council to help them, if they wanted to. They could leave the Watch and seek permission to join Il Trosa, and given the life they endured, he couldn't see that the Council would refuse.

Another woman stepped out of the first van, coming to stand beside Sempre, and Baron had to fight not to stare. It was Lita, the pack's mage.

He'd first met her many years ago, when she was a young woman, and over the years, he'd been startled by the rate at which she'd aged. It was a known side effect of the magic the Watch abused, but once again, he wondered at what sort of woman would throw her life away, inch by inch, just to dabble in the spirit world, where the living were not welcome and there were severe consequences for trespassing.

As Sempre finished her current rant, Baron opened his mouth to reply, but Caroline beat him to it. And thank goodness for that, he thought sardonically. For all Caroline's loyalty to Il Trosa, the Watch seemed to respect her more than most, and he hoped she would be able to talk sense into them where he had failed.

He glanced at Andre, seeing him observing Caroline closely, while maintaining the impression of merely acting as rear guard for their small group. Well, if the man had wanted an opportunity to watch the alpha female in action, he couldn't have asked for a better set up. It was going to take some serious negotiating skills to get them past this latest road block.

Genna furtively eased out of the van while Sempre and Il Trosa's alpha argued. It was hot in the van, with ten shifters crammed into the tight space, and she was grateful that they didn't have to make more trips like this. Usually it was just a handful of the Watch who went on any given journey, one van sufficient. The main reason they kept three of them was for when they chose to move camp. Some were within walking distance of each other, but others were too far, the vehicles required to move their meagre supplies and the weaker members of the pack, though even then, many of the wolves were expected to travel on foot, a long day of running to reach their new camp.

Seeing that there was no protest to the growing number of shifters leaving the vans, Genna stepped a few metres away and stood in the shade of one of the trees. Trying not to be too obvious about it, she looked over the shifters who had come with Baron. Caroline, she had heard about. Apparently the Il Trosa alpha had lived with the Watch for a short period, and everyone old enough to remember her held her in the highest regard. It was a shame she'd chosen to return to her Den, rather than forging a new life with the Watch.

Then there was that assassin who'd caused such havoc when he'd come looking for Dee, shooting one of their shifters dead and threatening to kill the rest of them, without the slightest hint of remorse. Genna wasn't sure what he was still doing here, having been under the impression that the Council kept a tight leash on their guard dogs, but his presence was unsettling, and she resolved to keep an eye on him.

Beside the assassin was another man. Tall, muscular, blond, holding a gun that clearly packed a hefty punch. He had a military air about him, his attention focused on Sempre, but he was still able to keep an eye on the other shifters, and Genna had no doubt that if any of them tried anything suspicious, he would be all over it in a heartbeat. His steady focus was intimidating... and yet oddly appealing at the same time. He was clearly a man in control, answering to Baron, but not held under his thumb, the way the Watch's males were. She glanced sideways at Sven, one of their own males, who had dared to come to the doorway of the van. To the door, she noted with disdain, but not out of it entirely. He was more dog than wolf, she thought sadly. Trained, collared, so beaten down he didn't know himself any more. And she paused to reflect that if a woman had been kept in that condition, she would be considered nothing more than a sex slave, righteous anger spewing forth from various sectors of society about the inhumanity of such oppression.

Did it make any difference because he was a man? Because he had, ostensibly, at least, chosen this for himself?

Genna stopped to wonder about that. She'd always been told that the males joined the Watch willingly, that they knew their place and their future role in it before making that decision.

But Genna wasn't so sure. She, herself, had been lured here with promises of magic and wonder, otherworldly power and the answers to unsolvable mysteries. While all that had been true, there had also been a darker, bleaker side to this new life that she had never been told about, constant bickering over food and shelter, lower ranking wolves downtrodden and cast aside. By the time she'd learned the truth of her new life, she'd already been converted and all thoughts of escape had come far too late. So perhaps these males had only been given half the story. Promised endless sex and otherworldly magic, only to realise, once they'd accepted the trade, that the other side of it was a life of slavery, of control, of servitude to unsympathetic masters.

But the man standing there with a gun, with those watchful eyes and masculine physique… he was nothing like the men of the Watch. He was powerful. Independent. A fully functional member of the pack, rather than an optional extra.

Genna's first thought was to wonder what it would be like to sleep with him. That was the only purpose of the men in the Watch, and she'd been trained to see them that way, walking sex dispensers with no desires or expectations of their own.

She couldn't see this man that way. He might be interested in a woman, she mused, might be tempted to spend a night in one's bed, but only on his own terms. There would be no coercing him, no manipulating him into giving more than he wanted to. The idea was refreshing, and entirely more alluring than Genna wanted to admit.

But more than that, she found herself wanting to know more about him. When had he become a shifter? Where had he learned to use a gun? His weapon was far superior to the small pistols the Watch were supplied with, and she was curious both as to how he would have learned to use such a powerful piece, and how Il Trosa came to have them in the first place.

Could they buy more? Could they supply them to the Watch? Though their run-ins with the Noturatii were few and far between, there was always a risk things were going to suddenly go south, and they would be hard pressed to defend themselves against submachine guns and grenades with simple pistols.

What did he think of his alpha, she wondered. Her own relationship with Sempre was strained at best, terrifying at worst, and it was hard to believe that a man as strong and independent as this one would bow to Baron if he didn't truly respect the man.

It was a captivating mystery to be explored, but one she would likely never get the chance to solve. This meeting was going to be as brief as possible, and there was little chance of finding time for idle chat.

"You betray us!" Sempre shrieked suddenly, and Genna spun around to see her facing off against Caroline, Sempre's face red with indignation, while Caroline looked calm, though resolved.

"I betray no one," she replied firmly. "No more than you betrayed me when you handed me over to a Council assassin. The conditions of the Treaty dictate that a census must be taken of all of our respective members. That means you have no grounds upon which to ask for Dee to be absent. She is a confirmed member of Il Trosa. She will stand at the census, as will you and your pack, or you break the conditions of the Treaty. Are you so eager to find out what the Council would have to say about that?"

The threat worked, though it made Sempre more angry in the process, and Genna sighed at the thought of how foul a mood she would be in once they got out of here and back to their forest.

"I break no Treaty," Sempre said stiffly, drawing herself up to her full height. Which was an inch or so shorter than Caroline, Genna was amused to see. "Clear the road. We shall proceed to the meeting point."

It was a short walk to the manor, only a hundred metres or so, but as one, the shifters around her turned and clambered back into the waiting vans. A display of solidarity, Genna wondered, as she followed without a word? Or blind obedience to someone who couldn't see past the end of her own nose?

# CHAPTER TWENTY-TWO

An hour later, Tank stood on the wide lawn where a folding table and chairs had been set up in the centre. The census had been taken, and Tank had carefully written down the names and ranks of every member of both the Grey Watch and the Den, duplicating the list and handing the copy to Sempre. She'd stared at Dee and glowered the entire time, while Dee, to her credit, had stared back, calm and composed, not willing to be intimidated. From what Tank had heard of the story, the last time she and Sempre had met, Dee and Mark had kicked the wolf's butt, and Sempre no doubt remembered the incident, her defeat fuelling her anger.

After the census was complete, the alphas had turned their attention to other matters – a discussion on each pack's encounters with the Noturatii; the members of their respective packs who had been killed over the past year – a sore point given that two of the Watch had been killed by Il Trosa; introductions of any new recruits. That had been an interesting one. Baron had introduced Dee with a minimum of ceremony, sending her swiftly back to the gathered shifters at the side of the lawn before Sempre could throw a tantrum about the presence of the Destroyer, and then a young woman from the Watch had been called forward. She was introduced as Genna, her name called out clearly, and Tank eyed her with curiosity. She was young, maybe only twenty years old, and though it was hard to tell beneath her grey cloak, he thought she looked rather gaunt. Her cheeks were hollow, her expression guarded, and it surprised him that the Watch would let one of their new recruits suffer from malnutrition.

As she reluctantly shook Baron's and then Caroline's hand, she glanced up at him, their eyes meeting across the lawn, and Tank felt a jolt as that dark, hollow gaze met his. There was a great depth of emotion in those eyes, anger, guilt, and a weariness that Tank could relate to only too well. It was the same look that had stared at him from out of the mirror for weeks after he'd been freed from the Noturatii lab, an almost helpless disgust with the world that was matched only by a stubborn determination not to let its hardships beat him.

Tank immediately knew that he had to talk to this woman. What had she been through to make her so hard at such a young age? It wasn't uncommon for shifters to recruit those who were down on their luck, orphans, petty criminals, the homeless or unemployed. But the look in her eyes was more like that of someone who had been through a war zone. And thanks to his service in the military, Tank had seen enough of those in his life to recognise the result.

But that conversation would have to wait, he acknowledged reluctantly, if they even got the chance to meet at all. Sempre had made it clear that this meeting would last only as long as was absolutely necessary, and with the Grey Watch looking on like a pride of lions guarding their cubs, and Il Trosa facing off against them, guns still at the ready, he didn't like his chances of getting a private moment to introduce himself to the woman.

But perhaps he shouldn't discount the possibility too quickly, he thought a moment later, seeing that a new development was about to take place.

Nikolai had disappeared a few minutes ago, Tank idly wondering where he had gone, and he reappeared now, with the other three Ukrainians in tow, each carrying a tray of glasses filled with a clear liquid. Water for the hot, tired shifters, Tank thought with a smile, liking Nikolai even more. He was a straight forward, no-nonsense man, and this ridiculous stand off was no doubt annoying the hell out of him. It was about time someone broke the deadlock.

The four men split up, working through the crowd, handing out the drinks, and while a few of the women refused – presumably out of resentment rather than lack of thirst – most took the glass willingly.

Tank watched as one of the women took a large sip, and immediately choked, spitting half of it out. "What is this?" she asked hoarsely.

"Best Ukrainian vodka," Tank heard Nikolai say. "Mixed with lemonade. Because you Brits don't know how to drink." The complaint was said with a grin, taking the barb out of the words, and the woman looked startled, glanced at Sempre, who was still deep in discussions with Baron and Caroline, and smiled back.

"Thank you," she said softly. Nikolai winked at her, then moved on to the next woman, who couldn't get her hands on a glass quick enough.


Re-joining her pack mates, Genna sighed with relief as a tall, thickly built man offered her a tray full of drinks. She took a glass, but didn't drink straight away, too caught up in her own curiosity about Il Trosa.

Whenever Sempre or the senior wolves spoke about them, it was with derision, complaining about their use of technology, the risks they took in exposing the shifters to humanity, their greed and inability to put aside physical desires to pursue the more spiritual aspects of life.

But what they had left out was the overwhelming sense of solidarity among this supposed foe. When Dee had been brought forward for her introduction, several of the men had watched over her with all the attentiveness of a mother bear guarding her cub. They were trained fighters, their weapons more advanced than the Watch's, every member maintaining a grim focus on their opposition that would make even seasoned soldiers apprehensive. They worked as a unit, the guards moving to cover weak points without being told, the men respecting the women, and vice versa, their clothes clean, but not overly showy, and Genna had to reassess Sempre's opinion of them as materialistic egotists. It would be nice to be able to choose her own clothes for once, she thought with longing, growing rapidly tired of the plain grey robe that she wore every time she took her human form.

Besides which, Genna thought with a stab of resentment, it was hard to care about the spiritual side of life when you were constantly hungry and cold and damp, fighting for food and a place to sleep. And while technology could certainly be over-relied upon, an excuse for laziness, there was a certain logic to keeping a computer around with an internet connection, the ability to look something up in the vast sea of information that was floating around the world's servers.

Glancing at the tall, blond man again, Genna took a sip of her drink, expecting plain water, but then she swallowed quickly, shocked by the strong, sweet taste, and glanced around at the other women. From the looks of them, they all had the same thing – vodka, if Genna's guess was right, though she hadn't tasted the spirit in a long while – and they were all being as clandestine about it as she was. Alcohol, while not forbidden in the Watch, was generally not available. It wasn't a priority for anyone heading into town for supplies, and a few small attempts at brewing their own in the forest had gone badly, apple cider turning to vinegar when it had become contaminated with bacteria.

Suddenly, Genna burst out laughing, seeing the ridiculous charade for what it was. They were a bunch of grown women, each with exactly the same drink in their hands, and each pretending they were doing nothing more than sipping water as they stood around a garden tea party.

Genna turned to Luna, standing beside her, and deliberately clinked her glass with hers. "Cheers," she said happily, taking a longer drink. Standing a few metres away, the man who had given her the glass winked at her and took a glass for himself, raising it in a silent toast before taking a drink, and that simple gesture seemed to break the tension in the women all around her.

Small laughs broke out, and then small conversations, those standing at the edges of the group daring to talk to members of Il Trosa, and Sempre looked around at the sudden noise, glaring daggers at her pack as they relaxed their carefully guarded stances and began to mingle. Oh, the horror of it, Genna thought sardonically, as she began to slowly work her way towards some of the shifters from Il Trosa. But there was little Sempre could do. She was caught in deep conversation with Baron and Caroline for the moment, and later... well, she could hardly punish the entire pack for having a friendly chat, could she?

Tank almost laughed as he watched Nikolai work the crowd of Grey Watch women. He would be flirting at one moment, offering serious words of advice the next, and then suddenly cracking jokes, slowly convincing even the most serious of the women to open up and start having a little fun. It didn't take long for the rest of Il Trosa to join in – with a few exceptions, of course. Silas was busy watching the discussion between Sempre and Baron. Andre was keeping to himself – no doubt a concession to the fact that he made everyone nervous as hell. And Dee was standing beside Mark, both of them avoiding the main crowd, for obvious reasons. While Baron and Caroline had both argued firmly in favour of Dee being allowed to remain during the meeting, it was clear that many of the Grey Watch were apprehensive about her presence, and there was no point pouring fuel on the fire.

Tank exchanged polite words with one or two women, vague sentiments to the effect that he was glad they'd been able to come, and then he turned around, meaning to check on Baron and Caroline at the centre table when he suddenly found himself face to face with Genna.

"Good morning," she said, eyeing the gun he still carried with more curiosity than trepidation. "You're a high ranking wolf, right?"

It was fairly blunt, as far as introductions went, but he was willing to go with it for the moment. "2IC to the alphas," he confirmed. "I'm Tank."

"Genna," Genna said, though she had already been introduced to the gathering. "How long have you been a shifter?"

It was more like an interrogation than a conversation, and Tank hesitated as he considered how he could turn it to more friendly terms. "Eight years. I was in the military before I was recruited."

"Where do you get your weapons from?"

Say what? "That's an awfully pointed question for a newly converted wolf," Tank observed, an undertone of warning in his voice. What game was this woman playing? He wasn't entirely sure it was safe to be discussing weapons supplies with one so new to the Watch, especially considering their rather rocky relationship with the group of late.

But to his surprise, Genna looked instantly contrite. "Ah, I'm sorry," she apologised. "I wasn't… I didn't mean to pry. I mean, you probably talk about that sort of thing with Sempre, or Lita. I was just…" She trailed off.

"You were just what?"

"You have better weapons than us. Which helps, when you go up against the Noturatii. I was just… wondering."

Interesting. A newbie, already concerned with the Endless War and wondering how best to arm her pack. No, Tank thought to himself, confirming his earlier opinion. This was no ordinary woman.

"Have you used a gun before?" he asked gently, not wanting to inadvertently prod a raw wound. If she had been in a war zone, she might not like to talk about it-

"No. Never. I just like to be prepared."

Well, that was nicely vague. Perhaps he was approaching this from the wrong angle. "How did you come to meet the Watch?" he tried again, hoping to learn more about her.

"Working a dead end job. Sempre tracked me down, told me a bunch of… stories." There'd been a clear hesitation before that final word, and Tank wondered what she'd been about to say instead. "The rest is history." Then she looked up at him, a perplexed, quizzical look on her face. "You're not like our males."

Tank glanced involuntarily at one of the men from the Watch, loitering at the edge of the lawn, trying hard to ignore Kwan and Aaron, who were trying to make conversation with him. "Thank God for that," he said, not bothering to disguise his feelings on the topic.

"You don't like the way we treat our men."

"Can't say I do, no."

"Good," Genna said, surprising him once again. "Neither do I."

"How old are you?" he asked suddenly, aware that he was constantly off balance around this woman, and not sure how she managed to be so forthright, and so mysterious at the same time."

"Twenty-one. Nearly twenty-two."


Genna cringed internally as she saw Tank wince at her age. This conversation was a far cry from the one she had been hoping to have with him. It was a long time since she'd had a real conversation with anyone, after spending so much time in wolf form with the Watch, and she couldn't remember a time she'd ever had the chance to talk to a man as attractive as Tank. She was making a dog's breakfast of it, overcompensating for her nervousness and no doubt coming across as confrontational. The men of the Watch had been no help either, not prone to conversation, answering direct questions, but never asking any of their own, and she was well out of practice at small talk.

"Look, I might be out of line in asking this," Tank said suddenly, and Genna felt the first blooming hints of a serious crush coming on, his handsome face suddenly creased with worry lines as he looked at her, "but is the Watch looking after you well enough?"

How the hell was she supposed to reply to that, Genna thought wildly. The answer was a resounding no, but to say so was a betrayal of her pack, which her conscience, however misguided, would not allow. And aside from that, there was no guarantee that Il Trosa would treat her any better. She didn't know these people, she reminded herself sharply. She had no reason to trust them.

Tank seemed to understand her hesitation, and he nodded, staring down at his gun in quiet contemplation. And then he asked, "Do you have a phone?"

"No," Genna replied immediately. "We're not allowed them. Sempre has one, and a few of the more senior women, but not the rest of us." That, she reasoned, was a simple fact, not a betrayal of any of the pack's values or secrets.

"How good is your memory?" he asked next, and Genna suddenly caught on to where he was going with this.

"Excellent," she told him. It wasn't, but if he was going to give her something to memorise, then she would damn well remember it.

"Good." He rattled off a number, repeated it several times, slowly, and then asked her to tell it back to him. She did, creating patterns in her head, rhymes and clues that would help her remember the number, months or years down the track.

"If you ever need help, call me. I can't guarantee I'll be able to get to you," he added apologetically. "But it's worth a shot."

"Why would you help me?" Genna asked without really meaning to. There was something about this man far more captivating than a firm set of muscles and a handsome face. His eyes held shadows that seemed to rival her own, and though this was neither the time nor the place, she was desperate to know more about him.

Tank just shook his head. "You know where we live?"

"In the Lakes District," Genna replied, feeling a stab of guilt shoot through her. This was one of the men she had betrayed to the Noturatii, their sworn enemy, who were at this very moment probably hunting down the elusive estate that Tank called home. She was a fool. That phone number was never going to help her, not after their home was burned to the ground and their members killed at Noturatii hands. She had never regretted anything more.

"We're not too far from Penrith," Tank told her. "Less than half an hour. Keep it in mind. If you ever need anything."

Genna nodded, then forced herself to turn and walk away. This was a good man. A decent man. While she was a traitor to his pack. And in that short conversation, she had revealed far more of herself than she ever intended to… and learned more about him than she had ever wanted to know.


It was early evening by the time the Grey Watch piled back into the vans, and as she climbed into the cramped space, Genna reflected that the day had gone rather better than anyone had expected. After sharing a round or two of drinks, Il Trosa had put on a generous lunch buffet, complete with cold meat, bread, cheese and salad for the humans, and raw steaks for the wolves. Sempre had been unhappy with the unexpected hospitality, trying hard to maintain her defensive stance, but Nikolai and his three Ukrainian friends weren't having a bar of it, going out of their way to get to know the members of the Grey Watch, making sure everyone had something to eat and drink, inviting various people to shift and play as wolves.

The more senior members of the Watch had declined it all, maintaining a firm aloofness that was, in Genna's eyes, entirely ridiculous. But despite her guilt and regrets over involving the Noturatii in their lives, she had still managed to have some fun, Nikolai all but dragging her into a game of chase.

She hadn't spoken to Tank again, but she'd watched him, feeling pangs of longing as she let her eyes linger on his handsome features, aware of an irrational stab of jealousy as she'd seen him talking to several of the women from the Watch.

On the whole, she'd been most impressed with Il Trosa, finding them far more down to earth than the rumours around the Watch had implied. And privately, she felt it was a great shame, and a greatly overlooked opportunity that they weren't spending more time here. These wolves seemed to have a wealth of information on the Noturatii, strategies for fighting them, an excellent command of their security systems and weapons that made their estate far more defensible than the Watch would ever be.

They also had a great deal of information on the world at large. Genna had spent an hour or more just eavesdropping on conversations, whether they involved simple celebrity gossip, long range weather forecasts or a debate on the latest policy from the government. The Grey Watch was weaker for their lack of information, and she could only hope that one day, Sempre and the senior wolves would realise that.

Buckling herself into her seat, Genna took one last glance out the window as the engine started and the van pulled slowly down the drive. Il

Trosa's shifters were gathered at the front of the manor, some waving, some simply watching them go, and, unable to help herself, Genna's eyes lingered on Tank's face.

The men of the Watch were going to seem forever dull and unappealing after even this short meeting with him. And she found herself sending up a desperate prayer that the Noturatii would fail in their efforts to find the estate in the Lakes District. All the shifters would be back next year, of course, at the next annual meeting with Il Trosa, with the faint hope in Genna's mind that relations could be repaired to those of concerned allies, rather than bitter foes with a common enemy. And next year, she could see Tank again. Practise her conversation skills so she made a better impression the second time around.

But only if the Noturatii failed where she had begged them to succeed.

# CHAPTER TWENTY-THREE

**16 Years Ago**

Caroline stared at the bag on her bed, reluctant to close the zip. It was eight weeks since she'd arrived in Italy. Eight weeks that had been some of the strangest in her life – and given what it had looked like so far, that was saying something.

Her training was finished. And far from the harsh punishments and stern lectures she had been expecting, the entire experience had been rather... liberating, if she could put a word to it.

The ghosts of the past were perhaps not entirely laid to rest – Andre had cautioned her that such things often took years to fully resolve themselves, and were prone to popping up at the most inopportune times – but they had certainly been pacified, far more than Caroline had ever thought possible.

So now she was going home. Back to England, to re-join her Den in the Lakes District. It was a nerve racking prospect. She'd disobeyed Kendrick, betrayed Il Trosa, run away to live with the Grey Watch... would they accept her back again? The Den had never officially accepted her into their ranks, and there was still the possibility that they would reject her when the vote was taken, sending her swiftly back to Italy until another Den could be found for her to join.

But the anxiety surrounding the welcome that waited for her was a small issue compared to the much larger reason why she was reluctant to leave.

She was never going to see Andre again.

The cause of her attachment to him was both obvious, and baffling. He'd been the perfect gentleman, polite, calm, diplomatic, and yet at the same time, pushing her to explore aspects of her past that were terrifying and painful. And she'd come out the stronger for it.

On the one hand, she should be glad to be rid of him, his patience infuriating, his quiet persistence nagging and nagging at her until she gave in, his relentless probing doing a number on her nerves.

But on the other hand…

The sad truth, she acknowledged, as she forced herself to close the bag and check the room one last time, was that she had fallen in love with him. He was so different from the men she had known before. Gentle. Compassionate. Soothing. And yet also a fiercely proud warrior, lethal, strong, admirable. It was a combination she hadn't known could exist in a mere mortal, and she feared that it would forever ruin her for other men, the bar set far, far too high for anyone else to ever reach it.

When Caroline arrived at the bottom of the stairs, Adriana was waiting for her – her official escort back to England. "What, no collar this time?" she asked, seeing the woman's empty hands, unable to supress the streak of rebelliousness that still lingered.

"No collars. No chains, no cages. It's simple, really," Adriana said, with a hint of predatory amusement. "You've had your second chance. You betray Il Trosa again, and this time, your life is forfeit. I have no need to keep you in chains."

The stark assessment of her situation was rather more confronting than Caroline had been prepared for, and she swallowed hard. And resolved that she wasn't going to do anything to give Adriana the slightest reason to doubt her.

Footsteps announced Eleanor's arrival, and behind her, Andre appeared as well. Caroline had been hoping, longing to see him one last time, but his presence would also make this goodbye that much more difficult. She would miss him like she'd lost one of her own limbs, and the last thing she wanted to do was cry in front of a Councillor and this other, far less temperate assassin.

"Best of luck," Eleanor said, with her usual poised elegance. "It's been a pleasure having you here." That, at least, Caroline could believe was the truth. Eleanor had always been steadfastly honest, and yet painstakingly polite throughout her visit, and if she'd held any further reservations about Caroline's behaviour, she was sure the woman would have said so.

"Thank you," Caroline said simply. Her gratitude was a paltry gift in return for all the Council had done for her, but it would have to suffice. "I won't let you down."

She turned to Andre last, gritting her teeth in an effort not to cry. "Good luck with your assassin thing," she said, knowing it sounded stupid, but not knowing what else to say.

Andre held out his hand for her to shake, looking like he wanted to hug her, but knowing it would be inappropriate. "May Sirius guide your days and guard your nights."

Caroline nodded, adopting a slight scowl to keep her lip from trembling. Then she picked up her bag and followed Adriana out of the villa, forcing herself not to look back.


Andre watched as Caroline left, head held high, back straight, every bit the proud and powerful woman he knew her to be. Her future would be tough, that much was certain. But he also had the utmost confidence in her, knowing that she had the perseverance to face her own demons, and the intelligence to become a warrior worthy of Il Trosa.

"Well done," Eleanor said, turning to face him, once the van had eased down the driveway and disappeared around the bend. "How do you feel?"

Like a piece of his heart had just walked away, never to return. Falling in love with his student was a gross breach of protocol, and he'd done everything in his power to keep his emotions in check, not daring the slightest word or action that might give him away. "I think she's going to do well," he said, working hard to keep his voice steady. "It's been an honour to be able to help her."

"And hopefully to help yourself in the process," Eleanor said, more insightful about his demons than he was comfortable with.

"That too," Andre admitted, knowing there was no point in denying it. Caroline's struggle with her past had stirred up some deep emotions in him, the pain of losing his parents once more fresh and raw, though now it also contained a measure of peace, the ability to mourn the past, but not let it control his future. He'd booked a week of leave, eager to return to the Italian Den for a short while, to visit his parents' graves and make his peace with the ghosts of his past.

"Have a good rest while you're away," Eleanor said, knowing there was a car coming to collect him in a little over an hour. "You've passed the third stage of your training. Your tutors are most impressed. But don't let yourself get complacent. When you return to the villa, you'll be heading out to Russia for a three week training course. And believe me when I say the next part of your training is going to be the hardest yet."


Kendrick was waiting at the entrance when Caroline and Adriana arrived at the Lakes District estate, four armed guards standing behind him, their faces cold and stern. He entered the code for the gate without a word, waiting while the heavy iron barrier swung open. Then he stood back, his arms folded, simply looking Caroline over.

"I'm sorry," she apologised immediately. She'd had plenty of time to reflect on the past two years during her time in Italy, the distance giving her a sense of perspective that she'd missed while she'd been confined within these walls, and her contrition for the way she'd treated these people was heartfelt.

Kendrick had rescued her from a hellish life. Trained her. Respected her. Everyone here had welcomed her as a member of the family – a far better version of the concept than the one she'd grown up with – and she'd thrown it back in their faces, disrespecting their rules and their safety, abandoning all the good she'd found here in favour of the wild forest and the damp ground, when she'd run off to join the Grey Watch.

At Andre's request, she'd considered whether she would prefer to return to them, rather than coming back to the Den, a suggestion that was quite unexpected, but that she'd taken seriously all the same.

It had been a surprisingly easy decision to make. She'd loved the Watch, genuinely enjoying her time with them, the wilderness, the rugged life, the sense of surviving day by day. But after only a few minutes' reflection, she'd realised that she couldn't go back to live with them. She owed Il Trosa too much. They'd spent a huge amount of time and effort training her, teaching her, spending their hard earned resources on a person who, they had hoped, would become a strong and useful member of their pack. It was not a debt she could repay easily, but she was going to do her damnedest to try.

"Caroline has completed her retraining, and the Council assures me she's ready to return to your Den," Adriana said, her voice containing neither pride in Caroline's achievements, nor censure at her failings. "She has fully merged with her wolf, and is prepared to take the oath of loyalty, if and when you see fit to accept her."

"Indeed," Kendrick said, his gaze never leaving Caroline's face. "And what do you have to say about that?"

"I know I've failed you," Caroline said, knowing more than a simple apology was required. "I know you took a huge risk in recruiting me, and I haven't upheld my end of the deal. All that changes today. I will honour your rules. I will respect your culture. I will do everything in my power to be a useful and productive member of your Den."

"That's quite the turn around," Kendrick said, finally uncrossing his arms and coming forward to meet her. "And the Grey Watch?"

"My home is here," Caroline said simply. In the weeks to come, she knew, actions would speak louder than words. But for now, words were all she had, and she could only hope that Kendrick would believe the sincerity of them.

"Then come inside," Kendrick said finally, after a long, tense silence. "It's time you took your oath, and we gave the Den a chance to vote on your right to remain here. I believe in you, Caroline," he added, nodding to Adriana, who ghosted away out the gate as if she had never been there. "I still do. I hope you don't prove me wrong."

The future was in her own hands, Caroline knew, as she followed him up the drive. There was a wide array of possibilities, avenues for failure, and opportunities for success stretching out ahead of her, and watching these stern faces, silently weighing her worth, she promised herself that she would never give them a reason to regret this second chance. She would win every battle. Defend every life. Safeguard the future of this Den as closely as she would have guarded her own child. She would prove her worth to this eclectic family, come hell or high water.

Failure was simply not an option.

# CHAPTER TWENTY-FOUR

**Present Day**

Andre stood beside Caleb, watching the latest round of Games with a grin on his face. The last three weeks had been going exceptionally well, the shifters overcoming their initial wariness of each other to form close friendships, and a wealth of information had been shared – combat techniques, strategies to fight the Noturatii, theories on shifter magic and philosophical discussions on the future of Il Trosa. There had been plenty of fun as well, late night drinks, card games, chases in wolf form and a few friendly fights as various shifters had pitted their strength and skill against wolves from other Dens.

In just a few days, the Densmeet would be drawing to a close, the visiting shifters sent back to their respective Dens. But first, there were still a few more Games to be held, and tomorrow, Eleanor would be arriving from Italy, the official visit from the Council to deliver their report on the past year.

The Nochtan-Eil had been performed, a ceremony that both farewelled the fallen shifters, and celebrated their lives. Annabelle had performed the ceremony perfectly, a beautiful event that would stick in Andre's mind for a long time.

As far as the Games went, everyone had been having a great time. They had kicked off with the traditional deer hunt, three deer brought down and devoured in a messy feast. Then there had been a tracking challenge for the new recruits, a simple game that had required them to follow a scent across the estate, the first one to reach the goal receiving a prize.

Next was a team challenge, the wolves split into small groups, each team consisting of shifters from a variety of different Dens, and they'd been instructed to complete a series of tasks, ranging from simple tracking exercises to complex challenges in which they'd had to work together to navigate obstacles, climb trees, or move heavy objects from one place to another. The catch had been that for the entire duration of the game, all shifters had to be in wolf form, unable to communicate verbally. It was a test of team work, the teams having to manage the whole of their communication and strategy-making using only body language and wolf sounds. A few scuffles had broken out as frustrations flared, but Andre had to admit at the end of it that everyone had learned a great deal, the game as much a training exercise as it was a way to blow off steam.

And now they were in the middle of one of the most difficult exercises. It was an obstacle course, with challenges that included opening gates with complex locks, climbing ladders, crawling through tunnels and solving puzzles. Each challenge was simple enough by itself, but the trick was that each shifter was only allowed three shifts to complete the entire course. They had to choose which form to be in to begin the course, and then make careful decisions each time they wanted to shift. Did they really need their other form to complete the challenge, or could they manage it in their current form? The results were often hilarious, with wolves trying to enter codes into keypads with their claws or open boxes with their mouths, or humans trying to dig through hard ground with their fingernails to find a buried item. One shifter had even tried to complete the tarzan swing in wolf form, gripping the rope with his teeth, and then falling off halfway through when his mouth slipped, and the watching onlookers had been in fits of laughter throughout the entire day.

In truth, it was designed to test the skills of the most experienced wolves, though anyone who wanted to have a go was welcome to try, but most of the participants were inevitably forced to drop out part way through when they found a challenge impossible to complete in their current form, and were left without any more shifts available to them.

Andre had to admit he was entirely impressed with Caleb for coming up with some of the challenges. The man had been a credit to his Den throughout the entire Densmeet. He was somewhat introverted, eschewing the larger, rowdier moments, but sharing plenty of quiet conversations in smaller groups. He'd handled the planning of the Games with precision, catering to shifters of varying ability levels, and when Andre had assisted him with various tasks, he'd given clear instructions and offered heartfelt gratitude each time. All in all, he was shaping up to be a fine candidate for service to the Council, and Andre was looking forward to giving him a shining recommendation, come the conclusion of the Densmeet.

Now, Andre was watching Dee, John and two of the Russian shifters attempt to finish the course. So far Nikolai, Caroline and Sabine were the only ones to have completed it. There were a few more contestants still to go, but the field was rapidly narrowing.

Dee seemed to be stuck at a particular challenge, the task to open a box and retrieve a marble from inside. She was in wolf form – still with one shift available to her, but she'd apparently decided not to use it just yet, and Andre chuckled to himself as he imagined the conversation she was having with Faeydir about the challenge. The wolf had managed to release the lock, but now the catch was stuck, and he wondered how long she would persist before deciding to shift.

Just as he thought she was about to give up, Faeydir unexpectedly solved the problem by deliberately knocking the box to the ground. The impact jolted the catch and the box flew open, the marble rolling off into the grass. A few quick sniffs later, and Faeydir had found the object, picked it up in her mouth and deposited it into the hole that finished the challenge.

Further up, John was tackling the final challenge of the course – a ladder-bridge, laid horizontally across carefully arranged stacks of boxes. While it was an easy task in human form, he had no more shifts available, and was being forced to try and navigate the narrow, slippery rungs of the ladder on his paws instead.

But he was both patient and persistent, taking each step with the utmost care, placing one paw, testing his balance, then easing his weight forward with all the focus of a predator sneaking up on a flighty and nervous prey before lifting his next foot and repeating the exercise.

It took a long time, but at last he'd crossed the ladder, jumping down to the ground and loping across the finish line. Andre checked his time – while there was no time limit, the winner was determined by who completed the course the quickest – and noted that he was a serious contender for first place.

The watching crowd broke into applause, and Andre headed back to the start so the next contestant could begin.

By the time seven o'clock came around, the last of the shifters had either completed the course, or given up, and Andre got together with the other adjudicators to compare times. As one of their newest recruits, he was surprised to see that Dee had successfully completed the course, no doubt due in part to the ingenuity of her unique wolf. But she wasn't even close to winning the competition, her time one of the longest.

"The winner," he announced, after a brief consultation, "is Olek, with a time of twenty-three minutes and nine seconds." A cheer went up from the Ukrainians, the others congratulating him with applause and slaps on the back.

"Second place goes to John," Andre went on, "with a time of twenty-five minutes and thirteen seconds, and third place to Sabine, twenty-seven minutes forty-one. Congratulations, everyone."

"Now, before you all head off to celebrate," Baron said, "let me remind you we have a long day tomorrow. Eleanor will be arriving in the morning, and we have the scavenger hunt in the afternoon. So have a good evening, and may Sirius guard your nights."

The next morning, Baron was waiting out the front of the manor. Tank had left early to collect Eleanor from Inverness airport, the Council's private jet flying her in from Italy. Right on schedule, he heard the sound of the van approaching. In general, Baron had little time for the political intricacies of the Council, but Eleanor was a clear exception. She'd done the Den some serious favours in the past, and was a far more straight forward person than the majority of the Council members.

The van rolled to a stop, and Eleanor climbed out without waiting for Tank to open her door for her. That was another thing he liked about her, the ageing woman having no time for misguided acts of chivalry when her own independence would serve just as well.

"Good morning," she greeted him, her English flawless, if accented. "It's good to see you again."

"You too, Ma'am," Baron replied politely. "It's an honour to have you here. I hope you had a good flight."

"The Densmeet has been going well?" she asked, collecting her bag out of the van. Baron held out his hand to take it from her, but she merely smiled, and shook her head. Amused, Baron quickly led the way into the manor. It had started to drizzle, so he didn't waste any time getting inside.

"Couldn't ask for better."

Eleanor paused in the foyer. It was still early, few shifters up and about yet, and she cast a covert glance around the room, finding that they were alone for the moment.

"And how are our candidates going?" she asked softly, a question that surprised Baron. He had assumed that Andre would be giving her regular updates on both Caleb and Caroline, but he was pleased with the chance to weigh in on the subject, nonetheless.

"Better than I could have hoped. Caroline's developed quite the knack for putting out fires. Caleb's quiet, but dedicated. You have two excellent candidates right there." He paused, then asked, with a touch of concern, "How are the Council coping with all this?" He'd heard nothing from them since Andre's announcement about the death of Amedea, and knew that the past weeks had to have been rough on them.

"Bearing up well enough. These are difficult times. We've managed to settle the political issues in Italy, but there's no telling when the next drama will flare up. I've been looking forward to meeting Dee," Eleanor went on, smoothly changing the subject.

Baron smiled. "I think she's a little nervous about meeting you. And

Faeydir… well, I expect you'll be a little surprised at her wolf. Even after this long, she still comes up with odd things that surprise the rest of us."

Eleanor gave him a mysterious little smile. "Indeed. Well, let me put my things away, and then I'll join you in the dining room. I hope I'm not too late for breakfast."

In one of the offices in the Noturatii's main base, Miller sat at a long table covered with a myriad of papers, laptops, maps and diagrams. There were six other men who had been covering the Lakes District with him, frustrations growing each day as they visited property after property, and seemed no closer to solving the mystery of the second pack's location.

"We found two possible matches in the southern area," David was saying, and Miller fought to concentrate as weariness tried to overtake him. "One of the estates has been in the same family for three hundred years. The family checks out, but that doesn't mean they couldn't be harbouring shifters on the side."

"Hm, no good," Hank said, studying the map of the estate. "Too much open ground that's visible from the neighbouring property."

"Shifters have been known to work with humans," another man said, reopening a familiar argument that Miller was rapidly getting sick of. "Maybe they've befriended the neighbours."

"Or bribed them," another man put in.

"Not likely," Miller said tiredly. "You keep that shit going from generation to generation, and sooner or later, one of the grandkids is going to get suspicious and start talking. Civilians are nothing if not unreliable. What about the other property?"

"A sheep farm. Plenty of open space, but lots of forest as well."

"Wolves living with sheep?" Hank scoffed. "Come on, are you serious?"

"They're wolves with human minds," David said angrily. "Just because they eat meat doesn't mean they're going to kill their own livestock. They've got to be smart enough to cover their own tracks with a legitimate business."

The arguments had been going on for hours, one of the men putting forth a likely property, only to have the others argue him down. At this rate, they were going to cross off every single property on their list, and have nothing to show for their efforts. The shifters had to be there somewhere!

"Miller!" Miller jumped at the harsh shout, Jacob marching into the room moments later with a file in his hand, agitation written all over him. He took one look at the table, and swore blackly. "Fucking hell, are you still messing about with that bloody map? No, whatever," he snapped, when Miller went to reply. "We've got news. Take a look at this." He thrust the file at Miller. "Look!"

Opening the file, he saw that the first page was a photo of that shifter they had captured earlier in the year, the one who had escaped after the lab explosion, and he quickly turned to the next page. An image of the same man, but in a far different location than the lab. This one was in a petrol station, a large white van parked beside him, the petrol pump in his hand.

"CCTV," Jacob snapped. "Look at the location."

Miller did, turning to the next page, the report on where the photograph had come from, and when... and his jaw dropped as he took in the information.

"Scotland," he said in awe. "Inverness. Two hours ago? Are you serious?" This was big news.

"Our computers have been running facial recognition scans," Jacob informed him, all but jumping out of his skin in excitement. "The dog is in Scotland! We've managed to get our hands on some of the traffic monitoring feeds. He was heading south. We lost track of him somewhere around Tomatin."

"What the fuck are they doing in Scotland?" one of the men asked, reading the file over Miller's shoulder.

"What does it matter?" Jacob shouted. "Recruitment drive? Buying weapons? Who cares? The point is, the bastard's in Scotland, and we have a very narrow window before he disappears off the radar again. So what are you waiting for?"

Miller's mind was racing as he rapidly threw a plan together. "We'll need a strong team," he said pragmatically. "Twelve men. Guns. Explosives. Body armour. The whole bit."

"To take down one man?" someone asked incredulously.

"Who says he's only one man?" Miller replied. "He could have friends with him. And we've all seen what kind of hell breaks loose when a bunch of them get together. So I want to go prepared. No fucking this one up, you hear me?" The men around him nodded in agreement.

"And I want dogs," he added, turning to Jacob. "The shifters can fight in wolf form, so we're going to need to level the playing field."

"On that note," one of the men interrupted, "Research and Development have been working on a little experiment. We read the reports of the attack on the lab. It said that the wolves were wearing body armour. So we've put together a little gift." He tapped a few keys on his computer, and then spun it around. On the screen was an image of a Rottweiler, one of the Noturatii's trained scent dogs... and he was wearing a Kevlar vest.

"Oh, get out of town! That's brilliant."

"Move," Jacob ordered sharply, shoving Miller away from his computer. He scanned through a few files, checked a staff log, and sat back with a look of glee on his face. "We have six dogs that can be at the base and ready to roll within two hours. Think that'll be enough?"

"Perfect," Miller replied. "We'll need a plane to get us to Inverness. It would take too long to drive."

"Done," Jacob promised, typing rapidly into the computer.

"All right, everyone," Miller told the men waiting eagerly all around the table. "Hank, get the rest of Delta Squad and meet me at the weapons store. David, you're on logistics. Find the last known location of that van and see if you can work out where it was headed. Adrian, meet the dog handlers as they come in and brief them on the situation. We've got two hours until we roll, people. Move it!"

# CHAPTER TWENTY-FIVE

Cassandra Morris stared at the trees around her in dismay. She checked her phone again, praying that the thing would miraculously start working, but the screen remained stubbornly blank, the battery having gone flat about fifteen minutes ago.

She was an idiot, she acknowledged to herself, glancing around again, hoping that something would look familiar.

But no luck.

She'd been so excited about this trip, the end of high school, a week away camping with her friends, and from the campsite, she'd spotted a high peak in the hills that had looked perfect for a photo of the scenery.

The climb up here had been long, but not too strenuous, the ground rocky, the bushes becoming gradually thicker until she'd emerged out the top of the trees to see what was an even more beautiful view than she had imagined.

All had been going well… until she'd gone to climb back down, and realised that she had no idea which way she'd come.

She cursed under her breath, trying to remember the layout of the camp site, any landmarks that might set her on the right path.

Nothing.

Fuck.

Oh well, she sighed to herself. This wasn't the most remote part of Scotland, after all. There were farms and houses dotted throughout the countryside, and if she was careful, if she started walking now, then it was only a matter of time before she had to run into one of them.

Picking a direction at random, she set off down the hill. She checked the position of the sun, to make sure she didn't end up walking in circles, and resolved to keep a positive outlook. All she had to do was find a road. A walking track. Another hiker who could tell her where to go. It was summer, after all, and Scotland was chock full of tourists this time of year.

Keep your chin up, she told herself, refusing to give in to the fear that niggled at the back of her mind. And next time, she must pay more attention to where she was going. Or better yet, not leave the path in the first place.

Fifty-five shifters were gathered out the front of the manor, ready and raring for the last of the Games to begin.

This final challenge was a scavenger hunt, a series of tasks outlined on a list that had been given to each group. Some were simple – collect a pine cone, for example, or find a flower of a particular type, while others were more challenging – form a wolf pyramid, standing on each other's backs, or catch a fish from the river. Each task accumulated points – more points for the tougher tasks – and there was a strict time limit. Every wolf on the team had to be back at the starting point in exactly two hours, or severe penalties were imposed for each minute they were late. It was a game of strategy as much as one of skill, as each team had to decide which tasks would take the least time to complete, and yet earn them the most points.

They were split into six teams, each team containing a mix of wolves of different rank, varying ability and with a range of ages. They were allowed to shift as many times as they liked, but at the same time, each team contained at least one person who didn't speak the language of the others. Each team had been given a backpack to store their collected items and a camera to take photographic evidence of their other feats.

As he wasn't officially a member of any of the Dens, Andre had been disqualified from entering most of the Games, but Nikolai had argued for his inclusion in this one, something the other shifters had enthusiastically agreed to, though to even out the odds, he'd been put on a team with George, the oldest and weakest wolf, so that his exceptional skills wouldn't give his team too great an advantage.

Once again, the game wasn't just for fun – it was a test of skill and teamwork, and the prize for each member of the winning team was a £100 online shopping voucher.

Caleb stood to one side, Eleanor beside him – the two of them the only shifters not participating in the game – and waited while the teams looked over their lists of tasks and debated where to begin. The estate was expansive, with several miles to run to get to some of the tasks at the far side, and back again, and he checked his watch, counting down to three o'clock, the official starting time for the game.

"One minute," he called, glancing around the huddled groups. The muttering from each team stepped up a notch, then the shifters spread out, each team having chosen an objective and selected the best route to get to their first challenge.

"Ten seconds," Caleb called, and the last of the shifters took on their wolf form, ready for a mad sprint into the forest.

"Five, four, three, two, one. Go!"

With a chorus of barking and growling, the wolves took off, several of them actually tripping over each other as they raced for the forest, and beside him, Eleanor let out a laugh.

"Ten pounds says Andre's team wins," she murmured to him, as she watched the wolves disappear, and Caleb was surprised. He hadn't taken the elegant, poised woman to be the betting type.

"I'll put my money on Nikolai's team," he said with a grin. "That man's got more tricks up his sleeve than a magician on show night."

Eleanor laughed. "That he does. All right," she said, turning to him and offering her hand for him to shake. "You're on."


Cassandra was breathing hard as she slogged her way to the top of a hill. This landscape was deceptive. The wide open spaces made things look closer together than they really were, and she'd decided to climb this hill to get a better view of her surroundings, thinking it would only be a short, ten minute climb.

It must have been twenty minutes later when she staggered to the top, sweat pouring from her, making her wish she'd brought more than just her small water bottle with her. She seemed to have been walking for hours, though without her phone working, she had no real way of knowing the time. So far she'd found nothing of any use, no roads, no signs of habitation, just endless forest and open fields dotted with sheep.

Surely it couldn't be much further now?

But when she reached the top of the hill, her heart sank. She'd come to a stone wall, a good sign, as it meant she was probably on farm land and could surely follow the wall to some sort of dwelling. But attached to the wall was a large sign, proclaiming in bold, red letters 'PRIVATE PROPERTY. KEEP OUT'. There was a length of barbed wire running above the wall, just in case anyone got any ideas about trespassing, and Cassandra stood there for a long moment, weighing up the pros and cons of entering the property.

She looked down at the broad valley below her... and there! Through the trees, she spotted a roof. And then more of the building – a large manor, by the looks of it, several miles off, but it was still her closest option for finding her way back to her friends. And while the occupants of the property were likely private people and wouldn't be happy with an uninvited guest, she was sure that once she'd explained that she'd got lost while hiking and only needed to find her way home again, they couldn't be too angry with her.

Satisfied with her new plan of action, she carefully climbed the wall, squeezing between the rough stones and the barbed wire, taking care not to rip her clothes in the process. Then she dropped to the ground on the far side, stumbling as the hill headed downwards in a steep incline, and resumed her trudging walk. At least this part was downhill, she thought, heading for the valley floor and across the centre of the property.

Not much further, she told herself cheerfully. Just a half-hour more, and she would be on her way back to camp, a good meal and a warm fire waiting for her.

Skip slithered down the tree, careful to keep from scraping her legs on the rough bark. She'd just completed the latest task for her team – climbing a tree to a height of at least five metres, and Alexei had snapped a photo of her once she was at the top.

She reached the lowest branch and Tank reached up, catching her slight weight as she slid off the branch and lowering her to the ground. He'd given her a boost up as well, the lowest branch too high for her to reach, and she'd felt as light as a feather as his powerful arms had lifted her.

The next task on their list was to try and fit their entire team into a hollow log. Apparently Alexei knew where one was, the team having taken to communicating via hand drawn pictures, since he spoke almost no English and Nikolai was stationed on a different team, unable to translate for him. Stowing the camera, they all shifted into wolf form and took off towards the clearing at the centre of the estate. The log was at the far end... but Skip had barely taken two steps when a large wolf leapt out of a bush to her right, with a flurry of teeth and loud snarling, and she leapt a foot in the air, yelping in fright. An instant later, Tank was right back beside her... but even as her heart raced, Skip was aware of the sly click of a camera, and she realised she'd just helped Nikolai's team complete another of their tasks.

Tank, too, realised what had happened before he caused Nikolai any serious damage, and the rest of his team emerged from the bushes, snickering in wolf form before shifting and laughing out loud.

'Scare one of the other teams' was on the list of things to do, and Skip tried to look annoyed as she picked herself up off the ground and shifted.

"Very well done! Show me picture," Nikolai said, laughing, then he bowed to Skip, hand over his heart. "My apologies, little wolf. But you scare so well! Look at your face!"

Skip did, the rest of her team crowding around to peer at the camera, and indeed, her wolf was wearing a twisted expression of utter horror, tongue flopping sideways, eyes opened comically wide.

Revenge was in order, and she glanced sideways at Tank, receiving a nod in return, even as she continued to feign interest in the photo. 'Steal a shoe from another team' was also on the list, and Nikolai had just volunteered for the task.

In a flash, Tank had tackled the man, flipping him upside down and ripping his shoe off. And then, before the rest of his team could come to his defence, Tank shoved the shoe inside his jacket and shifted, the shoe vanishing along with the rest of Tank's clothing.

So that the other team couldn't return the favour, Skip and the rest of her team mates shifted in a heartbeat, their shoes now safely out of reach of the others, and Nikolai swore fluently in Ukrainian as he picked himself up off the ground.

"Oh, very funny," he said, trying to sound angry despite his amusement. "But you wait and see. Nikolai has a few more tricks up his sleeve. You will see."

Down by the river, Caroline was trying to concentrate. The younger wolves on her team – Kwan, Aaron and one of the Russians – were busy building a tower of rocks. The team with the highest tower was the only one to get points for this particular challenge, and they'd taken to the task with diligence... and a little illicit ingenuity, propping up sections of the tower with sticks, filling in cracks with leaves, and even using mud as makeshift cement to hold the thing together. It was nearly a metre tall by now – surely tall enough to win the points – and, less interested in this particular challenge herself, Caroline had volunteered to keep watch while they were busy. There were various tasks on the list that involved ambushing or stealing from other teams, and at the start, she'd been keeping a close eye on the surrounding area, so that no sly wolf would be able to sneak up on them.

Now though, she was finding it hard to pay attention, an entirely distracting sight taking place a short way off. Not thirty metres from where she stood, Andre's team had arrived. The trees here were well spaced, giving them plenty of room to grow their branches outwards as well as up, and apparently Andre had been chosen to complete his team's task of having someone climb a tree.

He'd removed his jacket, gun holster and the larger of his knives – for all that they were on their own territory, the more senior members of the pack were always, *always* armed. And he'd laid the weapons reverently on the ground, giving stern orders to George to guard them with his life. He'd nodded solemnly, and had faithfully stood guard ever since, not taking a single step away from the pile.

But after a few moments, Caroline had paid no more attention to the weapons lying on the ground. The sight in the air was far more captivating.

Covered now in only a t-shirt that made his muscles stand out in defined ridges, Andre had lithely leapt for the lowest branch, hauling himself up with no more effort than it took Caroline to lift a loaf of bread. He'd climbed quickly, checking each hand and foothold, each movement smooth and deliberate, his balance perfect, and he'd made the whole thing look so damned easy.

God, she needed to get the man out of her head, Caroline thought, aware that even as she scolded herself, she was still watching him climb back down, one of his team mates having taken the required photo. Smooth, controlled, he seemed to *flow* down the tree, rather than climb. In no time at all, he was perched on the lowest branch, jumping down and landing in a perfect crouch, his thighs momentarily hugged by his trousers in a way that was thoroughly indecent. He tossed his shoulder length hair out of his face in an entirely masculine gesture, and Caroline forced herself to look away.

Too late, though, to avoid being caught by her own team. The young Russian had seen her watching, and he smirked at her, not unkindly, but with the knowing look of one who sympathised with her, but was amused nonetheless. He said something in Russian and let out a dramatic sigh, patting Caroline on the shoulder. 'Ah, young love,' he could well have said, and then laughed when Caroline felt her face heat.

"Are you done?" she snapped at Kwan and Aaron, perhaps more sharply than she'd intended, and they both nodded.

"There's a bird's nest in the holly bush near the eastern cottage," Kwan announced, stowing the camera after taking a shot of their prized tower and checking the list. "We need a photo of one, so we should head there next."

# CHAPTER TWENTY-SIX

Miller was about ready to scream in frustration. After the dogs had arrived, his team – eight men including himself, plus the six dogs handlers – had rushed to the airport and taken the plane to Inverness, landing in the early afternoon. Three SUVs were waiting for them when they arrived, and they'd all piled in, driving at breakneck speeds to the last known location of the mysterious van that the shifter had been driving.

But that was as far as they'd got. A check in with the nearby stores and petrol stations had yielded nothing, nor had talking to the locals. No one had seen the man, or noticed the van. Plenty of white vans around, after all, one man had observed drily, and Miller was infuriated at the idea that they could be so close, and let the man slip through their fingers once again.

They were making one last stop at the local supermarket before they gave up, Miller asking to see the manager and showing him the man's picture. A shrug and a shake of the head sealed the deal – they were getting nowhere here – when one of the delivery staff happened to walk in the door. He hesitated when he saw Miller and one of his team standing around – they were both tall, intimidating men – but then the manager called him over.

"Hey, Bob, you know this guy?" he asked in a thick Scottish accent, and the delivery guy gave the photo a cursory glance… and then took a longer look.

"Why do you need to know?" he asked, and Miller immediately knew he had seen the shifter.

"These gentlemen are looking for him," the manager said, nodding to Miller and his partner.

"And you are?" the man asked, not rudely, but with the natural caution of one dealing with intimidating strangers.

"Oh, excuse me," Miller said, pulling out his fake police badge quickly.

"Detective Ashton."

The man raised an eyebrow at that. "This guy in some sort of trouble?"

Miller thought fast. If he was reading the man correctly, he was likely friends with this shifter, whether or not he knew the truth of what he was, and was just as likely to try and protect him if he perceived Miller as a threat. "No, not in trouble," he said quickly. "We need to contact him concerning a member of his family. Rather urgently, actually." He was becoming rather an expert at pulling lies out of his arse, but the stories he concocted worked more often than not.

"Oh," the man said, frowning with concern. "Then yeah, I've seen him. A couple of weeks ago, up on the Windybyrne Estate. You know the one?"

"I'm sorry, I don't."

"Not many folk do. They're the private type, keep to themselves. We did a big grocery delivery there a little while back. That guy was helping us unload. Here, I'll get you the address."

Minutes later, Miller was off again, his heart racing, adrenaline pumping, the two other cars screaming along behind him.

Hurtling up to the front door was a bad move – aside from the lack of surprise, the shifters could have humans on the property working with them, and while the Noturatii had no problems with shooting civilians on principle, it was to be avoided where possible. Dead bodies tended to attract attention, after all, and a big part of their job was keeping the existence of the shifters a secret from the general public.

So after checking the address, and then consulting a map of the local landscape, they'd settled on a more covert plan. One edge of the estate ran close to a public road, a narrow lane that led nowhere in particular, and wasn't likely to have much traffic even at the busiest times of year.

They pulled up at the designated spot, leaping out of the vans and rapidly donning Kevlar vests, helmets, arming themselves with multiple weapons. Miller was taking no chances this time around. He'd seen the destruction that the shifters could achieve back in the lab, and while he expected no more than half a dozen shifters at most – assuming they didn't hit the jackpot and find their missing captive alone – he'd brought along a full squad of fourteen men and six dogs.

The dog handlers strapped the custom made Kevlar vests onto their animals, not just covering their torsos, but caps that protected the dogs' heads as well – a design that had been taken directly from the shifters' own use of canine body armour.

Once they were all ready, Miller led the squad to the edge of the property and scanned the landscape. They were at the end of a wide valley, forest covering a large portion of it, a clearing visible through small breaks in the foliage.

Then he froze, listening intently… There, in the distance! Barks. A short howl. The tell-tale sounds of the presence of shifters.

"Let's go," he ordered, gun at the ready. "Straight down the hill to the edge of that clearing. Be ready for anything. There's no telling what these animals are capable of."

Reaching the bottom of the hill, Cassandra paused to check her direction. Yup, she was still going the right way. She could just see the top of one of the turrets on the manor through the trees, the sun still to her left. She opened her water bottle and drained the last of the liquid, not so worried about conserving it now that she was within reach of a house.

Her path was taking her along the edge of a wide clearing, but she kept to the trees as she went, not wanting to take the slightest chance at being distracted and losing her way again.

She'd just about made it past the clearing and was about to start climbing the hill again, when movement caught her eye. She paused and looked out across the field. Maybe it was a deer? Or a flock of birds? But no, she realised, as she peered through the leaves to get a better look. On the far side, there was a tall, blond man, who looked like he was taking a photo of something. Oh thank goodness! She was found at last! She was about to head over to him, to ask for his help, when a large dog bounded out from inside a fallen tree not five metres from where the man was standing.

Cassandra hesitated at that. She wasn't generally afraid of dogs, but on a private property like this, it was possible they were guard dogs – particularly one of that size – and she didn't fancy being bitten for trespassing before she had the chance to explain herself to the dog's owners.

Then a second dog bounded out of the tree, then a third… holy crap, there were seven of them! What the hell kind of dogs were they, anyway, she wondered. They were a mix of grey and brown. The brown ones looked like some sort of hound, but the grey ones… if she didn't know better, she would have said they were… wolves? That couldn't be right. There were no wolves in Scotland. And there was certainly no way people would be allowed to just keep them as pets.

But then as she watched, one of the smaller wolves approached the man and…

Cassandra nearly fainted. The wolf had just… No, it couldn't be. Wolves didn't just turn into humans. It was impossible.

Was she dreaming? Hallucinating? What the hell was going on here?

Miller gestured for his men to wait as they approached the edge of the clearing. They'd moved quickly at first, then a lot slower as they got closer, not wanting to give themselves away too soon. The ground was littered with leaves and keeping their footsteps quiet was a painstaking exercise in patience. There were plenty of rocks and shrubs to use as cover, but they moved with the utmost caution, knowing that the wolves had excellent hearing and eyesight well accustomed to pinpointing prey.

Finally, they reached a rocky outcrop a few metres from the forest's edge, and paused to assess their enemy.

There were eight of them. More than he'd expected, but then again, that's why he'd brought a sizable squad with him. To be prepared for anything. He signalled for four of the men and two of the dogs to circle around and flank the group, then settled down to assess their capabilities.

Their escaped captive was in human form, seeming to tease a young woman as she danced around him, trying to get a hold of something in his hands, and Miller watched in consternation as the pair struggled. Several men and several more wolves stood around them, laughing and joking, and something about the scene struck an unexpected chord. This was the man who had withstood torture, stared down his enemies from inside a steel cage, shot a man in the head in cold blooded murder and promised Miller himself that one day they would settle their differences in a fight to the death. And here he was, playing with a young woman, a teenager maybe, the girl holding no fear either of the man, or of the wolves standing around her.

"Sir?" Hank whispered from beside him. "When you're ready."

Miller was about to signal the attack when one of the wolves suddenly shifted, turning into a middle aged woman. As before when he'd seen the animals shift, the sight was both startling and captivating, the transition smooth and effortless, unnatural, and yet the most beautiful thing in the world. The woman had long, flaxen hair, an indulgent smile on her lips, and she scolded the escapee, causing his shoulders to sag almost comically as he pouted and handed over whatever it was he had to the young woman.

It was like watching a family picnic. Friendly rivalry, good natured teasing, some of them playing while others stood around patiently and waited for the others to get on with things. And it struck him once again that there was so much he didn't know about these people. After the lab had blown up and Melissa had been shot, he'd been furious, putting aside his curiosity to focus on his job, on paying back the damage they had done. He'd lost good friends in the explosion, and that anger and grief had kept him from thinking too deeply about the shifters themselves for a while.

Now, though, after crossing more than half of Britain to get here, and summoning a small army to take them out, he was dismayed to find himself suddenly having second thoughts.

The girl in particular was a concern. Either they were going to kill her, or she would be captured and taken back to the lab. He shuddered to think what Jacob would do to her once she was there, but the thought of simply shooting her horrified him. She was so young. So innocent…

"Sir?"

"On my count," Miller murmured, shoving his misgivings aside and holding up three fingers. Two. One.

The men moved as a single unit, up and out of cover in a split second, guns drawn, dogs straining on the ends of their leashes as Miller aimed his gun straight at the escapee and yelled, "Freeze! Nobody move or you all die!"


Tank had fired his first shot before he even knew he'd drawn his gun, taking out one of the men who had appeared like ghosts out of the forest. He shoved Skip behind a tree, then dived for cover himself, a bullet grazing his shoulder, and he watched one of the Polish shifters go down. The rest of them scattered, and he cursed, popping off round after round as he realised that he and Marianne, the alpha female from the Norwegian Den, were the only ones who had guns. Fuck!

But the others weren't going to let that stop them, he realised with a rush of dread. One of the Russians, still in wolf form, went for one of the men, leaping for his throat, a hideous, gurgling scream emerging from the man before he died. But then one of the man's team mates shot the Russian.

Tank took out another man, then spun around as Skip screamed. She was staring behind them, and he realised there were more of them in that direction. But that wasn't the worst of the day's surprises.

Beside the men, straining at the end of their leads, were six dogs. Huge dogs, mastiffs and Rottweilers… and they had Kevlar body armour covering them from head to tail. Tank ejected his clip, reloaded the gun, and cursed with every foul word he knew.


Peering into the bush where Kwan insisted there was a bird's nest, the sound of the first gunshot made Caroline's head snap around. She was in wolf form an instant later, head cocked, ears twitching as she sought out the source of the sound.

The second shot had her bolting through the trees, heading for the clearing without a second thought. The rest of her team were at her heels, camera and backpack abandoned, game forgotten.

As she ran, they crossed paths with a dozen more wolves. There was Baron, his wolf huge and black in the undergrowth. Silas and Annabelle, Nikolai right behind them, more wolves rushing down from higher up the hill.

Howls started up throughout the forest a moment later, positioning calls as the entire pack worked to locate each other, to determine the source of the gunshots.

And then a sound that had Caroline doubling her speed, heedless of the danger she was running into. The sound of a scream, and after eight years of living under the same roof, her heart was in her throat as she recognised Skip's anguished voice echoing off the hills.

Cassandra watched the wolf-humans in horrified fascination. Several more of them changed into people, and her mind raced to try to make sense of what she had just stumbled into. Was this some bizarre science experiment? A testing lab for a new chemical weapon? Super soldiers being bred for an undercover war?

She had just about made up her mind to turn around and get the hell out of here, back up the hill the way she'd come, when the other men arrived, soldiers, by the look of them, dressed in camouflage green and carrying military style guns. For a split second, she thought maybe this was a war game, a training exercise for a covert arm of Britain's army…

Until the first shots were fired, and all hell broke loose. A scream lodged in her throat before she could give it voice as she saw one of the werewolves get shot, another one returning fire, and she sank to her knees, petrified into immobility, her mind scrambling for a prayer that would let her reach the end of the day alive.

Waiting with Eleanor by the manor, Caleb frowned as a harsh noise ricocheted off the hills. "What the hell…?" He jumped to his feet, abandoning the coffee they'd been sharing. "Is that… gunshots?"

Eleanor joined him, listening carefully. The first few shots were quickly followed by a volley of rapid fire, and there was no more denying it.

"We're under attack," Eleanor concluded quickly. "Go. They'll need your help."

But Caleb shook his head. "You're a Councillor. I am not leaving you here undefended-"

"Your pack is in danger," Eleanor insisted. "And I'm not nearly as fragile as I look. No one joins the Council without being a seasoned warrior. And I come with my own protection," she added, pulling aside the edge of her jacket to reveal a handgun.

Caleb glanced off into the forest again, then back at Eleanor, torn between two equally vital duties.

"Go!" Eleanor snapped, pulling out her gun and heading for the manor – as defensible a spot as she was likely to find, and that made up Caleb's mind.

Already running for the forest, he checked the gun at his side, the extra clip in his pocket, and then he was running on wolf feet instead, his howls joining the melodic echo filling the forest, a haunting backdrop to the drums of war.

Miller wasn't surprised when the shifters scattered and returned fire. He dived for cover behind a rock and lined up each shot carefully. While he was under orders to capture as many of the animals as possible, it was a foregone conclusion that some of them would die. But even so, he tried to aim for non-fatal shots, leg wounds, abdominal wounds that would disable the shifters, but that could be treated once they got them back to the Noturatii base.

His heart rate kicked up a notch when the shifters in wolf form attacked his men – they had a suicidal kind of courage, and he rapidly reassessed his expectations of the fight. The escapee had taken shelter behind a rock, the young woman behind a tree, but even though he was reluctant to hurt her, he knew his men wouldn't share his reservations. Suddenly one of them leapt up and dashed for the girl, grabbing her in a headlock and using her as a shield as he fired at the others.

Five of the eight shifters were on the ground by now, two injured, three dead, and he was struggling to focus on the others…

All at once, the sound of howling filled his ears. He should have expected that, he berated himself mentally. There was no reason to think they would all be in one place. But he'd come here expecting four or five of them, and finding eight at once had made him assume they'd found the whole group.

But no, he realised, his blood turning cold in his veins. That wasn't the sound of one or two extra wolves. The hills echoed with howls, the sound of heavy bodies crashing through the undergrowth, the noise coming ever closer. And Miller realised just how big a mistake he had made. Wolves flooded out of the forest, filling the clearing, racing towards him and his men. A dozen. Two dozen. Thirty of them…

Holy fuck, he thought, slamming another clip into his gun. They'd stumbled into a fucking shifter convention. There must be fifty of them, all swarming out of the hills, hell bent on ending his life, and the lives of his teammates.

There was only one chance for survival now, and he dared to take his eyes off the shifters for a moment, glancing around at his squad. Six dogs, Rottweilers and mastiffs. The biggest, meanest, toughest animals they could get their hands on. He had to force his throat to start working as his fear tried to smother the sound before it could escape.

"Release the dogs!"

# CHAPTER TWENTY-SEVEN

It took Silas only a split second to assess the battlefield as he raced into the clearing, and a moment later he'd changed course, heading back into the tree line, closing the distance between himself and the Noturatii where there was more cover.

Tank was already putting his gun to good use, he was glad to see. Two of the Noturatii were already dead, but so were some of the wolves. He glanced around, looking for suitable cover where he could shift and make use of his own gun... but then he saw the man holding Skip hostage. He'd backed himself up to a large rock, using it to cover his back while Skip was used as a body shield... and Silas saw red. No one harmed Skip. Ever.

He darted behind a tree and shifted, aware that he was partially exposed in his current location and dismissing it as a mere inconvenience, and he lined up a shot. The men wore helmets, body armour, but their faces were still exposed, and it was the work of a mere moment to pull the trigger, planting a bullet in the man's right eye, Skip not even flinching as the bullet came within an inch of her ear. The man tumbled to the ground, dragging Skip down with him, but Silas was on them a moment later, grabbing Skip's arm and pulling her to her feet. She came willingly. She wasn't the most experienced in battle, and certainly not a strong fighter, but she'd been trained in what to do in these situations, and he was relieved to see that she didn't seem put out by the rough treatment. He pulled out his second gun and thrust it at her.

"Take this," he told her, "and get back to the manor."

Skip didn't argue, just took the gun and checked for an escape route, then began a careful withdrawal up the hill.

Now, Silas thought, taking cover behind the rock and scanning the field. Who would be the next to die?

Baron hurtled onto the battle field, outraged that his pack was being attacked on their own turf. How the hell had the Noturatii found them? He could see six men, assumed there were more hiding in the rocks and bushes, and mentally ran through a list of who would be armed among his own pack. Caroline, Tank and Silas would have guns. Annabelle, Marianne, Nikolai. Andre, of course. There was a chance some of the others from the foreign Dens would have guns as well, but the bulk of their number were unarmed, and would be forced to fight in wolf form, if they were to have any chance of success. But wolves could still be taken out by bullets, and-

Baron's blood ran cold as he suddenly saw the dogs, released from their leashes and rushing to meet the wolves head on. Oh fuck. Six of them, and that was enough to make even him hesitate. He was a big wolf – many of those with him were, their size on average larger than the grey wolves of the wild – but even so, Rottweilers and mastiffs outweighed them all. There was only one way they were going to win this fight, and he didn't hesitate to put it to use now.

He dived for cover behind a tree, shifted and glanced around, spotting John racing down the hill a little to his right. "John!" he yelled at the top of his voice. "Dogs!"

John's childhood had been brutal beyond all reason. He'd been converted young, and from the time he was a teenager, his wolf had been used for sport as a fighting dog, battling against big, mean brutes bred for nothing but killing. But against all odds, he had survived. Which meant he was one of the few wolves here capable of bringing down a Rottweiler by himself.

John slowed a fraction, assessing the risks, choosing a target, and a look of unholy glee appeared on the wolf's face. Then he barked, increased his speed and flung himself into battle, tackling two of the dogs at once.

Baron shifted again a moment later, knowing that odds of six to one were a death sentence even for a seasoned fighter like John, and he felt a rush of relief as he saw Nikolai heading towards them. He was a big wolf, not quite as large as Baron, but solidly built, more muscular than the average shifter, as the grey wolves were naturally lean, and he'd more than pull his weight in a fight against the dogs. He was in human form at the moment, keeping the trees between himself and the Noturatii as he approached, and he paused behind a large pine, glanced out, and then fired a shot. Baron saw a man fall to the ground a short distance away, glad that one more of their enemy was dead… and then he stopped in his tracks, standing dumbly in the middle of the battle and risking getting himself shot as he stared at Nikolai in disbelief.

After shooting the man, Nikolai had looked around, seen the dog bearing down on one of the Russian shifters, and… vanished. A light crackle of electricity was the only sign that he'd ever been there, and then he reappeared a moment later, right beside the dog, leaping up to catch its throat in his jaws as the dog seemed as stunned by his sudden appearance as Baron was.

Holy fuck, Andre had been right. Nikolai had learned to teleport! Baron's surprise lasted only a moment longer, as he saw another dog heading for Aaron, and sprinted towards him to cut it off. But the dogs had the advantage here, he realised. Size and numbers aside, they wore body armour, greatly reducing the target area where the wolves could get a grip on them, the parts of their body they could bite and tear.

The Noturatii had prepared well for this, he acknowledged with a heavy heart. And he sent a prayer to Sirius to receive him with honour into the afterlife.

Fucking hell, where were all the wolves coming from, Miller thought desperately, shoving another clip into his gun. There were more and more of them, flowing like water out of the trees, and he watched as three of them tackled one of his men, gore spraying and a blood-chilling scream cut off with a gurgling sound.

There were a dozen shifters with guns, back in human form, firing from behind rocks and trees, but they almost needn't have bothered. The wolves worked as a team, a true pack mentality at work here, small groups breaking off to circle around one of his men and cut him off, using distraction and harassment techniques to keep him off balance until one of them could go in for the kill.

He glanced around for the young woman he'd seen before, horrified at the thought of her being killed in this bloodbath, but she was nowhere to be found. Did that mean she was alive and in hiding, or lying dead in a bush somewhere? His gut churned with uncertainty, and he fought to keep himself focused on the fight.

There was that warrior woman he'd seen back in the lab, dressed in black leather and sheltering behind a fallen log as she kneecapped one of his soldiers, sending him to the ground for the wolves to finish off.

And holy fuck, there was Trench-Coat, minus the coat this time, but the last time Miller had seen him, he'd been using explosive-tipped arrows to blow up half the lab. He was every bit as lethal now, calm and controlled in the midst of battle, ignoring a bullet that caught his arm as he shot a soldier right between the eyes.

Miller glanced around for his men, and a cold weight settled in his chest. There were only three of them left now, including Miller. And he himself was still alive only by virtue of his vantage point, nestled in between a cluster of rocks that made it difficult for even the wolves to sneak up on him.

But there were dozens of shifters left, though a handful of furry bodies lay dead on the damp grass, and Miller imagined he could hear a bell tolling, a long way off, a distant echo through the hills. *Ask not for whom the bell tolls,* he recited morbidly. *It tolls for thee.*

John grappled with the two dogs in front of him. One was a Rottweiler, a huge ball of solid muscle, strong, but not as quick as he could have been. John darted in, grabbed his leg and bit down, then released the limb a split second later, bolting away while the dogs gave chase, then spinning back to attack again.

If he'd been fighting just one dog, it was a simple case of go for the throat and hold on. Once his jaws were in place, is was just a question of time before he managed to cut off the dog's air supply.

But when fighting multiple targets, focusing on just one left you vulnerable to the others. So a quick strike and retreat strategy was needed.

Baron and Nikolai were tackling a mastiff together, struggling to reach the throat with all the Kevlar in the way. And Tank was in the thick of it now, blood turning his white fur red. He'd grabbed onto a dog's leg, biting hard, working his jaws until the limb was nothing but a mangled strip of flesh. But the need to tackle the dogs created a serious risk - while the wolves were fighting with them, it left them exposed to the guns of the Noturatii.

John dashed forward again, using his smaller size and greater speed to grab a dog's throat as he slid beneath him, latching onto loose skin and ripping. It wasn't a deep wound, hadn't got anywhere near the arteries or veins yet, but it was a start. And his next bite on that flap of skin would go deeper.

Patience, John reminded himself, suddenly feeling claustrophobic and trapped. He was in a field, he reminded himself, as the next dog came for him. Not in a fighting cage. These were his pack mates around him, not leering spectators placing bets on which dog would be the one to tear him to shreds. The old scars on his body pinched as he remembered the wounds that had caused them, the teeth and claws that had paid no mind to the fact that he wasn't a mindless beast, but half human.

He sent a prayer skyward as he prepared for the next attack. But it wasn't a prayer for Sirius to receive him into the afterlife, though he knew that was the customary request when facing a battle that one wasn't likely to win. Instead, he asked for strength, for courage, for a cold brutality to rival that of his enemies. He would bring glory to the House of Sirius, not by dying with honour, but by painting the ground with the blood of the Noturatii.

Andre fired at one of the dogs fighting John. There were four left now, and only three Noturatii men. The bullet hit the edge of the Kevlar vest, making Andre curse in Italian. Such a small target, and a constantly moving one… even with his skills, it would be more luck than anything if he managed to hit something vital on the raging animals.

He longed to shift, to go and fight the dogs as a wolf, but with three armed men still lurking amongst the rocks, he didn't dare leave them unattended.

He skirted around to his right, keeping low, behind the rocks as much as possible. There was one, his back to Andre, shooting at the wolves trying to fight the dogs. He waited, and then got a split second window as the man altered his position slightly. It exposed his neck for half a second, but that was more than enough. Andre's bullet slid through skin and muscle, neatly severing the carotid artery, and the man went down in a gurgle of blood and foam. Two more to go. Not long now…

Racing through the forest, Caleb made a beeline for the clearing at the bottom of the valley. Moments ago, he'd run across Skip, heading back up the hill with a gun in her hand and a terrified look on her face. He'd intercepted her – in wolf form, so she wouldn't be alarmed, thinking he was a soldier come to attack her – and then he'd shifted, checking whether she was hurt, and listening as she blurted out a hasty report on the situation down below. Noturatii. Guns. Dogs. She wasn't clear on the finer details, and Caleb didn't wait to hear more. He was off again in a heartbeat, back in wolf form, preparing himself for the carnage that waited below…

What the hell…?

Caleb slowed to a halt, his feet suddenly silent on the bare earth in this part of the forest. There was a woman crouched in the bushes ahead of him, and at first he thought it must be one of the shifters, one not skilled at fighting, trying to retreat, as Skip had done. There was no shame in recognising that a battle was beyond one's capabilities, after all.

But there was something furtive about this woman, and as he got closer, he realised he didn't recognise her. He sniffed deliberately, letting the light breeze carry her scent to him… Human! And from the looks of her, not one of the Noturatii.

What the hell was a human doing on the estate? She was staring at the battle, so he knew she'd seen the shifters, the guns, and the secrets that could not be allowed to escape.

Caleb rose up to his full height, raised his hackles, and growled.

Cassandra spun around with a cry as she heard the low growl behind her, and she was on her feet in an instant, adrenaline overcoming her paralysed fear as she faced the beast that stood not five metres from where she hid. She backed up a step or two, stopping when she felt the bush behind her. Where could she go? She went to move right, but the wolf moved with her, head low, teeth bared...

In a sudden burst of panic, Cassandra broke cover and ran, trying to head up the hill, but every time she found a gap in the undergrowth, the wolf was right there, blocking her way. So she ran through the tree line at the edge of the clearing, blind panic setting in, the men and the guns and the other wolves forgotten as she desperately sought a path to escape her own grizzly death.

## 14 Years Ago

Andre stepped into the cold, stone-walled room, feeling his heart beating in his chest. But far from the rapid thudding of a terrified rabbit that had expected, he was quietly shocked to know that it beat with its usual slow, steady rhythm, his breathing quiet and regular, the gun in his hand a familiar weight, as if it was an extension of his own arm. His mind, on the other hand, was being nowhere near as obedient as his body.

Inside one of the iron cages was a woman, twenty-four years old, by the name of Lorne. She was lying on the bed, unconscious, as she'd been drugged to make this as easy on her as possible. Her hands were tied behind her back, her clothing stained with mud, her hair a bedraggled mess.

She'd been a new recruit from the Den in Germany, joining the shifters eagerly, completing her training with enthusiasm... until she'd hit the six month mark in her first year, and suddenly changed her mind. She'd tried to run away, getting only as far as the nearest town before the Den's alpha had caught up with her and dragged her back, and then handed her over to the Council when she couldn't be reasoned with.

After two weeks during which a diplomat for the Council had tried to talk her through her doubts and fears, she'd tried to run away again, and the Council had finally called for Andre.

He approached the cage, and a burly guard unlocked the door. Andre stepped inside and looked down at the woman, taking a deep breath, his heart still beating slow and regular, his hands steady, his skin cool. Could he do it, he wondered silently? Two Council members were at the door, watching. The guard waited beside the cage. Could he really kill this woman, unarmed and completely helpless?

He raised his gun, aiming straight for the middle of her forehead. A quick, painless death, the final grim mercy he was able to offer her. She would not suffer. Il Trosa had no regard for torture as punishment, never prolonged the death of even one of their worst enemies for longer than was absolutely necessary. Others might torture, might take pleasure in the pain of others, but Il Trosa would stand by its honour, regardless of the hellish morals of others.

A wave of nausea hit him suddenly, along with a burst of adrenaline, a thrill of power that was completely at odds with the horrified disgust at what he was about to do. He was going to take a life. Not a Noturatii enemy, not a politician on the wrong side of the law or a police officer turned to corruption. But a young woman whose only crime had been to make a bad choice, one that, on reflection, she found herself unable to live up to.

Without allowing himself any further time for thought, Andre fixed his eyes on the girl's face, sent a silent prayer to Sirius, and pulled the trigger.

And his training, he now knew, was complete.

# CHAPTER TWENTY-EIGHT

**Present Day**

Miller watched as the shifters tore apart the last dog. It had been terrifying to watch them fight, the one with all the scars in particular. Hank had been shot just moments ago, the last of his men still alive, and Miller sat motionless in the sudden and eerie silence. They knew he was here. He had no back up, was on his last clip of ammunition, and had no possible chance of retreat.

He was a dead man.

He waited as the shifters gathered around his hiding place, some of them shifting to become human, others staying in wolf form, hackles raised, teeth bared, and he found himself hoping that his end would come with a swiftly delivered bullet, rather than being torn apart by those teeth. Was it a lack of courage, he wondered, heart pounding in his chest, or merely good sense?

Trench-Coat was staring at him now, not bothering to keep in cover. And there was no need, really. He could shoot the man, but what good would that do? There were a dozen more men standing there ready to shoot him the instant he moved. He recognised the leader of the pack from when they'd come to the lab, a huge man with dark hair and a short beard. Their former captive was back in human form now, but it had been a shock to see him shift, his wolf huge and white, the most beautiful animal Miller had ever seen. Until his fur had turned red, thick with blood, and it had been like looking at a demon, a spirit of rage come to life, dripping with gore as he tore flesh and shattered bone.

Warrior woman was also there, cold fury on her face, and he found himself fearing her anger more than the others. She wouldn't let him die quickly.

"Come out," Trench-Coat ordered, sounding impatient. "Put your gun down and your hands up." Miller's heart sank further. Rather than just shooting him, it sounded like they wanted to interrogate him instead, and after seeing the brutal methods the Noturatii employed for that purpose, he could well imagine the horrors that awaited him. Perhaps he should try fighting his way out after all, forcing them to shoot him rather than handing himself over for weeks of pain and torment.

Suddenly, a crashing sound came out of the forest to his left, an unholy snarl and a woman's terrified scream, and the shifters turned to meet this new threat, the ones closest to the forest aiming their guns at the sound, the ones further away keeping their eyes locked on Miller's hiding place.

A human woman suddenly ran out of the trees, a wolf at her heels, a look of terror in her eyes. She pulled up short as she saw the gathered crowd, dead bodies lying in bloody puddles, half a dozen guns pointed right at her, and if the situation hadn't been so profoundly serious, Miller would have found it almost comical, the way the shifters all hesitated, glanced at each other, more shocked by the appearance of the girl than they were by the presence of a dozen Noturatii.

But then the reality of her arrival hit Miller like a freight train.

She was a human, he realised quickly. Not a shifter, not if these men and women didn't know her as one. A human who had seen the battle. Had seen the wolves shift. A leak in their carefully guarded secret, and a threat to everything that Miller fought to protect.

He lifted his gun to aim at her... and found that he simply couldn't do it. He'd shot shifters, men and women, as humans and as wolves... but he couldn't shoot an innocent girl. His conscience would haunt him forever...

But it seemed Trench-Coat had reached the same conclusion as he had: the girl was a security leak that put them all at risk. With none of Miller's hesitation, he lifted his gun, looked the woman in the eye, and pulled the trigger.

She hit the ground, a bullet lodged directly between her eyes.

The wolf who had been chasing her shifted, and Miller recognised him as another man from the lab – the one with only one eye. He glanced around the battle field, disgust and grief written all over him, and then he spotted Miller. His gun was out in an instant-

"Don't shoot him!" Trench-Coat ordered, just in the nick of time, and One-Eye hesitated, glancing from Miller to Trench-Coat, to the dead girl in consternation.

"Is she one of yours?" the Leader asked Miller, eyeing him through a gap in the rocks.

"No," Miller called back. "I've never seen her before. She's not with us."

"Then what the fuck?" the Leader demanded of One-Eye.

"Human," One-Eye said shortly. "Hiker, maybe. Found her at the far end of the clearing."

"Fuck!"

"What was I supposed to do?" One-Eye demanded, clearly unhappy about both the situation and the Leader's reaction to it.

"No." The Leader shook his head, softening his tone a fraction. "Not your fault." He looked like he was about to throw up.

But it was Trench-Coat who really got Miller's attention. Utterly stricken, his face was pale, his hand shaking, and it was with an effort that he holstered his gun. Miller felt a sickening kind of relief that he hadn't been the one to pull the trigger, and felt like an utter bastard for daring to have the thought.

Good God, and the Noturatii thought these men were vicious beasts, without conscience or morals. But Trench-Coat was feeling the weight of the girl's death far more deeply than Miller, and as it was, Miller was fairly sure he wasn't going to sleep for a week.

Another man slowly approached the dead girl, an older man with streaks of grey in his hair. And in one ridiculous moment, Miller noticed the absurd detail that he only had one shoe on. Where had his other one gone? The man crouched down beside the girl and closed her eyes reverently. "May your soul ride the night winds," he said, in a thick accent that sounded vaguely Russian, "and Sirius guide your spirit to the next world."

That broke something in the rest of them, jarring them out of their focus on Miller and the girl to realise that their dead comrades lay in the grass all around them. Miller did a quick headcount – eight shifters were dead, a dozen more nursing bad wounds, stoic and silent, though their pain was evident in their eyes.

One woman moved, crouched down beside a dead wolf and ran her fingers reverently through the thick fur. Then she said, in a strong French accent, "I have measured your steps, this last day that you run." The rest of them joined in, making Miller feel like he was trespassing on a sacred and private ritual. And he realised in that moment that everything he knew about the shifters was completely and utterly wrong.

*"Greet our brethren at the gate,"* they recited. *"Bold warriors, brave and true.*
*Wait for me in the Hall of Sirius until the setting of the sun,*
*When I will join you."*

Tears fell from the French woman's eyes, and then she suddenly stood up, drew her gun and marched towards Miller, no doubt intent on ending his life-

"No," Trench-Coat said, stepping in her path. "We need him."

The woman spat something in French, and Trench-Coat replied in the same language. "Merde," the woman said, when he'd finished speaking, and she holstered her gun with a look of utter disgust.

"Come out," Trench-Coat said again. "No one will harm you."

It was the look on his face, rather than his words that made Miller pay attention, and he set his gun carefully on the top of the rock where they could see it, then slowly emerged from behind his shelter with his hands held up in surrender. He didn't know what the man wanted, but a strange instinct was telling him that he was trustworthy. Despite these most bizarre circumstances.

"You guard our secrets from humanity just as closely as we do," Trench-Coat said, then pointed to the dead girl. "She's human. Probably a hiker. Probably staying with friends or family, not too far from here. They'll be looking for her." He swallowed hard, and Miller was struck by the strange thought that he was fighting back tears. "We can't cover this one up," Trench-Coat said, his voice shaking just slightly, cold resolution in his eyes. "We don't have the time or resources to explain how an innocent girl ended up dead in the middle of the forest with a bullet in her skull." He looked Miller straight in the eye. "But you do."

It was true, Miller realised joylessly. The Noturatii had a long reach, access to police departments, spy organisations, political figures… they had the means and the power to invent a story, move a dead body without attracting attention, break the news to the girl's family in a way that would not arouse suspicion.

They were going to let him live, he realised in shock. They were going to let him walk away, because they needed him to make the dead girl conveniently disappear, and there was no other way for that to happen.

Miller nodded. It was the most pragmatic solution, and ironically, not in violation of his own orders. The directive to keep their war a secret from humans overruled any and all other operations, missions and goals. He was well within his rights to let this mob of shifters walk away, no questions asked, if it meant that their secrets stayed hidden from humanity. "So how do we do this?" he asked.

The Leader stepped forward. "You have a vehicle?"

Miller nodded. "West of here, at the border of this property."

"How many bodies will fit in it?"

Miller glanced around at the dead soldiers. "Maybe five?"

"Then we'll escort you back to your car. Help you load what we can into it, and we'll clean up the rest. You take the girl with you, and do whatever it is you do to make this go away."

Miller took a step forward, preparing to go and collect the girl's body, but the Russian-sounding man, the one who had closed her eyes, stepped between him and the body. "I will carry her," he said, then turned to the others. "But I'll need someone standing guard. I don't trust this Noturatii to keep his word."

"I'll go," the former captive said, then he turned to Miller, a predatory grin on his face. "It would be a pleasure to get *reacquainted.*"

Miller nodded his agreement, knowing he couldn't argue, and making a mental note not to do anything to further antagonise this man. Several other shifters rapidly gathered five bodies, and Miller was impressed with their strength as they hefted them onto their shoulders, paying no attention to the blood that rapidly soaked their clothing.

"This is the second time I've let you walk away with your life," Trench-Coat told him, just before he turned to leave, warning and speculation in his voice. "Don't count on there being a third."

"I won't," Miller told him seriously. He waited for another bizarre moment, as the former captive gave the Russian-sounding man his shoe back – had he lost it in the battle? If not, how had the captive come to have it? And then a moment longer as the man put it back on.

"Once you reach the car, wait half an hour before you let him leave," the Leader ordered. "We'll need time to clean up here and be on our way before he calls in reinforcements."

"I wouldn't bother," Miller said, not expecting them to believe him. "You'd be long gone before they ever got here."

Then the two men led the way up the hill, the others carrying the bodies following behind him. He had sorely underestimated these people, he mused as he walked. They felt more grief at these events than the Noturatii ever would. They didn't quarrel or bicker over their course of action, no misguided shooting themselves in the foot just to get revenge at him. They were a united front, a military unit with the finest training he had ever seen, the ability to put aside petty squabbles for the greater good, and the discipline to focus on the most urgent issues, leaving heartfelt emotions for later.

By nightfall, the entire place would be deserted. And in this part of Scotland, he was sure, the shifters would never be seen again.

Baron watched Nikolai and Tank lead the Noturatii man up the hill, his heart heavy in his chest. Annabelle was still sitting beside Sabine in the grass, the younger woman dead, her body in wolf form.

A tally of the dead was the first order of business, and Baron was grieved to realise that two of his own Den were among them – Nate and Eric, two of the lower ranking wolves. They'd fought bravely, died for their pack, and a funeral would be held for them once they were back at the estate.

One of the Ukrainians was also dead, along with several of the Russians, and Marianne, the alpha from the Norwegian Den.

Fuck, what a mess.

"Get the bodies back to the Manor," Baron ordered, wishing he could give everyone more time to mourn. "We need to be off this estate as soon as possible. Wash the blood off, pack your things, and be ready to move. Caleb, go get a couple of rubbish bags. Any body parts need to be collected, but the rain will wash the blood away." The sky had clouded over in the last half an hour, and it wouldn't be long before they had a downpour.

The shifters began to move reluctantly. The wolves' bodies were carried reverently, tears flowing, faces grim. The stronger shifters carried the bodies of the remaining Noturatii men, while the weaker ones dragged the dogs over the ground. In less than ten minutes, the entire clearing was empty, blood stains on the grass the only remnant of the brutal battle.

Back at the manor, Eleanor was waiting, and when she heard the news, she closed her eyes and muttered a prayer in Italian. Baron explained what they'd decided about Miller, and she sighed. "The best we can do under the circumstances, I suppose. I don't like the idea of letting him leave, given that he's seen our faces, but there's not much else we can do."

"Where's the plane?" Baron asked, knowing there was no way to accommodate this many people at the Lakes District manor.

"At Inverness," she replied, immediately picking up on his train of thought. "It can be ready to fly this evening." Baron nodded. That much, at least, would be a relief, to have all the foreign shifters out of Britain and on their way home.

"What about the bodies?" one of the Polish women asked.

"We'll cremate them, and return the ashes to you," Caroline answered quickly, appearing at Baron's side. "We don't have time to get clearance through customs on such short notice."

The woman was clearly unhappy with the plan, but she didn't protest, understanding there was little other option at the moment. She nodded, lips pressed into a tight line, then headed up the stairs to get cleaned up and pack her things.

In less than an hour, everyone due to leave was packed and waiting out the front. "Caroline, Silas, Raniesha, Alistair," Baron ordered, forcing himself to continue putting aside his own grief until his pack was safe. "You drive them all to the airport, then get back here as fast as possible. We'll be ready to leave when you get back. And change the licence plates. If the Noturatii tracked one of the vans here, we don't need them following us all the way back home."

All of the Den's vehicles bore fake number plates, and they were changed regularly to minimise the risk of detection. There was a stack of spares hidden in the back of the vans, along with the tools to have the plates swapped in a matter of minutes.

The rest of the shifters were scrambling to pack up the estate, their bags packed, vacuum cleaners humming away as they removed all traces of wolf fur from the carpets. George was in the kitchen with a handful of assistants packing up the last of the food. The bodies were all wrapped and lined up at the door, ready to be transported back to the estate. The rain had started, a heavy downpour that would wipe the last traces of blood from the forest.

Just as the vans were getting ready to leave, Tank and Nikolai arrived back, reporting that the Noturatii man had left with the bodies, as planned. There were two other vehicles aside from the one he had taken, but that was the Noturatii's problem. The shifters didn't have time to move them, and if the Noturatii knew where this estate was, there was no point trying to hide them anyway. They were never coming back here – the Densmeet in future years would have to be relocated to another country, since this place was no longer secure.

"I'll be staying with you," Eleanor told Baron, waiting by the door. "We have business to discuss before I go back to Italy."

Baron nodded, not really caring one way or the other. The Councillor was more than capable of looking after herself, and practical enough to know that he had bigger things on his mind.

It was Andre who really had him concerned. During the battle and the clean up, he'd been cool and calm, issuing instructions to the others, checking that nothing was missed, offering words of comfort to those who had lost loved ones.

But Baron had seen the look on his face just after he'd shot the girl, had seen the trembling in his hands and the desolation in his eyes. And it was as clear as day that the girl's death was affecting him more than he was prepared to admit.

The Council's assassins were trained to put aside their emotions, to focus on the mission, the bigger picture of protecting their species, to deny even their own conscience if that was the decree of the Council, and he had the utmost admiration for those who volunteered for the role, knowing that their species would never have survived as long as it had without them.

But no one could deny themselves forever, he reasoned. Sooner or later, the life of violence and killing had to catch up with them. One way or another.

# CHAPTER TWENTY-NINE

Sean watched the vans pull up out the front of the Manor, prepared for a grim greeting. Baron had called him a few hours ago with news of the attack in Scotland, and he'd promptly packed his bags and prepared to leave, knowing they wouldn't want him sticking around once they arrived.

After the visit from the Noturatii several weeks ago, three mysterious visitors had shown up, two men and a woman who had introduced themselves by showing him that peculiar symbol on their hands that Baron had told him about. Since then, they'd been ghosting around the estate, checking security, guarding the perimeter, but thankfully there had been no further intrusions from the Noturatii, and the three of them were packed and ready to leave as soon as the shifters returned. He'd been given no real explanation on the visitors other than that they were some sort of security force, and while they'd all been perfectly polite during their stay, he found them to be rather intimidating, and he was just as glad to be away from them.

He was right about the grim mood, Sean acknowledged, when Baron got out of the van. A scowl was fixed to the man's face, and he simply muttered a gruff 'thank you' when he saw Sean, handed him an envelope full of cash, and watched as he climbed into his car and drove away. They would be in contact again, when they next required his services, but until then, as far as Sean was concerned, the shifters didn't exist. He'd never met them, knew nothing of the existence of otherworldly beings right under humanity's nose, and would give his wife an enthusiastic report about his 'fishing holiday' when he got back home. Nothing to see here, folks. Just move along.

Caleb paced the library, surprised that Caroline had called him in for a chat. Baron was busy, organising the grieving Den, planning how the hell they were going to dispose of so many bodies, and he'd rather expected Caroline to have been at his side, juggling the thousand small tasks that were going to keep them both snowed under for days to come. For all that they butted heads at every opportunity, when the shit hit the fan, the pair of them worked together like a well oiled machine. They were both a credit to their Den, and he knew that the rest of the shifters couldn't have been prouder of their work, the way they held everyone together and overcame the seemingly insurmountable odds that were constantly stacked against them.

So while he knew that Caroline cared deeply about her pack, she rarely showed it in words of sympathy or compassion, preferring to let her actions speak more clearly about her intentions.

"Let's talk about the hiker," she'd said bluntly when Caleb had arrived in the library, and he'd stared at her in surprise. "Thoughts? Feelings? Regrets?" she'd probed with an air of caution, and Caleb had realised that he was being far more transparent about his feelings surrounding the incident than he'd realised. But putting those feelings into words was difficult, pride and guilt and remorse eating away at him.

He should be above this, he scolded himself, as Caroline watched him pace. Baron and Caroline dealt with far worse crises on a regular basis.

"What was I supposed to do?" he asked finally, a harsh edge to his voice. "She was standing in the middle of the forest, watching you all shift and shoot each other. She was a security risk that could have brought down our entire species."

"What do you think you should have done?" she asked calmly, watching him carefully to see how he reacted.

"I don't know. Taken her prisoner? But then what? She still knew secrets she wasn't supposed to know."

"I'm not trying to interrogate you," Caroline interrupted, sounding far gentler than he had expected. "This isn't a trial for a crime. It's just a discussion about how you're dealing with what happened."

"I'm fine," he snapped, not liking the fact that his doubts and guilt were so exposed.

"That's what Tank said when he got back from the Noturatii lab," Caroline pointed out. "And everyone could see, clear as day, that it wasn't true."

Tank. Fuck. A higher ranking wolf than Caleb, and he'd fallen to pieces for a while there. Caleb still wasn't sure of all the details involved, either what he'd been through inside the lab, or what had finally led to him being able to deal with it, but Caroline had a point, he admitted to himself reluctantly. If Tank had moments that were hard to deal with, then was it such a bad thing that Caleb found himself in the same situation?

"So in hindsight," Caroline asked, repeating her previous question, "given the time and space to think about it clearly, what would you like to have done differently?"

Caleb thought about that, recalled the shock of finding the woman there, the fear that his pack was being slaughtered at that very moment, the knowledge that she couldn't be allowed to just walk away. "Nothing," he said finally, sinking into a chair. "I hate what happened. I hate this whole fucking war, and the people who die fighting it, and the people who die without even knowing why. But… given the situation over again, I would have done the same thing. Or maybe even just shot her myself. When I confronted her, I guess I was hoping that I could capture her, take her to you or Baron and let you decide what should be done. But that would be horribly selfish in the end, wouldn't it? I couldn't decide what to do on my own, so I cover your hands with her blood, instead of my own."

Caroline nodded, a slow, thoughtful gesture that showed she understood. "Sometimes we have to make terrible decisions," she said softly. "And hating those decisions doesn't mean that we don't have to make them. And knowing that we have to make them, that there is no other choice, doesn't mean we can't hate what we had to do."

It was a strange relief to hear it so simply put. In a nutshell, she was saying that he did the right thing, but he was still allowed to feel like a complete and utter bastard for having done it. Sometimes there wasn't just one right way to feel about things like this.

"I have work to do," Caroline said apologetically, standing up and heading for the door. "But have a think about it. And if you want to talk again, I'm always here to listen."

It was a strange side to Caroline that he didn't see very often. But he knew that her concern was real, even if bluntly expressed, and he nodded.

"Okay. And thank you. I'll keep it in mind."

Caroline nodded, then left the room, leaving Caleb alone with his thoughts.


"He feels guilty as hell, but also recognises that it was the right decision," Caroline reported to Andre later that night. He'd been keen to assess how Caleb was reacting to the hiker's death – though he hadn't actually killed her, the man had certainly been instrumental in the event – but Andre had been unable to question Caleb himself. Not only would it have been rather inappropriate, but it would also have yielded very little useful information, with Caleb far less likely to open up to him than to one of his own Den mates.

The problem now was that, having been invited into Andre's room and given him her report, Caroline was strongly suspecting that Andre was having the same conflict of conscience as Caleb. Usually when she spoke to him he was polite, attentive, considering her opinions with a calm patience that she'd come to treasure during her time in Italy. Now, he was sounding almost impatient, avoiding her gaze, focused on the screen of his laptop as he typed rapidly, though she couldn't see what he was writing.

But what the hell was she supposed to do when a highly trained assassin was having a crisis of conscience? She could hardly do what she'd done for Caleb and give him a heartfelt debrief. He was the one who was supposed to be entirely reasonable and in control, the one who helped other people solve their moral dilemmas, rather than suffering from those dilemmas himself.

"Thank you," Andre told her, still making notes on his laptop. "I appreciate your help."

"How much longer is this assessment going to go on?" she asked, leaning against the door frame. Perhaps it was an impertinent question, but she was fishing for ways to continue the conversation, to try and tease out a little more of how Andre was feeling, and since small talk had never been her strong suit, she was left with direct questions on issues of significant importance.

"A few days at most," Andre replied. "For one thing, I need to return to Italy with Eleanor when she leaves. With the ban on travel lifted, I have little more excuse to stay here without arousing suspicions." The announcement came with so little warning that it left Caroline feeling rather dismayed. After so many weeks, she'd got rather used to having Andre around. Though, in all that time, they'd still never managed to have a real conversation, a chat just about themselves rather than business around the Den. Neither of them had referred in the slightest way to their past in Italy. "But aside from that, my assessment is basically complete. I'm going to speak to Eleanor tomorrow and tell her that I wholeheartedly recommend Caleb for service to the Council."

It was said in such a deadpan voice that it took a moment for the words to sink in. "You're recommending him?" she repeated, not sure why she was surprised at the news. Caleb was a most capable shifter, an excellent fighter, providing a calm and soothing presence at the top end of the ranking, between Tank, who was often more playful mischief maker than 2IC, and Silas, who could strip paint off walls with his glare alone.

"Absolutely," Andre said, glancing up at her. "He's calm under pressure, he excels at strategic planning and he thinks outside the square. That's exactly the sort of man we need."

"I'm thrilled to hear it. Caleb will be delighted."

"It's not all done and dusted yet," Andre said, and Caroline caught a hint of weariness in his voice, a tone she'd never heard from him before. "All I can do is make my recommendation to the Council. The final decision still lies with them. Now, if you'll excuse me," he added, turning back to his computer, "I have a few things I need to finish up here."

It was a dismissal, and not even a particularly polite one. It was far enough from his usual manner that it made Caroline pause, rather than simply leaving him in peace, as she would normally do.

But what could she really say about it? Andre seemed tired and stressed, so clearly the world was caving in? Since coming here, he'd been dealing with one drama after another, first with Dee, then the Noturatii lab, then spending all his time trying to find subtle ways to assess Caleb without arousing suspicion. The life of an assassin was tough. It was no wonder he might get a little worn out at times.

But the nagging feeling that something more serious was going on wouldn't go away. It was years since she'd been with him in Italy, years that had hardened and refined him, so that the man sitting in front of her now was a far cry from the young assassin-in-training who had sat and talked with her for hours over coffee and sunsets, the one who had taken her soul apart and put it back together again, and who had made her fall hopelessly in love with him.

But then again, she was no longer the lost, lonely girl she had been then. And so she dared to do something that broke all protocols when dealing with an assassin. She waited until he looked up at her, impatience on his face, and said, "We never talk about Italy." A momentary confusion crossed his face, so she pressed on, before he could dismiss her again. "You've been here for weeks. You've seen our Den inside and out, you've worked and played and fought with us. But we never talk about anything other than business, how best to run the Den, how to deal with the Noturatii. Why don't we ever talk about the past like old friends?"

Andre looked down, seeming more tired than angry about her sudden interrogation. "We were never friends, Caroline. You were my student. I was your psychologist. That relationship required a certain professional distance."

"That was fifteen years ago. We're both adults now. The world is vastly different from the way it was then."

"I'm an assassin," Andre continued to protest, irritation colouring his voice. "I travel constantly. I kill people for a living. I exist in the shadows of society – human and shifter – and that kind of life is not at all conducive to making friends."

"You're friends with Heron," Caroline said stubbornly, wondering why she was pushing this so hard. He didn't care for her the same way she did for him, that much was obvious. She could just leave it at that... but for the past fifteen years, she'd lived with the nagging feeling that there was a gap in her life, a missed opportunity that just wouldn't go away. And if she didn't find a way to resolve that tension now, she would likely never get another chance. Andre would be leaving, and she would probably never see him again. "You've had great long chats with her about the Den, about your childhood, about the things you've been doing for the past fifteen years."

"I grew up with Heron!" Andre said in exasperation. "She was like a second mother to me."

"And that's my point. Okay, so you grew up with her, but you still manage to maintain some kind of relationship with her, despite your lifestyle, despite not seeing her in years."

"What the hell do you want from me?"

"For you to see me as an equal. Not the fragile girl who was scared of her own imagination. I'm an alpha now. I run this Den. Baron and I have held back the tide of the Noturatii for years together. We recruit new shifters. We make choices that risk other people's lives – that cost them their lives, on occasion. In the nicest possible way, Andre… I don't need you any more. So why can't we move past this professional distance you insist upon?"


Andre struggled to find an answer to Caroline's insistent questioning. This was one of the things he had always admired about her, her persistence, her tenacity in reaching for something she wanted to achieve. But right now, that same persistence was driving him insane.

There were two very good reasons for the need for distance between them, neither of which Andre could admit to. The first was that he was currently assessing her for a position on the Council, and for that, he needed to remain objective. He was supposed to assess her on her skills as an alpha, her intelligence, her prowess in battle, not let his opinion of her be coloured by personal bias. But of course, there was no way he could tell her that. The rules for his current job were that potential Council candidates were never, ever aware of the fact that they were being assessed until the Council had made a decision. On the one hand, once someone knew they were in the running for the role, they were instantly on their best behaviour, more careful in their decisions, more diplomatic in their relationships, and in order to know who a person really was, how they reacted in normal, day to day situations, it was imperative that they continue to behave as they normally would.

The other issue was a more tactful reason. If a person knew they were being assessed, and they didn't make the final cut, it could breed resentment that was counterproductive to the smooth running of Il Trosa and the expectation of loyalty to the Council.

And then there was the second reason, even more complicated than the first, one which he was fairly sure he'd managed to hide from even the Council, since if they'd known, they'd never have given him this assignment. The truth was that, even after all these years apart, the assignments he'd completed, even the women he'd slept with from time to time… he was still hopelessly in love with Caroline.

And that was never, ever going to fit in with the life of an assassin, constantly moving from place to place, constantly in danger, never knowing if this mission was going to be his last, if he would finally meet an enemy who would succeed in killing him. No one could live with that kind of uncertainty for long, the knowledge that their partner, their lover might leave on an assignment and never come home.

He opened his mouth to reply, scrambling for something that would sound reasonable enough to Caroline for her to leave this issue alone. But what came out of his mouth was nothing at all like what he'd been intending to say.

"I killed a girl," he said, blindsided as the guilt and regret and grief leapt out of him like a living thing. "I shot an innocent woman, who did nothing more than accidentally get lost."

Caroline closed her eyes. He thought for a moment that she was going to reach out and take his hand, and he prayed that she didn't, knowing that it would break the last threads of control he had on his surging emotions. But she didn't move, just stood there, arms folded like a shield in front of her, abject sorrow on her face.

"There was no other option," she said softly, a mantra that Andre had told himself a thousand times. "It's a tragedy, I know, but the sad truth is that that is the price of our own survival."

But Andre shook his head, knowing she had missed the point. "It's not that I killed her," he tried to explain, forcing the words past the lump in his throat. "Anyone could have shot her. You. Baron. Nikolai. And you'd have hated doing it, and hated yourself for it, and mourned the loss of an innocent life even before you did it. But I didn't. I didn't regret what I was doing. I didn't hesitate. I just looked her in the eye and pulled the trigger. And I didn't feel a thing." He looked at her pleadingly, eyes searching hers for the answer to unanswerable questions. "What have I become?"

Andre waited, heart in his throat, as Caroline lowered herself to one knee in front of him, elbow resting on the desk, putting her almost at eye level with him. He waited for a lecture – the most gentle, most well meaning of lectures – about the price of being an assassin, of protecting their species, of the emotional distance that was required for the life he had chosen. Because he had chosen it, Andre reminded himself. He could have picked a different option, become a historian, perhaps, and worked to further the interests of their species in an entirely less violent way. He had chosen to give up his soul to death and killing, and now he was reaping the rewards of that choice-

"A wise man once told me," Caroline said, her voice barely more than a whisper, "that if you don't like who you are, then you are the only person with the power to change that."

It was such a simple statement. And yet the moment she said it, a whole barrage of ideas and questions and doubts suddenly crystallised in Andre's mind. The answer was right there, hidden in plain sight, just waiting for him to discover it.

The moment of clarity was so profound that it blocked out all other rational thought. Without waiting another moment, Andre leaned forward, giving in to years of pent up frustration and longing, abandoning the control that had ruled his life for as long as he could remember. He cupped her face in his hands, and kissed her.

# CHAPTER THIRTY

Andre's response to her overly simple advice was far from what Caroline had expected. She'd been anticipating a long discussion, objections about the responsibilities he held, the sacred vows he had taken before the Council, the years of training that had been invested in him.

What she got instead was a kiss, the likes of which she had been dreaming about, fantasising about for the past fifteen years. And she returned that kiss with all the passion of years of unfulfilled longing.

Without a word, without either of them really deciding to do it, Caroline found them both on their feet. Andre's arms were a tight band of muscle around her waist, the stubble on his chin tickling her face, his lips warm, his body a column of heat and power against her own.

Years ago, she might have felt overwhelmed by his sudden affection, letting him lead, awkward and uncertain as to how to return the attention. But the years had changed her, for all that her desire for him was undimmed, and moments later, she was steering him across the room, his hands sliding beneath her t-shirt to stroke smooth skin, hers stripping his jacket from his shoulders, neither of them able to manage their usual grace and balance as they stumbled backwards, feet bumping into each other as they tried to maintain as much physical contact between them as possible.

"Are you sure-?" Andre tried to ask.

"Shut up," Caroline replied. "God, it has been so fucking long…"

So long, indeed. The last man Caroline had slept with had been her arsehole of a boyfriend, back before she was recruited. Over the years, her curiosity about sex had grown, fervent imaginings replacing her previous distaste with the act, but she'd never managed to let her guard down enough to take the plunge. There was no one in the Den she was particularly attracted to, and finding a random stranger in a pub for a one night stand had never appealed. But her imagination had more than filled in the gaps in her experience, and she found herself breathing hard, body hot and thrumming as she felt Andre's body against hers.

"Far too long," Andre agreed, breaking away from her for only long enough to strip his shirt off, and then his arms were around her again, mouth pressing kisses down her neck, hands fumbling with her belt.

By Sirius, he was divine, Caroline thought, running her hands over hard shoulders, defined abs, his breaths coming fast and shallow. The firm ridge of his erection pressed against her thigh through two pairs of trousers, and then he was tugging her shirt over her head, sliding his hands down inside her underpants, her trousers open and hanging off her hips.

He was going to struggle to get her leather trousers off, so Caroline backed him up against the bed and gave him a shove. He went down willingly, falling backwards onto the sheets, and she used the moment to rip off her boots, then peel tight leather down her legs, not bothering to be seductive about it, just trying to get the damn things off as quickly as possible.

Seeing her intentions, Andre joined in, sitting up to unlace his own boots, toeing them off and peeling away socks to be flung carelessly out of the way. Then she was on top of him, straddling his narrow hips, pressing herself against his groin, her underpants creating a delicious friction against her sensitive flesh.

There was nothing tender or cautious about their foreplay. They were both hard, stubborn, tenacious people who knew their own minds, both brutal warriors in their respective arenas, and romance didn't feature anywhere on the agenda for this evening. Caroline took the lead, surprised but gratified when Andre let her, and he lay back on the bed, a look of almost desperate anticipation on his face as she undid his belt and stripped his trousers and underpants down his legs.

Andre lay on the bed, feeling like the whole situation was surreal, as if he was dreaming and was due to wake at any moment. He lifted his hips to help Caroline in her quest to unclothe him, and felt his erection spring free, the air of the room cool against such heated flesh.

When she climbed back on top of him, she was entirely naked, bra and underpants having disappeared in the last few moments, and he simply stared at her, hands slowly climbing from hip to shoulder, and then around to cup her perfect breasts. They weren't the largest he'd ever seen, but they overflowed his hands, and Caroline let out a moan as he massaged them, feeling his cock throb, trapped beneath her thighs.

Long term relationships were an impractical hindrance for an assassin, but sex most certainly wasn't, and he'd had his share of one night stands with other assassins – there were a dozen or more women in the ranks, and they suffered from the same frustrations as the men, in the long run. Occasional nights of pairing up to relieve the tension was an accepted part of the assassin's lifestyle, an entirely appropriate convenience, as neither party harboured any expectations of long term commitment or emotional entanglement. And while the interludes had been physically satisfying, they'd also left him with a lingering emptiness, as if each one had only served to remind him of the things he could never have.

This time, it was completely different. His skin felt more sensitive, his ears revelling in the harsh pants of Caroline's breathing, the faint moan as she rocked herself over him, and he let go of her enticing breasts to hold her hips, encouraging her to rock more firmly over him, the pleasure sublime, though he wasn't yet inside her.

He tugged her down to kiss her again, squirming beneath her as her breasts pressed against his chest, and then he tilted his head up to capture one in his mouth. The scent of her skin was intoxicating and he teased her nipple with his tongue, his hands roaming down to circle her waist, as if he couldn't stand a single moment without touching her, as if there were simply too many tantalising dips and curves on her body to be explored. She was a lean, hard woman, her stomach washboard flat with defined abs. Her biceps stood out plainly, her thighs holding her balanced above him without the slightest hint of strain, and he reflected for a moment that it was a relief to know that he wasn't going to hurt her. Sex between assassins tended to be rather athletic, a way to work off excess energy as well as relieve sexual tension, and he knew there was no way he could be the gentle, considerate lover that many women would have preferred.

There was nothing soft about Caroline. But he also had no fears that he was going to take advantage of her. She was nothing if not blunt and forthright, and if he did anything she didn't like, she wouldn't hesitate to let him know.

But Caroline wasn't objecting in the slightest to the vigorous treatment. If anything, she was urging him on, fingernails in his shoulders, feet digging into the bed to gain better leverage, and then, before he was quite prepared for it, he felt her rise up, eager fingers fumbling for his erection, and he was sliding inside her.

He let his head fall back, a moan of indescribable pleasure rumbling out of him. She waited a moment, mouth parted, eyes closed in bliss, and then she was moving again, rocking back and forth, her hands stroking his chest, then reaching up to cup her own breasts – a task that Andre quickly took over for her.

It wasn't going to last long, both of them too worked up, the stress of recent events putting them on edge as much as the frustration of years apart, and the instant Caroline moaned, her sheath contracting around him, Andre let himself go, his orgasm pulsing out of him, pleasure tingling from his toes all the way up his spine.

Long moments later, he came back to himself, Caroline lying on his chest, his arms around her shoulders, his softening penis still inside her. The soft harmony of their breathing was loud in the quiet room. And the slow, even draw of Caroline's breath suggested she would be asleep soon.

He gently nudged her over to the side, feeling himself slip out of her, and then grabbed a handful of tissues from the bedside table, handing them to her so she could clean up a little. There was no conversation as he tugged the blankets up to cover her. No gently whispered reassurances, no sweet nothings to murmur into her ear. He got up, closed his laptop, switched off the light and climbed back in beside her. She wrapped an arm around his waist, and he pressed a kiss to her forehead.

And lying there, in the darkness, with Caroline falling asleep beside him, Andre finally allowed himself the tears that he had been denying himself all day. For the dead girl. For himself. For a lifetime of missed opportunities.

Andre had been awake for an hour already when he finally heard Caroline stir. It was just after five in the morning, but the sunlight was already filtering in around the edges of the heavy curtains.

He turned to face her, able to see her clearly in the dim light, and a look of concern crossed her face as she registered the fact that he was already fully dressed.

With a sigh, Andre got up and opened the curtains, letting the grey light of early morning fill the room.

They stared at each other for a moment, Caroline sitting up in bed, unconcerned about her nudity, Andre trying to find the words to explain what he needed to say. "I owe you an apology," he said finally. "Last night should never have happened." He winced as he said it, knowing the words sounded heartless to the extreme. "It's not that I regret it, or that I don't... care about you," he rushed on. "But I have responsibilities and duties, and I'm leaving in a few days…"

Would she understand? Had she expected this, knowing his job for what it was? Or would she hate him, call him a heartless bastard for his selfish behaviour?

The thing was, last night when he'd made his decision, the one about his career, not the one about Caroline, it had seemed so simple, offering him the one backdoor to all his troubles and doubts, an end to the killing and violence.

But now, in the cold light of day, he had to admit to himself that it was far more complex than he had realised.

Regardless of the choices he made about his own life, Caroline still had hers. He was days away from completing his assessment of her as a potential Councillor – a duty he was determined to fulfil, regardless of any other decisions he made about his life. If she moved to Italy, it was to a life of complex responsibilities, further training, study, the weight of the survival of their entire species on her shoulders. He had no right to go butting in and complicating things further for her.

And then there was the Endless War. Just because he wanted to bow out of it didn't mean it wasn't going to continue for every other shifter on the planet. And whether or not she was elected to the Council, that reality was never going to go away for Caroline. She was the alpha of a stable and successful Den. He was a drifter, subject to the whims of others.

But once again, it seemed he had underestimated Caroline. "I know," she said simply. "I know you have to leave." She seemed calmly resigned to the inevitability of it, though he was perversely relieved to hear just a hint of disappointment in her voice. He seemed to be going out of his way to make life awkward for her, and then he was happy when he succeeded? What the hell was wrong with him?

"Please don't think that last night was a casual thing." He hesitated, then pressed on, knowing that what he had to say couldn't make things any worse. "I've been in love with you since Italy. And I will cherish every moment of what happened here. But my life is not my own. Nor will it be, until we find a way to end this war." If Andre got his way, that day might come a lot sooner than most people were expecting. But there was no point saying so now. If he was wrong, it would only cause more disappointment in the long run.

Caroline didn't react to his sudden profession of love. But perhaps that was simply her pragmatic way of seeing the world. No fuss, no drama, just taking each day as it came, whether it brought sunlight and hope for the future, or the perpetual dangers of the Endless War.

Without a word, she got up. Searched around for her clothes, dressed in silence, and only when she'd laced her boots and straightened the worst of the wrinkles did she face him again.

"I have no regrets about last night," she told him frankly, looking him in the eye. "I know what your responsibilities are. I'm not asking for anything you don't have to give. And for the record… I've been in love with you for just as long. And we both know that's never going to work out for us."

With those final words, she quietly let herself out of the room, shutting the door softly behind her. And the thing that pissed Andre off most about that was not that she had no expectations of him. That was simple pragmatism, and nothing he could hold against her. No, what really made him grit his teeth and want to curse at the sky was that she was right – as far as a real life went, as far as commitment and emotional stability and any kind of real future… he simply had nothing to offer her.

And it was about time that all that changed.

# CHAPTER THIRTY-ONE

Three days later, the Den was slowly returning to a semblance of normality. A funeral had been held for Nate and Eric, a heartfelt ceremony held on the back lawn by moonlight, new plaques added to the memorial wall, and the traditional chants and prayers to Sirius performed as a tribute to their courage and sacrifice as warriors of Il Trosa. The bodies of the other shifters had been cremated and the ashes boxed to be sent back to their respective Dens.

Baron and Caroline had given an extensive report on the attack to Eleanor, who had passed it on to the rest of the Council. Condolences were pouring in from the other Dens – being attacked was bad enough, but for it to happen during the Densmeet was a blow that had everyone's emotions on edge, and amongst the heartfelt sympathy were several comments reaffirming the growing view that Il Trosa's current strategies on the Endless War were inadequate. Despite agreeing with some of the sentiments, her anger over the attack still raw, Caroline knew there was little she could do to change their current course. It was an issue for the Council to decide, the best minds in Il Trosa already employed to tackle the problem, but the answer to the crisis remained as elusive as ever. Every strategy they could devise contained inherent risks that could do as much harm as good.

There was an incinerator in the basement, and they'd put it to good use, disposing of the bodies of the Noturatii men and their dogs. Alistair, their PR guru, had managed to track down the elusive news report on the death of the hiker – elusive, because the Noturatii had apparently done their job well. The official story was that the girl had wandered into a hunting ground on private property – covered by all the appropriate permits and warning signs – and been accidentally shot by one of the hunters. For the sake of the family's privacy, few details had been released, and it was a relief to know that for once, their enemies had proved as useful as their word.

After giving her reports on the other Dens, Eleanor had announced that she was eager to be heading back to Italy. The Council's plane was standing by for the journey as soon as Eleanor gave the word, so it wasn't a surprise to Caroline when Eleanor approached her, requesting a private meeting with her, Baron, Andre and Caleb: The verdict of his assessment for service to the Council.

As promised, Andre had handed over his final report on the matter several days ago, and Eleanor would have discussed the selection with the other Council members by video call, no doubt reaching a rapid conclusion, given how thorough she knew Andre to be. And with the meeting now set up, Caroline had to assume that it was good news. If not, Eleanor would likely have simply returned to Italy without speaking a word of it. Caleb himself was still unaware of his assessment, and if he hadn't been chosen, there would have been no point in letting him know anything about it.

And so the five of them now sat in the library, her and Baron feeling a swell of pride in one of their finest shifters, though Caleb was no doubt feeling rather baffled by the meeting. "Is this about the dead hiker?" he asked immediately, once everyone was seated.

"Not at all," Eleanor said. "It was a most unfortunate situation, of course, but you did nothing to warrant any kind of reprimand. If anything, your quick thinking saved us all a lot of trouble – albeit with an unpleasant ending."

Caleb nodded, seeming to relax a little with the official pardon for his actions. But then the confusion returned, as he no doubt wondered what this could be about, if not that.

"I have some news for you," Eleanor said, apparently deciding there was no point in drawing this out. "And I think it may come as a surprise. You have been told that Andre remained at your Den because of a tense political situation in Italy which made it unsafe for him to return home. And that much, at least, is true. But he also had another purpose in staying here. He has been assessing you for service to the Council."

Caleb's shock was palpable. His eyes opened wide, his jaw dropped, his gaze flashing over to Andre, then to Baron and Caroline, as if astonished that they would dare to keep this from him. "Me?" he squeaked out at last. "I'm not... I don't... I haven't the skills needed for service to the Council."

"On the contrary," Andre spoke up, and Caroline steadfastly avoided his gaze. What she'd said to him the other day was true – she had no regrets about sleeping with him. But somehow she hadn't anticipated how difficult it would be to still have him around the manor, now that she knew what she had been missing all these years, and with the firm knowledge that it was most definitely a one-time event. So she'd gone out of her way to avoid him, while trying to keep the tension between them a secret from everyone else. So far, at least, she seemed to have been successful. "You have excellent skills as a warrior," Andre went on, addressing Caleb. "You have a solid grasp of the old language, and you're a superb strategic planner. There will be additional preparation required once you get to Italy – assuming you accept the post, of course," he added as an aside. "But you're more than capable of completing the training, with the appropriate instruction."

"I only have one eye," Caleb protested, which made Eleanor laugh.

"I'm not recruiting you as an assassin," she pointed out drolly. "Aside from anything else, you haven't the temperament for it. But one of our historians is about to retire, and he's looking for a protégé to pass on some of his extensive knowledge to." She smiled, a warm affection lighting her eyes. "I think you would fit the bill rather nicely."

Caleb didn't seem to know what to say, so she asked, "Would you like a few days to think about it?"

Caleb shook his head. "No, Ma'am. It is the highest honour to be offered such a position. I wholeheartedly accept."

The smile on Eleanor's face was bright and welcoming. "I'm so glad. I'll be returning to Italy in a few days. If it's not too soon, I'd like you to come with me."

"Of course," Caleb agreed, then he turned to Baron and Caroline. "You both knew about this?" he asked, then went on without waiting for an answer. "I had no idea. That whole time in Scotland, I thought Andre was just… killing time."

"I couldn't think of anyone better suited to the job," Baron said warmly. "We'll miss you. And I hope you'll stay in touch, as far as your duties will allow it. But we couldn't be more proud of you."

"Thank you."

"I'm sure you have plenty of things to prepare before we leave, so I'll let you go and get started," Eleanor said with a smile. "Unless you have any further questions?"

"No, not at the moment. Thank you so much. This is a great honour." Caleb left the room, and Caroline stood up, assuming that the meeting was over.

"Just a moment," Eleanor called her back. "We have one other issue to discuss."

That was news to Caroline, and she sat down again, her mind racing to imagine what the problem could be. Don't go jumping to conclusions, she told herself sternly. It was probably just a follow up on the attack in Scotland, new security measures from the Council, perhaps.

"I'm afraid Caleb is not the only one who's been kept in the dark," Eleanor said, a sly grin creeping over her face, though Caroline couldn't begin to deduce the meaning of it. "Andre had another assignment to complete while he was here. He handed in his final report two days ago, and the Council has reached a decision."

"A decision on what?"

"On you." Eleanor pulled a sheet of paper out of the stack she had in front of her and slid it across the table to Caroline. "This is a letter, signed by the Council, formally inviting you to join us as a Councillor."

Caroline stared at her blankly. Was this some kind of joke? "Excuse me?"

"I've been assessing you as a replacement for Amedea," Andre explained patiently, and Caroline took the time to notice that he lacked Eleanor's enthusiasm for the proposal. "You've been accepted. They're offering you a seat on the Council."

Stunned, Caroline reached out and took the letter. It was signed at the bottom with eleven signatures – the entire Council – and she had to read it twice to get it to sink in. A Councillor. Her? "Why me?"

"We made a selection of four potential candidates," Eleanor explained, not at all put out by her shock and hesitation. "We sent emissaries to assess each of them. And yesterday we took a vote. It came in in your favour, eight votes to three."

There was a heavy silence, as Caroline read the letter again. Yup, there was her name at the top. And all those signatures at the bottom. "I don't know what to say."

"Take a few days to think about it," Eleanor said gently. "I realise this is a big decision. And you're likely to have a lot of questions, so feel free to come and find me any time, day or night, if you want to talk things through. In the meantime, here's some more information about the intricacies of the position." She handed Caroline a small, ring-bound book. "There's extra training provided, so don't be alarmed if you feel you're not up to speed with some of the responsibilities. This is more an overview, to give you an idea of what you'd be signing on for." She fixed Caroline with a steely look. "I have the utmost confidence in you, Caroline. You would not have been selected for this position if you weren't capable of fulfilling it."

With a reassuring smile, Eleanor got up, nodded to Andre, and the pair of them left the room, leaving Caroline staring at Baron, who was giving her an odd, scrutinizing look.

"You knew about this?" she accused him angrily. How dare they just drop this on her like this? This was huge! A massive responsibility with implications affecting the survival of their entire species!

"I did," Baron replied. And Caroline wanted to hurl a huge pile of accusations at him, but knew they would all be useless. Of course he couldn't have told her. Andre would have forbidden it, the same as he'd forbidden them both from telling Caleb about his assessment.

And Andre... fucking hell, she suddenly realised. She'd slept with the man who was assessing her for a position on the Council. She wasn't familiar with all the regulations that governed the behaviour of Council emissaries, but there were surely rules against that. She could only assume that Eleanor didn't know.

What the hell was she supposed to do now? Leave her Den? Her family? Leave Skip, and Tank, and Silas, and know that if the shit really hit the fan, the species unable to fight their way out from under the claws of the Noturatii, then it would be partially her fault, a consequence of the decisions made by the Council, which could just as easily bless, or damn the lot of them.

"I need to be alone," she muttered, staggering to her feet and stumbling out of the room. Baron made no attempt to follow her.

# CHAPTER THIRTY-TWO

**6 Years Ago**

The Den was in an uproar.

Anna, the current alpha female, sat at the long table in the library, watching the chaos around her with calm composure. Beside her, Baron looked like he wanted to throw up. All around them, the members of the Den were expressing their displeasure at Anna's latest announcement, shouting, swearing, some gesturing wildly to punctuate their angry pronouncements while others paced, hit things, overturned chairs.

And in the midst of it all, Caroline sat silently, mind racing, her safe and stable world suddenly on shaky ground.

Anna was resigning as alpha. And she was moving to Italy, abandoning her Den, her duties, her family. The Den was reeling in shock.

It was five years since the death of Kendrick, her husband, who had been alpha up until his death, when Baron had taken over. And though no one was quite willing to admit it, since that time Anna had hardly been exemplary in her fulfilment of her duties. She'd taken frequent trips to Italy, shown little interest in rebuilding their Den, left the vast majority of responsibilities up to Baron, and while more than a handful of their members had petitioned for a leadership change, the problem then remained the same as the problem now – there was no other female in the Den both willing and able to take control.

Heron would have been the first choice, the most senior and most experienced of the females, but for reasons that few among their number understood, she had steadfastly refused to challenge Anna for rank.

Raniesha fancied herself another good bet, but Caroline knew for certain that she would never gather sufficient social support to hold the rank. And Skip, of course, was far too young, and had neither the skills nor the desire to hold such a position of responsibility.

Which left Caroline.

Privately, she scoffed at the idea, sure that the Den would never support her, convinced that she was too hot tempered, too brusque and lacking important social skills to ever make a real play for the role.

The real problem was that, in the absence of a willing and able female, the Council would be forced to send in a new female selected from another Den, a strong, experienced wolf with the skills and personality to become alpha. While this was a sound plan in the long run, a strong female needed to keep the Den stable and functioning well, in the short term it was a nightmare. No one liked having new wolves of high rank brought in. It would create resentment among the females and dissention among the males. It sparked weeks, if not months of status fights, as everyone jostled for rank and with Baron as their alpha male, a powerful personality and formidable opponent, the new female would be up against serious opposition to ever get a say in anything. Feuding between the alphas made everyone tense and anxious, which led to more squabbling down the ranks. And though it was ultimately a sign of the Council taking care of its people, the need to bring in a new alpha was also taken as something of an insult, a declaration of shame and failure in the Den, as they had been unable to recruit and train a suitable female of their own.

But as Caroline sat there, running over all the possibilities in her mind, she happened to glance at Silas.

He was watching her, a grim, calculating look on his face. He seemed to weigh her carefully, unhurried in his assessment… and then, totally ignoring the ongoing chaos around them, he gave her the slightest of nods.

Caroline's eyes opened wide in surprise. It wasn't a totally new idea, Silas having brought it up several years ago in far different circumstances than this, but Caroline had assumed that it had been merely a bait, designed to get her to focus more on her training and strengthen the Den. She'd never imagined that he could actually mean for her to…

Bloody hell. She glanced at Baron, who was busy cursing under his breath. A new alpha meant one hell of a headache for him as well, and he caught her gaze, rolled his eyes and looked away, before seeming to do something of a mental double-take. He glanced back at her, then quickly over to Silas, the highest ranking male after Baron… and a strange calm seemed to come over him.

Across the room, Caleb, the next in rank after Silas, was pacing the room. Not one for displays of temper, he was nonetheless agitated about Anna's announced retirement, lost in dark thoughts – their Den had been through enough chaos and trauma in recent years, nearly having been shut down at one point before Baron had stepped in and taken control, and this did not bode well for their continued future stability. It took a long moment for Baron to catch his eye, and then he nodded clearly, but subtly at Caroline. Half a dozen arguments were still going on around the room, and no one else was paying them any mind.

Caleb glanced over at her and rolled his eyes, but then he paused, as Baron quirked one eyebrow upward and added a faint hint of desperation to his expression. It was fascinating, as Caroline watched. So many conversations going on around the room, and the most serious of them were being conducted without a single word. Such was the way of it, when half their lives were spent in a form that could not speak, when they were dependent on body language to convey a wealth of meaning in situations from the most mundane to the most drastic of emergencies.

Caleb gave her another look, long, lingering... and then he nodded, a grim, resolute expression on his face.

Baron turned back to Caroline and nodded once, and with that single gesture, she knew she had, by some bizarre quirk of fate, just secured the most senior female rank in the Den. With the three top ranking males on her side, and no other female a serious contender, her victory was all but assured.

The idea was terrifying.

Not that it meant she wasn't going to have to fight to get there. The rest of the Den might not get on board with the plan quite so quickly, and if she was entirely honest with herself, Caroline had absolutely no idea how to be alpha anyway. It was a role chock full of responsibility and ritual, fraught with danger, with Caroline expected to lay down her life for her Den, should they come under attack.

But now that the decision was made, there was nothing to be gained from delaying her move.

She stood up, feeling her heart racing, and announced, "I petition for the role of alpha."

It took a few moments for everyone to pay attention, looks of confusion, disbelief and even anger shot her way. "What?" someone asked, so she repeated herself.

"I petition for the role of alpha." She turned to Heron, the one female who ranked above her, and stated simply, "I challenge you to a status fight."

It broke the rules of status challenges, as she would be skipping several males in rank for the fight, but with things the way they were, no one seemed to care about the paltry details at this stage.

Heron stood up, normally a calm, genteel sort of woman, but in this instance, she was livid, face red, having just broken off a long verbal tirade at Anna about her abandonment of duty, so this latest challenge just seemed to infuriate her more.

"You have neither the experience nor the social pull to hold the rank of alpha," Heron declared flatly, the rudest thing she had ever said to Caroline, and there were several gasps across the room as the Den looked on.

"Baron?" Caroline asked, ignoring the insult. "Do we have leave to fight?" Perhaps technically she should have asked Anna, as the ranking female, but after years of neglect and her impending departure, it wasn't likely anyone would take her seriously anyway.

"You have leave," Baron said calmly, standing up to lead the way out onto the back lawn.

Caroline followed, Heron glaring at her all the way, and as they faced off across the damp grass, the Den forming a wide circle around them, Heron drew herself up with dignity and announced, "I will not be throwing this fight." It put voice to the thoughts a lot of the Den must be having. It wasn't unknown for a higher ranking wolf to deliberately lose a fight to allow another to climb the ranks. There were a number of reasons why someone might do so, but in the end all of them came down to the same point – rank in the Den was not just based on physical strength and skill. There were also complex social structures in place, which meant that a wolf with significant social support, perhaps because of clear leadership qualities, or niche skills, like hacking, for example, could climb the ranks even if his or her fighting skills were not up to scratch. But in this case, that was clearly not going to cut it. "I will not see this Den weakened and be put at risk by an inferior alpha just because we have a seat to fill."

"Understood," Caroline said simply. In truth, she preferred it that way. At least if the fight was real, then she'd know one way or another whether she was worthy of leading the Den. And if not? Well, then, she'd done her best to hold them all together, and whatever fallout happened after that was not her fault.

She and Heron both shifted, the older wolf strong and experienced, giving her the edge despite her age, and they locked eyes, each trying to stare the other down.

"Begin," Baron said from the sidelines, and then it was on, no hesitation, no spare moments to plan or strategise. Just two lithe, furry bodies flinging themselves at each other, snarls and growls filling the air as they tumbled over each other, neither one pulling any punches.

It took upwards of twenty minutes for the fight to end. And when the conclusion came, it was with Heron lying on her side on the blood-splattered grass, her sides heaving as she gasped for breath, Caroline standing over her, teeth bared, tail high, the clear winner.

"Caroline now outranks Heron," Baron announced, amid a host of jeers and shouts of victory from all around them. "But don't go thinking that means you're alpha," he warned her firmly. "You have two more males standing between you and the top spot. So take a day or two to recover, if you need it. But then it's back to business."

Panting harshly and dripping blood all over the grass, Caroline nodded. This was the first, but most certainly not the last fight she would need to win to claim her place as alpha.


Three days later, Caroline was once more striding across the lawn, the Den gathering around her. Silas was her opponent this time. Two days ago she'd fought Caleb, and won, which had come as a surprise more to herself than to anyone else. Now Silas was the last wolf standing between her and the rank of alpha, and the quiet words he'd spoken to her this morning echoed in her mind.

He'd pulled her aside, out of the kitchen at breakfast, and murmured, "You know you have to challenge me soon. And understand me clearly, Caroline..." He'd glanced around, to check they were alone, and then muttered, "You cannot beat me in a fair fight. You and I both know that." It was true – Silas had taught Caroline almost everything she knew about fighting, and while the student could sometimes grow to outshine the teacher, that was certainly not the case in this instance. "And if you want to hold rank for any length of time," he went on, "then this fight needs to look *good*." He looked her in the eye. "So I need you to hit hard, move fast, and leave the rest up to me. If the Den doesn't believe this is real, they'll never pull in behind you."

Caroline was too much of a pragmatist to be offended by his declaration that he could win the fight, and she was not nearly clever enough to know how to stage one effectively. So she had to trust Silas to hold to his word. He'd been the one to get her into this situation, after all. Not much sense in setting her up as alpha if he was just going to kick it out from under her now.

The fight was hard and vigorous – by Caroline's standards, it was as real as they came, Silas a tough opponent, a very even match that she was genuinely struggling to beat at times. Which was probably just as well, she thought in hindsight, when she'd finally pinned him to the ground, both of them bleeding, and secured his surrender by choking the air out of him whilst simultaneously sitting on him with her full weight and digging her claws into his belly. If the fight was good enough to almost convince *her* that it was real, then the rest of the Den should be no problem.

As Silas climbed to his feet and offered his hand for her to shake, Caroline looked around at the silent crowd, feeling more nervous than ever about the situation.

The last few days had been fraught with tension, as firstly, Anna had left, not even sparing them the courtesy of waiting until a new alpha was found, and then there had been endless discussions on the possibility of Caroline taking over the role. Baron had been an absolute rock, standing firmly beside Caroline the whole way – a surprise to her, given that their relationship had often been on shaky ground. Some of the Den had legitimate concerns, a number of which Baron had answered by stating that there was a mandatory period of extra training from the Council for any new alpha, to get them up to speed with all their various duties and responsibilities.

"In the absence of further challenges, I claim the rank of alpha," Caroline announced. "How does the Den answer?"

A full public veto would see her booted from the role, regardless of her rank. She waited, holding her breath as the Den considered their answer.

"You run fast and true," Silas said finally, the first to answer the question. "And I will follow."

"I will follow," Caleb said next, and then Heron, Raniesha, Skip, until every voice was repeating the sentiment.

But if Caroline should have felt any kind of pride or satisfaction at her latest achievement, it was strangely absent. Instead, all she felt was the heavy weight of responsibility. These wolves had chosen to support her, despite many of them having very real doubts about her ability to fill the role, and gaining the title of alpha was just the first step in proving to them all that she had what it took to lead.

She was not going to let them down. She had much to learn, many adjustments to make to her life, and after the mess that Anna had left for her, there was no way in the world she was going to take a backseat position where Baron was concerned. If he thought he could get away with continuing to run the Den singlehandedly, with no one to check his more outlandish ideas, he had another thing coming. He was her closest and most loyal ally, Caroline knew already, but he was also going to be her toughest opposition.

# CHAPTER THIRTY-THREE

**Present Day**

Caroline sat on the back patio, alone for the time being, a glass of vodka in her hand as she tried to calm her jittery nerves.

She'd spent the entire day thinking, pacing her room, then running in wolf form to try and clear her head. She'd read the booklet Eleanor had given her, and sat with the woman for a couple of hours, asking her questions – not because she particularly wanted answers, but because she knew it was expected of her. And after all of it, she was no closer to a decision than she had been when Eleanor had first delivered her unexpected news.

The back door opened, and Caroline glanced around to see Baron stepping outside. She swore under her breath. He was the last person she wanted to see right now, desperately needing time alone to think, and she hopped off the wall she was sitting on, turning to face him with a glare. "What the fuck do you want?"

"Nice to see you, too," he replied blithely, taking a seat on the wall she had just vacated. "I thought we could have a little chat."

"Eleanor said I could take a few days to make a decision," Caroline snapped, sure that he'd come to tell her she was perfect for the job and what the hell was she waiting for? "So I'm taking some time, thinking about it, and I don't appreciate-"

"Whoa, hang on," Baron jumped in, holding up his hands. "Let's call a truce here, shall we? There have been moments in the past – not many, but enough – when you and I have managed to put down our swords and have a heartfelt discussion without the need to lock horns. And I'd like to have a go at that now."

That made Caroline pause. In truth, for all their frequent disagreements, she respected Baron more than she'd respected almost anyone else in her life. So she stepped back. Took a deep breath. Came to sit down on the wall again and waited for him to speak.

Baron looked her over slowly, an expression of genuine affection creeping over his face. "Kendrick would have been proud of you," he said softly. "He never stopped believing in you. You've gone from rebellious teenager, to lethal warrior, to alpha of the entire Den. And now you're up for Councillor. He would have been proud."

Caroline said nothing, but felt her face heat at the praise. It wasn't often that Baron bothered to affirm or compliment anything she had done.

"I firmly believe that you would make a magnificent Councillor," he said next. "You have an eye for strategy that few can match. You're selfless, to an almost ridiculous degree." When she went to protest, he went on. "When Anna stepped down as alpha, our Den was facing the worst crisis it had seen since Kendrick died."

That was true enough. Kendrick's death had come out of nowhere, a raid by the Noturatii that had seen half their Den wiped out in a single day, a gaping hole left in their ranks with Anna badly injured and left in a coma, and no males of sufficient rank or training to take Kendrick's place as alpha. Left without a rudder in a wild and dangerous storm, the Council had stepped in, all but ready to shut down the Den and move its remaining members overseas. That Baron had pulled them back from the brink was nothing short of a miracle. And it was perhaps an overstatement to say that Caroline had done the same, when Anna stepped down, but not by a huge degree.

"You stepped up to the post," Baron went on. "You completed the Council's training, you got Silas to teach you to fight. Like an alpha, not like a force of nature bent on destruction," he added with a laugh, at her insulted look. "And you pulled the Den in behind you, when half of them were just as ready to stab you in the back and call it quits.

"And now you're staring down the barrel of a position on the Council. I know exactly what's going to happen in the next few days. The Den is going to vote on your appointment." The vote was the last formality in the election process, and a clear majority was needed to make the appointment official. Caroline still had her doubts about whether they'd side with her, but apparently, Baron held no such reservations. "And they're going to approve it," he said confidently. "Then you're going to accept the posting in Italy, pack up your things here, and move in with a bunch of stiffs whose favourite thing in the world is to talk policy all day long." He smiled, and then the look faded, turning pensive instead. "But if you head into that battlefield in the mindset you're currently in, you are going to hate every single minute of it." Caroline turned to him with a glare, but Baron wasn't done yet. "Not only will you hate the job, but you'll hate yourself for hating it, and you'll hate everyone else for putting you there – the Den, Andre, the Council itself. Because," he said, emphasising his words carefully, "you have been living in a cage of your own making since the moment you set foot inside this Den."

The words cut too close to the bone, the truth suddenly a living, breathing thing, a ghost given life by his words. "I don't know what the hell you're talking about," she bit out harshly.

"Look at yourself, Caroline. Look at the work you do. You never cut yourself any slack. You don't let yourself fail. You won't admit when you're tired. You won't lean on anyone else. You won't ask for help when you don't know the answers. You've set this impossible standard for yourself, and you see anything less as total and complete failure.

"You think I never screw things up?" Baron went on, continuing right along with his rant. "No, scratch that, of course I do. But I'm aware of it. The rest of the Den is aware of it. Hell, the fucking Council is aware of it. But the Council doesn't beat me up over it because they all know, from personal experience, how fucking difficult it is to run a Den. The rest of the Den knows, but they don't throw it in my face, because they're all terrified that if I'm not here, one of them will have to do this job instead. So understand, Caroline, that no one expects you to be perfect. No one except you."

He was right, Caroline had to admit to herself, even if she couldn't quite get the words out. That was what she felt each and every day, every time they were attacked by the Noturatii, every time they had to make a decision on a new recruit or on a battle strategy. It was the bars of her self-inflicted cage, tightening around her, a constant warning that if she didn't get it right this time, didn't fight hard enough, didn't make the best choice, then the cage would close around her and crush her once and for all.

If she was entirely honest with herself, that was what she had felt when Eleanor had offered her the position on the Council. Just another cage, a stronger one this time, with thicker walls, with the ceiling bearing down on her if she made the slightest mistake.

She was no stranger to the challenges that the Council faced on a daily basis. They wrote the rules that kept their society a secret. Chose the location for each Den. Determined how many members each one could have, passed judgement on new recruits, decided strategies for fighting the Noturatii and safeguarded the future of their species. It was terrifying to think that Caroline would soon be among their number, making decisions that could make or break their future. How the hell was she going to deal with that, when it wasn't individual lives on the line, but the future of their entire species?

But walking away from the challenge also wasn't an option, because that, in itself, was a failure. A failure to stand up to her responsibilities, to use her skills and knowledge to steer this eclectic family towards a brighter future. And failure was never, ever an option.

"Being appointed to the Council can be the greatest honour any shifter can receive," Baron told her softly. "It's a chance to change the course of history, to balance tradition with progress, to bring to light new ideas that can be mined for tremendous rewards.

"So go to Italy if it's what you truly want. No one would stop you, and just so you're aware, I admire the hell out of you for even considering it. Being offered a position like that would scare the shit out of me. But if it's just another cage, just another set of duties and expectations heaped upon you by other people… I'm just saying maybe you should think twice."

He stood up, not expecting a reply, and for the moment at least, Caroline had none to offer. He'd ripped her most private fears wide open and exposed them to the light of day. And she was mortified to feel tears pricking at her eyes as she suddenly remembered the only other man who had ever managed to do that to her, and remembered also that he was forever lost to her, having himself chosen obligation and duty over personal satisfaction, the decision keeping him from her as surely as if he were locked in a cage of his own.

"The door is open, Caroline. No one is keeping you in your cage except yourself. So isn't it about time you stepped outside and had a look at what else life can offer you?"

With that final question, Baron turned and walked away, leaving Caroline with more questions, and more doubts than ever before.

The following evening, Caroline was once again standing on the back patio of the manor, but this time she was far from alone. The entire Den had gathered, along with Eleanor, who was overseeing the ceremony, and Andre, who was lurking in a corner, keeping to himself. It hadn't just been Caroline avoiding him, she realised as she stole covert glances at him through the crowd. He'd been going out of his way to avoid her, as well.

"As you are all aware," Eleanor was saying, "Caroline has been proposed as a candidate for the empty seat on the Council. We have made this decision after careful deliberation and a thorough investigation into her skills and attributes, and we have the utmost confidence in her ability to guide Il Trosa with kindness and wisdom.

"But our opinions are not the only ones that matter. You, also, all have a voice. And so, having given you all twenty-four hours to consider this matter, I am calling the vote. Your decision will be upheld as the final voice on the subject. An affirmative vote will see your alpha rise to the position of Councillor, to oversee the future of our species. A negative vote will nullify her candidacy and close the matter permanently. So I ask you all:

Consider this choice seriously. Place your vote honestly. And consider not just your own feelings, but the future of Il Trosa in this decision."

Caroline watched the proceedings with an odd sort of detachment. She had yet to officially accept the position, spending the day going over and over Baron's words from last night, making a decision, only to find herself second guessing it five minutes later, and she must have changed her mind twenty times by now, each time thanks to a new reason that had suddenly popped into her head.

The real problem, as far as Caroline saw it, was the question of what she would do if she turned the offer down.

Last night, Baron had asked her what she really wanted in life. After nearly six years at the job, the role of alpha no longer scared her the way it once had. For all the pressure she placed on herself to do it well, she had become good at it. Not perfect – as Baron had said, they both still made mistakes – but good enough. Good enough to hold her Den together. Good enough to recruit new shifters and train them to be productive members of the team. Good enough to hold her own against Baron, to steer them through a crisis, to put up with the inevitable squabbling and in-fighting that popped up now and then.

But the question of what she really *wanted?*

That was a tough one, not because she didn't know the answer, but because what she wanted had seemed for so long to be an unattainable goal. In her mind's eye, the answer was clear. Herself. Andre. Her Den, all around her. A new family, to replace the old, hideous one that she'd abandoned all those years ago, the larger one that lived on the estate, and the private one that lived in her heart.

But Andre had chosen another path. And that made all the rest of it seem hollow.

Perhaps it was time she finally moved on from him, Caroline counselled herself gently. She'd wasted fifteen years longing for the impossible. She had a chance for a new start now. A boyfriend, maybe? It was a long time since she'd had one, but there were plenty of honest, respectable, reliable shifter males around. There was one in France whom she'd met on occasion, who had tried to flirt with her once or twice. One of the Ukrainians in Scotland had given her a smile and a wink, and if she'd been paying more attention, maybe it could have come to something.

As either alpha or Councillor, a partner wasn't out of the question. And going to Italy wasn't abandoning her family here, Caroline reminded herself. It was just looking after them in a different way, a very important way that valued their lives just as much, even if she wasn't here to see them every day.

Eleanor's voice cut through her musings, and she realised that the Den was ready to take the vote. "The affirmative vote will be to my left,"

Eleanor announced loudly, holding out her hand to indicate the side of the patio, "and the negative vote will be to my right. Proceed."

There were seventeen shifters in the Den, sixteen who could place a vote, since Caroline didn't get to vote for herself. Which meant she needed a majority of nine to seven to succeed. Anything less, even a draw of eight-eight, would be taken as a negative result. For all that it kept its democratic processes to a minimum, Il Trosa took its members seriously when it counted, and for a role as important as Councillor, no risks were going to be taken.

She'd expected to be nervous about this. She expected her Den to vote honestly, not to place emphasis on personal loyalties or simper about for favours by giving their approval, but the prospect of being voted out by her own Den was a very real one, a terrifying denouncement of her skills as a leader. She'd led the Den to the best of her ability, not always being able to grant them what they would have desired, but always making decisions with their best interests in mind. And she'd expected to be standing here, shaking in her boots at this most definitive of judgements on her success or failure as an alpha.

But instead, she felt only numb. She watched with no particular attention as the shifters moved, slowly, taking their time, giving the decision all the consideration it deserved. And when the last person had moved, had chosen a side and cast their vote... Caroline couldn't help but stare in shock as her jaw dropped.

It was unanimous. A unanimous vote in her favour. Caroline stared at the clustered group of people, unable to believe what she was seeing.

"The vote is called," Eleanor announced, a clear note of pride in her voice. "Sixteen for, none against. Caroline Saunders... Welcome to the Council."

# CHAPTER THIRTY-FOUR

Andre let himself into Eleanor's room, having knocked on the door just moments ago, and he wasn't surprised to see her hard at work, reviewing documents on her computer, typing notes next to some report or other.

"Andre." She smiled up at him, setting her work aside to give him her full attention. "What can I do for you?"

Andre fingered the letter in his hand, typed clearly, folded neatly and nestled in a plain white envelope. "There's something I need to discuss with you." He handed her the envelope, noting the surprise on her face as she took it. "I'm formally seeking permission to resign from my service to the Council."

Eleanor stared at him, the sudden announcement completely unexpected. "Well. That's certainly a surprise," she said, glancing down at the envelope, but not opening it. "What brought this on?"

Andre sighed and paced across the room. "It's been a long time in coming," he admitted. "The Council was surprised, right from the moment I made my choice to become an assassin. And rightly so. It's not something I would have considered, but for the circumstances at the time. It's been an honour to defend our species, but it's not just shifters and the Noturatii being killed in the war. It's innocent humans getting caught in the crossfire. Not just one or two, but dozens. Hundreds, if you add them all up over the years. And with things the way they stand, we currently run the risk of becoming the very thing we've always claimed to abhor – mindless killers willing to destroy anyone who puts us at risk. There may be honour in defending our species, but there is no honour in killing innocent bystanders to do it."

Eleanor nodded gravely. "This is a most serious request. I needn't ask if you've thought it through – clearly you have – but it comes as quite a shock, nonetheless. I'll speak to the Council about it. But if they approve your resignation… have you considered which Den you would like to join? Assuming one of them will accept you?"

That was the next complication in Andre's plan. He couldn't join any Den without a vote being taken from its members, a majority needed to earn him a place in their ranks. And there were plenty of wolves out there who would be more than a little reluctant to have a former assassin living under their roof.

"I thought perhaps the Den in France," Andre replied, "if they'll have me. I know some of the shifters there, and I speak French well enough."

"I had thought you might consider the Italian Den," Eleanor suggested mildly.

Andre shook his head. That was where he'd lived with his parents for so many years, and the memories, now soured by their deaths, made it an unpalatable option. At first, of course, he'd considered England. It had been his childhood home, after all, even if most of the shifters he'd known then were now dead. But the main draw card for England had been Caroline's presence, and once she moved to Italy to join the Council, there was nothing left for him here.

"I'll put it to the Council tonight," Eleanor promised. "I must say, though, I'll miss you. And not just because we need every soldier we can get. You're one of the best assassins in Il Trosa. But more than that… it has always been a pleasure working with you, Andre. You're a true gentleman. I'm going to miss that."

Andre nodded, but didn't return the sentiment. In truth, there was little about the nomadic life of killing and violence that he was going to miss.

"There is one other issue I'd like to discuss with you," he added, after a moment. "One that needs to be put to the Council, though I don't expect they're going to like it."

Eleanor raised one graceful eyebrow. "Oh?"

"It concerns our strategies for fighting the Endless War." Eleanor's expression instantly turned guarded, and it was no surprise. It was a topic that had caused the Council no shortage of headaches in recent years, and Andre could only hope that his position as assassin would persuade them to take his suggestions seriously. "We've been fighting this war for centuries. And in the past, the tactics of keeping our heads down and staying as hidden as possible were sound. In the middle ages, the superstitions of the general public gave us little other choice, and since then, we've struggled to rebuild. We've grown our numbers to three thousand members, we've spread across Europe and into Russia, we've acquired land and significant wealth, and in this latest age of information, access to weapons and technology that we couldn't have dreamed of in ages gone by.

"But so have the Noturatii, and for the entire time I've been in your service, it's been nothing but a tit-for-tat trade off. We kill one of them, they kill one of us. We buy new guns, they buy new grenades. They have more than three times the manpower that we do, and it is my fervent belief that if we continue fighting them on their terms, sooner or later, we are going to lose."

Eleanor was listening closely, but he could already see the counter-arguments gathering in her mind. She wasn't liking this one bit.

"There is only one way we're going to win this war," Andre went on, reciting the speech he'd spent the last two days rehearsing. "And before you dismiss it on purely conceptual grounds, I hope you'll give me the chance to explain my perspective in full."

Another raised eyebrow, but Eleanor nodded. "Go ahead."

"We need to go public," Andre said, seeing the instant denial in Eleanor's eyes. But she'd promised to hear him out, so he continued. "It's the one thing the Noturatii truly fears, and the only thing they are powerless to prevent. Whenever we've considered the idea in the past, it's been on the basis of a sudden announcement to the world at large. And with that comes the extreme risk that public sentiment will turn against us.

"But what we've never really considered is putting together a plan to tease out public opinion before they actually know about us. There are a dozen or more ways it could be done. We have PR agents in every Den, who monitor the news and kill any story that hits too close to the truth about us. What if we started letting a few of those stories slip through the net? Let social media start a few rumours, build a few conspiracy theories. There have been dozens of times in the past few years where we've wanted to enlist the aid of humans – police, doctors, veterinarians, biologists. Maybe we can start doing that, screen some likely candidates, reveal our secrets to a select, trusted few, and see how they react. It could take years to move all the way towards an official 'coming out', decades even, but we can make good use of that time by testing out public sentiment on the concept. Influencing the opinions of the public, even. Look at gay rights, for example. A few decades ago, homosexual acts were a crime. Now we've got gay marriage legislation in countries across the world, gay rights activist groups, government support. We can't just sit around and wait for the world to like us. We need to give them a healthy nudge in the right direction."

Eleanor opened her mouth to reply, but Andre wasn't done yet. "But more than just going public," he went on, "if we're to provide a strong defence against the Noturatii – because the instant they figure out what we're doing, they're going to be all over us – then we also need to boost our numbers. The Council has put limits on the size of each Den – again, a sound strategy in the past. We needed to stay small enough to avoid public attention. But if we're going to match them in battle, we need to match their numbers, if not exceed them."

"New shifters means new territory," Eleanor pointed out, not disagreeing with him, but rather pointing out pragmatic limitations to his plan. "Even if we let the Dens recruit as many people as they liked, they don't have room to house them all. This manor, for example, is running close to capacity, and they couldn't handle any more than twenty-five shifters at most."

"Exactly," Andre agreed. "But there are other options, besides expanding the existing Dens."

"Humanity is slowly creeping over the entire world. There's not much wilderness left in which to keep an extra six thousand wolves."

"Not in Europe, no, there's not." He let the statement hang… and the wary caution that grew in Eleanor's eyes told him that she was following his train of thought perfectly.

"North America is off limits," she said flatly. "The possibility of expanding into Canada has been discussed in the past, and you and I both know the reasons why we can't do that."

Andre shook his head. "No one has heard from the North American shifters in over three hundred years. For all we know, they could be extinct, just like the bears. I'm not saying we just pack our bags and move in – that could lead to a shifter war, as we're both well aware. But isn't it time we started putting out a few feelers? Try to find out if Canada is still occupied territory or not?" As a general rule, the shifters of each species were notoriously territorial. And Eleanor was right – they had more than enough reason to fear those who had once inhabited the North American continent. Their magic was deep and powerful, far more potent than anything the wolves could hope to fight. "That side of the equation is a way off, at any rate," Andre said, not wanting to get caught up in the details of the argument right now. It was more the concept that he was trying to get across. "The first question to be answered is whether going public is a viable option – if we plan our tactics well, and take things slowly, that is."

Eleanor still didn't like his plan, but he could see in her eyes that he'd struck a chord, that she would at least have to consider it.

"You play dice with our very existence," she said coldly, a far cry from her usual polite manners, and Andre nodded, aware of the enormity of what he was proposing.

"Isn't that what the Council has been doing for the last six hundred years?" he asked, though not without respect for her reservations.

Eleanor sighed, and Andre knew he had won. "I'll bring it up with the Council," she said reluctantly.

"I've detailed a proposal for how it could work," Andre said immediately, handing her the second envelope in his hands, a far thicker one than the first. "And if they wish, I would be happy to attend a meeting in Italy to discuss the matter further."

Eleanor stared at the envelope for a moment… and then she burst out laughing. "It seems I have underestimated you, Andre. You are turning out to be quite the force to be reckoned with."

Caroline sat opposite Eleanor at the table in the library, staring at the sheet of paper she had just been given. It was a contract confirming her appointment to the Council, the letter detailing her duties, responsibilities, the training to come and the consequences for failing at any of the listed tasks.

"Once you reach Italy, you'll take a formal vow before the Council," Eleanor was explaining, "but for now, it's just a case of signing the paperwork. Are there any last questions you have before we wrap this up?"

Caroline shook her head. She picked up the pen and fingered it restlessly, pretending to read through the document, though her mind was far away, her eyes not focusing on the words.

Even now, she'd never formally agreed to join the Council, though Eleanor must have taken it that she had, after their long chats and Caroline's questions on political protocol and living arrangements.

She removed the cap from the pen – a beautiful calligraphy pen, engraved with Celtic-looking symbols. She stared at the line where she was to sign her name…

And then she thought of Kendrick. The first day she'd met him, all the suspicions she'd harboured about his intentions. Meeting Silas, and being trained by him, until her muscles were screaming and she could hardly breathe. Trying to shoot her family, meeting up with the Grey Watch, her trip to Italy, and then all the years that had followed, making friends, fighting for status, battles with the Noturatii, recruiting new members.

She felt like she'd lived three lifetimes in her thirty-five years.

Baron's words from the other night came back to her. She had been living in a cage for her entire life – first, the one created by her parents, a cage of grimy walls and yelling and violence. Then one of anger, as she struggled to let go of the hate she felt for them, for her old life. And then there was the one that was entirely of her own making. Her perfectionism, if she could put a simple label on it, a cage of expectations and regrets and doubts that had choked her for long enough.

Caroline replaced the cap on the pen and set it gently on the desk.

"I'm sorry," she said to Eleanor, heartfelt words, though they flowed from her more freely than she had imagined they would. "But I cannot accept this offer. I decline the position on the Council. I wish to stay with my Den."

As Eleanor stared at her in undisguised shock, Caroline felt lighter and freer than she had done in years.

Melissa sat before her laptop in her flat, feeling a deep wave of satisfaction. After sending her letter to Headquarters, there had been no response for a long time, and she had almost given up on the hope of ever having her ideas taken seriously.

But here it was, the reply she'd been waiting for. And it was everything she had hoped it would be.

Professor Ivor Banks, the head scientist in Germany, had written a long and detailed reply. There was some effusive nonsense at the start about appreciating her dedication to their cause and praising her creativity in solving their ongoing problems with their research.

Then there was a short paragraph that said the Professor had sent her suggestions about extra training to the defence department, who were now looking into the level of staffing needed to provide basic combat classes for all their employees and running budget projections for such a thing. It was as much as Melissa had hoped for, and more than she had expected. Of course, they couldn't just rewrite their entire training plan overnight. That kind of investment took time and money of the sort that didn't just fall out of the sky. But they were considering it, seeing it as a valuable strategy for their future success, and the validation gave her a warm glow.

And then she read the final part. The part about her ideas on the experiments. And when she saw what the Professor had written, she jumped out of her seat, crowing with glee, dignity be damned as she pranced around her flat in delight.

He loved her ideas! He found the possibility of multiple voltages per shift to be entirely plausible, and was going to arrange extra funding for her to conduct her experiments!

Take that, Dr Evans, she thought gleefully. That would teach the good Doctor to ignore her staff.

Getting a hold of herself, Melissa sat down again to finish reading the letter, feeling her heart speed up as she read the final part. If she'd been excited before, now she was absolutely ecstatic. Not only was the Professor impressed with her ideas, but he was coming to England personally, to review the team's experiments.

He was due to arrive in a few days' time, and would personally oversee the first of the tests Melissa wanted to run, assist her in analysing the data and make suggestions for further improvements that could hone their results.

It was a dream come true. Validation for her ideas, recognition from Headquarters, and the chance to meet Professor Ivor Banks in person. He was one of her heroes, Melissa having read every report he'd ever written on shifter physiology, and she'd been constantly impressed and inspired by his work.

Melissa opened a new file and began typing frantic notes. There was so much to prepare for before his arrival, and she was determined that everything would be set up and ready to go, no detail left unattended.

# CHAPTER THIRTY-FIVE

Dee sat in the library, facing Eleanor and Andre on one side, and Caroline and Baron on the other, wondering what on earth this meeting was about.

In the last few days, there had been no shortage of crises to solve, dramas to settle and official meetings aplenty to thrash everything out. The latest slice of chaos had been concluded this morning, with Caroline's startling announcement that she had turned down the post in Italy.

The Den had taken the news rather well. There had been a predictable amount of shock, a dozen questions about why and declarations that she was turning down the opportunity of a lifetime, along with plenty of confused faces. But then Caroline had given them an extremely simple explanation for her decision. "I love my Den," she had said. "I love seeing you all every day. And I couldn't imagine giving all that up to go and live with a bunch of politicians in an ivory tower."

They'd accepted her reasons with surprising calm – Dee wasn't well versed enough in high-end politics to grasp all the implications of the decision, but she was glad to have Caroline stay, nonetheless. For all that she could be tactless, blunt and domineering, she was also loyal, intelligent, and cared more about this Den than anyone Dee knew. And then Tank had given Caroline a cheeky grin, and declared, "Damn good thing. It would have been a nightmare trying to find a new alpha." And that had been that.

Eleanor had declared her intention to leave early tomorrow, and as far as Dee knew, that was the end of any official business for the time being, so she was a little surprised when she'd been called into a meeting with not just Andre, but Eleanor as well. It was rather nerve racking to find herself face-to-face with a member of the Council, and she wondered if she'd done anything wrong.

"A serious issue has come up," Eleanor began, once everyone was seated, her eyes focused on Dee. "And time is of the essence, so unfortunately, I'm not going to be able to give you long to think about this. I received a call about the Den in Italy this morning. They recently converted one of their new recruits, and the conversion hasn't taken. The wolf is showing all the signs of going rogue."

Dee felt her blood run cold at the announcement, and she instantly knew what Eleanor was going to say next. And then she decided a moment later she couldn't stand the tension, so she blurted it out herself instead.

"You want me to remove the human from the shifter," she said grimly. "Or is it the other way around? You want to keep the human and get rid of the wolf?" She felt Faeydir stir in her mind at that thought. Killing wolves was something she strongly objected to, regardless of the circumstances, and Dee was anticipating quite the argument from her animal side if that was what was being asked.

"No, you were right the first time," Eleanor said quickly. "We'd like you to remove the human." She glanced at Andre, who so far had said nothing. "Andre brought it to our attention, after the last time you were asked to perform such a service, that it might be appropriate to create a sanctuary for separated wolves, should a situation like this arise. Allowing the human to live isn't a viable option – I'm sure you're aware of the security risks that would create. But there's no reason why we can't keep the wolf, and care for it appropriately."

That was a relief, and Dee felt a jolt of satisfaction from Faeydir. *We're still going to be killing a human,* she reminded the animal sharply, thinking that she was being rather insensitive about the situation, and Faeydir meekly whined in her mind, a wolf version of an apology.

"We've been doing some investigating, and have secured a parcel of land in Romania that should be perfect for a wolf sanctuary. The Romanian Den is rather eager to lend a hand and have volunteered to run it. It's not set up yet, but they have the facilities to be able to care for a single wolf for a couple of months until the proper arrangements can be made."

That, too, was a relief. While she liked the idea of a sanctuary for stray wolves, neither Dee nor Faeydir liked the idea of one having to live all by herself. But if she was to stay with the Romanian Den, she'd have plenty of playmates to keep her company.

"When do we leave?" Dee asked, not looking forward to the task, but knowing that delaying it wasn't going to make it any easier.

"First thing in the morning," Eleanor replied. "Once a shifter starts to turn rogue, we've only got two, maybe three days before they go completely mad. And after that, we're not entirely sure that removing the human side would actually solve the problem. We may just be left with a crazed wolf at the end of it all."

Dee nodded. "I'll pack my things. How long will I be away for?"

"That raises another important point," Eleanor said. "I understand that

Andre has already spoken to you about the possibility of spending some time with the Council, to have your abilities assessed, and for us to make some more investigations into the nature of your rather unique wolf. And given that you and she are going to be in Italy anyway, would the two of you be willing to stay on for a little while?"

Dee hesitated at that one. While she'd notionally agreed to go to Italy, the thought of being poked and prodded like a lab rat was not an appealing one. "I'll ask Faeydir," she said, turning her thoughts inward.

To her surprise, Faeydir was rather intrigued at the idea. By her understanding, the Council wolves were advanced warriors, tasked with protecting their species, and Faeydir quite liked the idea of spending time in such revered company. There would be tests involved, Dee reminded her, lots of questions about Faeydir's past life, an analysis of their abilities. That earned her a mild growl, though Faeydir remained generally in favour of the idea, and Dee told Eleanor as much. "Faeydir agrees, but she's a little concerned about the tests you might run. As am I. So we'll come, but on the understanding that we can refuse any given test, if we feel it's not appropriate."

"Agreed," Eleanor said easily. "We have no intention of making you uncomfortable. And given what you're able to do for rogue shifters, we see you as an asset to our cause, rather than a threat to it. Please understand, our investigations are far more a product of curiosity than any perceived danger from you."

"Okay, then. I'll go and start packing." With a smile from Eleanor, and a nod from Baron and Caroline, she got up and headed up the stairs, excited, but also nervous about this next stage of her adventure.


After Dee left the room, Eleanor stood up, and Baron went to follow, until she motioned him down again. "That's all from me," Eleanor said, gathering her papers. "But I believe Andre has something he would like to speak to you about."

Baron shrugged and nodded, and took his seat again.

Once Eleanor had left and closed the door, Andre hesitated, trying to choose his words carefully... and then shook his head, deciding to just bite the bullet. "I wanted to let you know that I've decided to resign as an assassin," he said bluntly.

Baron looked mildly surprised, but that was the extent of his reaction. All things being equal, it was probably something he didn't feel directly affected him too much. But Caroline's reaction was much more dramatic. She sat up straight, eyes wide in shock, and spluttered for a reply. "You what?" she managed finally. "Why?"

Andre sighed, not wanting to bring up dark memories again, but knowing that they both deserved an explanation. "What happened in Scotland wasn't an isolated event," he said grimly. "Too many innocent bystanders are being killed in this war, and for my part, I've grown tired of being the one to pull the trigger."

Caroline swore under her breath.

"I can well understand your perspective," Baron said. "None of us like this war, and I can't imagine that being on the front lines of it every day would be an easy thing. But you've served the Council well. There's no dishonour in realising you've reached your limits."

Andre nodded. "It wasn't an easy decision. But now that the Council has approved my resignation, I'm left with another problem. As I'm no longer an assassin, I can't live with the Council in Italy any more. I need to find a Den to join. I'd like to make a formal request to join yours."

Baron raised an eyebrow. He looked Andre up and down, glanced at Caroline, and let out a long-suffering sigh. "Oh God, here we go," he muttered, rolling his eyes.

"What?" Caroline demanded, and Andre braced himself for the latest round of bickering between the two to start up.

But rather than snarling back at her, Baron simply laughed. "I've seen you get angry," he said to Caroline, amusement sparkling in his eyes. "I've seen you cry, I've seen you laugh – maybe only twice in my entire life, but even so. But what I've never seen," he went on, leaning forward gleefully, "is what it looks like when you fall in love."

Caroline gaped at him, speechless and completely flustered. "What? What the fuck makes you say that?"

Baron snorted. "The other morning, you came out of Andre's room, reeking of him like you'd been rolling around in his work-out gear. And that was *after* you'd taken a shower," he added with a grin. Caroline turned beet red, and Andre sighed quietly. Fucking hell, he'd forgotten all about that. Every wolf in the house had probably picked up their scents on each other, and would have known exactly what had been going on in his bedroom that night. Hell, even Eleanor probably knew, though if she did, she'd been the epitome of discretion.

"So I have no doubt that Caroline would gladly accept you as a member of our Den," Baron said with a smirk. But then his expression turned grim. "But I'm afraid I'm going to have to say no."

Caroline's head snapped up at that. "You what?" she demanded. Unfortunately for her, it was one of the overriding rules of Il Trosa – while the whole Den got to vote on whether a shifter could join them or not, either of the alphas had the ultimate right of veto – they could absolutely refuse a shifter membership, for any, or no reason. "How dare you?"

"How dare I?" he repeated, a hint of anger in his voice now. He looked Andre up and down with a cool, calculating look. "I'm not handing this

Den over to a poncy upstart imposter. I spent the last ten years caring for my Den, my family, and if you think you can just waltz in and take over from me, you've got another thing coming-"

"What? I'm not petitioning for alpha!" Andre interrupted, shocked that Baron would jump to such a conclusion. Okay, so he was the better fighter, but that didn't mean he wanted to kick Baron out of his place as leader. "If you like, we can have a status fight, just to-"

"Status fight? What the fuck will that prove? Everyone knows you'd win-"

"I'll lose!" Andre said, rolling his eyes. Christ, it was like trying to reason with a five year old throwing a tantrum.

Baron glared at him. "You're the better fighter by far. So if you lose, everyone will know you threw the fight."

"And that's the point. It's not about who's the better fighter. It's a public declaration that I intend to support your leadership. For Christ's sake, Baron, your entire Den is not going to abandon you and fall in behind me just because I know how to kill people better than you." The idea was patently absurd. But apparently, he'd underestimated just how much Baron was threatened by him. It was a common problem that assassins faced, but after several months under the same roof, he'd somehow assumed that Baron would have moved past any petty rivalries.

Baron stared at him, eyes narrowed. "Why don't you want alpha?" There was genuine curiosity in the words, as well as an ongoing undercurrent of warning.

"I'm retiring as a Council assassin," Andre said wryly. "The last thing I want to do is heap myself up with a whole pile of new responsibilities." His lips quirked upwards in a faint smile. "Frankly, I could use a holiday."

"That sounds... reasonable," Baron conceded after a moment. And then asked, "I have your word on that? You won't challenge me for alpha?"

Andre nodded. "I do expect to end up as a high ranking wolf. But no, I have no intention of making a play for alpha."

Baron considered the idea for a moment. "Caroline?" he asked, turning to her.

"Yes," she said immediately, eyes locked on Andre. "He can join the Den."

Andre almost sighed in relief. He'd rather anticipated this conversation going the other way, with Baron welcoming him, a powerful addition to his Den, and Caroline putting up opposition. She was the reason he was choosing this Den, after all, but after their night together, he was honestly not sure how she would react. They'd both declared their love for each other – awkwardly, but honestly – but since then they'd both been avoiding each other like the plague, and he hadn't dared to simply assume she'd want to resume their fumbling relationship just because he did. Even so, it wasn't going to be easy. They came from vastly different worlds, had years of catching up to do before they could really claim to know each other again... but after long weeks of watching her from the shadows, of weighing her every action and measuring her every word in his assessment for the Council, Andre was more convinced than ever that she was the one for him.

Though aside from that heartfelt declaration that she'd accept him into her Den, Caroline was currently giving nothing away.

Baron looked from him to Caroline and back, and Andre wasn't entirely sure what he was seeing on each of their faces. But finally, he sighed. "All right. Fine. We'll take a vote with the Den, and if they agree, you can join us."

Andre smiled, feeling lighter, and younger than he had in years. "Thank you," he said sincerely. "You won't regret this."

# CHAPTER THIRTY-SIX

"What the hell are you doing?" were the first words out of Caroline's mouth, once Baron had left the room.

"Exactly what I said," Andre replied, hoping he hadn't misread her. "Retiring. And hopefully, joining your Den."

"You're throwing away a perfectly good career. One that benefits Il Trosa immeasurably."

Andre smiled wryly. "And didn't you do exactly the same thing just yesterday?" he said gently, not intending any reprimand in the statement. He fully understood her reasons for turning down the appointment as Councillor, and if he'd been a little more selfish than he was, he might even have been relieved by her decision.

That stopped her in her tracks, and Caroline looked away, a faint blush creeping up her cheeks. "But why here?" she pressed. "Why do you want to join this Den?"

He'd thought it was obvious, but if she wanted to hear it out loud, he had no problem telling her. Facing up to his own long-running affection for her was a drop in the ocean, now that he'd taken the plunge and resigned from his career. "Because I love you," he said simply. "I meant what I said the other night. I fell in love with you back in Italy, fifteen years ago. And I figured it was about time I did something for me, for a change."

"But I... you can't... It's not..." He waited while she fumbled for words, feeling strangely at peace with the whole situation. It had taken him far too long to acknowledge how he felt, even to himself, and it was a relief to finally be able to say it out loud.

"But why me? How can you love me?" she demanded. "I'm stubborn. And hot tempered. And argumentative, and I haven't the slightest tact or diplomacy."

Andre had to laugh at that. Unable to resist any more, he got up and came around to her side of the table, lowering himself to one knee beside her and taking her hand. "I'm just as stubborn," he said cheerfully. "And after years of listening to politicians beat around the bush and phrase every banal statement in the most diplomatic way possible, it's a relief to find someone who will just say what they think for a change. You're more courageous than anyone I've met: facing your own demons takes a lot more courage than facing a horde of rampaging Noturatii. And you're a fine warrior. Not that I couldn't give you a few pointers," he added with a wink, and Caroline managed to look both amused and offended by the suggestion.

"So I can honestly say you are everything I've been looking for in a woman. And more than I had ever hoped for. But the real question," he added, surprised at his own sudden nervousness, "is will you have me? I get out of bed at ridiculous hours of the morning. Our bedroom will constantly be littered with weapons. On the plus side though, Baron doesn't seem to like me. So I could annoy him with that for the next decade or so. Just in case you ever run out of things to argue with him about yourself."

Caroline laughed, the first one he'd heard from her in a long time, and he couldn't help but smile. "Of course I'll have you," she told him, trying to sound gruff, and failing. "Who the hell else would ever put up with me?"

Standing on the manor's back patio, the evening still light, despite the late hour, Andre found himself facing a crowd of apprehensive shifters, and tried to remain calm. Having gained the approval of the two alphas, and finally set things right with Caroline, he had high hopes for a bright future with this Den.

The rest of its members, however, had yet to share his point of view.

"We're not going to support you as alpha," Raniesha called, the latest in a long list of questions and objections in response to his request.

Baron had announced this morning that Andre had requested to join the Den, giving everyone almost a full day to consider the idea. And they'd all gathered here about half an hour ago for the official vote.

However, in keeping with proper ritual and tradition, Baron had first asked whether anyone knew of any reason why Andre shouldn't be allowed to join the Den.

And all hell had broken loose.

"I make no petition for alpha," Andre answered plainly. "I have the utmost respect for Baron and the way he has led this Den through very trying times, and I fully intend to fall in under his leadership."

"What about the status fights?" Alistair asked pragmatically. "You can hardly expect us all to fight him one by one. It would be a huge waste of time. Not to mention terrifying," he added under his breath.

"I propose a different solution than usual for determining Andre's status," Baron replied. "It's a foregone conclusion that he could defeat anyone here with little difficulty..." The only reply to that statement was a low growl from John, and having seen him fight the massive dogs in Scotland, Andre was prepared to tolerate his objections. While he was still confident that he would win against the boy, it would undoubtedly be a tough battle. "...so I suggest that instead of starting at the bottom, Andre starts at the top and works down. How far he falls is more a question of whether he can gather any social support for his position, than of whether he can hold it by force."

"Here we go again," someone muttered, and Andre cringed. A new member in the ranks tended to inspire numerous fights, not just surrounding his own status, but that of many other members of the pack, as everyone jostled for position within the sudden change in social dynamics. The Den was clearly not looking forward to that sort of upheaval.

"Are there any other objections?" Baron asked, and Andre braced himself.

But it seemed the Den had finally run out of steam, so it was time to move on to the final part of the ritual.

"Then I call the vote on Andre's petition to join the Lakes District Den," Baron announced, loud and clear. "The affirmative vote will be cast to my left, the negative vote to my right. Proceed."

For a tense moment, nobody moved. There was a muttering through the crowd, and then Simon asked, "Can I make a conditional vote?" There was a murmur of agreement through the crowd. "I'll accept Andre as a member of our Den, but only on condition that he doesn't challenge you for alpha."

Andre sighed. Apparently, his heartfelt words hadn't been enough to quell that particular objection.

But Baron shook his head. "That's not how it works. The vote is binding, regardless of what happens in the future. But I will say this: If you don't trust him to keep his word, then I would suggest you shouldn't be voting in his favour."

It was a fair call, Andre knew, and one he should have expected. For all that Baron had given his approval for Andre to join them, he was too much of a fair and diligent leader to ever try and coerce his Den into making a decision against their better judgement. So he waited, the gathered shifters eyeing him cautiously, as they tried to make up their minds.

Finally, one of them moved. It was Dee, head held high, marching boldly to the left. An affirmative vote.

George moved next, to the right, a doubtful look on his face.

The rest of them followed, some deciding quickly, others lingering in the centre of the patio, and no one made any attempt to hurry them up. This was too important a decision to be taken lightly, one that could dramatically alter the social dynamics of the Den and impact all of their futures.

Finally, the last person moved, Caleb, who was still considered a member of this Den until he left with Eleanor in the morning, and Baron counted the heads to tally the vote. "The vote is called," he announced. "Eleven for, six against. Andre Damasio... Welcome to Misty Hills."

On the back lawn of the estate, Baron and Andre faced off against each other, the entire Den gathered around them. It was time for their much anticipated status fight, and while the result was supposed to be a foregone conclusion, that didn't stop the shifters from being on edge, emotions running high, more than a few of them apprehensive about Andre keeping his word. Jeers and insults flowed freely, the shifters eager to show support for their alpha, for all that this fight was staged.

Andre had already moved into Caroline's room, and if it hadn't been so damned amusing, it would have been nauseating to watch them together, the way they stared at each other with love-struck eyes and snuck private kisses when they thought no one was watching. As Baron had said, he'd never seen Caroline in love before, and the result was both bizarre and fascinating.

And now they just had one last issue to resolve – the status fight, in which Baron was no doubt going to find out that Andre was indeed the superior wolf, but was going to win the battle anyway.

"Come on Baron," someone called. "Show the princess who's boss."

"You fight like a poodle!" someone else yelled at Andre, who merely rolled his eyes.

"Don't expect me to go easy on you," Baron told Andre, just before they shifted. "You're about to find out what this alpha's really made of."

"Oh, shut up," Andre said with a grin. "Much more of this poncing about, and half the people here are going to fall asleep. I know you're nervous about all this" he mocked Baron cheerfully, to be answered with a low growl, "but I wouldn't want to bore our audience. So if you're done with the speeches... let's dance."

Both men shifted, circled each other, teeth bared, hackles raised, growls filling the chilly evening air... and then they attacked.

# EPILOGUE

Miller stared at the email he'd just received. He'd seen the news report a few days ago, the dead hiker now officially the victim of a tragic but entirely unintended hunting accident when she'd wandered onto a fenced and clearly marked private property. Nonetheless, it was a relief to see the official confirmation that the operation had been completed successfully. Less so to see that his superiors were praising him for his quick thinking and diligence in covering up this tragic secret. In Miller's own mind, he'd done nothing remarkable, and in helping to create a bunch of lies to feed to a family that had lost an irreplaceable part of their lives, it was quite possible that he was actually a complete and utter bastard.

Whatever his personal reservations, he had to admit that the PR team had done their job well. The problem of a dead body lying around had officially gone away, swept under the rug with a chorus of official sympathy for the family and a sigh of relief as the cops they'd bribed had quickly fabricated a hunting permit, pardoned the hunters as having done nothing wrong and offered apologies and unlimited support for the family, should they need any assistance in having the body transported, or fending off the media, or arranging a funeral.

A medical report had also appeared out of nowhere, not entirely a work of fiction as the cause of death had, in fact, been a single bullet wound to the head. The post mortem said that the girl was dehydrated at the time of her death, she had blisters on her feet, indicating she had been walking for some time, and there was debris in her hair and dirt on her clothes, making it a plausible suggestion that she'd climbed through a fence onto private property.

So as far as the Noturatii were concerned, it was problem solved, back to business as usual. Miller had submitted the required report on the attack at the shifter base in Scotland, but expected nothing more to come of it. As he'd pointed out in the report, the shifters would be long gone by the time a second team went to investigate, and with such a massive security breach, they were never likely to show up at that location again.

But as far as Miller was concerned, the whole incident was far from done and dusted. After seeing the actions of the shifters, their compassion for the death of a stranger, their rituals and beliefs in an afterlife, Miller was reassessing the Noturatii's entire stance on the shifters' existence.

They were a bizarre quirk of nature, that much was certain. But in a world where scientists worked every day to hybridise animals by crossing genes with other species, where genetically modified food was becoming more and more common, and where gene therapy for humans was rapidly gaining ground as a viable option for the future, it was hard to justify a mindset that said that just because something was weird, it was necessarily evil.

Terrorism was the usual catch cry of those in power, the need to prevent devastating attacks on targets impacting national security. But as far as Miller knew, such an attack had never actually been planned, threatened or carried out by the shifters. It was far more likely that terrorism threats would come from your regular, garden variety, human terrorist group, and he was seriously questioning whether it was worth throwing so much money, time and effort at a threat which had never actually materialised.

The moral questions of what they were doing were greater still. In Scotland, he'd seen that young woman, with the short hair and baggy shorts, playing and laughing with their former captive, and no matter how he tried, he couldn't get the image out of his head. He still didn't know if she had survived the battle, and when he'd started having nightmares about her, he'd actually welcomed the macabre scenes, the girl dying in his arms in some of them; in others, her wide, innocent eyes accusing him of horrific crimes. It was a harsh reminder of what they were actually doing. By capturing these people – people, not animals, Miller now steadfastly believed – and torturing them, separating them from their families and loved ones, experimenting on them and killing them in horrific ways, weren't they just bringing to life the acts of terrorism that they purported to be trying to prevent?

But despite the easy conclusion that what they were doing was wrong, the question of what to do about it was a lot tougher. When he'd joined the Noturatii, he'd been told in no uncertain terms that the only way to leave the organisation was in a body bag. And it was a mark of his horror and guilt over the whole situation that he was actually starting to consider that a viable option. He could, of course, go public about their whole organisation, and wait for the outcry from the community to drown them all. But tempting as that was, he was also aware that the shifters had wanted to keep their existence a secret just as much as the Noturatii did. He wouldn't be doing them any favours by outing them all. Hell, it was just as likely that the public would turn on them, naming them the abominations that the Noturatii believed them to be, and the last thing he wanted to do was inadvertently bring about the end of their species.

But what else could he do?

One thing was for certain, Miller knew, as he closed his laptop and prepared to go home, his work at an end for the day. There were changes in his life that were long overdue. And it was about time he started taking them seriously.

# ABOUT THE AUTHOR

Laura Taylor has been writing since she was a teenager, spending long hours lost in imaginary adventures as new worlds and characters spring to life. The House of Sirius is her first published work, a series of seven novels following the wolf shape shifters and their war with the Noturatii.

Laura lives on the Central Coast of NSW, Australia and has a passion for nature, animals, hiking, and of course, reading.

https://www.facebook.com/LauraTaylorBooks
laurataylorauthor@hotmail.com